THE UNWANTED BRIDE

AN ARRANGED MARRIAGE ROMANCE

NADIA LEE

To Chris and Alex. Thank you for your love.

1

HUXLEY

"How's business?"

The question is innocuous, and delivered in a sweet tone that says my grandmother Catalina Huxley is merely curious. But I know better. The sentiment hidden beneath those two words is *I hope your agency fails so you have no choice but to join the firm.*

"Great. Got more work than we can handle, so we're hiring. Why, you know anyone who's interested?" My words are honeyed, my smile polished as I let out a puff of smoke from my cigar. It's a vice I indulge in around the Huxley side of the family because I need something to soothe my temper. Sometimes whiskey just isn't strong enough to cut it.

"Of course." Her smile remains as glitteringly brilliant as the chandelier over our long table. Everything about her is polished and expensive, from her glossy, dark hair to the deep blue dress that fits her slim form. Very few lines mar her elegant face—just a couple of furrows between her eyebrows that her cosmetic surgeon couldn't get rid of. They came from years of unconscious frowning while dealing with criminals who deserved to be put behind bars. Underneath that concerned maternal expression is a Machiavellian heart that makes Lucrezia Borgia look like Florence Nightingale. Grandma spares no one, not even her own grandchildren. "I'd love to refer a few."

"Awesome. Looking forward to meeting them." She's going to send me saboteurs. If she could, she'd find a way to sue my agency out of existence, except that she knows that I'd fight back, and I fight dirty. She doesn't want that kind of mud splattered on her pristine reputation as a highly successful former prosecutor.

Part of me wishes I could just throw my hands up in the air, say *fuck you all* and walk out, but some old guilt holds me back—I don't want Grandma to focus all her intensity on my cousins. They've told me to go see a therapist, but what's the point? No therapist has the power to travel back in time and stop me from being the ignorant moron who endangered his cousins. Ares still bears the scars.

Her housekeeper brings us small plates of tart samplers and coffee. Grandma has a definite preference for desserts, and today it's bite-sized tiramisu, chiffon cake and some kind of berry-topped custard.

My eyes flick to the gloomy sky outside—a storm is coming. Rain doesn't bother me, but it's a good excuse to end this farce early. I should've known better when I walked into Grandma's dining hall and saw no one except her and my mother Jeremiah.

The latter is sipping Merlot and also puffing on a cigar. She must've just eviscerated some opposing counsel and won a major victory for her client. Merlot and a cigar is how she celebrates every triumph. If she could, she'd drink her opponent's blood, but that's frowned upon these days. And the Huxleys prize their reputation.

Wonder what she'd drink if I finally caved in and agreed to join Huxley & Webber? Maybe her prized Pétrus 2009? A five-figure wine, but she'd find it worth it. I'd opt for hemlock—I'd only join the family law firm if my ad agency went bankrupt and all my money somehow vanished.

"Don't you think you're wasting your education?" Mom says conversationally.

Dammit. *Need to make an excuse and get out of here.* "People do a lot of things with law degrees." I should just order cards with the statement printed on them and pass them out like Halloween candy to the elders. There's a reason my cousins call them The Fogeys—TF for short. I give the nickname my stamp of approval.

Her auburn hair glints under the light as she tilts her head and regards me. She got her delicate looks from Grandma, but only idiots underestimate her. That pitiless, cast-iron heart of Grandma's? Mom got that, too.

"You should reconsider your choice of career," Grandma declares, probably tired of my resistance.

"And your future," Mom adds. "What being part of this family means."

"For the millionth time, I'm not joining the firm." *What's going on here?* It isn't like them to be so overt about this demand. They gave up that particular mode of convincing me when my ad agency landed its first multimillion-dollar contract.

Not knowing all the facts is unsettling, especially since they obviously want me to play a role. The last time I trusted a family member, I was lied to and used. Not making that mistake again.

Mom's gaze flicks to the coat of arms above the wall behind Grandma. A trio of silver wolves on a shield with the family motto. "*Pietas et unitas,*" she murmurs.

"Loyalty and unity," Grandma says, translating the motto. Like I could ever forget it.

The three words are hammered into you from the moment you're born into the Huxley family. A special cane is commissioned, with the family motto embossed in silver filigree down the side, as a gift to every Huxley baby.

Just because my father happens to be a degenerate—but highly successful—movie producer doesn't mean the family passed up the chance to try to indoctrinate me. I got a cane, too, which—last I remember—is somewhere in my closet. Mom and her family were gleeful when Dad had zero interest in or time for me, and let them mold me as they wished.

But their efforts didn't really take. Probably because I also went to boarding schools in Europe with my six half-brothers, and they weren't brainwashed into doing whatever their mothers' families wanted. Besides, it was my half-brother Emmett's mom who spent more time with me in a single month than my own mother did my entire first eighteen years.

I give both my grandmother and mother a pointed look. "You

promised you'd leave me alone if I went to Harvard Law. I never promised to practice law afterward."

"I thought you were going through a phase." Grandmother's tone says she's disappointed that I'm still going through that phase.

"Huxley & Webber is *your* dream." I spread my hands, encompassing them both. "Not mine."

"It's not anyone's *dream*, Huxley. It's the family legacy."

And the legal empire they built with their partners—the Webbers.

"And we all benefit from it." Grandmother pauses briefly, looking for an acknowledgment, but I merely stare. "If you're so averse to the idea of being a lawyer, how about marriage?"

The abrupt question causes me some mental whiplash. What's this about? Is she having a grandbaby craving like my father? Every time he sees his "rival"—who doesn't even know he exists—he goes crazy and calls me and my brothers to demand a grandchild.

"Marriage?" I ask warily. When you're dealing with these two, the less said the better. They're masters of twisting your words.

"You can't live alone forever."

"I'm a *very* happy bachelor."

"Could become an even happier husband," Mom says, then lets out another puff of smoke.

I don't buy the cool façade. There had to have been some sort of deal I'm not aware of, designed solely to fuck me over. "What did Dad offer you?"

"Nothing. We aren't interested in grandchildren—not immediately, anyway—but rather a cementing of the families. The Webbers have two girls. About the right age. Pretty enough," Grandmother says.

My face twists in displeasure. "No." Being married to a Webber would mean getting entangled in Huxley & Webber. I'd be hooked like a fish, and all they'd have to do was reel me in. I'm already in more than I'd like because of my unwitting role in my cousins' abduction, and I don't want to get dragged deeper.

The family can scream *pietas et unitas* until they lose their voices, but I create my own destiny. *I* decide the direction of my life and *I* take the steps to forge my future. That means no fucking Webber is going to be my wife.

"Just keep an open mind," Mom says, "and think about it."

"You might just fall in love with one of them in a meet-cute," Grandmother adds, her eyes twinkling, betraying how pleased she is with herself. Must've slogged through more than a few romantic comedies to come up with *that* line. She usually likes horror and police procedurals.

Her dedication is terrifying.

"Yeah. When the sun rises out of my ass." I stand up, leaving the dessert and coffee. "I need to get going before the rain starts."

Mom frowns. "Rain doesn't bother you," she says. I was raised in Europe, then spent seven years in Massachusetts. The sky could spew hail, and I'd be fine on the road.

I look at these two women, whom I both love and hate. "No, but parricide would."

THE ENGINE of my new Lamborghini roars as I drive away from the Huxley estate. The family should change its motto to whatever the Latin is for Make Huxley Our Puppet. We agreed that if I went to Harvard Law, they'd leave me alone. I never promised to take the bar or become a lawyer, much less join Huxley & Webber. That's my mother's dream—probably my grandmother's too. But it isn't mine.

Perhaps my graduating top five in the class gave them hope. Grant suggested intentionally flunking out, but why should I look like a dumbass? The classes were easy, and it isn't my fault my classmates couldn't do better than they did.

Uncharacteristic sullen clouds sit low in the SoCal sky, hiding a full moon. They're swollen with rain, and the roads are mostly empty, since most Angeleno drivers fear rain like a zombie apocalypse.

Even after my declaration, Grandmother asked me to spend the night at her place for my own safety—*ha!*—but I declined because I'm not an idiot. She's likely planning to ply me with the best whiskey and scotch from her liquor cabinet. For all I know, she might've planned a not-so-subtle "meet-cute" with one of the Webber girls accidentally falling into my bed.

Impatience wells. My family isn't stupid: they're all Harvard-educated lawyers. They should get the hint that being part of their legal empire isn't my life goal. I'm building my own domain in advertising—the 4D Agency.

I am nobody's puppet.

Another wave of resentment rolls through me at the memory of Grandma saying we've all benefited from the legacy—by which, of course, she means *me*. Trying to guilt me into believing that I've taken from the family without giving anything back pisses me off. Dad, who's not a member of the Huxleys, paid for my education and upbringing in full because he's a firm believer in throwing money at things he doesn't have time for. Mom's always been busy with her legal career—after all, she's gotta pull her weight—and the Huxleys didn't have to contribute a penny toward my law degree. They've never done me a favor, not even free legal advice. Whatever legal services I've needed, I've paid for.

Grandma better not be referring to birthday and Christmas gifts. Shopping is her secret hobby, and she buys everyone's present at least three months early.

Fifteen minutes later, the flat gray bellies of the clouds finally split and water pours down. Visibility deteriorates until anything more than four yards away looks like a hazy shadow. The wind picks up, blowing the rain at a sharply slanted angle. The raging weather reflects my grumbly mood, and it's surprisingly soothing.

I make a tight turn around a corner, the Lambo responding like a dream. Beethoven's "Egmont" overture rises dramatically from the speakers as I maneuver on autopilot. It's the best time to be on the road —just me and the fury of nature.

Something jumps out in front of the car. I slam on the brakes, stopping just an inch short of hitting it.

"What the *fuck*?"

The headlights reveal a woman in a thin T-shirt and jeans, soaked to the bone. Her dark, stringy hair hangs limply around her face and shoulders. A drowned rat would look better.

Frustrated irritation surges. If she wants to die, she should find a way that doesn't involve an innocent motorist. She rushes around the hood and bangs on the passenger-side window, shouting something.

I narrow my eyes. Is she one of those scammers who act hurt and try to squeeze drivers for money? *Lady, you picked the wrong mark.*

I crack the window open. "Fuck off." My foot starts to step on the gas. I've got no time for this BS after my "talk" with my grandmother and mother.

She sticks her fingers into the gap in the window, forcing me to stop again. "Wait, please! Sorry I jumped out like that, but I *really* need a ride," she shouts over the rain.

Riiiiiight. And I have the intelligence of an amoeba. "Uber."

"Nothing's available! Please. I *have* to get to the Ronald Reagan Medical Center."

Definitely a scammer. I'd bet both my balls my car didn't touch this crazy woman, and if she thinks this is her payday...

Well, she thought wrong. And she's stupid to assume that sticking her fingers into my window will keep me from leaving. I will not be manipulated, especially not by some third-rate loser who thinks she's smarter than me. She'll pull those fingers out fast when I floor it. If she doesn't, she'll get hurt, but that's her problem, not mine.

"Better luck next time, sweetheart," I grind out. "Sure you'll be able to find a more malleable sucker somewhere in this city."

"Please! I *have* to get to my mom!"

The shakiness in her voice makes me hesitate. Or maybe it's the desperation in those wide, baby-blue eyes.

She's probably a serial killer, says the cold, rational part of my mind that enabled me to graduate top of my class at Harvard.

Grandma's meddlesome voice joins in. *Yes, definitely a serial killer. If you'd just stayed here at home like I offered, then you wouldn't be dealing with this.*

My head throbs. The last person I want to think about is my grandmother.

"*Please.*" It's more a sob than a word.

On cue, the rain pours down even harder. I look around, searching for the girl's car. Nothing. I'm the only person on the road because nobody else in SoCal is dumb enough to drive in this weather at this hour.

I should just leave—it's the smart thing to do. But what little humanity is left in me says I can't abandon her like this. I wouldn't be able to bear the guilt if on tomorrow's news there was a story about something terrible happening to a lone woman who just wanted to go to a hospital.

My hands flex and unflex around the steering wheel. If she's crazy, I can handle her. And driving her to the medical center won't be a big deal. It's worth a clean conscience and all that.

"Get in." My voice is anything but gracious, but she doesn't complain as she runs around and hops in, dripping all over the brand-new leather seat.

Without commenting on that, I take off toward the hospital.

"Thank you so much," she says. "I'll pay you for the ride."

The sincerity in her voice is amusing for its naïveté. "Do I look like an Uber to you?"

"In this car? No. Which is why what you're doing means so much." She looks at me like I've single-handedly slain a dragon and solved world hunger, making me want to squirm. I'm not the heroic type by any means. At the same time, it soothes my temper, frayed from having to deal with my irritating family who can't even abide by their own promises.

It's hard to tell what she really looks like, since she's so wet, but her eyes are beautiful, with long, dark lashes and slightly slanted outer corners. Expressive, too. Exactly the kind Dad would love, except she should stay away from any man like my father. He impregnated seven women in a four-month span, which is how I was born, along with six half-brothers. Supposedly he hasn't made any more babies, but I'm not so sure his second vasectomy has held. It failed before; it could fail again.

But hopefully he's sterile now. The world doesn't need more children to suffer through fucked-up childhoods.

The girl rubs her arms. Soon her teeth are chattering loudly enough that I can hear them over Beethoven. The A/C is blowing icy air, which is how I like it, but it's probably too chilly for her. I turn it down. "Better?"

"Thank you." Her beautiful eyes focus me, then crinkle as she smiles. "You're really nice."

"It's just the A/C," I say gruffly, slightly uncomfortable at the thanks.

The warm smile she flashes at me lances my heart. "Yeah, but a lot of people wouldn't notice. Or maybe wouldn't care." She sniffs.

More like she's surrounded by assholes who don't give a damn about anybody. I keep my mouth shut to discourage her from sharing more.

"My half-sister wrecked my car and didn't bother to get it repaired yet," she says, then expels a frustrated breath.

I grunt, so glad I don't have a half-sister who drives like a drunken teenager. If I did, and if she wrecked my car, I'd put her on a one-way flight to Africa with my brother Noah. He doesn't believe in luxury travel. His goal is to take the best wildlife shots possible, which means rolling around in dirt, bugs and snakes until he can position himself to get the photos he needs.

"So what's wrong with your mom? A car accident?" As soon as I say it, I bite my tongue. It's none of my business. I'm never going to see her again.

"No. She collapsed, and..." She takes a shaky breath. "Why do people collapse, do you suppose? Low blood sugar?"

When the pause stretches, I realize she's waiting for a response. I shouldn't engage. But the sight of her pleading eyes makes my resolve weaken. "I'm not a doctor, so I wouldn't know." The women in my family don't faint. They make the other party do so with fear.

"She's too young to have something serious, I'm sure. She's not some health freak, but she's fit enough."

I don't tell her that just because you look okay from the outside doesn't mean your insides are in top shape. Young and seemingly healthy people get diagnosed with cancer all the time. One of my friends' fathers died in his forties of stomach cancer that way.

Soon we pull into the entrance of the ER. The area is a madhouse, with an ambulance pulling up, people shouting. Coming from a wreck, judging from the way a mangled man on a stretcher is bleeding.

"Thank you. Here..." My hitchhiker reaches into her pocket...and pulls out the saddest-looking dollar bill I've ever seen. She flushes. "Um, sorry. It's all I have, but wait. Lemme Venmo you." She grabs her phone from a back pocket, but it's also soaked. "Shit." She pushes buttons, but obviously nothing's happening.

Or maybe it is responding, but she's playing dumb. Honestly, I don't care. I didn't drive her here for the money. Still, a glimmer of respect stirs in my heart that she's at least trying.

Curiosity over how she plans to get out of the situation she's in keeps me quiet. If she has no cash and her phone isn't working, what are her options? Write me an IOU? A check? Ask me to drive her to an ATM? But would she do that if the situation with her mom is urgent enough for her to jump in front of a car?

"Here." She takes the pen I keep on the console and writes on the dollar bill. "This is my number. Please call me and I'll send you the money." She looks down at the wet seat. "And I'm sorry about your car seat. I'll pay for this, too."

She lifts the damp bill, waiting for me. I stare at it for a while. *The number's probably fake,* the cynic in me says. Still, she's waiting, so I accept it gingerly between my index finger and thumb.

She beams at me. "Thanks again!" She runs out, disappearing into the ER.

I look at the limp bill and toss it on the seat she was occupying just seconds ago. "Hope your mom's okay," I mutter. The car suddenly feels empty and quiet as I pull out to head home.

2

GRACE

—TWO YEARS later

"STILL WORKING?" Elizabeth says as she exits her office. As always, she's in a beautiful designer dress—something in a pretty pink today—and her golden hair is perfectly styled and curling around her shoulders. The makeup on her face is just enough to bring out her gray eyes and highlight her model-perfect cheeks.

She's one of the heirs to the Pryce family fortune, as well as being the head of the Pryce Family Foundation and my boss. Most importantly, she's my savior. If she hadn't agreed to take a chance on a kid with a history degree from UCLA nobody wanted to hire because the economy was terrible and "oh gosh, what are we supposed to do with a history major, ha-ha-ha" I would've been so, so screwed.

When people learn that my father is Nelson Webber, they assume I grew up in luxury and have never experienced money problems. He's a very successful lawyer, and the Webber family is wealthy. What they don't know is that he resents my having been born. Only if I hadn't been conceived—or, failing that, hadn't survived—he could've denied that he'd ever seduced a particular young woman. Or that he got her pregnant and then abandoned her because he didn't have the balls to fess up to his wife.

Nelson is to himself the greatest tragic hero and victim, made to suffer endlessly. Mom and I are a burden he must bear for a "minor youthful indiscretion"—even though he was thirty-seven when he slept with my mom, who was only twenty-four. He often forgets that he hasn't given Mom a penny in child support. He used a fake name with her, and then ran as quickly as he could when she told him she was pregnant. She only found out who he really was when his photo was all over the news because he was the lead counsel for a sensational lawsuit involving a giant pharmaceutical company sixteen years later. She didn't chase after him for anything because she had her pride and realized he never wanted to be a responsible human being. Also, she was making enough money to support us.

But when she first became ill and started having to go to the hospital just as I was finishing high school, everything changed. Mom never earned enough to have much in savings, certainly not enough to pay for the outrageous hospital bills, and I confronted Nelson at his house, where I was blocked, and then at his law firm.

He would have continued to ignore me, except I changed tactics and went directly to his father, Andreas Webber. After a paternity test, Andreas told Nelson to man up and do the right thing or he'd sue Nelson on by my behalf for neglect, abandonment, unpaid financial support and everything else I was legally entitled to.

"I just need to check some personal emails," I say with a smile.

"Good. I was wondering if we were working you too hard. There's a catered lunch in the breakroom if you want. I'm out for a lunch date." Her entire being glows as she says it. Despite being married for years, she still acts like a teenager having her first crush. She flutters her fingers. "See ya."

Tolyan gets up from his desk and accompanies her out. I think of him as *that scary Russian* rather than *Elizabeth's personal assistant* but don't have the courage to say it out loud. The man gives off a weird, dangerous vibe that is completely at odds with Elizabeth's sweet personality. And he stands out among the gentle souls at the foundation. If that man has a gentle soul, I'll eat my toenails.

I turn my attention back to my computer and look for the weekly update from Johns Hopkins Hospital, where my mom was transferred a year and a half ago. Andreas insisted that she be treated by Dr. Adlai Blum, the world's foremost specialist on cerebral infarctions, which is what finally put Mom into a coma two years back. Nelson flushed, probably upset at how much it'd cost, and his wife Karie protested, but neither could afford to cross Andreas.

There it is. Like clockwork.

Your mother's condition hasn't changed much, but the new therapy we started last week is very promising. Many patients in her situation have shown some improvement over time. She's still relatively young, and I think she is a good candidate.

Dr. Blum's messages are never long, but always in layman's term and to the point, which I appreciate. The previous doctor flung dozens of technical words at me, and always acted like it was a bother to explain himself. Despite Dr. Blum's cautious words, I'm optimistic. The last time I visited her in Baltimore, her lashes fluttered and her fingers twitched in my hand. The more I spoke to her, the more she responded, and I know she could hear me. *And that means she's getting better.*

Attached to the email is a picture of her in a private room with the purple hyacinths I sent for the week. Every Monday, the local florist delivers a different bouquet, so that when Mom opens her eyes, the beautiful blossoms will be the first thing she sees.

I'd love to be there with her for that moment, but I need to make money. Although Nelson reluctantly agreed to pay for most of Mom's care, his wife Karie isn't as generous. She demanded I chip in as much as possible, so I ended up shouldering two thousand dollars a month. If my job didn't pay so well, and if Andreas hadn't let me live in one of his condos rent-free—even if it does come with my half-sister occasionally barging in to "borrow" my stuff because she somehow manages to get the key—I'd be eating nothing but ramen noodles and living under a bridge.

Actually, if it hadn't been for Andreas, Nelson would've let the doctors take Mom off life support within a week of her arriving at the ER on that stormy night. He honestly wasn't willing to do anything to keep her alive from the very beginning. If I hadn't shown up when I did, she might not have survived at all. The grumpy stranger who gave me a ride didn't just get me to the hospital—he probably saved my mom's life.

Who was he?

The guy never contacted me. I didn't give him a wrong number. I double-checked before handing him the dollar bill to make sure. I try to pay my debts, and never take anybody's generosity or kindness for granted.

And he treated me with more kindness and patience than the situation warranted. In retrospect, nobody would've blamed him if he'd just driven off. I most likely sounded crazy and incoherent. Panic tends to do that.

One thing I know for sure: his car was fancy. Like, *really* fancy. I didn't quite catch the make, but I can still smell the new-car smell and feel the way my dripping body sank into that soft leather. How much might it cost to take care of the seat I probably ruined with rainwater?

It was so nice of him to let that go when he didn't have to. And his action—well, *inaction*—reminds me that most people in the world are good, even if I did get the short end of stick in the dad department.

I make a quick voice recording for Mom so the hospital staff can play it for her. "Hey, Mom! Today's another beautiful day! I'm at work, organizing another fundraiser for the foundation. The money is going toward helping children with cancer. Isn't that amazing? I'm lucky to be part of an organization that cares so much about people.

"I know you're alone now, and I'm so sorry about that. As soon as you wake up, we're going to be together. I'm not letting you stay so far away again. We can move to someplace nice and quiet, like maybe Montana. I've never been, but I hear it's beautiful. And you can have a gorgeous flower garden, just like you always wanted. I have to go now, but I'll send another note soon. Love you." I make a kissing noise, then end the recording and send it to Dr. Blum.

Montana. Ever since Mom collapsed, I've been saving every penny possible for our future. Thankfully, Andreas is paying for all the utilities at the condo—he said that was the least I deserved for all the years I'd been deprived. I shop at thrift stores and raid garage sales for everything I need. I rarely do what most people my age would consider "fun," and all my friends, except for Adam, drifted away when they realized I was just "too cheap to live a little" with them. And Peter, of course. I don't even know how I ended up with a boyfriend when I lead such an unexciting life.

But the sacrifice is worth it. I need to be able to take care of my mom when she gets better. Nelson isn't somebody I can rely on. Andreas isn't either—not because he's as reptilian as Nelson, but because he's so busy it's impossible to see him unless you work at the firm or make an appointment months in advance. Being his grandchild doesn't grant me any special access.

Still, I make a mental note to do something special for tonight. I'm going to make shrimp scampi and a chocolate cake to celebrate Peter's promotion. He's a lawyer at Huxley & Webber now, but when he was interning at the firm, he let the poor eighteen-year-old me sneak in to meet Andreas and plead my case. I'll never forget his kindness, and when we reconnected last year, it just seemed right that we end up together.

I want him to know I appreciate him.

3

GRACE
HOW WEIRD.

I⊤'s already nine, and Peter still isn't home. His assistant said he left the office around seven thirty, so I timed my cooking so everything would be done as he walked through the door. The dinner's cold now. So is the kitchen, for that matter. The sauce I made for the shrimp and pasta sits in an unappetizing, congealed lump. The vinaigrette I whipped up for the salad has separated, oil forming a layer on top of the balsamic vinegar.

I run a hand down my black dress. It's a classy piece I picked up for twenty bucks several years ago. I've only worn it twice, and underneath it is some sexy underwear and silky thigh-highs I bought on sale with a Christmas gift card—for the perfect end to our evening and celebration. Peter deserves it after working so hard for the promotion, coming home late and exhausted for months on end.

What happened? A car accident?

I text him again. And again, nothing. He hasn't read my earlier messages, either. Worry begins to mount, and my anxiety spikes. This reminds me eerily of the time Mom became seriously sick for the first time when I was in high school. She didn't come home when she was supposed to, didn't answer the phone like she was supposed to.

Is Peter okay?

My phone buzzes, and I immediately check the screen.

—Adam: Hey, GG, you coming to the party?

I frown.

—Me: What party?

—Adam: The one to celebrate Peter's promotion.

The world seems to spin a bit.

—Me: Is this a surprise party?

—Adam: No. Everyone in the office knew about it. Kacey planned it last week. I thought Peter invited you?

No, he didn't. Hasn't uttered a word about it. And why didn't Kacey say something when I contacted her earlier? As his admin, she knows his schedule.

—Me: Must have slipped his mind. Where's the party?

—Adam: At SportsBrews. Right across from the office.

I know the place. It's famous for serving specialty beers from local microbreweries. But it's even more famous for its late-night snacks for lawyers burning the midnight oil. Everyone at Huxley & Webber has spent time there at some point.

—Me: I'll be there soon.

I drive my ten-year-old Corolla over to the bar. Even from the street, it's obvious the bar's packed with lawyers in their fancy suits and confident swagger. The firm is one of the best in the country, and most associates there behave like they're God's Chosen. But then... I guess God must really love you for you to be able to attend an elite law school. You can have all the talent and drive in the world, but circumstances can keep you from realizing your full potential. I think about my perfect LSAT score, and the fact that I'm never going to be able to attend a law school.

I park on the street and go in. Buzzing conversations provide a counterpoint to Kurt Cobain's vocals on the sound system. I look around for Peter—the lanky six-two frame in a charcoal-gray suit, topped with a golden head. He's not near the door, so I start pushing through the crowd.

About halfway into the bar, slurred words come from a nook to my right. "At some point, y'know, you just need to move on."

Peter?

He's standing with his back to me, one arm wrapped around a brunette in a red dress with a magenta scorpion tattoo on her shoulder. I inhale sharply as shock punches my gut. The design is something I'll never forget—it's the tattoo my half-sister Vivienne got the day she wrecked my car, which happened to be the day before Mom was rushed to the ER. Viv had been worried about her tattoo parlor being in a bad part of town, and didn't feel safe driving her Maserati there. I ignored her babbling, not realizing that she was planning to filch the key to my car from my bedroom and take it instead.

Of course, she denied she was responsible for the crash. Karie said I would need to pay for the repairs, until the police showed her security footage from a gas station near where Viv fucked up my car.

After that, I put a small security camera in my bedroom to make sure Viv will never be able to lie about taking my things and get away with it. I would've been so screwed without the cops' help.

What the hell is Peter doing with Viv? And why is his arm around her like she's his date?

She says something to him and trots away without seeing me in the crowd.

Now that Peter's with just guys, his shoulders relax a little. A lawyer to his left says, "Where's your girlfriend?"

Yeah, what about your girlfriend, *Peter?*

I can see a just-between-you-and-me-boys smile on Peter's face in the reflection on the window.

"You didn't hear what I said earlier about moving on? It doesn't just apply to cases, man. Everything in life. Including women. It isn't like we're really compatible," he says. "I only slept with her because I thought she could help my career."

What?

"She was crushing on me hard, you know? And I didn't want to be mean, especially since she's Andreas's grandkid."

"Why was she crushing on a bastard like you?" one of the lawyers says. *Guy talk.*

"Because I'm hot?" Peter laughs. "Nah, I did something nice for her once, and after that she wouldn't leave me alone. It was a little pathetic."

That wasn't how we reconnected. He couldn't figure out what was wrong with his fob because it refused to unlock his car in a Home Depot parking lot. I recognized him instantly, although it took him a few minutes to remember me. I fixed the fob by replacing the battery—it happened to me once—and he asked me out for coffee.

I might've been happy enough to run into him again that I was a bit too friendly for his taste. But that doesn't give him the right to trample on my gratitude and affection.

Waves of tremors rack me. Humiliation and pain pool in my belly like acid.

"And sort of useless." He sounds annoyed. "I thought the least she'd do would be to tell Andreas or Nelson how hard I'm working. Try to help out with my career if she wanted to really be useful." He shrugs. "It's fine, though. I've upgraded. Viv is better anyway." He tilts his head in that particular way, and I can tell he's smirking. Bet he's smug that he's been given the promotion he wanted, thanks to Viv. And here I thought he was working to *earn* the promotion.

Disappointment drips through the ignominy of my situation.

He opens his mouth to say more, but I step forward. I've heard enough. "Peter."

He stiffens, then turns. "Grace! Wow. What are you doing here?"

"Oh geez, let's see..." I tap my chin, then snap my fingers. "Oh, that's right—I was told my boyfriend was having a party to celebrate his promotion."

"Well. Yeah." His eyes are bright with rapid calculation. He's probably wondering how much I heard and what he can say to get out of the pile of shit he stepped into. Finally, he smiles. "Great! Glad you could join us."

I shake my head. The men around him look at each other, shifting their weight. *Are they embarrassed they got caught, or worried that I might badmouth them to Nelson?* Either way, it's gross.

"Are you? Did you cheat on me with Viv to get ahead?"

He knows the game is up. "I wouldn't call it *cheating.*" He gives me a patronizing smile.

My temper rises. Does he think his lawyerly talk is going to work on me? "Of course not. It's called sleeping your way to the top because that's all you're good for."

The smile vanishes. "You aren't that good in bed, at least not enough to marry. So what value do you have if you can't help with my career?"

"Should I repeat that to Nelson?" I say in my most saccharine voice.

He shuts his mouth and merely glares.

I laugh mockingly. "Thought so."

His face turns pink. The humiliation of being caught and told off in front of his colleagues is likely too much for him to handle. "You know what? In law school, which you'll never go to, they teach us to deal with facts. And here are the facts of this case: same bed, different woman, and that was all it took! Viv is fantastic, and she makes more sense for me in every way."

Oh my God. He slept with my half-sister in *my* bed? Disgusting! I just bought new sheets, too!

"She's going to Harvard Law, you know," he says.

"And?" I snort. "She hasn't graduated yet, has she?"

I *know* she won't graduate. My money's on her dropping out before the first year is over. She wasn't qualified to be admitted in the first place. The only reason she got in is because I took the LSAT for her last year. Karie practically ordered me to, saying that if I didn't, she'd make sure I took on a bigger share of Mom's medical expenses. The amount she demanded was ridiculous—five thousand a month, which I could never afford.

"Pretty sure that's some kind of extortion," I told her. "And thus illegal."

She just shrugged. "Oh well. I guess if your mom dies it'll be because her only child didn't care enough."

I couldn't ask Nelson for help, since he stood next to Karie the entire time without saying a word. And if I'd brought it up with Andreas, Nelson and Karie would both deny it, claiming I misunderstood. Andreas is aware of his son's shitty personality, but I'm not sure how he'd react if Nelson, Karie and Viv all insisted I was misrepresenting the situation. And that was assuming I'd even be able to see him. He's always busy, and his assistants hate shifting his appointments around for a nobody like me. I resent that my situation leaves me with no choice but to accept the little charity the Webbers deign to bestow on me to keep me quiet.

"Give her three years, and she will," Peter says. "You're just jealous because she's better at everything than you."

"Fine. Just replace my sheets and bed. I'm not sleeping in a bed you soiled with Viv."

"Ha! You're lucky I fucked you at all."

"So you *aren't* going to replace them?"

He smirks. "Sue me for 'em."

Sue him? Something dangerous shifts inside me. "If that's the way you want it."

4

HUXLEY
AHH, SHIT.

I COME to an abrupt stop exactly one step into the glitzy dining room at Uncle Prescott and Aunt Akiko's home in Bel Air. The marble floors and crystal chandeliers twinkle and shine, looking like an ad for prosperity. It's almost as if the room itself is happy.

Should've known better.

When my uncle and aunt invited me over for dinner, I said sure. They said it was because they missed me, and—unlike my grandmother—they don't pressure me to join the firm. And they certainly don't ask me to marry for "the legacy." Also, unlike Mom, they don't stand around gazing at me with vague disappointment and disapproval that I'm not doing what every Huxley is supposed to, what the family motto demands.

They didn't inform me that Grandma and Mom were dining with us—two people I've been doing my best to avoid seeing as much as possible in recent months because I'd rather not be forced to defend myself in court for strangling them.

Akiko comes over, her serene smile never faltering despite the overt tightening of my jaw she has to have noticed. The petite Japanese woman could smile calmly while treading water in an ocean full of starving sharks. As usual, her black hair is in a bun, her makeup subtle and perfect and her outfit expensive but understated. The perfect wife for a lawyer who's often involved in high-profile cases.

"Huxley, so good of you to come by! We missed you so much!" She hugs me.

Under any other circumstances, I'd return the hug and say something warm in response. Instead, all she gets is a short grunt.

"Isn't it lovely that Prescott offered to host a family dinner?" Grandma beams.

She can play innocent until the second coming of Jesus, but I'm not buying it. I glance at my watch. "You know what? I just remembered an appointment I forgot about."

"Oh, nonsense," Mom scoffs. "Madison said you were free."

Fuck. If they already spoke to my assistant, they really put a lot of thought and effort into this. "Sometimes she forgets."

"Then fire her," Grandma says. "An assistant who can't keep track of her boss's schedule is less than worthless."

"I'm not firing her." Madison is an excellent employee and presents herself well to our clients. Not only that, she has an uncanny ability to know what I need even before I ask. And she's never given me a gift I didn't like. As opposed to my grandmother, who sent me a gold-plated business card with my name and the Huxley & Webber logo last Christmas. Apparently, it was meant to be *aspirational.*

"Shall we sit down?" Uncle Prescott says. He's a tall man—albeit a couple inches shorter than me—and possesses an imposing intellect and voice. Not that he speaks loudly, but his tone brims with confidence.

His three sons are just like him in that regard. Thankfully, none of them took after his ex, an unhinged bitch he married when he was young and foolish. Even the smartest of us make mistakes when our hormones are in the driver's seat.

Ares and the twins, Bryce and Josh, are standing behind the elders. They're still in suits, probably having arrived from work. I shoot them a dirty look. If The Fogeys plotted to fuck me over, these three should've watched out for me. We don't let each other get screwed over.

They shake their heads fractionally. Ares and Josh mouth, *We didn't know.* Bryce mouths, *I was stuck in court all day!*

I expel a resigned breath. My cousins probably did the best they could. They respect my career decision, even though they've joined the firm and are "having a blast." Well, the last part is what Grandma claims, so who the hell knows? But if any of them aren't happy at Huxley & Webber, I hope they leave rather than listen to the family motto and stay. You only live once.

"I made a wagyu roast with Japanese-style citrus sauce and a few side dishes that I've been dying to serve at a big dinner," Akiko says with a smile. "We have both warm and cold sake. Plus a lovely plum wine."

If I can't leave, I might as well enjoy the food. My aunt is an exceptional cook. If she ever opened a restaurant I'd take my brothers there, except she only serves two-bite portions. For some bizarre reason she acts like she loses a year of her life for every bite people take of her cooking.

The table at Uncle Prescott's home is long enough to seat twenty-six. When he pissed Mom off about a case at one of the previous family dinners, she gestured at the expanse and remarked that the length might be compensating for something. With any luck they'll get into another spat over some obscure legal point and forget about my existence.

I make sure to sit as far away from the naggers as possible, taking a seat next to Josh. He leans over. "Want me to text your assistant and have her fake an emergency meeting?"

"Thanks, but it won't work. Mom already checked." If Madison fakes something, Mom will find out. She hates being misinformed or inconvenienced, and she's tenacious when she feels wronged. I wouldn't want to unleash Jeremiah Huxley on my poor assistant.

The meal starts with an appetizer of fresh maguro and tai sashimi, two slices each. Aunt Akiko's refusal to fill your belly hasn't changed one bit over the years. My cousins always snuck over to my place during summer and winter breaks to raid my pantry and fridge when we were younger.

"How's Joey treating you?" Mom asks casually.

I can feel myself tensing up. Just thinking of Dad's overzealous assistant, who looks like the unfortunate love child of an alien pervert

24

and an orange, makes me want to break the lacquered chopsticks in half.

"Is he still sending you women?" Aunt Akiko says, her eyes comically wide in faux shock. She's always deliciously scandalized at the degenerate workings of America's upper echelons.

But she knows the answer. Everyone does.

Grandma looks like she's dying to hear me say it. Meanwhile, my cousins cast me looks full of sympathy.

"Joey treats me the way he does all my brothers," I say icily.

"Well, that sounds fair. Would you like some warm sake?" Akiko says.

"The cold one, please." I keep my tone polite. No matter how annoyed I get, she *is* my aunt.

The serving staff places a bottle and a white glazed cup only slightly larger than a thimble next to my plate. I reach for the emergency cigar I carry for situations like this.

Aunt Akiko opens her mouth, but then presses her lips together instead. Everyone present knows this dinner isn't going to end well, and it'll be worse if I don't get my cigar fix when dealing with my stubborn grandmother.

"Your father just wants a grandchild to bounce on his knee...as we all do." Grandma sighs theatrically. She must've taken some acting lessons.

"The only things he wants on his knee are young chicks with huge, bouncy tits." Just because I try to be polite doesn't mean I'm going to agree with her.

Aunt Akiko chokes on her plum wine, and Uncle Prescott pats her back. Mom smirks—she probably warned Grandma that line wouldn't work—and Grandma is scowling. My cousins are staring at the empty plates like somehow they can conjure more sashimi.

"It's disrespectful to speak of one's father that way," Grandma says.

"But factual." I let out a puff. "There's a reason Emmett and Griff don't let him near their kids." My brothers are too smart and sensible. Dad's idea of great outings for toddlers is Hollywood galas and movie sets.

Her mouth tightens into a stubborn line. "*I* want a great grandchild to bounce on *my* knee. Don't you think that's the least you owe the family, since you won't join the firm?"

"No. And wouldn't your orthopedic surgeon disapprove? Think of your age."

Her face turns red. My cousins bite their lips to contain laughter. The last time we were together, Grandma complained about how horrible her surgeon was because he couldn't get rid of her knee pain. The man's unvarnished response, that her knees had simply worn out from old age, was unacceptable. She will continue to fight the passage of time—demonstrating an admirable strength of will...as long as it isn't directed at me.

The second course is served: salad topped with salmon roe. I stare at the pale white dressing and little sprouts, doing my best to hide my distaste. Aunt Akiko looks so proud. She loves her veggies. I can choke 'em down as long as the dressing is good enough to disguise the grassy flavor. If God wanted me to eat five servings of grass, He would've made it taste like steak.

"But don't worry, I'm definitely going to do the right thing," I say, then puff again.

Grandma's complexion returns to normal at the possibility that I'm going to acquiesce to her demand. "Which Webber girl are you interested in?"

She's been pushing them on me, like her choices are in any way superior to what Joey has been offering. At least he picks girls with "tits and ass," even if they generally don't have the brains to match their other assets. If all I wanted was a quick fuck, they'd be serviceable enough. After all, that's what he's aiming for. Dad doesn't necessarily want me married. He just wants a grandchild.

Grandma, on the other hand, wants me to marry like a proper, respectable Huxley. And not to just any woman—to a Webber. But there are only two available, and neither is particularly appealing.

"It's difficult to decide, since one is idiotic and the other is frivolous," I say.

"Viv got into Harvard Law," Josh points out, although his expression says he's not sure how that happened.

Bryce rounds his fingers into a cock-sized cylinder and moves his arm up and down.

Of course, the motion doesn't go unnoticed among this gathering of lawyers. Aunt Akiko glares at her stepson, while I snort and Uncle Prescott tries to maintain a serious façade.

Time to rescue him. "Whose dick did she suck? She sure as hell didn't get in on her brains."

"Huxley!" Grandma's scandalized tone is totally manufactured. Not even she can believe Vivienne Webber got into Harvard Law. The girl's dumber than a piece of gum on a sidewalk.

"I don't know what's been promised in the marriage contract, but I'm not marrying her. Besides, she doesn't really want me, either. Don't the conditions specify that it can be any Webber and any Huxley?"

"For the sake of flexibility, we chose that for the Webber side. But not ours. You're specifically listed in the contract we signed."

"You signed a contract behind my back?" I say. "One that stipulated *I* had to fulfill certain obligations?"

"If you'd joined the firm, it wouldn't have been behind your back," Mom says.

"This is illegal on so many levels. You know better."

"Oh, no, I assure you it's quite legal and proper." Mom smiles. "When you saw how your friend—Matt—was fighting with his family over whether they should continue treatment for their terminally ill father, you drafted a power of attorney that'd kick in if you were comatose for over twenty-four hours. Remember?"

"Yeah, so you could unplug me in the event." I refuse to be hooked up to a machine so I can "live." Merely breathing isn't living as far as I'm concerned, so I picked Mom for the job, since I didn't want to burden my brothers with such a heavy decision. Furthermore, I couldn't trust them to not prolong my life, clinging to a pointless hope that I'd miraculously wake up with no ill side effects.

"Correct. And remember that half-pipe accident you had?"

A cold panic clenches my stomach. I love snowboarding, even though I can't indulge often. But my last trip ended in a nasty fall. I was certain I'd die.

Except the doctors managed to save me.

"You were, in fact, comatose for two days."

"Are you kidding?" I grind out as the pieces click into place. Mom didn't just want the ability to unplug me, but to control all my affairs in such a case. And I acquiesced; it seemed fair, given what was being asked. She might have the heart of Machiavelli, but she still has a heart.

"You gave me away in marriage while I was in a coma?" I demand. "What's *wrong* with you?"

"The Webbers didn't complain."

"Did you disclose that I could be brain dead?" I ask.

She shrugs. "They didn't ask. Besides, it wasn't like the news of your accident was exactly a secret."

"And if I hadn't woken up? What would you have done? Give one of them instead?" I gesture at my cousins.

"Obviously I can't ask them to do more than what they've already done by joining the firm," Grandma says. *Unlike you.* "It wouldn't be fair. The marriage deal will strengthen our alliance, and more importantly, it'll create an heir who can mediate between the two families."

Too many big egos. Not enough space at the firm. "And let's see. We'll get a bigger percentage of the firm because you're giving me up for one of their third-tier losers nobody wants."

Grandmother folds her hands placidly in front of her.

"*You* could marry Andreas," I say, trying to keep my voice civil. "You're both old and widowed. A geriatric romance. It's all the rage these days, what with people living so long."

She rolls her eyes. "Don't be ridiculous. We are not on the contract. And in any case, we're far too old to produce a child."

"Have you looked at the other girl? She isn't stupid," Uncle Prescott finally puts in.

"She spends twenty-five thousand dollars a month, and that doesn't include rent because Andreas set her up in a condo for free." Ares gave me the scoop on the other sister during a poker night. Apparently, this daughter is such a mess, the family is all hush-hush about her. Only the innermost circle knows—even most people at the firm are unaware of her existence.

"Wives are expensive, sweetie. But twenty-five a month is certainly within your capacity," Mom says.

My patience is wearing thin. It's the same bullshit conversation my grandmother and mom and I always have. This is why I do my best to avoid them. "Fucking her isn't worth that kind of money."

Grandmother turns positively apoplectic. "Huxley Lawton Lasker! She could become your wife!"

I'm not finished. "And if I ever decided to trade up, I'd need to pay her alimony too. Screw that."

"Prenup," Ares murmurs.

I give him a death glare. *Whose side are you on?*

I start to stand. Aunt Akiko looks at me, a futile hope in her eyes. "The nearest powder room is under renovation, so you'll need to use the one off the living room."

"I'm not going to the bathroom."

"But I haven't served the main course. The wagyu roast."

"I'll have to take a rain check." I go around the table to lay a quick kiss on her temple, then turn to the head of the table, where my grandmother sits like a queen. "If you try to pressure me to marry a Webber again—just *one* more time—I will elope with whomever Dad picks out next."

5

GRACE

THE SECOND WHISKEY burns down my throat and joins its companion in my otherwise empty belly. I probably shouldn't be sitting on a barstool drinking, but alcohol seems like a great option for consoling my wounded soul after that shitshow of an evening I just had. The bar is blasting Rihanna's "Breakin' Dishes." I wish I could break some dishes and burn Peter's clothes. But the plates at my place are mine, and he took his good clothes to the dry cleaners this morning, so there's nothing worth setting on fire.

—Adam: Are you okay? Where are you?

That's his tenth text, maybe twentieth... Something like that. I would answer him, but I have no idea what to say. He probably heard all there is to know from the other lawyers at the bar, assuming Viv hasn't told him already. She hates it that Adam's such a good friend to me. A girl like me doesn't deserve somebody like him.

The fact that my mom was the "other woman" in her parents' marriage has put a bright scarlet letter on me, figuratively speaking. When I pointed out that it was Nelson who decided to lie to my mother and cheat on his wife, she screamed like I'd poured rat poison down her throat, then called me a "fucking cunt." Viv's older brother Mick's reaction wasn't much better, as he worships his father. He pushed me, then smacked the back of my head hard enough to stun me. Karie said everyone should calm down, then threatened to cut off payments for Mom's bills if I dared to make a fuss or tell Andreas.

Karie isn't scared of anybody except Andreas. Probably because he isn't impressed that her father was a judge or that she graduated from Vassar with a degree in French lit. Furthermore, she feels the need to ingratiate herself with him to advance Nelson's career at the firm. By all accounts, he doesn't cut anyone any slack if they don't perform, family being no exception.

It sucks that no one's on my side. Mom would always be on Team Grace, but I'm not going to upset her by telling her what happened with Peter, even though I'd kill for some of her warm support to help soothe my pain.

I glare at my empty glass. There isn't enough alcohol in the world to make me feel better. *So...revenge?* I've never really pursued it before, but that seems like the only option left.

Except... *What would constitute good revenge in a situation like this?*

In romance novels, heroines sometimes sleep with their shitty ex's dad, but Peter's father passed away when he was in college. His older brother's out, since he's a degenerate alcoholic who's in jail for assaulting his girlfriend. It's not revenge if you downgrade.

I scan the people in the bar again. The place is near a couple of law firms with lawyers Peter has talked—well, sneered—about. I could sleep with one of them, just to show him.

Loud laughter and cheers erupt from a large group to my left. From the conservative suits and boasts of "spanking the opposing counsel," they're definitely lawyers. They also sport smiles as slick as Peter's, their teeth just as bleached.

I shake my head inwardly. *What am I doing?* Sleeping with a random guy isn't going to hurt Peter. He wouldn't even care. Our relationship ended, unilaterally, a little while ago.

My actions going forward shouldn't involve spiting Peter. I should only sleep with someone who makes my belly flip and libido sing. A guy who's at least a hundred times better in bed than my ex, which shouldn't be that difficult. He wasn't always that great, especially when he was tired from work. Huxley & Webber works their associates hard. Or maybe Viv rode him too hard.

Ugh. I need to stop thinking about that or I'm going to puke.

Maybe I should get a guy who isn't a lawyer. Just look at my life. No decent attorney anywhere, except for Adam.

I signal the bartender for another drink. She gives me a look, but this is *definitely* my last one. Spending money on whiskey isn't going to solve my situation. The idea of doing laundry tonight is exhausting, but no way am I sleeping in that bed with the sheets Peter and Viv fucked on. I already feel gross. If I hadn't showered this morning, I'd drive back home to disinfect my body with extra-hot water and bleach.

—Adam: Peter's a fucking asshole.

The understatement of the century. Bet Adam never cheats on his boyfriend. Always treats him with respect, too. I stare at the screen glumly. Why can't I find a man who loves me unconditionally and thinks I'm hotter than sliced bread?

A lawyer from the rowdy group comes over, stands next to me and says something to the bartender. He leans annoyingly close, even though the bar isn't *that* crowded, and brushes against my bare arm. Then he pushes his jacket back and places his hand on his waist, his elbow almost poking my side.

He's dressed in a dark suit, with a shit-eating grin that reminds me of Peter when he thinks he's being extra clever. I used to think it was sort of cute, but now it just looks smarmy.

The bartender puts my whiskey down. As I reach for it, the guy knocks my hand out of the way, grabs the drink and downs the whole thing in one swallow.

"Hey, that was my drink!" I say.

He blinks at me, like he can't believe I have the audacity to complain. "Says who?"

"Says me. I ordered that whiskey."

He rolls his eyes. "It didn't have your name on it, sweetheart. And I ordered a whiskey too."

"That actually *was* hers," the bartender says.

"Nobody asked you," he sneers at her, his expression dripping with condescension. Apparently, a fancy law degree makes him better than her. What a dickface.

"Nobody asked you to take up my space, either," I say. "Or to steal my drink. Why don't you apologize to the bartender who corrected you so you can quit making an ass of yourself, then run back to your group? They obviously don't mind putting up with your poor manners, and I'm not interested in interacting with rude people. Oh, and pay for that whiskey before you go."

His face turns red. "You think you can get away with talking to me like that? I'm a fucking lawyer, bitch. I can sue your ass."

"For what? Teaching you manners? I should bill you for doing the job your mother didn't. And speaking of lawsuits, I'm the one with the grounds to sue. You smacked my hand out of the way when you stole my drink, which is technically battery and assault."

He's incandescent scarlet now. People probably don't talk back when he says he's a lawyer and threatens to sue. He steps forward and tries to physically tower over me, the gesture meant to intimidate. If he can't win with words, he's going to win with physical force.

My mouth dries a little, my heart picking up speed. An overpriced suit and an even more overpriced degree don't mean the man's too good for violence. Mick has shown me how low men can go when they think they can get away with it. And I'm always on my own.

"Back off, asshole," says a cool, gravelly voice.

I blink as a brick wall of a man places himself in front of me like a fortress. He's tall, and solidly built underneath the well-fitted suit. His shoulders are wide, his waist trim. The man keeps in shape.

"Who the fuck are you?" Mr. Lawyer says.

"The guy who's going to break you in half if you don't cool it. You don't come to a bar, take a lady's drink and then yell when she points out that you've made a mistake."

His voice isn't loud, but there's steel underneath, like a well-honed knife. Menace radiates from him, and I bet he's dying for an excuse to hurt Mr. No-Manners.

I lean over a little to see the jerk's reaction. His face is radish red. "Who the hell do you think you are to talk to me like that? Do you know who I am?"

"Mmm... Let's see..." Mr. Fortress gives it some thought. "Nobody."

"He's right. If you have to ask, 'Do you know who I am?' you are nobody," I add, in case nobody bothered to teach him that, either.

"Shut up, bitch!" The lawyer guy jabs his index finger into my savior's chest. "Listen, asshole—"

Mr. Fortress grabs his wrist with the viciousness of a striking snake and twists.

"Ack!" The lawyer guy drops to his knees, his face twisting with pain. Probably nothing is broken, but the angle looks incredibly uncomfortable.

Fortress follows the wristlock with a kick that makes the guy double up and whimper. "Fuck!" he wheezes. "I'm gonna sue your ass!"

"Excellent. My lawyer will be in touch. Jeremiah Huxley. Perhaps you've heard of her."

6

HUXLEY

At the mention of Jeremiah, the man goes flaccid faster than an eighty-year-old with performance issues. Huxley & Webber is on retainer, and although this matter doesn't technically pertain to my business, she'll handle it because she always wants to handle anything related to my legal affairs.

All I wanted was a stiff drink or three after leaving Uncle Prescott's house, and getting involved in a scene wasn't in the plan. But at the same time, I couldn't let some asshole physically bully a woman half his size. Although she was doing her best to hide her fear, I noticed the slight pallor of her face, her hands clenched and arms vibrating with tension when he started to use his size and strength to intimidate her.

He slinks away to his buddies. They start talking to him and throw some furtive—and a few overt—looks my way. The asshole himself stands with his back to me, shrugging and obviously trying to play the encounter off as no big deal. But his hands are trembling slightly, and he sticks them in his pockets. *That's right, motherfucker.*

"Thank you," the woman says. Her voice, now devoid of aggressive sarcasm, is sweet and melodious with a hint of a smoky undertone, like a great cigar. I like the way it flows.

"My pleasure, believe me." I check her over to make sure she's okay, then bring my eyes back to up to meet her gorgeous blue ones. They sparkle even in the bar's dim light, reminding me of the sunny Pacific. "Can't have a lady getting abused by some jerk. Besides, I respect that you didn't back down. Most would've cowered." I take the seat next to her.

"Showing fear would've only emboldened him," she says, a steely light in her eyes.

Amusement tugs at the corner of my mouth, as a sliver of respect slides into my heart. "True enough. But still, with the size difference, you looked pretty brave there."

She wrinkles her little nose. "Not really." Her voice drops low, and I'm forced to lean closer to catch her words. "I was actually a teeny bit afraid. It's just that backing down is exactly what bullies want."

There's the lingering fire from the whiskey on her breath. She smells warm and sweet, like peach cobbler spiced with cinnamon. "But that's exactly what bravery is. Standing up for something even when you're afraid."

She exhales softly. Her heart-shaped face is stunning this close, especially as it's framed with long, wavy hair that's a brown so dark it's almost black. Charming freckles dust the bridge of her nose, and she has cherry lips that make me want to have a quick taste to see if they're as sweet as they look. But the best feature is her eyes—wide and clear, in a stunning shade of baby-blue. They shine with intelligence, humor and a glint of steel. A smart woman with a spine. Something hot stirs in my gut, displacing the tension from the aborted dinner.

When was the last time I felt anything remotely like this? And this fast?

"You have really pretty eyes." She gives a short laugh. "I guess you probably hear that a lot."

It takes a second before I can recover. It's like she's reading my mind. "Not really."

"Seriously?"

"The people in my life don't generally notice my eyes." My brothers are...well, guys. And unsentimental, except when it comes to their women and children. Grandmother and Mother are too preoccupied, plotting ways to get me to join the firm or marry one of the worthless

Webber girls. And the women I've dated were always too busy cataloguing my watch, my clothes, my car and my house. Or the possibility that I might be a bridge to my father, who would undoubtedly make them all into stars if only he would come to know about their existence.

She arches a skeptical eyebrow. "You must be surrounded by a lot of oblivious folks."

I laugh. "They have different priorities."

The bartender brings me my scotch, and I push it to her. "Here. To make up for that whiskey."

"Oh, no, it's okay. You aren't the guy who stole my last one."

"So? My treat."

"Well... If you insist. Thanks. I'm Grace, by the way." She extends a small hand.

I take it in mine. As my senses revel in the softness of her skin, a searing jolt runs through my spine. "Huxley," I say.

She takes a big swallow of the scotch, her eyes holding mine, then dropping to my mouth. Her hand is still in my grasp. Then her lips purse and she frowns. I have an absurd impulse to kiss her and tell her to forget whatever is irritating her.

She replaces the glass on the bar. "Okay. Please tell me you aren't a lawyer."

"Why?"

"Because all the lawyers in my life have turned out to be jerks. Except for my best friend, but that's different."

The family resentment that's been simmering in my chest for so long abates a bit. I wish I could record this woman's distaste for attorneys and send it to Grandmother, who thinks that I was born to go into the legal profession. "Well, you're in luck. I'm most definitely not a lawyer."

"What a relief. I'm all lawyered out for the day. Probably for the century."

"Get sued?"

"No." Her eyes flick down briefly, a rueful smile twisting her beautiful lips. "I walked in here to pick up a rival lawyer and have a little revenge on my boyfriend, who cheated on me—"

I lift my eyebrows. *Hard to believe.*

"—and then had the gall to say it was because the sex wasn't great."

"Your boyfriend is a spineless idiot. Infidelity is a coward's way out for people who don't have the guts to end a relationship face to face. He also probably felt deep down that he couldn't measure up to a woman like you." A woman who stands up to a bully, then makes me laugh, is able to soothe my temper *and* turns me on? That's a unicorn.

She flushes and shifts, like she isn't used to hearing how wonderful she is. Her boyfriend is an asshole who probably couldn't find her G-spot with a GPS.

"Well, I am, again, *not* a lawyer...but we could go for it anyway." I keep my tone light enough for her to dismiss it as a joke, but hold her eyes and give her a slow smile.

She considers, giving me an intent, slanted look. As each heartbeat passes, I realize I'm actually growing restless at the possibility she might say no. It's a novel feeling. I've never cared about a woman's response like this before. There was always another one just around the corner, just as good. But I have a feeling Grace is one of a kind.

"Mmm," she says meditatively, glancing in the direction of the group the asshole ran off to. "So far, those were my options. A bunch of guys who are about as attractive as hairless orangutans."

Despite myself, it makes me laugh.

She leans closer until our cheeks are just a hairsbreadth apart. "But I think," she says hotly into my ear, "I just found what I was looking for."

7

GRACE

Huxley and I spill into a gorgeous suite at the Aylster Hotel. I didn't want to take him to my place when the sheets that Peter and Viv used are still on my bed. We deserve better. So when I told him, "Your place," he brought me here.

The lights come on automatically, casting a soft glow everywhere. I don't have time to appreciate the beautifully appointed suite because the instant the door shuts, my back is being pressed against the cool wall.

His mouth claims mine, his tongue plundering me. He tastes like scotch, hot spice with a hint of smoke that's intoxicating and sexy. Something dangerously exciting I've never felt before sizzles in my veins. It feels like every inch of my skin is on fire.

I whimper, digging my fingers into his powerful shoulders. I angle my head to deepen the connection.

With a soft groan, he puts a hand on the small of my back and pulls me closer. He's all lean muscle and excitement—*exactly* what I've been looking for.

Yes, there was a zing that went up my spine when I looked into his beautiful blue-gray eyes at the bar. The tingly sensation that shivered through me when I got a sniff of his spicy cologne. The sudden dryness in my mouth when we shook hands, and how shockingly warm his bare skin felt—how my body seemed to sing as my blood heated.

But the most important thing is that he defended me against others unconditionally, without question or expecting anything in return. That's never happened, not since Mom collapsed two years ago. It's probably the reason I opened up to him more than I normally would have. And why I'm going to spend the night with him.

For the next few hours, I want to feel worthy of protection and care. Deserving of respect and some very hot sex.

I run my hands along his body. He has to be six-six, maybe taller. And underneath the expensive suit is a hardness that hints at massive strength.

A strength he used to keep me safe.

Another whimper rises in my throat, then gets trapped in our fused mouths. My breasts are crushed against him. Even though the layers of fabric, the contact feels more erotic than anything I've ever experienced. His free hand travels along my leg, then cups my ass, the touch sending sparks of heat through me.

Crossing my arms behind his neck, I move my leg along his pelvis restlessly, my clothes riding up and bunching around my upper thighs. He groans at my eagerness and slips his hand underneath my dress, smoothing it over my belly, which quivers at the touch.

"Jesus, you're so soft."

I smile at the lust-roughened voice. It makes me confident and sexy that he wants me so badly. "Yeah? Is that good?"

"*Very* good. Just how a woman should be."

"Then show me exactly how you'd treat a woman who wants you right now."

I let out a surprised yelp as he picks me up. He kisses me as he carries me effortlessly past a door and into a softly lit room. Our bodies slide against each other as he lets me down, and I bite my lip at the way my nerve endings have come alive. I'm hyperaware, hypersensitive. And all we've done is kiss.

He lowers the zipper on my back and pulls the dress over my head. He lets out a sharp exhalation at the sight of my underwear—the black lacy bra, garter belt and sleek silk stockings...and nothing else.

Heat blazes in his darkened eyes as he takes me in. The tent between his legs grows bigger and tauter. I smile, drunk with desire and power. It's so hot to see a man show his naked need.

"Like what you see?" I say, feeling naughty and bold.

"Enough to devour you now."

My eyes on his, I take a slow step back, undo my bra and let it fall. "Then what are you waiting for?"

His eyes flare, then he's on me, like a flash of lightning. My back hits the mattress with a soft bounce, and I laugh. But it soon turns to an anticipatory shuddering of breath when he threads his fingers through mine and spreads my arms, leaving my breasts completely exposed to his burning gaze.

"Pretty, pretty girl." He dips his head and makes a lazy circle around one nipple. I shiver, the tip of my breast aching for more. From the tension in his hands I know he's going crazy for me. But he's reining himself in to prolong the moment. And the only reason a man takes his time is because he wants his partner to enjoy herself, too. Consideration I suddenly realize I've never received from Peter.

Huxley nips my nipple, just hard enough to sting but not enough to hurt, as though he knows my mind has wandered off for a bit. I banish Peter from my thoughts, this room, the planet and reality itself. He doesn't deserve to be in bed with us, not even as a memory.

Huxley soothes the ache by licking my nipple, then pulling it into his mouth and sucking it hard. My back arches as liquid heat unfurls, pooling between my legs. He knows exactly how much pressure to exert, how to use his tongue and teeth to tease and arouse.

Every rational thought vanishes from my head. I pant, arching my back, writhing and rubbing my thighs along his pants. He's nestled between my legs, and I tilt my pelvis, cradle his thick length along my dripping core. His cock pulses so hard I can feel it through the clothes.

Ah yes.

His breathing roughens; I rock myself against him shamelessly. It feels so, so good, but it isn't enough. I'm just at the cusp without anything to push me over.

My fingers tighten around his. "Huxley."

"Impatient for my cock, aren't you?" He rolls his hips over mine, and I moan at the delicious sensation.

"Greedy for it." I'm so close. I've never been wound this tight or felt like I'd die if I didn't come soon.

"Spread your legs. Show me how greedy you are."

I do it, pushing them apart as far as possible and leaving myself utterly exposed. The cool air on my heated pussy stokes my craving.

"So pink. So wet." He purrs the words like a satisfied panther.

"For you."

"Good girl."

He shoots me a grin, the heat in his eyes intensifying. My heart pounds with anticipation of his cock gliding into me.

Instead, he moves down, his hands still holding mine, and buries his face in my dripping flesh.

I've had oral sex before. But what he does is nothing like I've ever experienced.

He's lapping me up, licking me, sucking me, devouring me like he hasn't been fed since forever. It's as though his mouth was created for this. My back arches as he takes his fill between my thighs, and I scream as an orgasm rips through me.

Instead of stopping or wanting to take his turn, he keeps going, pushing me harder and faster to another peak, higher than the one before. But he's not letting me come down, and I twist as another wave of need mounts even higher. His hold on my hands provides me an anchor, and I move my pelvis, rocking against his face. He groans with approval. The vibration pushes me over again.

Every cell in my body quivers. Breathing is a struggle. I've never experienced anything like this before in my life. The only thing that can reliably give me multiple orgasms is my vibrator, but no more than two, and the climaxes are nowhere near this mind-blowing.

"Take off your clothes," I manage between panting breaths. "I want to feel you."

He pulls away. His eyes are burning, and his mouth and jaw glisten with my juices. The contrast between the lewd sight above his neck and the neat three-piece suit is shockingly erotic—and makes me feel powerful that I've destroyed a cool, well-put-together man's control.

Just like I did when I unhooked my bra, he keeps his eyes on mine as he strips out of his clothes, each piece falling to the floor with a whisper. I sensed his body was lean and powerful, but what's left after the veneer of civilization has been peeled off takes my breath away. The sheer width of his shoulders, slabs of muscle all over the tall frame, and the tight six-pack and...

Oh my God.

I slowly sit up. His cock is even bigger than I expected. Dark veins pulse along the long, thick shaft so hard the head is touching his belly. But what's even more shocking are the silver ring and bead sparkling at the head.

Without thinking, I reach out, then stop. Is it okay to touch it? I've never seen a pierced penis before, and don't know what the proper protocol is.

He laughs softly, the sound washing over me like rich velvet. "Go ahead."

Flushing, I stroke the metal carefully. It's warm and smooth—and a bit slick from precum. His cock jerks, the veins darker and more pronounced.

"Never seen a pierced dick before?"

"Never. Did it hurt?"

"Nope. And it's going to feel amazing for you."

He puts on a condom and possessively loops my long hair around his fist. Then his mouth is on mine; I part my lips, welcoming him in. His free hand moves along the sensitive skin of my neck, shoulders; his thumb brushes over the center of my palm where all the lines cross.

Everywhere he strokes, pleasure pulses, then streaks through me and pools between my legs, as though his touch is turning even the most mundane parts of my body into erogenous zones.

I've never been with a man this attentive to me, this *tuned in* to my reactions. My head spins as my back arches again and mounting pleasure rushes up my spine. Everything is too much but not enough at the same time. I want this man inside me *right now*, feel him stretch and fill me. I want to experience the wild rebellion that lurks under that conservative three-piece suit.

The empty aching in my pussy grows so intense, I whimper against his mouth. I want to feel him inside me so badly, but he takes his time, even though his own body is shaking with need.

Push him over the edge.

I recall what he said about spreading my legs to show him how greedy I am for him. Placing my hands on my knees, I part them as widely as I can in offering and temptation.

"See how wet I am? See what I want?"

The tendon in his neck tenses, the vein in his forehead pulsing. His face twists, and something dark and hot and delicious shivers through me in anticipation and warning as a guttural growl starts in his chest.

His large hand grips my hip. "You sweet little slut." His voice is low, but seething with undisguised desire.

How's it feel to lose control? But I can't control myself around him either, so we're even. "If wanting you makes me a slut—"

He pushes in; the words are strangled in my throat. He's so big, the pressure is enormous as he drives in. And the silver bead rubs against the inner wall of my slick pussy, stimulating me in a way I've never experienced before. I feel so full and overexcited. My toes curl.

"Oh my God."

He laughs. "Not even all the way in yet." He pushes forward hard and hilts himself, sending sparks shivering along my nerves.

It's all I can do to suck in air. He feels even bigger inside, and the pulsing of his cock feels like some kind of primal mating heartbeat. Or maybe I'm too in tune with him. Whatever the case, it feels like I'm burning up.

"Hold on to your knees," he orders, then retreats slowly, only to start thrusting with a power and speed that drive me wild. The bead and ring bump into spots in my vagina I didn't know existed. And each time, pleasure strikes like a lightning bolt. I scream, writhe... Beg him to stop, to keep going forever...

I no longer know what I'm saying or doing. The only thing I can chase is another peak. But the second I reach it, he pushes me higher, then higher again. My vision turns hazy; I'm hot and shaking with more orgasms than I can count. Somehow, through it all, I manage to hold on to my knees. And he rewards me for my effort. Calls me a good girl. Tells me how much he loves my tight pussy and how beautiful I am when I climax.

Another peak, and all I can do is lie there, mouth open in a soundless scream as I shake, feeling like I'll die from pleasure. Finally, he clutches me tightly and shudders against me, his face buried in the crook of my neck as his entire body goes rigid.

I let go of my knees and close my eyes as he slowly relaxes, hoping to prolong the moment before he turns over and falls asleep. I sense him get up and pad away. *Hmm... What next?* I've never had a one-night stand before, and have no clue what to do now. Since he left first... Is it a sign I should get going? Except I can't even lift a finger at the moment.

The sound of flushing and running water. A moment later he returns, and the mattress dips. He spreads my legs and puts a cool, damp towel on my flesh. It feels surprisingly soothing. And makes me feel cared for and treasured.

Once he's done, he wraps his arms around me, the gesture oddly protective and...*possessive?*

"That's a lot of firsts for one night," I blurt out, my voice slightly raspy from screaming.

He frowns. "Are you saying you were a virgin?"

I chuckle. "No. But... A one-night stand. A pierced..." I gesture at his cock. "A guy bringing me a towel afterward. And—" I shut my mouth.

"And what?" His tone is lazy, beckoning me to take my time.

I blink, trying to recall how it went after he started to drive into me. Finally, I say, "Damn."

"What?"

"You didn't touch my clit even once after we got naked and I came."

He considers for a moment. "Did you want me to?"

"No. I mean... It doesn't really matter. It's just that usually I can't really finish without some stimulation there." And Peter always rubbed it a few times to get me excited enough, like Aladdin rubbing the lamp just enough to get the genie out, no more. Then he made it sound like somehow it was my body that wasn't responsive because other women weren't like me.

"Well, now you know you can come without it. You're welcome."

I laugh at the cocky pride in his voice, then lay my arm over his chest. It's nice to be held afterward and laugh.

His body radiates a comforting heat, and I nestle closer. My eyelids start to drift lower as exhaustion pulls at me.

"What's your favorite breakfast?" he asks softly.

"Mmm...? Um...Belgian waffles with whipped cream and berries, topped with powdered sugar," I mumble. It was what Mom ordered when she wanted to spoil me. There was a diner not too far from where we lived when I was a kid, and the owner always gave her a small discount and asked us how we were doing and if we needed anything. In retrospect, it's obvious he liked her. I wish *he*'d been my dad. Then we would've been happy even if we lacked the material abundance of the Webbers.

Not gonna make the mistake Mom made. Gonna marry a man who loves me and treats me like a queen, I think drowsily as Huxley places tender kisses on my forehead.

8

GRACE

I AM *WRECKED*.

That's the only word that comes to mind as I carefully get up and roll out of bed. Huxley is sound asleep and doesn't stir.

The nightstand clock says four thirty-seven. Muscles I didn't know I had protest as I move around the bedroom, gathering my clothes. *Holy moly*. My legs tremble, my thighs and calves as sore as if I ran a marathon last night.

Well. It might as well have been—a marathon of orgasms.

Still, it's best to leave now and avoid an awkward conversation. We can end on a high note—a great night of sex and some talk and laughter. If Huxley were local, I might stay, but he's not. I sigh as I take in the gorgeous hotel. As intrigued as I am about him, I don't have the resources or bandwidth to start a long-distance relationship, especially with my mother in a hospital in Baltimore. That's the only long distance I can manage right now.

After I put on my clothes, I look back at the bed. Huxley hasn't moved.

Goodbye, Huxley. I'm never going to forget you.

It's impossible to forget a man who's shown me what is possible in bed...

You know... He'd probably adjust his schedule to fit yours. And this isn't a regular room or suite. See that kitchen there? He might be in town for longer than you think, the part of me that doesn't want to give him up argues.

Or it might be his last night in town. We don't know.

So stay and ask.

Given my luck, he's only in L.A. because his flight got canceled.

Mom and I were happy until she got sick. Then I thought we'd caught a break when my biological dad came for us, until I learned what a gutless, soulless jerk he was. Peter seemed perfect too—until yesterday.

I don't want to mar one of the best experiences of my life by discovering more about Huxley. If that makes me a chickenshit, so be it.

I arrive home a little after six. I take the elevator to the top floor and unlock the door to my condo. After dumping the keys in the bowl by the door, I start toward my bedroom. *Need extra sleep.*

Then I stop dead. *Peter and Viv.*

Making a face, I turn and head to the couch, kick off my shoes and stretch out, one arm over my head. *A couple of hours' nap, then laundry, then hit the grocery store.* Then record something for Mom, so the nurse can play it for her. Ever since the doc said hearing my voice could help, I've been doing my best to send a different recording every day so she knows she's not listening to the same thing over and over again.

Oh, shoot. I should get back to Adam. But not now; it's too early. Maybe after starting the laundry...

I drift off, only to be yanked back to full wakefulness by giggles. Not just any giggle, but *a man giggle.*

What the hell? It's not the neighbors—the unit's impeccably soundproofed because Andreas hates noise.

I get up and grab a skillet from the kitchen. Given the security and the location of the building, I doubt it's a burglar, but you never know.

I open the bedroom door, skillet raised high, then stop. "*Peter?*"

He's lying on my bed with Viv, both of them naked and gross. From the way the sheets are draped across them, her hand is on his crotch. Probably what made him giggle like a castrato.

"What the hell? Knock before you come in," Peter yells.

"Knock? It's *my* room! *My* condo."

Viv jumps in. "No, you're just living here rent-free like a parasite!"

"Really?" I gesture at the living room with the skillet. "Want to make a call and see who's right?"

She shuts up. She knows Andreas doesn't approve of her. She thinks it's because she isn't super smart like the other people in the family. But my money's on her shitty personality.

"Don't be a bitch. I was just leaving anyway." She hops out of bed and runs off to the en suite bathroom.

Peter stares after her like an idiotic, hormonal teenage boy. I grind my teeth. I should be hurt at seeing the betrayal in person, but I'm just irritated that they're in my home when I want to rest. Instead of the skillet, I should've brought a can of Raid.

"Get off your ass and get lost before I call cops for trespassing," I say. "Don't *ever* come back." The shower starts in the bathroom. I'll have to deal with Viv later.

He shakes his head, his butt still on my bed. "Nope. I should get to live here until I find a new apartment."

"*What?*"

"I moved out."

"When? Why?" I demand, my mind furiously processing what's going on.

"Last month. I thought it made sense for me to live here with you. Saves money. I sold my old couches and TV for a decent price."

Blood roars in my head, and I tighten my grip on the skillet. "Just so we're on the same Kafkaesque page... You decided to move in here without telling me because you're too cheap to pay rent for your own apartment?"

"Not cheap. Smart."

"And you also thought it was *smart* to bang her"—I point at the bathroom—"behind my back when you don't even have a home to return to anymore?"

He glares like *I'm* the problem. "This is the least you can do for me."

"Why? Because I won't tell Nelson Webber what a wonderful lawyer you are?"

"Exactly. Be reasonable. Without me, nobody would've known you're Andreas's granddaughter anyway," he sneers.

My gratitude for his one act of kindness five years ago dies a painful yet cynical death. "You asshole!"

"Calm the fuck down. Do we have to be this difficult?"

"Yes! Yes, we do!" I rush to the dresser and pull out the drawers with a few of his casual shirts, shorts, socks and underwear. I should've poured bleach on them all and set them on fire anyway!

I throw them in his face. "Take your crap and *get out!*"

He pulls a shirt off his shoulder. "Come on! You owe me! It's gonna take some time to find a new place!"

"Are you fucking kidding me?" I shake the skillet at him. "What I owe you is a hard swing to the head with this frying pan!"

"That'd be assault and battery."

"It would, wouldn't it? And what would you do? Sue me? You know what... Do it! I'm gonna make this worth a lawsuit!" I put both hands on the skillet and swing it at him.

His eyes widen as he ducks. He rolls off the bed and lands on his side with an ominous *crack.*

Did he...break something? I wonder, half hopeful and half uneasy.

"Aw, fuck!"

He's talking, so he can't be hurt that bad. How disappointing. "Get. The fuck. *Out!*"

He crawls along the side of the bed. "I think I pulled something in my back." He glances up hopefully.

"What are you looking at? Move your ass."

"Can you help me get up?"

"I'm not touching your filthy, cheating body, okay? Get out before I brain you." I lift the skillet in case he's too stupid to get the hint. My God. What the hell is wrong with him? How can a guy with an Ivy League education be this idiotic?

He stands gingerly and gathers his things. I can't decide if I'm lucky he's at least in boxers. After Huxley's penis in all its bejeweled glory, other dicks sort of look small and sad.

"Don't forget to replace my bed and sheets," I say, making a face at a noticeable wet spot.

"Fuck you." Then he hobbles out as quickly he can before I hit him for real.

I exhale to control my temper. It's ridiculous and infuriating that my relationship with Peter didn't hit its lowest point last night. What kind of fool did he take me for, anyway? Did he honestly expect me to let him live here after I found out he'd cheated on me?

The door to the bathroom opens. I'm still holding the skillet, although I won't need it to deal with Viv. She's even dumber than Peter.

"Get out, and don't ever show your face around here."

"You don't own this place," Viv sneers.

"Yeah, well, neither do you. And it's me Andreas picked," I say, twisting the knife a little. Viv wanted this condo. It's in a nice, safe area and close to downtown.

"Only because he feels sorry for you. You're just a manipulative, greedy bitch trying to squeeze money out of everyone!"

The words bounce right off. Her opinion means nothing, because she's never been fair or nice to me. Why bother listening to her anyway? "Exactly. And I'm also going to tell you that you and Peter need to replace my bed and sheets."

"Get a job and replace them yourself. Or is honest work beneath you? Emotionally blackmailing people is all you can do, isn't it? If it weren't for you, Andreas wouldn't have been so hard on Dad."

"If Nelson had kept his dick in his pants—where it *belonged*—none of this would've happened. Do you think I want to be his child? Or be related to someone like you?"

Viv screams, then looks around for something to throw. That is her go-to when she can't win an argument. She grabs a bottle of toner from my vanity and lifts it over her head.

"Throw that and I'll tell everyone in creation that you didn't take your own LSAT."

She hesitates. That perfect score I made for her is the only reason she got into Harvard Law. Her college transcript is average at best.

"You wouldn't dare," she says, the bottle still poised over her head.

"Why? Because it's illegal to take the test for someone else?"

Her eyes glitter. "Exactly."

"So is coercing somebody to take it *for* you. How do you think it'll look when I go on TV and tell everyone I had no choice because my stepmother threatened to end my real mother's care and let her die? You and Karie have a lot to lose because you're proud Webbers. Me? I'm just a nobody, so..."

She bites her lip, then finally throws the bottle on the bed, where it bounces a couple of times. "*You.*" She points a quivering finger at me. "You better keep your mouth shut if you want your cunty mom to live!"

9

HUXLEY

Sleep fades as my consciousness starts to assert itself. I feel so damn good as I laze in the soft bed, my face on the plush pillow and my body on twisted sheets. The morning after a visit with my family always starts with my mood somewhere south of zero, but not today.

Grace.

Just the thought of her makes me smile. My internal clock says it's still early. Maybe a morning shower together would be good. With me washing her *very* thoroughly. I'd love to see my cum on her wet, naked body, her eyes glazed in orgasm, her nipples hard, and her mouth soft and swollen from my kisses. By then our breakfast should arrive. We can eat and then do it again, this time in bed. I'd love to have her for dessert.

I reach over to stroke her long, silky hair...and my fingers touch nothing but cool sheets. I crack my eyes open. *She isn't here.* The bathroom's quiet—and the door's open—so she isn't in there, either. No sound coming from the living room or the kitchen either. No scent of coffee. Nothing to indicate another person in the residence.

I sit up and rub my forehead. Displeasure tugs at my attention like a splinter stuck under my nail—not enough to hurt, but enough to make itself known. I glance at the nightstands and the desk. No note.

If it weren't for the ripped condom wrappers, I could have dreamed the whole thing with Grace.

Why did she leave?

The sex couldn't have been the problem. She came hard multiple times, her pussy spasming around my tongue, my fingers, my cock. She clung to me like I was her lifeline. I asked her what she liked for breakfast so I could instruct the concierge to send our breakfast at nine thirty sharp, all the while patting myself on the back for bringing her to the Aylster Residence my brother Seb still has a lease on, although he doesn't live here. I chose this place because it was closer than mine and traffic was a shitshow. Plus, the concierge is damn convenient.

But I didn't count on Grace fleeing the scene as I fell asleep with her in my arms. My mood craters, and a shower doesn't help. By the time breakfast arrives, there are practically thunderclouds over my head.

I stare balefully at the Belgian waffle, all the attendant fixings and the three-egg omelet with cheese and bacon. I choke down some coffee, but don't touch the food. My stomach is clenched too tight.

I don't feel any better when I arrive at my place. Should've driven us here even if the traffic *was* shitty last night. Then she wouldn't have been able to leave so easily—Uber and the like can't get past security without alerting me first.

I glumly stare at my mansion. It merely stands, stately, the stained-glass windows sparkling and the rock garden as Zen as the one I saw in Japan. Everything is as it should be, except my mood.

How am I going to find her again? I got the sense that the bar wasn't her usual spot. She said her ex was a lawyer, but the city has over eighty-five thousand licensed lawyers. If she went to the bar to find a lawyer who was better than her ex...

That bar is a hangout for Huxley & Webber's rival, Highsmith, Dickson and Associates. Most of their attorneys are from Ivy League schools or Stanford, and the massive firm has its fingers in hundreds of legal pies. And they generally employ very good lawyers.

"Hi there!" comes a high-pitched, cheery voice from...*above?*

I look up at the big tree in the yard. A blonde in a leopard-print dress straddles a branch about seven feet off the ground. The outfit is cut so low, I can see the tops of her areolas. She's put a soft cloth over the branch to ensure she doesn't chafe her toned thighs, and the skirt is riding so high I can see half her bare ass. I'd bet both eyeballs she's going commando. With Grace, it was hot. But this chick—it's just vulgar.

If I had normal people for parents, I'd be at least slightly alarmed that a stranger had invaded my home. As it is, what I feel is a little resignation and a lot of fury.

What the fuck, Joey?

"Get down here!"

"I'm Jane." She smiles and waves like a pageant queen.

"And?"

She bounces on the branch, one hand over her quivering tits. "I could be *your* Jane if you'd just come up." She lets out a tittering giggle, unfazed by my impatience. Or she's too dumb and oblivious to notice. "Do you know that every woman in my family had twins? So we could have twins. One that looks like you and one that looks like me! Wouldn't that be cute?"

"More like terrifying," I mutter. Joey has been sending me progressively dumber and dumber women to procreate with, trying to satisfy my father's need for a baby he can take to Hollywood parties. Apparently, I'm smart enough to compensate for a lack of IQ in the baby's mother.

"So let's *do* it!" She leans forward, arching her back and opening her mouth to show me her tongue. The sight is outright third-rate porn. Actually, I don't think even third-rate porn does this anymore. "Come *ooonnn.*"

She brings down her torso low enough that her breasts pop out of the dress. Instead of covering herself, she laughs. "Oops! Guess the girls can't wait."

My skin crawls. "Get down here. *Now.*"

"Make me!" She giggles again and sticks her tongue out.

Just how old is she? Twelve?

"Come and get me, Tarzan," she says breathlessly, then cups her breasts and pushes them toward me.

No. *No!* I can feel brain cells gasping and writhing as they die. Time to end this shit.

"I haven't done any skeet shooting in a while, and it's time I got some practice in. To avoid getting rusty."

She lets out a theatrical gasp. "Are you threatening me?"

"Nope. Just informing you of my plans for the day." I start toward my house.

"Wait! I can't get down on my own!" she yells.

"How'd you get up there?"

"Joey helped me."

"So call him." Maybe I'll shoot both of them. Joey could look like a clay target if I dumped a bucket of white paint on him.

"Wait!" she screams again. She probably has a twenty-word vocabulary, the top one being "wait."

"If you aren't gone by the time I get out..." I give her my most charming smile, the one that makes even my mom nervous.

It scares "Jane" more than a gun, because she lets out a small shriek. "Oh my God! Joey never told me you were a serial killer!"

"I'm not. But I could make an exception."

10

HUXLEY

MY FOUL MOOD PERSISTS, and hasn't improved much by the time brunch with my brothers rolls around four weeks later. It doesn't help that I've been to the bar near Highsmith every night and haven't run into Grace. My feeling that it wasn't her scene was correct.

And it certainly doesn't help that Joey sent me two more women, neither of which was an improvement over "Jane." Actually, Jane was the best of the bunch. Where does he *find* these women? And does Dad know about it...?

Of course he does. He probably approves all these women. To my chagrin and disgust, I can easily imagine Dad playing "me Tarzan, you Jane" with women a third his age.

I should just hire somebody to beat the hell out of Joey. Wonder if any of my brothers knows somebody who knows somebody. Money's no object. Keeping Joey permanently away from me is.

On top of that, my grandmother isn't even trying to talk to me anymore. She sent me ten different wedding invitation designs, all of which have my name and a blank for the bride's, since I haven't chosen which Webber yet. Then came fifty bouquet options. Why the hell does she think I care about what flowers should be at the matrimonial farce I don't plan to participate in?

Then she texted me that it'd be tragic if I was cut off from the family, and I had to stare at the message, trying to figure out what she was *really* trying to communicate.

Has she forgotten that I have my own money, my own career and my own last name? Maybe threats like this work well on Uncle Prescott and some others in the family—although I can't visualize them working on Mom—but I'm immune. If getting cut off means no more Huxley & Webber on retainer, so be it. Highsmith, Dickson and Associates would love to have my business.

I park my Lamborghini in front of Emmett's mansion. I spot a few other cars, including the Bugatti Noah loves so much. It's a little shocking that he hasn't gotten a custom paint job to make it look like cheetah skin. And more shocking that he got here before I did.

Emmett's place has gone through some renovations, mainly to accommodate his and Amy's little daughter Monique. There's a pink baby grand in the center of the great room that looks out onto the lush garden. Monique apparently wanted to play a pink piano after seeing another girl playing one, so that's what Emmett got her.

Right now, the gigantic home has only us brothers. When we have our brunches, Amy prefers to hang out with my other sisters-in-law— four of them, since Noah and I are the only bachelors left, although even he has an all-but-wife girlfriend now. We told them we wouldn't mind if the ladies wanted to join us, but they said it was our man-bonding time, and they didn't want to intrude.

Which just shows how smart they are, because the purpose of our brunch is exactly that. It's always been just the seven of us. We were in the same grade in the same schools, and always had each other's backs because we knew from early on that we couldn't necessarily count on our parents. So what if our father was a legend in the movie business and there were seven women who could've taken on a maternal role? They were busy and had their own interests. The only one who came close to being a mother figure to me was Emmett's mom, but only because she's nice and unassuming, not because she's boring or had nothing better to do.

So even though we've been out of school for years, we make sure to spend time together. To see what's up with each other's lives. And, of course, give each other shit, because that's just how we roll.

I'm the last to arrive. All seven of us were able to make it here today, in the huge dining room with a massive brunch spread. Emmett has catered the meal because he doesn't want to kill us with his cooking. To be fair, none of us are any good in a kitchen. Ted Lasker gave us many things—dark hair, square jaws and enough money that none of our mothers needed to work to provide for us while we were growing up—but not culinary ability. Of course he probably can't wipe his own ass without Joey, so wielding a knife in the kitchen... Not a good idea.

I grab some sausages and bacon and sit down with a mug of strong coffee.

"Playa del Carmen is a great choice for a month-long birthday celebration," says Nicholas. "But a little crowded with all the gringo vacationers."

"Whose birthday is this?" I ask. Nicholas is so whipped he might just go ahead and book an entire resort for a month for his wife.

"My mom's," Emmett answers. "She wants to have a quiet vacation on the beach."

Emma is the polar opposite of Dad in every way. Sane. Rational. Loves peace and quiet. Enjoys reading romance and mysteries. Not a big fan of parties, and she stays away from most of them except for Dad's birthday bash because he's impossible otherwise.

She's nothing like the other six mothers, either. God must've taken pity on Dad to let him dazzle a woman like Emma enough to spend a night with her. But of course, he botched it by returning to his degenerate lifestyle the next day and promptly impregnating the rest of our mothers.

They had no desire to put aside their own interests and careers—from modeling to photography to being a rich jewelry heiress—while my brothers and I were little. They voted to ship us off to boarding schools. A lot of our brothers like to blame Dad for that decision, but if you think about it, it's obvious he never cared about us deeply enough to ponder where we should get our education. As long as we didn't die, he was fine.

The boarding schools were convenient for my mother, who was never around because her legal career demanded everything she had to give. But not Emma. She moved to Europe to live near the schools and acted as our guardian. She taught me to be a better man than my father, and even tried to teach us how to cook, saying it was an essential life skill. In addition, when I was fighting for the right to steer my own future, she was the one who told me to take my time to consider what I truly desired.

"Follow your heart, Huxley. You only get one life. Don't live it for someone else."

The woman might not have given birth to me, but spiritually she's been more of a mom than Jeremiah ever was. And I love her for it.

"Rent out an entire resort with a private beach," I say. "That way she can just invite the people she wants."

"That's the plan," Emmett says.

"Good. It's the least she deserves." My eyes fall on the Belgian waffle on Noah's plate, and I scowl. *Still can't figure out why Grace ran out on me.* I checked with the Aylster concierge in case she'd gotten in touch that way, but nothing.

Noah must feel my gaze. He looks up from his phone—he's always on his phone, checking social media feeds. "What? You look like that stick up your ass suddenly got bigger." Then he munches on the waffle with sheer bliss radiating from his face. He's never met a carbohydrate he couldn't fall in love with. But he manages to maintain a lean frame, probably from chasing all those cheetahs he loves so much. He's a wildlife photographer, albeit a part-time one, since he doesn't need the money. None of us do, thanks to the early investments we made with Emmett and Grant, who are financial geniuses.

"Probably just met a chick who wouldn't succumb to his charms." Sebastian shoots me a sly grin.

"Who?" Noah says, finally putting down his phone.

"No way!" Grant says. "Hux would never bother."

"Exactly. Women are dime a dozen for him." Griffin yawns. Probably his children kept him up all night again—he never lacked for sleep until his wife popped out three at once. He teaches, does an enormous amount of research and publishes like his life depends on it—he is in academia, after all—but he never, ever had to give up sleep for what he wanted to accomplish.

"Besides, if he puts his mind to it, I'm sure he can charm any woman." Nicholas's words are measured. He has a calm, settled way of speaking that makes you instinctively trust him. I wish he'd do some voiceovers for our bank commercials, but he's not interested. He is as intensely private as Griffin, who does everything in his power to hide who his parents are. To the point that his mother has complained that she "isn't some serial killer to be ashamed of."

Seb snorts. "I have it on good authority that he took a girl to the Aylster a month ago. She didn't leave until zero dark thirty the next morning."

Outrage pulses in my heart. "They *told* you? What the hell happened to client privacy?"

"Oh, it's alive and well. Thing is, *you're* not the client." Seb looks positively smug. "They have a log of who comes in and out. And apparently you're interested to know if the lady in question ever came back and left you a note." He turns to the others. "Which she didn't."

"Bro..." Griffin shakes his head.

"Women don't like it when you're desperate," Grant says. "It repels them."

"Thank you, Captain Obvious. How's Aspen doing?"

"Shut up." He and his wife Aspen are still engaged in a minor cold war over his refusal to be reasonable about her idea of investing in an old college friend's bar. His reluctance has nothing to do with the business plan being shitty. Rather, it's personal because the friend happens to have a penis.

"It's only fifty thousand bucks," Emmett says. "Let it go. Besides, your wife is smart. She wouldn't mix business with anything personal."

Frustrated irritation sparks in Grant's eyes. "Have you seen the way that motherfucker looks at her?"

"Nope. But I know who Aspen married," Emmett counters.

We nod. Grant merely sighs. He probably knows he's wrong but doesn't want to admit it to his wife. None of us knows how he gets around with an ego that big. "Fine. It isn't like we'll become destitute if the bar fails."

Nicholas lifts his coffee mug. "Now you're talking."

"So, back to that stick up your butt... If it's not the girl, what is it?" Grant says, obviously trying to turn the topic away from his disagreement with Aspen.

Asshole. "My family is pressuring me to marry a Webber. My grandmother in particular absolutely refuses to leave me alone. She set up four dates for me and one of the girls! So that I could 'get to know and appreciate my options better.'" My hands clench. I fantasize about strangling The Fogeys so often my knuckles ache.

"How did they go?" Grant asks, eyeing me cautiously.

"They didn't," I say, in a you-know-me-better-than-that tone. "Then yesterday, she sent a huge brass plaque that read *Huxley Lasker-Webber* to the office to hang outside my door."

Emmett and Nicholas spew out their coffee. Noah makes a strangled noise and slaps his chest to dislodge the last piece of waffle he shoved into his mouth. Griffin's mouth actually hangs open.

"Well... At least she put your last name before the *Webber*," Grant says.

"Thank God!" I throw my hands in the air.

"The empire needs its heir married and producing baby heirs," Seb says.

I shudder. "Ugh. No. I'm not a lawyer, which disqualifies me from being an heir to Huxley & Webber."

"He's right." Noah finally says something rational, only to ruin it by laughing and adding, "You don't sell your heir to the highest bidder."

"There was no bidding." If there had been an auction, it would've been better because then I would've bid to make myself permanently unavailable.

Noah blinks. "So the family got nothing?"

"There's a contract," I grind out.

"Can't be legal," Griffin says with a dark scowl.

I clench my teeth. "Unfortunately, it is. I got stupid and trusted my family with a POA once." I revoked the power of attorney so fast, Mom burst out laughing. Being hooked up to a machine will be better than getting used by my family again. I read the entire infuriating contract twice. "If I fail to marry a Webber within two years of signing, I'm to hand over twenty-five percent of my ownership stake at 4D Agency to my grandmother." The veins in my head almost popped when I read the clause. It still makes my blood boil.

Emmett winces in sympathy. "Huxley & Webber isn't one of the best for nothing."

"Legalized human trafficking." Noah moves his chin up and down in an I-knew-it nod. "Well, look at it this way, Hux. At least you're the prize."

I shoot him a death glare. "Not funny."

He shows me his palms. "Hey, don't hate me. I'm not the one sending you a Lasker-Webber name plate. Just pointing out the silver lining."

"So your options are...?" Griffin says, always pragmatic.

Just thinking about them makes my head throb. "An idiot—"

He grunts. He hates dumb people because he has to deal with them every semester when they swarm his office to argue their grades.

"—and a spender."

Nicholas cocks an eyebrow. "A spender?"

"Burns through twenty-five thousand a month," I say, recalling what Ares told me. "And the Webbers don't even talk about this one publicly, so there's gotta be a lot more wrong than just some frivolous spending habits."

"Like what?"

I shrug. "No idea. But Andreas agreed to throw in a million bucks *if* she's the bride." Bryce mentioned that the other daughter being an option at all is probably Andreas's doing. For some reason, the old man seems to like her better than Vivienne. Probably because nobody can be as annoying and lacking in common sense as that disgrace of a human being. Or...my cousin is totally wrong about Andreas's motives, and what he really wants is to offload a seriously flawed grandchild.

Onto *me*.

"Wow," Seb says.

"Maybe she has an extra nose." Noah scratches his own in contemplation. "Or a scar on her forehead. I mean, not a lightning-shaped one—that'd be cool. Wait, I know!" He snaps his fingers. "A face tattoo!"

Griffin's mouth twists. "Be serious."

"The money's probably to make up for the twenty-five K." Emmett steeples his fingers. "You put the million into a decent investment vehicle, it'll pay for her monthly allowance. Plus there'll be some left over to cover taxes."

"Uh-huh. And will it be enough to cover my pain and suffering?" I mutter.

"Well... Given how you are..." Grant shrugs. "Probably not."

"Too bad Alaric isn't a girl. He's so sensible," Noah says.

He's a Webber. A Harvard-educated lawyer, naturally. And... "He's large and tall, so even if he were a girl, he wouldn't be my type. I like my women small, pretty and with soft curves. Flowing, dark hair. Sweet tempered but a little feisty."

Seb looks at Griffin. "Sounds like he needs a Labrador retriever."

"Hunt around for the right woman," Nicholas advises. "How hard can it be?"

"You met yours at a high school graduation. I'm a little long in the tooth for that," I say dryly.

He rolls his eyes. "How about a fake engagement? You can't marry a Webber if you're engaged to somebody else."

"To whom?" None of my exes would be able to pull it off because nobody would believe I cared about them enough to go back to them, much less want to marry one. I wonder briefly about Grace, but the sad fact is that I may never find her again.

"How about Madison?" Grant says. "She's capable."

I make a face. "She's my *assistant*."

"So?" Noah points a piece of bacon at me. "She has feelings for you. She'll do a good job for a chance to cling to you in public."

I stare at him. "What are you talking about?"

"You haven't noticed? She's been giving you that 'oh please...fuck me, boss'"—he does a breathless falsetto for maximum impact—"look for years now."

I scoff. "She has not."

"My eyes don't lie. She's like that every time I stop by your office to drop off some photos." Noah sounds exceptionally convinced. The camera lens client wanted to use Noah's shots because he's one of the

64

best wildlife photographers. For the multi-year campaign, he even did shots of scenery other than cheetahs.

"I saw how overly attentive she was when Lucie and I visited your office to discuss the ad campaign for our collaboration project," Seb says. "She's on your wavelength. Knows what you want without you having to say it."

"How could you side with him? Of course she's attentive—that's her job! But trust me. The second I fired Madison, she'd quit giving a damn. Besides, even if she had feelings for me—*which she doesn't*—I'd still say no. I don't shit where I eat. Interoffice dating is doomed to fail."

"Fine. Forget Madison. You must still know somebody who can help you," Grant says.

"If you don't have even one hottie who owes you..." Noah's expression positively brims with pity. "You've lived your life wrong."

~

BY THE TIME the brunch ends, the sky is practically black.

"Damn it. Is it going to rain?" Griffin gets grumpier when the weather's crappy. Not because he's afraid of driving in the rain, but because he hates SoCal drivers even more when it's raining.

"Looks like it. Drive carefully," I say, climbing into my car. I'm not worried about my brothers doing something stupid. I'm worried about other drivers screwing up.

As soon as I'm on the highway, the water hits, and the road turns into a parking lot.

Fabulous. Just fantastic.

If a zombie apocalypse started during a rain, everyone in SoCal would be trapped in their cars and get their brains eaten.

After about five minutes of my staring at the barely moving taillights in front of me, my mind begins to wander. *Fake engagement...*

Nicholas's idea sounds like a romance novel. Of course, he reads a lot of them because his wife Molly loves them so much. He somehow manages to get her tickets to all sorts of popular signings and gives her his black AmEx to buy whatever books she wants. He even sent a private jet to pick her up because she often buys more books than she can possibly ship.

But even she doesn't spend twenty-five thousand a month. Seb's wife might, but Lucie is a jewelry company CEO. She works her ass off, and she's entitled to spend the money she's earned.

This secret spendthrift Webber girl probably has no job. Why work when you receive free money? I haven't heard anything about Vivienne getting such a generous allowance, so the mystery girl must've found some way to squeeze it out of Nelson, which couldn't have been easy. He's generous and indulgent with himself, but not with others. And he isn't a complete moron, so he'd be difficult to trap.

She's starting to seem like a manipulative, conniving woman. Maybe worse than Grandmother. I'd have to be on guard at all times to make sure I didn't get fucked over if I was dealing with her.

I narrow my eyes, loathing the situation. The mystery Webber girl is almost certainly worse than Vivienne. At least I know what's wrong with that one. Annoying. Stupid. Vapid. Spoiled. Fickle. Gather all the foibles of our mothers and take away all their positive aspects, and you have Vivienne Webber.

My mind whispers that I should choose the lesser of the two evils. At least pick the devil I know. But the idea is abhorrent. On the other hand, if I don't do anything, my family will eventually find a way to force me. A twenty-five percent stake is enough to meddle in the management of my ad agency, and Grandmother will do everything in her power to ruin my dream so that I'll have to live hers.

She's already sent me hundreds of texts, railing at me for not showing up for the dates she set up.

If I had a fake fiancée, I could take myself off the market long enough to fight this contract. My family is damn good, but so is John Highsmith. And he'll take the case just for a chance to show my grandmother.

But who owes me a favor big enough to play my fake fiancée?

The rain is now pouring down so hard I can barely see anything in front of me. It hasn't rained like this in a long time. In fact, the last time...

Wait a minute. That girl who said she'd like to pay me back. She only had a dollar or two and left me a number instead. I never called to collect, but I kept that dollar bill.

She may not be suitable, but it wouldn't hurt to check her out. Her gratitude when I dropped her off was sincere. If she can help, she will.

Well, well, well.

Maybe I didn't live my life so wrong after all.

11

GRACE

WHY, OH WHY, DOES ANDREAS HATE ME?

I TRY NOT to show how I really feel as I push my seafood pasta around on the plate. It's probably poisoned. Not because Karie's cook is a terrible human being, but because Karie is.

She loves to serve food like she's the one who labored in the kitchen, putting on a red and white apron with a big embroidered apple and holding a wooden spoon with some sauce smeared on it. But if you look closer, the dress on her gym-toned body is a brand-new Dior, her nails long and flawless, her makeup perfect. And no one has to look closely to see the bleached hair pulled up in a French twist and secured with a couple of pearl pins, or the fact that too many diamonds glitter on her ears and around her throat. Or listen that carefully to hear her sky-high stilettos clack on the marble floor. She's the picture of a woman who doesn't look like she spent more than a minute instructing her staff.

Nelson is sitting at the head of the needlessly large table in his ostentatious dining room in his pretentious mansion. He borrowed more money than he should have to purchase the place, most likely to alleviate a feeling of inferiority to his more successful brother. His wide-set brown eyes are narrowed, bringing out his crow's-feet. His prominent nose got the height his cheekbones didn't. The wide, square jaw line gives his otherwise slightly above-average features an impression of strength, which he uses to his advantage to soothe clients. He aims for dignified by refusing to smile, but merely ends up looking displeased. It doesn't help that his hairline has receded enough to make him appear about ten years older than he is.

I thank my lucky stars every day that I look nothing like him.

Mick sits to Nelson's left, a carbon copy of his father sans the hairline. He desperately wanted to go to Harvard Law, but failed. *Twice.* Once, when drunk, he cried about how unfair it was that he was "forced to settle" for Wake Forest because the Harvard Law admissions office was blind to his brilliance. From the way he went on, you'd think he'd been the victim of some unimaginable crime against humanity. But he's a DA in Los Angeles now, doing fine. It's more than he deserves.

Viv is seated next to Karie. They're so much alike—outwardly and inwardly—cold hypocrites, full of themselves.

Currently the four are talking to one another, sharing what happened during their week, how they're doing, gossiping about people they know. They make sure to bring up only people I don't know—God forbid I join the conversation. The only reason they invite me at all is because Andreas insisted that we have at least one bimonthly family meal together. He thinks it'll help me and the rest of Nelson's family "bond." Apparently he's under the illusion that the reason I'm like oil to their water is that we haven't spent enough time getting to know each other.

Karie likely hasn't disabused him of the notion, since he isn't just the head of the family, but controls Nelson's legal career. She's desperately hoping that Mick can join the firm once his stint at the district attorney's office is over. The fact that her nephew Alaric is killing it at Huxley & Webber drives her crazy because she hates Nelson's brother and his wife.

My phone buzzes. I check the message.

—Peter: Are you serious about the bill?

Guess he finally got the invoice for the bed and sheets I sent him. I emailed it to him initially, but it bounced because he blocked me. So I mailed it to his old address, since the post office is likely forwarding him his mail.

—Me: Yes. Why would you think I wasn't?

—Peter: I'm sleeping in the office because of you!

Oh, really? Let me shed some tears.

—Me: Gosh. If only you'd keep your dick in your pants...

—Peter: Why do you have be so difficult, Grace?

—Me: Good question! Upon reflection, it's probably because an asshole ex-boyfriend cheated on me and humiliated me in front of his colleagues at a promotion party I wasn't invited to.

—Peter: It was an honest mistake. Kacey fucked up. I already spoke to her about that.

That poor assistant.

—Me: Uh-huh. Did she also shove your dick into my sister's vagina?

—Peter: You're being unreasonable.

—Me: At least you aren't paying rent. Why don't you move in with your NEW girlfriend?

—Peter: It isn't that simple. Viv isn't that kind of girl.

—Me: What kind? The kind who'd let you move in with her? The kind you cheat on? Or the kind you bang to further your career?

—Peter: She's Nelson's real daughter!

If he meant to wound me with that, it doesn't work. I've never considered myself Nelson's true child.

—Me: So it's the career thing.

"Grace, it's rude to stare at your phone at the dinner table. Didn't you mother teach you any better?" Karie says.

I do my best not to clench my jaw. Karie never brings up my mom, not even asking how she's doing at Johns Hopkins, except to criticize. In a way I understand how bitter she must feel about the fact that my mom is "the other woman." But Karie never directs her ire at Nelson because she understands who has the power.

"Leave her alone. Who cares if she knows how to behave?" Viv says, obviously upset the focus of the conversation has shifted away from her. "I'm the one marrying *the* Huxley, anyway."

That name. Memories of my one-night stand come flowing back. My cheeks warm at what we did, and it's suddenly difficult not to squirm in my seat. *Huxley.* I wish I could see him again, but he's probably back to wherever he was from. I went by the hotel, but the front desk said the residence was unoccupied but not available for lease. The clerk, who had TRAINEE printed under her name, was reluctant to share any more information. It probably didn't help that I don't look like someone who can afford to live there.

"He's *sooooooo* hot," Viv says dreamily, practically fanning herself. "Like a god or something. I'm so happy he's going to be mine. Just think —*Mrs. Huxley...*"

I roll my eyes. It's going to be an *arranged marriage*. Hardly a river of romance. And how pathetic is it that Andreas feels the need to help her find a husband because he doesn't trust her to do it on her own?

I navigate to the Huxley & Webber site and look at the lawyers. There are three possible options for Viv: Ares, Josh and Bryce. Which one is she thinking about? And what has he done to deserve a fate worse than death? Lose an important case, maybe?

"I get shivery every time he looks at me," Viv says, still gushing.

Karie gazes at her fondly.

I can't stand it anymore. "What about Peter?"

It jerks her out of her reverie, which is perversely satisfying. "What about him?" It's practically a snarl.

"I caught you in bed with him last month. You guys might've spent more time together since then."

"Are you *judging* me?" Viv looks me up and down. "It isn't like I'm *married*. I just wanted to take him out for a spin."

I flutter my eyelashes. "You mean you just wanted him because you were jealous he was with me."

She flinches a little before snorting. "Why would I be jealous of *you*?"

"I don't know... Oh, wait!" I snap my fingers. "Remember that perfect LSAT?"

Viv turns bright red. Karie inhales sharply, while Nelson scowls. Mick trains his half-crazed eyes on me. "Watch what you say to my sister. I won't tolerate your bullying her."

I wish Andreas could see this for himself—no matter how many meals he forces on me and Nelson's family, we will never be a true family. "Stating a fact isn't bullying."

"It depends on intent," he says, his tone sharp with anger. But he won't do more than talk, not with the staff around.

"Oh look." I point my fork at the window. "There are clouds in the sky."

"So?"

"What will the poor sky do, now that I'm bullying it?"

"You little bitch!" Mick slaps the table hard enough to make the silverware rattle.

"Mick." Karie cuts her eyes to the server who's coming over to refill our water.

He lets out a breath, all the while staring death lasers at me. Well, whatever. He made it clear a long time ago that he'd always hate me because of my mom. I'm not going to waste energy trying to earn his love and approval.

Karie turns to Nelson. "Viv needs a new car for law school. Something that will help her fit in better. How about a Lexus?"

"I prefer a Maybach," Nelson says.

I'd prefer to leave and never come back, I think.

And then, like some divine intervention, the sky splits open and rain starts to fall. Nelson sighs—inclement weather supposedly aggravates his back pain. But big grins split Karie, Mick and Viv's faces. They're thrilled I'll be driving in the rain. They probably hope I'll get into an accident—maybe even die.

"Well—fun as this hasn't been—I should get going before the rain gets worse."

Nobody objects as I place my napkin on the table and get up. My sneakers squeak a little as I make a rapid escape from the miasma of elite pretension.

Outside the house the air is wet and oppressive, but I still take a deep breath of it. *Thank God, freedom!*

I head to my car and get in. The traffic's going to be terrible, and I'll spend hours sitting in it, but I don't care. My car has comfortable seats and music. Most importantly, it *doesn't* have Nelson and company.

The engine starts with its usual reliable growl and Garbage sing, "Tell Me Where It Hurts" from the speakers. My phone rings. No caller ID, but it could be somebody from the hospital. Dr. Blum's staff has called from unknown numbers before.

Hope flutters in my heart, tentative yet excited. Dr. Blum's email this week was so positive.

"Hello?" I say, trying to sound calm.

"Hi," a deep male voice says. "A couple of years ago I gave you a ride in the rain. I'm calling about the compensation you promised to me."

Everything inside me immediately deflates, then almost instantly swells back up in rage. "What the hell kind of scam is this?" Cursing under my breath, I pull the phone from my ear, about to hang up—

"I drove a young woman to the ER on a rainy evening. She promised to pay, but didn't have enough cash and left me this number."

Holy... I remember! "Which hospital was this?" I ask, just to be sure.

"Ronald Reagan Medical Center. The woman had dark hair and was soaking wet. Got rainwater all over my car seat."

My hand flies to my cheek. "Oh my God!"

"Do I have the right number?" A tinge of impatience roughens the voice.

"No, no! I mean, yes. Yes, you have the right number. I thought you'd lost it because you never called. But I'm glad we could finally connect." I smile, happy to be dealing with the kind stranger from before. People like him are the reason I believe the world is a great place and am hopeful about the future, no matter how hard my life feels at the moment. "How much do I owe you? I can Venmo you right now."

"Don't worry about the cash. Would it be possible for us to meet? Just for a coffee or something."

"Uh... I guess. Why?"

"I have a proposal for you."

12

GRACE

AN HOUR LATER, I arrive at Merry, the gorgeous café in the lobby of the Aylster Hotel. It's impossible to look at this building and not think of Huxley. I'll probably never forget him—every time I see the place it brings to mind the most erotic experience of my life.

A valet in a crisp uniform takes my car. I walk up to the entrance, trying to ignore both memories of Huxley and the feeling that I don't belong in this sea of expensive vehicles and casual affluence. But then, I've never felt like I belonged anywhere since I met Nelson. I feel so alone without Mom by my side.

I stop by the ATM in the back of the lobby and take out two hundred bucks. It should be enough to pay the stranger for the ride. *Or at least I hope it is.* He mentioned his seat getting wet, and if there was any damage to the leather, he may want me to pay for it.

Can't recall the exact make of the car. I was in a panic at the time, plus it was dark and raining. I can't even remember clearly what the driver looked like. But I definitely recall that his car was one of those super-expensive ones Mick sighs over all the time.

If he wanted you to pay for the seat that bad, he would've contacted you already.

Yeah, true, but then why is he contacting me *now* and saying he wants to see me in person? This can't possibly be over some cleaning bill... Can it?

Okay, no reason to get anxious yet. He hasn't said why he wants to see me. And if I ruined his seat, I *should* pay for it. That's the right thing to do. I just pray it doesn't break my little bank.

The cash stuffed in my purse, I make my way to Merry. Named after the wife of the current CEO of the Aylster hotel chain, it's one of the swankiest cafés in the city. Beautiful golden marble sparkles on the floor and walls, and Swedish crystal chandeliers hang from the high ceiling in a chic contemporary display. The place plays nothing but classical music at a low volume so people can linger over their drinks and converse with ease.

Coffee here costs a kidney and half your liver, but it tastes like liquid gold and has an intense jolt of caffeine to wake you up. I would never come here on my own—it's *way* out of my budget—but Andreas loves the place.

I probably should've suggested a different place—some cheaper café, I tell myself as I stand in the entrance. But I was so surprised to get a call from the man who helped me out that I forgot to try to change the venue. *Well, it doesn't matter.* No need to order anything. Just thank him again, give him the money and get out. How hard can it be?

I look around for the man. *He said he'd be in a white shirt and khaki slacks.* Most of the tables are occupied by well-heeled and even better-dressed patrons. Many of them have tall, asymmetrical tiered trays of colorful desserts and coffee and tea. Merry has an afternoon tea service, although most people get coffee. Andreas sure did.

"Grace?"

I turn and look up at the voice I never thought I'd hear again. *"Huxley?"*

He's as gorgeous as I remember—the beautiful eyes with a hint of silver, the straight and narrow bridge of his nose and the fullness of his lips. The sight warms my blood as my libido relives the sensation of having that mouth between my legs.

"What are you doing here?" I manage a calm voice despite the urge to fan my suddenly overheated face and neck. "Didn't you go back?"

His eyebrows pinch. "Back where?"

"To wherever you live? The front desk told me you weren't here anymore, so..."

He looks lost for a moment, then realization dawns. "You thought I didn't live in L.A.?"

"Well...yeah. Why else would we have come here that night?"

He laughs incredulously. "What a mess. I came here because I didn't want to waste time going to my place. It would've taken too long, especially on a Friday night."

I flush, embarrassed over my assumption. Then I notice that he's in a white shirt and khaki slacks. *Wait. Is he...?* "Okay, um, weird question: are you waiting for a woman you gave a ride to a hospital two years ago?"

He cocks his head. "Yes. How did you know?"

Oh my God. A smile splits my face. "That was *me!*"

He laughs softly, then looks at me again. "That's... Wow. Almost unbelievable." He puts a hand on my elbow protectively as he takes me to a table. There's some coffee in an elegant porcelain cup. "Want something to drink?"

"Uh... No, I'm okay. Maybe just some water?"

He gestures at a server, and a glass of water appears. I look at him, unable to process this turn of events. *He's* the one who helped me when I was at my most desperate, with nobody from the Webbers willing to give me a ride and Adam out of town. And this same man was the one who came to my rescue when that drunk lawyer started to get physical at the bar.

"I looked for you," Huxley says. "I ordered breakfast for us before going to sleep. But you weren't there in the morning, and..." He spreads his hands. "Grace, why did you leave?"

I shake my head. "I'm so sorry. I thought it might get awkward the next day. I, um, would've liked to see you again—like, *really* would have —but I'm just not in a position to be able to do a long-distance thing." Having Mom halfway across the country is more than I can handle.

He nods slowly. "And you thought I lived somewhere else."

"Yeah. I did." I can't *believe* how dumb that sounds now.

The sugary scent of desserts in this place is positively tormenting. My eyes slide to the trays full of delightful little pistachio cakes, brownies and mini-berry tarts. My mouth waters—I haven't had anything to eat since breakfast. But knowing how much it costs, I can't bring myself to order anything. I drop my eyes and sip the cold water to fill my empty belly. A sandwich at home makes more economic sense. I've fallen behind on my savings goal for the month because I foolishly splurged on the shrimp for the "congrats to Peter for his promotion" dinner and the whiskeys I bought at the bar. No more spending money on unplanned food and drinks until I'm caught up. Mom's going to be okay soon—I know it—and we'll move to someplace away from SoCal—and Nelson. A place with a backyard where we can plant the flowers she loves so much.

Huxley tilts his head, and the server immediately rushes over. "One of each set," he says, gesturing at the dessert trays. "And a bitter caramel tea."

"Right away, sir."

"That's a lot," I blurt out. On the other hand, he's a big man, so he might want the calories. *Why did I say that?* I squirm, feeling a teeny bit awkward that I commented at all. What if he thinks I'm trying to get him to share when the main reason we're here is for me to pay him? I clear my throat, paste on a bright smile and face him. "I'm sure you'll love them all. Anyway, I just want to thank you—again—for giving me that ride. I'm grateful you didn't just run me over, thinking I was some crazy woman."

He laughs. "The thought crossed my mind, but something about you that night convinced me maybe you weren't insane."

My grin widens. "Thank God."

"How's your mother?"

"On her way to recovery, thank you. I was so shocked when you finally called. I thought about you from time to time, and wondered if the lack of contact was a sign that I should just try to pay it forward instead." I clear my throat again. "Anyway, how much do I owe you? If it's like a hundred or something, I can pay you now, but if you want me to pay for, like, water damage to your seat, um, you may need to be more patient because I don't have a lot of money. I can probably do installments, though." It'll put me even further from my savings goal, but it'd be wrong for me to refuse to pay when he did me such a huge favor.

The waiter returns with a gorgeous teapot etched with pink-gold roses and places the empty teacups in front of me and Huxley, then starts the hourglass, its fine grains of sand sparkling as they drain steadily through the narrow gap. He sets three gorgeous sets with various desserts on the table, then leaves.

"Go ahead," Huxley says. "The pistachio cake is particularly good, especially with the bitter caramel tea. Same for the berry tarts."

I flush. Guess he must've noticed me eyeing the desserts. Wonder if he also figured out why I declined to order anything.

Maybe, my subconscious whispers. Every so often, Karie sneers that I "reek" of poverty, no matter what I do, because the poor "just have that way about them."

"It's my favorite combo," he adds with a warm smile.

I realize that despite the gruff attitude from two years ago, he actually is kind, and my heart flutters. I feel silly for being anxious over the possibility that he might ask me to pay for damage to his car. "Thank you." I take a bite of the cake. It melts in my mouth in a delightful cloud of buttery cream and sugar. *Holy cow.* It's nearly orgasmic. I close my eyes. "Mmm-mmmm."

Once I'm done with the bite, I open my eyes. He's looking at me with an intensity that betrays a hunger that has nothing to do with food. I bite my lip as heat of my own unfurls. Until I remember that he didn't call me for sex. He had no idea who I was. "So. The payment."

The heated haze in his eyes abates a little, and he makes a small, dismissive gesture. "Don't worry about that. I don't need money."

"Okay. Then what do you need?"

"A fake fiancée."

13

GRACE

"A...fake fiancée?"

"Correct."

The last grains of sand slide through the hourglass. I pour the tea into our cups and slide one toward him. The caramel scent wafts over us as I drop a cube of brown sugar in and stir it to give myself time to gather my thoughts. "Don't you have any friends you can ask?" In every romance novel I read, the guy always asks his assistant or best friend or something, not an old one-night stand.

He squints at me. "No. I'm not gay. As I believe I demonstrated when we—"

I almost choke on the tea. "I mean a *female* friend."

"I don't have any female friends."

"Why not?" Is there something wrong with his personality?

He shrugs. "Women want to sleep with me."

From any other guy it would sound beyond arrogant. But from him? Totally natural. Of course, women want to sleep with him. The redhead behind him has been eye-fucking him ever since she sat down, and she's with a date.

"Okay... I can see that. But why *me*? Other than the fact that I broke up with my boyfriend."

Slight satisfaction crosses his face at the mention that I'm still single. "You seem normal. Not clingy. And we have good chemistry."

"And if I want to sleep with you again...?" I say, half serious and half hypothetical, since he brought it up as the reason he has no female friends.

"Grace, we aren't going to be friends."

Why does that slide into my gut like a blade?

"You're going to be my fiancée."

My fiancée.

"Why do you need a fake fiancée?" I pat myself on the back for sounding cool, but my heart is fluttering like a flag in a hurricane. *Am I nervous or excited?* What's happening is so unreal.

Actually, everything involving Huxley has been surreal—the ride in the rain to the most amazing sex of my life to this.

"My family is trying to force me to a marry a woman of their choice."

"Can they do that?" I ask in surprise. He doesn't come across as a pushover. He comes across as the type who, if you push, will push back harder.

A corner of his mouth twists into a sardonic smile, his eyes darkening with anger tinged with self-directed annoyance. "Unfortunately, they found a way. I plan to undo it, but that requires some time. Which is where you come in. They can't force me to marry someone quickly if I already have a proper fiancée."

His family sounds pretty...*difficult*, to put it mildly. Their behavior reminds me of Nelson and Karie, who are always trying to force me to do things I don't want in order to benefit themselves and their children. "How long is the fake engagement going to last? And what's, uh...involved?"

"A few months. No more than a year, is my guess. You just need to attend a few family dinners and social functions. I'll limit them as much as possible so as not to disrupt your life more than necessary."

I can feel my face heat. "I only have two dresses." They're black and classy, but it's going to be obvious if I wear nothing but for those two to all of his events. Given the way he speaks of his family—and the fact that he drives an outrageously expensive car—my usual wardrobe of faded jeans and T-shirts isn't going to cut it.

"Don't worry. I'll pay for clothes, accessories—whatever you need. You won't have to spend a penny, and you can keep everything we buy for the ruse."

He adds the last part like it's a big incentive, but I'm not too worried about who keeps the items. "Do I have to give up my job or anything?"

"No. Nothing like that."

"Okay. I'd hate to give up my position." I won't find another job that pays as generously as my current one. If I can resell the things he buys me for the dinners and parties after we "break up," I might be able to hit my financial goals more easily. Still, a little voice says it won't be that simple. Life always throws you a curveball.

"What do you do that you're so enthused about?" he asks with a curious smile.

"I work at the Pryce Family Foundation. As a junior fund development specialist. You know, help raise money for various causes. I love it. How about you?"

"I'm in advertising. The head of the 4D Agency." His eyes sparkle.

"And you love that."

"Yup."

"Bet you're good at it, too."

"I like to think so. I fought my family to start the agency, and I'm not giving it up."

"They don't approve?"

He snorts. "No. If they could, they'd find a way to bankrupt it."

"That's terrible!" Empathy wells. His family sounds just like Nelson and Karie, who would do something similar to me, partially out of spite and partially out of a need to keep me down and control me. "Why would they do that?"

"Because they want me to join the family business. They don't like it that I'm doing my own thing."

My sympathy deepens. No wonder he's desperate enough to fake an engagement. I would be, too. "So everyone in your family is awful?"

"The older ones are. But my brothers are great." The bright smile returns to his face, making him look younger and approachable.

"How many do you have?"

"Six. Except for me and Noah, they're all married. Two have kids." His expression gentles with affection. "You have any siblings?"

"No. It's just me and my mom." I debate bringing up Nelson, but decide not to, since there's no way he and his family would want to be associated with me any more than I do. Their disdain for me couldn't be clearer. If I could, I'd pull the half of my DNA that came from Nelson and give it back. Like returning defective junk you don't want to Amazon.

Huxley holds my eyes. "I'll do everything I can to avoid disrupting your life. You don't even have to move in with me."

I nod. That works—it would probably be awkward to share a space with a guy I barely know. "Is your family going to believe that we're really engaged? What are we going to tell them? And the people I know?"

"We should stick to the truth as closely as possible. That way, there are fewer chances of screwing it up."

He's put some thought into this. "So, we met two years ago?"

"Right. When I gave you a ride to the ER, but then we lost touch. I was sad that I couldn't find you because I was attracted to you...even though you were soaked through." He grins, and I have to smile. "And when we just happened to run into each other again, and I knew you were the one I'd been looking for all my life. Love at first sight. Well, second." He says it like he's pitching an ad. Straight to the point, a little humor to leaven the seriousness of the business. No real sentimentality. But with such finesse that it sounds completely natural and believable.

I study him, all my nerves tingling. The easy, confident way he sits opposite me and the air of affluence about him say of course he'll be able to forge his own path and get what he wants. No other outcome is possible in his world. A keen intelligence shines through his eyes. Despite the kindness he's shown me, I've seen a hint of cynicism as well, when we first met and he almost drove away. And the brutal physicality at the bar against that ill-mannered lawyer.

But it's doubtful that Huxley hides that side of himself from his family if they're as big of a pain as he claims. And they're going to know he isn't sentimental enough for the scenario he's presenting.

"I don't think anybody's going to believe that you're the type to fall in love at first—or even second—sight."

He cocks an eyebrow.

"I can't picture it. I don't think your family will be able to, either." To be honest, I can't imagine him in love with anybody. If he ever marries —for real—he'll go for pedigree and credentials: somebody smart, beautiful and inoffensive.

He considers for a few moments. "Maybe you're right."

"So..." I nibble on my lip.

"There's no time to set up something with a longer timeline. And I need a way to ensure my family won't force a breakup."

"*Force?* How powerful are they?" Andreas could command Nelson to do many things, but the latter is sort of gutless and sniveling toward his father. Mick will do as he's told, too, because he wants to join Huxley & Webber once his stint as a DA is over. But Huxley doesn't come across as the type to walk around with his lips smelling like somebody's ass. He'd break anyone who tried to cross him.

"It's not a question of power, just deviousness. And they won't come after me." He gives me a level look. "They'll come after you."

"*Me?*" I squeak.

"You're the new element. They'll test how malleable you are. Then they'll do everything in their power to bend you to their will, or, failing that, break you."

And I thought the Webbers were shitty. "They sound positively delightful."

A wicked grin splits his face. "But I've got an idea. You'll be pregnant."

"I'll be *what?*"

"Not for real, of course. But they won't try to break us up if there's a baby involved."

"The line they won't cross?" If so, they're better people than the Webbers.

"Correct."

"But a fake pregnancy? Where are we going to find a baby for that?" I wave a hand. "Even if we end the fake engagement, they might want to be part of our nonexistent baby's life. I don't want to continue to lie to everyone forever."

A shrug. "We can tell them the pregnancy test was defective or something." He couldn't care less how his family reacts as long as he gets what he wants. My instinct is right—that he's unsentimental and much more ruthless than he lets on.

"Aren't you afraid of disappointing them?"

His eyes narrow, and a stillness comes over him. "They're trying to screw me over. Disappointing them will be a pleasure of biblical proportions."

Okay... "So, do I have to fake morning sickness or something?"

"Yes. And you're going to crave tuna and mashed broccoli."

"Ugh." I make a face. "Why?"

"Because that's what my mother craved when she was pregnant with me."

"Fine. But if I actually have to *eat* anything like that, the deal's off."

He lets out a laugh that ripples over me like delightful waves. "Deal."

14

HUXLEY

−3 weeks later

THE MOMENT my private jet lands in Los Angeles, I drive straight to my grandmother's mansion in the Pacific Palisades. Normally I'd avoid a family dinner, but since Grace and I plan to announce our fake engagement and the fake bun in her oven, this will be the best time to do it.

Pounce before they can strike.

Naturally, traffic is terrible. I can't decide which city is worse—L.A. or Paris. My two-week business trip was tiring, but at least I accomplished the key objective. The client acted like I was his savior for salvaging his disastrous perfume launch. Most think hiring a pretty and popular face is enough. But there's so much more. The client isn't in the business of selling perfume. He's in the business of selling a dream—of beauty, of love and the future.

Grandma's mansion is the main place of gathering for the Huxley family, and there are at least twenty vehicles parked around it as I pull up. I note the crowd sardonically. Grandma doesn't collect cars—she doesn't appreciate them and only has a Rolls-Royce because it's comfortable and projects the right image.

A huge, ornate tapestry with the Huxley coat of arms hangs in the foyer, so none of us can ever forget the family motto. Silver wolves snarl, while PIETAS ET UNITAS glints in gold.

My phone buzzes with a text.

—Grace: I'm stuck in traffic. Gonna be late.

—Me: No problem. Drive safely.

—Grace: Thanks. At least I have the ring!

I smile. I didn't have time to do the proposal in person, thanks to the emergency situation in Paris. So having a ten-carat solitaire ring from Sebastian Jewelry hand-couriered to her was the next best thing. It's not unique like the *moi et toi* engagement ring Lucie got, but it's a classic. And sticking to the classics is best when you're trying to spin a lie.

But my family also knows that I don't do vanilla. So I added my own touch by having our names engraved inside the band: *Grace Lain & Huxley Lasker, Always forever in love.*

And we've texted our basic information—birthdays, where we grew up, favorite foods and colors and music, things that a couple would know. It'd be pretty shitty if we got caught over some minor detail, but minor details are how projects cohere or fall apart.

—Grace: Also, I need to talk to you about something important. Can we do that tonight?

—Me: Of course. Before or after the dinner?

—Grace: Doesn't matter.

—Me: Let's play it by ear, but it'll probably end up being after. Doubt my family will give us a private moment once we announce the engagement.

—Grace: Sounds good.

Grandma's housekeeper Sally bustles out from the long corridor toward the dining room. Comfortably plump, she's been with the family for decades. Her silver hair is cut short, and her green eyes have lost a bit of their intensity, although she still misses nothing. "Huxley! Welcome. Everyone's here."

"There are more cars than I expected for a family dinner."

"She invited the Webbers."

"Did she now?" So Grandma has managed to strike first. Too bad I'm going to strike harder.

Sally gives me a professional smile. "They're practically family at this point."

"Of course." It's just like Grandmother to count her chickens in front of me to pressure me into doing what's necessary to hatch the eggs.

"Emma is here as well."

"She is?" Emmett said his mom was in Playa del Carmen for the month to celebrate her birthday. I sent a present to the resort for her.

"She was visiting Jeremiah, who decided to invite her over."

"Ah." Mom might be friendly with Emma, but she didn't invite her over for no reason. She knows I'll behave if Emma's around. The woman is like my second mother, and my family knows she'll be a buffer if I become upset enough to lose my cool.

"I know the way," I say before Sally offers to show me, like always. She seems to think everyone is a baby she needs to hover over. It's ridiculous to see the way she fusses over my mother, who is one of the most menacingly competent adults ever.

The long table is laden with drinks and platters of caviar, cheese and crackers. Guess we're toasting the family alliance. From the expectant vibe in the air, it's obvious I'm supposed to pick my bride tonight.

I can't wait until they realize I'm here to deliver the *coup de grâce* to their scheme.

One side is occupied by Grandma, Mother, Emma, Uncle Prescott, Aunt Akiko and my cousins. The other side is Andreas—then his oldest son Bill, his wife Patricia and their son Alaric. To the latter's right are Nelson and Karie and their children—Mick and Vivienne.

The setup looks like a two sides girding for battle, but it's actually a transparent attempt to lower my defenses. My family has no clue I'm in the process of hiring John Highsmith to undo the entire contractual fuckup. They're feeling secure, no doubt, thinking I'm trapped and they'll be getting greater control of Huxley & Webber and a bigger slice of the firm's profits. What I don't understand is the motivation on the Webber side. Are their girls so terrible that this is the only way to unload them? Surely Vivienne can find *somebody* on a dating app.

Or is it for the other one, who spends money like water? If she's pretty enough, she can get a sugar daddy. SoCal is full of them. The Webbers can start with their billionaire client list.

Emma looks a little uncomfortable surrounded by all the legal sharks. A lithe brunette with a face more beautiful than most movie stars, she's too kind and gentle to be tossed into the upcoming battle. From the way she's looking around the dining room, she isn't sure why my mother invited her.

Vivienne leaps to her feet. "Huxley! I just *knew* it!" She runs toward me, her arms spread wide.

"Knew what?" I step back just as she's about to wrap her arms around me. She ends up hugging the air.

"That you'd choose *me*!" She's so breathless, she sounds like she's been running the Boston Marathon. "I mean, I *am* the only suitable girl in the family."

She reaches out again, and I put a hand on her forehead to keep her away. "Suitable for someone who likes boiled vegetables for brains."

Emma blinks, then presses her lips together.

Patricia laughs. "Not all Webbers are equal. Some are winners and some aren't." Her eyes bounce from her son to Mick. Must be referring to the big case Alaric won in the face of excellent legal arguments deployed by the opposing counsel. Mick just lost one with a murderer due to a botched cross-examination of a key prosecutorial witness. Now a killer is walking free on a technicality. Both were all over the news in the last two days. "At least the loss won't affect the firm."

Alaric calmly takes a sip of wine, while Mick glares like he wants to snap her neck. I'd pay good money to see him try. Start the evening with a bang before Grace arrives.

"Let's not make a spectacle until it's time." I hand Vivienne off to Mick, then cross the dining room to air-kiss the hostess. "Hello, Grandma."

Her dark eyes glitter with pleasure. I haven't been this affectionate with her in years. "Hello, my dear. You look exceptionally sharp tonight."

I give her my most innocent, beatific smile, which never fails to charm her. "I'm looking forward to a fabulous evening." Then I hug

Emma. "Good to see you! I thought you'd be in Mexico. What happened? Emmett didn't get you a resort to yourself?"

She flushes. "He did, but I needed some legal advice."

"And she came to the best." My mother grins, then turns to me. "If you were a lawyer, she could've come to you."

"I already have the best lawyer, and wouldn't want to deprive the world of the best mind in advertising," Emma says. "You must be so proud of Huxley for what he's been able to accomplish. Did you see the new Sebastian Peery collaboration ad campaign he did? It's *brilliant*! I always told myself I didn't need a man to drop to one knee and offer me a ring, but that ad made me want to change my mind."

Her smile warms my heart. "Thank you."

Mom's expression doesn't falter. "So you've decided?" She picks up a glass of Merlot and peers at me, too sharp to let down her guard completely.

"Yes." I take my seat. "And I'm glad everyone is here so I won't have to repeat myself." I look at the people assembled.

Vivienne inhales audibly with anticipation, too stupid and self-centered to realize that she and I simply aren't happening. Karie shifts in her seat, looking down as though to hide a triumphant smile tinged with nervousness. She's smart enough to realize I have no feelings for her daughter, at least not anything positive. Nelson's smirk has turned smug. He's probably relieved to unload his defective goods on somebody else. Meanwhile, Mick looks annoyed—which isn't surprising, because he never liked me. Says I'm a stuck-up son of a bitch. Most likely it still pisses him off that I have the kind of legal pedigree he'd kill for but didn't get. It enrages him that I disdain it.

"I have found," I say slowly, letting the anticipation build, "the love of my life."

"Yes!" Vivienne jumps to her feet, her hand in the air like a kid volunteering in class.

"It's not you," I say before she can humiliate herself further.

"What?" she screeches, but stops when Karie put a hand on her wrist.

"Congratulations. I'm happy for you," Emma says.

"Thank you," I say, at the same time Mom lets out a quiet snort.

"Really, Huxley? The love of your life?" She couldn't sound more skeptical.

Time to put on the right mask. I mentally flip through my brothers' expressions when they're in love...then settle on Noah's face when he thinks of croissants from Bobbi's Sweet Things, minus the goofiness. "Yes. She's everything to me."

"Duty comes before love," Grandmother says.

"I know *amor* isn't part of the family motto. But trust me, this will be the perfect union of duty and love."

"How so?" Andreas's eyes are keen as he studies me. He's never taken me lightly, and he respects that I have plans not involving my family's legal business.

"She's pregnant with my child."

Emma gasps, then beams at me. She's probably the only one here who buys everything out of my mouth at face value. Guilt pokes at me for lying to her, but there's nothing to be done about it. I can't deviate from the script when Grace is going to be here any minute.

"How *could* you?" Vivienne yells, her face red and eyes redder with unshed tears. From the way she's reacting, you'd think she was a scorned wife. Once again, Karie lays a hand on her arm.

I turn to Grandma. "Your first great-grandchild."

Her cool mask cracks a little to show a glimpse of longing. Guess she wasn't kidding when she said she wanted a great-grandchild to spoil. Andreas presses his thin lips together, the gesture bringing out the fine lines around his mouth. His forehead creases as he narrows his eyes in thought.

"Pregnant?" Mom looks at me like a hostile witness. "How did you meet this woman? You've never mentioned her before." The antagonistic, lawyerly gleam in her eye says she wants to bring up the twenty-five percent stake of the agency to hand over to Grandma, but Emma is here. We aren't supposed to discuss such details in front of outsiders.

"We don't have the kind of relationship where I tell you everything." My voice is as smooth and cold as the marble in the mansion as I let my gaze sweep over Mom and Grandma. "But if you must know, we met a couple of years ago when I gave her a ride. We reconnected recently, and the rest is..." I shrug.

"Are you sure it's your baby? She could be lying." Vivienne's screechy voice cuts through the room.

I cock an eyebrow. "Sounds like a bit of projection there."

Fury and embarrassment color her face. Hurt glitters in her eyes, brimming with unshed tears. *She honestly thought I'd pick her. Good lord.* Just how did Andreas end up with a granddaughter like that? I'd wonder whether Karie cheated on Nelson, but Vivienne has her father's eyes.

"Don't be rude to my sister!" Mick's fist hits the table, but it's a muted blow as his eyes dart to Andreas, then flick back to me.

Chickenshit. "She insulted my fiancée. Not to mention my first child."

"*Fiancée?*" Mick's eyes nearly bulge out.

I smile charmingly. "Of course. I had to propose. After all, it was my duty. And we all know how my family *adores* the idea of duty."

Grandma's face is the weirdest combination of happiness and defeat. Mom narrows her eyes like she'd love nothing more than to cross-examine me until I fess up the truth. She's too smart to buy this at face value.

Emma nods. "It is the right thing to do," she murmurs, just loud enough for me to hear. She's probably thinking about how shamefully Ted treated her and the six other women who were pregnant with his babies. Marriage was off the table, but he'd pay for an abortion or child support, whichever the women preferred. He didn't want to waste mental energy on the babies in their wombs.

"You son of a bitch! You did this on purpose, dragging it out, stringing Viv along for years!" Mick shouts.

Next to him, Nelson looks the other way, a corner of his mouth twisted upward. It's a slightly sour expression, but he's probably relieved that his son is doing a good job of being the bad guy. Bill and Patricia drink more wine, looking everywhere but at the others. Alaric thumbs through his phone—probably annoyed that he's stuck here when he could be doing billable work. Only Andreas is observing me with an unblinking stare, as if searching for a weakness to exploit.

"I never promised to marry a Webber. What options did you provide? Her"—I gesture at Vivienne—"and some girl who's too busy spending twenty-five-thousand dollars a month to show her face anywhere. Why should I tie myself to either one? Would you have chosen one of them, Andreas?"

"They're my grandchildren. The question is moot," he says smoothly.

Spoken like a lawyer, but we all know the truth.

Karie shifts, then lets out an impatient breath. "The contract—"

"Will be broken," I say coolly. "John Highsmith will take care of it."

Grandma, Mom and Uncle Prescott glare at me like I've just backstabbed them in public. Andreas, Bill, Nelson and Mick look like I've just pissed all over their favorite dessert. My cousins drink more wine without making eye contact with anybody, and Alaric doesn't lift his head from his phone. Emma is the only one who looks clueless about what this means. She's unaware of the intense rivalry between Huxley & Webber and Highsmith, Dickson and Associates.

"You'll fail. Highsmith isn't good enough," Mom says stiffly.

I smile with satisfaction. She wouldn't be this tense if she wasn't at least somewhat worried. "We'll see. Regardless, I won't be marrying a Webber." I turn to my grandmother. "And you can stop setting up dates for me. It's disrespectful to my fiancée."

Just then, I hear a quick clicking of heels on marble and stand up. Grace walks in hurriedly, wearing a black dress that hugs her curves and heels that elongate her shapely legs. Her unbound hair bounces around her shoulders, and the fire-engine red on her siren's lips is hot.

Everyone at the table turns, and she halts. Shock and confusion settle on her face. It's understandable; I told her it was going to be just my family with about eight people at the most.

I walk to her and give her a brief kiss. "Some uninvited guests, although you'll love Emma," I murmur.

She nods vaguely as she takes in the scene. Unease tightens her brow. I place a soothing hand on her shoulder and turn to face our audience. *Showtime.*

"Everyone, meet my fiancée, Grace Lain."

A long stretch of silence follows. Emma looks at us with loving approval. On the other hand, Grandmother has an inexplicable expression overlaid with a glimmer of...triumph? Mom cocks an eyebrow, then reaches for the humidor closest to her with a soft chuckle. How can the current situation be a win for my family? Andreas's shoulders sag with...dare I say relief? Nelson slaps his forehead, and Karie turns red. Mick starts to laugh quietly, tears beading in the corners of his eyes.

Apprehension slices into my gut. Instinct screams that I've stepped into a trap, but how could that be?

Most importantly, how did they manage to set me up without tipping their hand?

Vivienne erupts, shattering the silence. She shakes off her mother's hand and launches herself at Grace. "You *fucking bitch!*" Her fingers are talons, ready to rip Grace's face off.

I shield Grace from the attack with my body, putting a hand out to keep Vivienne at arm's length.

"Nelson, control your child!" Andreas says sharply.

Nelson shakes his head before getting up and coming to drag her away. Vivienne continues to flail and scream expletives. Karie puts a hand over her daughter's mouth, but it isn't enough to muffle her.

Mick hisses something in Vivienne's ear and she finally quiets down, although her breathing is still rough.

Andreas lets out a long sigh. "Well. Now that order has been restored and everyone is here, it's time to toast to our families' union."

"I'm not marrying her." I tilt my chin at Vivienne. Even if I wanted to, I wouldn't, not after that display. I've seen three-year-olds who behaved better.

Dumbass, Mick mouths as me, then smirks.

"No need. Grace is also my granddaughter," Andreas says.

The words sink in, but suddenly the gears in my brain seem stuck. I follow his gaze, note it's on Grace—my fake fiancée, the one I chose specifically to help me avoid marrying a fucking Webber like my family wants. "What?"

"And you gave her a ride. A classic meet-cute sprinkled with a dash of destiny." Grandmother brims with satisfaction.

Mom puffs on her cigar with a victorious smile. "Straight out of one of those romcom movies. I wonder if your father will appreciate the irony." She shrugs. "It appears that you won't need John Highsmith after all."

Oh...fuck!

The pieces start to fall into place. That rainy evening... Grandmother knew I wouldn't stay, especially not when she offered me two options—join the firm or marry a Webber. She knew the route I'd take to get home. It would have been easy to place Grace on one of the streets I'd be on, and tell her to stop me. I should've realized it was weird there weren't any cars around. How would she have gotten there without one?

The sob story about her mother was a stroke of genius to stir my sympathy and make it harder for me to say no to her plea for a ride.

Then the convenient excuse of her phone not working and how I had to get in touch with her to get the money she promised to pay me because she only had a single dollar bill.

The one-night stand we had was probably The Fogeys' renewed attempt when it was taking too long for me to call her. Wouldn't put anything past them. They could've hired somebody to follow me. Grace could then position herself where I'd see her, then get me to sleep with her.

I don't know why she didn't stay. She might've wanted to appear shy and reluctant. But when I called, she couldn't disguise how happy she was. And she has made sure she never looked like the type who gets a three-hundred-thousand-dollar annual allowance. Wore cheap clothes. Pretended to be worried about not having money to buy dresses for my family's dinners and social functions.

She even told me I should ask a female friend to be my fake fiancée. But she must've known I don't keep a lot of women around as friends.

And I never suspected anything. Sheer rage and humiliation slam into me. What a fool I've been!

Pasting on a smile, I give them the clichéd slow clap. "Bra-*vo*. Very well done."

Grace turns to me. "Huxley..." Anxiety threads her voice.

Getting scared? Too late, sweetheart. You've already stuck your hand into a hornet's nest.

94

Mick's silent laughter grows audible. The sound is like nails on a chalkboard.

I force myself to unclench my hands and concentrate on keeping my breathing even. Everyone in the room seems to be pleased to have gotten what they wanted. But if they thought this would be the end, they thought wrong.

This is just one battle. I will win this war, no matter the cost.

15

GRACE

I'M USED to awkward and unpleasant meals. It's something you become immune to when you're around people like Nelson and his family. But the one at Huxley's place takes *tense* to a whole different level.

His family is acting gleeful and triumphant, which is both creepy and weird, while the brunette called Emma—apparently Huxley's half-brother's mom—is serene and seems genuinely happy for me and Huxley and our upcoming nuptials. If she suspects something's weird about our situation, she's doing a great job of hiding it.

Vivienne vacillates between sobbing and screeching, while Nelson and Karie content themselves with glaring at me. The latter's look in particular promises retribution. Mick can't seem to decide between anger and amusement. He scowls when he notices me, but smirks every time he glances at Huxley. Meanwhile, Nelson's brother and his family go along with Andreas, who acts as if this is just a friendly meal.

Tension and fury pour off Huxley, even though he's doing his best to maintain his calm. His knuckles are too pale, and the smile on his face doesn't reach his eyes.

"Are you all right?" Emma says to him.

"I'm fine. Just a little overwhelmed at the turn of events."

He's upset that he didn't know I was Nelson's daughter. I'm shocked that he's a member of the Huxley family. Don't all of them work for Huxley & Webber?

I wasn't kidding when I texted that I had to talk to him. Nerves clench around my throat. This isn't the best time, but my news isn't something I can hide from him, even if I wanted to.

My belly twists. I can't touch my whitefish in lemon sauce. It's lightly baked and looks perfectly cooked, but it smells off. The multigrain roll served with the entrée tastes sour and bitter. I reach for the water, then decide it feels strange in my mouth—with a slightly slimy aftertaste.

Huxley notices me moving my food around. He gives me a look and says, "You don't have to lay it on so thick," in a low voice.

"She's always been a picky child," Karie says. "I suppose Catalina's fish doesn't meet her expectations."

I give her a smile as fake as her breasts. "Morning sickness. I'm sure you understand. Now if you'll excuse me, I need to go to the powder room. Huxley, can you show me where it is?"

Fury flares in his eyes. Emma says, "You should take her there and maybe get her some ginger tea. It always settled my stomach when I wasn't feeling well."

He schools his face into a polished mask of warmth. "Of course."

We leave together, his hand at my elbow. Vivienne's gaze stabs into my back like a knife, but I ignore it. She's the least of my worries right now.

"You cheap whore," she mutters loudly enough that we can't miss it as we walk past her.

"I happen to be a *pregnant* cheap whore. Fortunately, I have a fiancée, so things should work out fine," I respond softly, so people on the Huxley side of the table won't hear me.

Vivienne turns scarlet, but she can't think of a better attack, not when Andreas is around. Launching herself at me a second time would upset him enough to earn her some sort of punishment. A hint of amusement and respect fleet over the fury that's been banked in Huxley's gaze ever since he found out I'm Nelson's daughter. A tiny bit of hope flares—he might be less upset now.

When we're sufficiently far from the dining room, he lets me go. I turn to face him, my brief optimism vanishing when I see his now-flat eyes. "Do you plan to call the engagement off?" I ask.

"Why? So everyone will learn I've made an even bigger fool of myself than they realized?" Rage and frustration twist his face. "It's already bad enough I told them I was in love with you. I'll look like an absolute moron now if I tell them I was just kidding."

"I'm sorry." I sag, overwhelming exhaustion pressing down on me with more force than I can handle. "The plan sounded great, and I never wanted to make things difficult for you. It's just... I didn't know who you were."

"Really? With your sister acting like that? When I know she must've said my name in front of you at least once or twice?"

"First, she's my *half*-sister. Second, she and I aren't close, in case you haven't noticed. And third, I thought everyone in your family worked at Huxley & Webber. Like, *everyone*. And I never saw you on the section of the firm's site listing all the lawyers and their credentials and specialties. So when Viv got all moony over marrying 'Huxley,' I thought she meant *a* Huxley—one of the people from the website."

His narrowed eyes scrutinize me for signs of deception. I hold his gaze. I have nothing to hide, nothing to be ashamed of. Still, my insides jitter uncontrollably with nerves that refuse to settle.

"And there's one more thing I need to tell you." I let out a soft breath. "I really *am* pregnant."

Shock slackens his face. "*What?*"

"I just found out last night." My voice doesn't shake, thank God, even though my hands are trembling badly. I fold them together.

Icy skepticism frosts his handsome face. "Is it mine? Actually, is it even real?"

The disbelief is warranted. I'm braced for it, but it still cuts deep. "I checked five times. Trust me, I didn't want this any more than you." Even as I say it, I'm sad for the baby in my womb. Just like me, it isn't wanted by its father. Actually, it has it worse than me. Mom told me she was so happy when she found that she was pregnant with me. I panicked last night for a long time. Then considered texting Huxley the news, but changed my mind because it seemed like something that should be related in person.

And right now, happiness is the last thing I'm feeling. Sympathy, pity and heartache fill my heart until I want to cry for my baby.

"And yes," I add. "It's yours."

He threads his fingers through his hair as he closes his eyes briefly, his mouth tight. "You've gotta be kidding me," he mutters, more to himself than me.

What am I doing? *He doesn't want this baby.* Maybe he hates children, or just doesn't want to have one with me. Either way, my heart breaks that my baby is going to have a father who might treat it as badly as Nelson did me. "I'm not asking you to take responsibility for the baby. I can't force you, and I'm not going to try." My baby won't beg for crumbs of affection from its own parent. I won't let that happen.

"Then why are you telling me this?"

"Because you should know. You're the father."

"You won't object to a paternity test, then."

"No." If I go through the paternity test now, I can spare my baby the kind of heartbreak and humiliation I experienced after Nelson outright rejected me when we first met. "I also won't make a fuss if you quietly end the engagement."

"Too late for second thoughts, not after that show you put on with your family. We will get married."

"It's foolish to go through with it when you're this angry. Besides, we were going to fake it for a few months, not actually get married."

"That was then. Things have changed. Believe me, I don't want to marry you. But I'm not going to disappoint Emma."

"Why do you care so much about her?" *Why can't your decision be about the baby, even a little?*

"She's like the mother I never had. She was always there by my side. If I abandon the mother of *my child*"—he sneers the words—"she'll be dismayed." He shakes his head. "Disappointed. Disillusioned, even. I won't have that."

"But getting married? We can't make such a big life decision to please one person."

"Then beg me. Getting on your hands and knees might do the trick."

I inhale with pain at his cruel demand. "You asshole."

"I've always been an asshole. It's just that I wasn't one to you."

He takes a step forward, invading my personal space. I stiffen my spine and glare up at him. I'm not backing down.

"Now. We are going to return to the dining room and you're going to smile and stop testing my patience. You've screwed me over quite enough already."

16

HUXLEY

I'VE BEEN PLAYED. Fucked over. And publicly mocked.

The dinner was a week ago, but the humiliation I've felt hasn't abated one bit. And it won't until I have my revenge.

"Are you okay?" Madison asks. She's a prototypical California blonde with long legs and toned body. Her eyes are blue—but a lighter shade than Grace's.

No. Don't think about that manipulative little bitch.

I can't believe I ever thought she was cute and sassy. How hard did she have to bite her cheek not to laugh when I asked about her mom? Did she have a good chuckle with my grandmother after I reached out to propose a fake engagement?

My phone buzzes with another call from Grandmother. She's been calling and texting at least five times a day. Mom's been trying to reach me too, but I refuse to answer. They'll try to gaslight me—insist that my meeting with Grace was fate, fawn over how the pregnancy is a sign that Grace and I are meant to be and praise me for doing the right thing for the family.

"You look a little tired," Madison says.

"I'm fine."

She nods. "This came for you from Huxley & Webber." Madison places a thick envelope on my desk. Her manner is deft and businesslike. If my situation weren't such a mess, I might've been tempted to ask *her* to be my fake fiancée, like my brothers suggested. At least she'd be good at it—and not fuck me over with my family.

But she's too damn professional to fool anybody. Who would believe she has any feelings for me when they see that smooth expression or hear her perfectly modulated voice?

"Do you know what it's about?" I ask.

"No. Legal hasn't looked at it, either. It's marked personal."

Probably Grandma and Mom trying an end run around my refusal to answer their calls and texts. "Put it through the shredder."

"Shouldn't you see what it is first?" If she's curious what's in the envelope, she doesn't show it. "It could be a legal matter."

"Don't care. Shred it, then pack it into an envelope and send it back to them. COD."

Madison's well-trimmed golden eyebrows pull together. "Is there something I can do to help?"

"Unless you can invent a time machine, no."

She nods again and leaves, bringing me a cup of extra-strong coffee a few minutes later. She knows exactly what I need when I'm upset.

—Dad: How come you didn't tell me you were engaged? I wasted so much time looking for good women for you!

—Me: Who told you?

—Dad: Your mother.

Of course. Since she couldn't get to me directly, she went to Joey. The texts are coming from Dad's phone, but Dad doesn't text. That's too much work. It's Joey doing the texting, undoubtedly feeling smugly important to be able to send messages as Ted Lasker.

—Dad: But maybe the time wasn't totally wasted. Since your fiancée is pregnant, if you want to have some extra fun, I have a few options. They're discreet.

As discreet as Jane's tits that wouldn't stay confined to her dress.

—Me: Joey, go away

—Dad: Come on! Can't you just give me credit for doing a great job?

—Me: I could...but first you'd have to be doing a great job.

—Dad: You're such an ungrateful jerk! At least we're invited to the wedding, right?

Hell no, comes to my mind instinctively. Dick cannons are my dad's idea of dignified and fun. My brothers and I should be grateful he didn't ask us to commission a giant replica of his dick for his birthday.

But then it hits me. *Why should I gift the Huxleys and Webbers a dignified wedding?*

—Me: If you can send the most amazing gift ever.

—Dad: We can manage that.

—Me: If it's impressive enough, who knows? Dad might get to bounce the baby on his knee.

—Dad: No. It might puke. But we'll take it around the city, show it the world it rightfully belongs to.

Translation: Dad plans to take the baby to every debauched Hollywood party he can squeeze into his busy schedule. He'll also shove the poor baby into his rival Josh Singer's face. I'm still not sure why Dad hates Josh Singer so much. He's just a guy who financed and produced a lot of artsy-fartsy films. Nothing like my father's history of producing megahits.

I send a quick email to the team in Paris to make sure the client isn't doing anything stupid—you never know with *artistes*—and head to the steakhouse. I'm meeting my brothers for dinner and to celebrate Noah's upcoming nuptials. He actually managed to convince Bobbi to marry him. *How* is anybody's guess—not long ago she wouldn't even let him buy a croissant at her bakery. Hopefully he didn't do anything stupid, like give her all his money. I don't worry about my other brothers, but with Noah, I do. When he becomes focused on something, he disregards everything else. He'll go on a trip to photograph some cheetahs, and sometimes it'll be weeks before anyone hears from him.

I pull up to the steakhouse and toss the fob to the valet. Just as I do, Mick emerges from the car behind me. He's in a suit with a thin white-gold tie pin. He apparently won his first case while wearing it, so now he wears it all the time as some kind of talisman. If he were actually good at what he did, he wouldn't need luck.

"Well, well, well. Look at the man who got duped into marrying a whore." He smirks, probably happy he finally has something to feel superior to me about.

"Say that again and you won't be able to make a court appearance for months." Griffin isn't the only one who can break a man's jaw with a kick.

Mick flinches slightly, then scoffs to hide the initial reaction. "What does it feel like to marry a girl like Grace?"

"I'm wondering why she's a Lain," I say conversationally, refusing to rise to the bait, then head to the entrance.

He follows me. He isn't giving up this opportunity to stick it to me. "Because she took her mom's name. Do you know her mom was—*is*? A slut who tried to wreck my parents' marriage. She's 'lain,' all right." He grins, waiting for a reaction, but when I don't give him the satisfaction, he says, "She shamelessly seduced Dad—*knowing he was married*—to change her lot in life, and it backfired. He didn't leave Mom for her, not even for the baby."

Well, that explains the last name. And the fact that Grace has never made a public appearance with the family. "And I'm supposed to feel...what?"

"Disgust for gold-digging whores? Like mother, like daughter!"

I study my nails nonchalantly for a moment. "There wouldn't have been a problem if Nelson had kept his dick in his pants, though, would there? After all, he knew he was married with children. Guess Karie and you two kids didn't mean much to him."

Mick's complexion is so red, it looks purple. He opens and closes his mouth a few times. As usual, he can't think of anything clever to say. If he thought he could get away with it, he'd throw the first punch. But he knows I can fight. You don't grow up with six brothers—one of whom is a kickboxer—and not know how to fight.

I hold Mick's eyes just long enough to establish that he's too chickenshit to do anything, then smile and turn to the hostess. "Noah Lasker. Party of seven."

She smiles back. "I see it. Right this way."

I follow her. Mick screams, "You got yourself a gold-digging, opportunistic, scheming *whore* for a fiancée! Soon she's going to be your wife! Good luck with that, loser! She'll fuck every guy in the city just because."

Rage swells. I start to turn, but he scrambles away. *Is it worth it to go after him?*

"Would you like us to call the police?" The hostess's words penetrate my red haze.

"No." With a gigantic effort, I wrench myself back under control. "That was the DA, believe it or not. I doubt a call to the police would accomplish much."

She shakes her head, muttering something, and takes me to the table where my brothers are. A few empty bottles stand on it. Noah stops in the middle of gorging on bread as I walk up.

"Did somebody wreck your new Lamborghini?" he asks.

Why does he think the only thing that gets me upset is wrecking a new Lambo? I haven't bought one in at least two years.

"Worse. Much worse." I grind my teeth at the memory of Mick's insults. I taunted him back, of course, but the person I really want to mock is *myself* for not doing more due diligence. I should never have asked Grace to be my fake fiancée without checking her out more thoroughly. How could I have forgotten how devious my grandmother can be? I just assumed someone like her could never be the vapid spender of the family, not based on the way she dressed and spoke. But the best con artists never show their true colors. I should've learned after the kidnapping incident involving my cousins. "I'm stuck. I have to marry Grace Lain."

I've already given it a lot of thought, and there simply doesn't seem to be a good way to get out of it. But at the same time, do I want to end things like this? It wouldn't materially damage Grace. She would still get to go back to her daddy and spend his money. So what if he's embarrassed about the way she came into the world? He obviously cares enough to fork over twenty-five thousand bucks a month.

She could've kept on collecting that money and stayed out of my life. Instead, she set her sights on me, manipulated her way into becoming my wife. Well, I'm going to ensure she doesn't get what she wants out of this marriage—money. She'll have to pay with her own money if she wants anything. I'm tempted to charge her for rent and utilities, but that would be beyond petty, even in my state.

The pregnancy is another bucket of gasoline over the fire. Does she think I'm going to buy her innocent act just because she can still look at me with seemingly guileless eyes? I'm not trusting anything out of her mouth without proof.

"Well... At least she's not a Webber...?" Emmett says tentatively.

The other brothers nod.

Just thinking about how she fooled me sends my blood pressure into orbit. "She's a fucking Webber in disguise! She misrepresented herself!"

"You sure? I've never heard of Grace Lain," Emmett says.

Nicholas pours a whiskey and slides it in my direction. I knock it back.

"She's the daughter Nelson Webber had with his side piece," I grind out.

Grant frowns. "Do you have to marry her? There's gotta be a loophole."

My hands shake with suppressed rage. "She claims she's pregnant with my baby."

"Well... Is she really?" Noah asks. He can't believe I would be so careless.

And I can't either. There's no way the baby's mine. It was just a one-night stand. I'm fanatical about condoms because I refuse to have a child I'm not ready for. Nor do I want to behave like my father, throwing money at accidental children like that's all there is to being a parent.

Every time I think about asking her to be my fake fiancée, I want to kick myself in the balls. "She thinks she's won, but I'm going to ruin that conniving little bitch." Both of my hands clench.

Noah slowly masticates some bread, a smidgeon of pity crossing his face. Bitterness flows through my veins. I don't want his pity. I don't want to be the object of *anyone's* pity.

I am Huxley Lawton Lasker. *Nobody is allowed to pity me.* And I hate Grace for putting me in this situation.

Sebastian clears his throat. "You might not want to judge so hastily. Just in case." He's referring to the time he almost lost his wife because he thought she'd screwed him over. He vowed to make her pay and she did. And then filed for divorce over it.

"She crawled into my bed!" It galls me that it was the best sex I'd had in a long time, if not my entire life. I actually liked her at the bar. Thought she was interesting enough that I wanted to pursue something more with her, not an urge I've felt with women before.

But it was just an illusion. I can't decide which pisses me off more—that she put on an act or that I bought it. How she must've laughed to herself! "Did Lucie crawl into yours?"

"No. But her sister crawled into my brother's."

"She's going to wish she'd never met me."

"How about the kid?" Nicholas says.

"I don't know. It probably isn't mine anyway."

"You sure?" Emmett asks.

"Gonna have to check, but I am extremely careful with contraception."

"Still could've failed." Griffin makes a circle around the table, at the result of our father's failed vasectomy.

"I didn't get a vasectomy from a second-rate doctor," I shoot back at him.

Griffin doesn't give me a nasty comeback, which is something, since he's grumpier than a hungry bear, and he doesn't back down from fights, physical or verbal. He just shrugs and says, "Neither did I, but..." He got his wife pregnant during a one-night stand at a masquerade party. And he's one of the most meticulous people I know. He wouldn't have forgotten to wear protection, and he would've made sure it wasn't expired.

Sighing, I squeeze my eyes shut for a moment. Gotta control my temper. It isn't my brothers' fault that I'm in the predicament I'm in. "Yeah. Sorry. I shouldn't have said that."

"It's cool. I know you're upset." Griff slaps my shoulder.

I shake my head, as though that will help my crappy mood. "We should have some fun here." My voice comes out grim. But damn it, I'm going to make sure we have a good time. This is the last time Noah's going to be at a brothers-only dinner as a bachelor. I'm not letting my problem bring everyone down.

Grant pours me my favorite scotch. We toast, and I knock it back. We order food and more alcohol.

But even as we toast and laugh and give shit to Noah about his tumultuous relationship with Bobbi and their upcoming nuptials, a corner of my mind stays on revenge. Nobody fucks with my life and gets away with it.

17

HUXLEY

PINK CHERRY PETALS float in the air over the riverbank, the cloudless sky a brilliant blue. The man drops to his knee, and the camera focuses on a small black velvet box. It zooms in as he opens the lid, showing an impeccably cut clear diamond surrounded by round blue diamonds. Cut to show the woman's face. The subtle lighting changes brighten her face as surprise, joy and love glow in her blue eyes.

The third attempt is romantic, with the right color scheme—lots of white, gold, silver and blue. The model was selected specifically for a particular type of ethereal beauty, so popular in Asia. But now I wish we had chosen someone with green or brown eyes. The cornflower blue reminds me of Grace. Her eyes are more beautiful than the model's. Larger, more expressive and even bluer. Every time she blinks, her long, thick lashes flutter like butterfly wings.

Stop thinking about her. I tried to keep her out of my mind all weekend, at home, at Noah's wedding, and afterward. But she keeps invading my head, and it doesn't help that Sebastian's wife Lucie is also currently pregnant. It's too early for her to show, but she's often nauseated and can't eat.

Is Grace okay? Is she constantly nauseated? Throwing up, perhaps?

Sierra seemed fine when she was with Griffin's triplets, but the woman is so sunny and optimistic she makes Pollyanna look depressed by comparison.

The fact that I'm worrying about Grace at all is irritating. She lied to me, trapped me in a marriage and turned me into a laughingstock in my family and with the Webbers. Who cares if she isn't feeling well? She should be racked with guilt, texting and calling to explain herself.

But she hasn't made a single attempt.

The only thing she has done is get her OB-GYN to send a paternity test kit to my office. It's a cotton swab to get some DNA from my inner cheek. I can't quite pinpoint what I felt when the kit fell out of the discreet padded envelope and into my palm. She must be damn sure the baby's mine. Otherwise, she wouldn't be so eager to have the test done.

A small part of me wonders if I was too harsh. But I shake off that niggling guilt.

I am *not* feeling bad for her. *My concern is for the baby.* The child, at least, is innocent. It deserves better.

Grace, on the other hand, deserves whatever treatment I hand out. If she hadn't lied, I would've shown her honesty and kindness. It galls me not to have seen through her deception. She seemed so sweet, funny and intelligent, with an admirable backbone. She's the only woman I've ever met who sparked an interest beyond simple lust.

Forget her. You have work to do.

The Sebastian Peery collaboration needs a new campaign for their spring collection that's going to be sold exclusively through Hae Min Department Stores in Korea. Lucie wants romantic, sweet and luxurious. So far, the campaign has *romantic* and *sweet* down, but I'm not feeling the *luxurious*, despite all the sparkling diamonds. Cherry blossoms are a nice touch, since they symbolize spring in Korea, but there needs to be more oomph—a visceral appeal. I make some notes for the team.

"Your ten o'clock is here," comes Madison's voice through the intercom.

"Bring him in, please."

A moment later, my door opens. Bryce is in a three-piece suit, of course—every male Huxley wears a three-piece suit when they're working—with perfectly polished, strait-laced shoes. Presentation is half the battle. He inherited the best features from his parents—midnight-black eyebrows that slant slightly above keen, dark eyes, and straight, dark hair that rarely looks messy even when he doesn't do anything to it, even though he prefers to style it so it lies slicked back. His skin is always golden, and he never burns. Mom often complains it isn't fair because she and Uncle Prescott turn scarlet with only ten minutes of sun.

"Anything to drink, sir?" Madison asks, her gaze briefly on Bryce, then shifting to me.

"Iced Americano," Bryce says.

"Nothing for me."

She nods and disappears, closing the door behind her.

"The prenup you asked for," Bryce says, handing me a thick document before taking a seat. "Jeremiah isn't happy about my handling it."

"Thank you, but you could've couriered it," I say, ignoring the part about my mother. She's not getting anywhere near my *personal* legal affairs again. "I'm not paying your hourly rate for the delivery."

He snorts. "That isn't why I'm here. Have you talked to Grace since the dinner?"

"About what?" My voice is too casual.

"About the wedding. And the terms in the document." Bryce jerks his chin at the prenup.

"No. She already knows we have to get married, especially with a baby on the way. And nothing in the contract should come as a shock to her."

He cocks an eyebrow. "She's going to fight. You specified you were not giving her a penny, that if she wants to spend money, she needs to earn it herself."

"I'm not an ATM."

"Yes, but she's going to be your *wife*."

"Precisely. And that's more than she deserves after she fucked me over." Bryce is the only one on the Huxley side who knows the humiliating truth behind Grace's and my engagement. You don't hide things from your lawyer if you want good advice, and I want the absolute best out of Bryce.

"And the mother of your child," he adds, like that makes a difference.

"I'll arrange for the baby. But that doesn't mean she gets to use my money for herself."

Bryce looks at me. "Do you honestly think she'll just hand the baby over?"

"You mean the meal ticket?"

Even after I quietly divorce her after a few years, the child will always be between us, and she'll do everything in her power to use it to squeeze what she can out of me. I doubt she'll downsize her spending after burning twenty-five thousand bucks a month for years. But in order for her to use the baby to get me to cough up the cash, she needs to be around to groom it into a tool of manipulation. And I know how far some women can go.

I was an unwitting participant in the toxic drama between Uncle Prescott's ex-wife Zoe when she became upset that she couldn't bend him to her selfish whims during their divorce proceedings. That psycho decided to abduct their children, probably trying to use them to get more alimony or something. I'm not going to let anything like that involve the baby. "If she doesn't agree to it, I'll fight her to the death. What's the baby going to learn if it grows up with a mother like her?"

The only thing my father did right with us is that he never tried to raise us himself. If he had, we would've turned into Ted Laskers—self-centered, irresponsible, inappropriate megalomaniacs. Grace as a mother would produce the same outcome.

Madison enters the office with coffee for Bryce, then pauses and looks at me for a beat before leaving. He takes a sip, then scrunches his face. "Nasty stuff."

"So why are you drinking it?"

"Because you don't have decent green tea."

"I told you last time you came by that I got matcha from Japan."

"Yeah, but you can't brew it for shit." He's particular about green tea, probably influenced by Aunt Akiko.

I roll my eyes. He complains about the lack of acceptable tea, but still never fails to ask for coffee every time he comes over. It's almost like he has a crush on Madison, but he does this with everyone. The man simply can't say no to free caffeine. "Fine. Finish your shitty coffee and get out."

"Ever the gracious host. How you manage to charm so many clients is beyond me. But I'll be nice to you—after all, you're about to get a shitty father-in-law." He snorts a laugh and takes a sip, then makes a face again. "Nelson is an asshole. Never liked him. My brothers don't either. Ares openly tries to humiliate him."

"Ares cuts everyone down." Not to mention he hates everybody and trusts no one. His mother messed him up by kidnapping him and keeping him in a shed in an isolated wooded area when her divorce didn't go the way she wanted. He almost died when a wildfire started in the area because his mother forgot she'd stashed her son out there.

I'm grateful he doesn't blame me for what happened. Zoe asked me to invite Ares, Bryce and Josh over to share some cookies she'd bought, and I was the naïve kid who made the call. I knew Uncle Prescott and Zoe were separated, but didn't think much about it. It turned out she wanted to kidnap all four of the children, but failed because Ares put up a fight. He was worthy of his name even as an eight-year-old.

Still, every time I see the burn scars on him, guilt wells up. Even though logic says I was only seven and couldn't have known better, my heart feels what it feels.

"You're either just like your family or the opposite," Bryce says. "You saw how Vivienne treated Grace, and what her family was like. Your fiancée looked surprised and a little flustered at the dinner."

"She's a damn good actress."

He shrugs. "Or maybe she really was flustered. Not everyone in this town wants to get into movies. You just think like that because it's how Ted sees the world."

I bristle at the comparison. "That's low." He knows how much I hate being told I'm in any way like Dad.

Bryce shows zero sympathy as he chugs down the coffee. "Truth hurts, man. Give her a chance. That way, if she turns out to be the bitch you think she is, at least you can claim the moral high ground. If she's actually an unwitting participant in all of this, you can avoid being an asshole to an innocent woman."

"Why are you telling me this?"

"Because you are driven, maybe too much so. When you set your sights on something, you don't care what or who you trample over to get it. One of these days, that's going to come back to bite you in the ass. As your cousin—and your lawyer—I'd hate to see you suffer. By the way, this advice is free. You're welcome."

"Did Grandma ask you to say this to me?" My voice hardens at possible betrayal. My cousins always supported my decision to pursue my own thing and thought Grandma was too controlling.

"No. I side with my clients, and she isn't one. I just don't want you to regret anything. Grandma won't live forever."

"She'll outlive us all," I mutter, but I don't make a point of it. Bryce lost his Japanese grandmother a month ago, and he's taken it harder than his mother. Which is odd, since he wasn't that close to the woman.

"She's old, Hux. She loves you and wants the best for you, in her own way. She'll be gone soon, and then it will be too late." He shakes his head. "By the time you learn the truth, it's always too late."

Only the scent of coffee lingers after he leaves. I stare at the prenup. If Bryce stopped by in person to advise restraint, he probably thinks I'm being too harsh. When I asked him to draft me a prenup, the only thing I thought of was how to destroy and humiliate Grace. But...

Sebastian also said I should tread carefully, just in case.

Fine. I'll give her a chance to explain. I'm not too proud or stupid to ignore well-meaning advice from smart people who care about me.

I get on the intercom. "Madison, do I have any lunch appointments this week?"

"No. Would you like me to make one for you?" she asks, attentive as usual.

"No, thanks." Grace and I aren't going anywhere that requires a reservation.

I pick up my phone. I'll give my fiancée one more chance.

18

GRACE

Monday is nobody's favorite day, but this particular one starts out a mess with the venue for our next fundraiser event telling us there may be a problem because of an upcoming workers' strike. I sent messages asking if they can help finding another venue for the charity art auction, but the contact hasn't responded. That poor woman's inbox is probably exploding with email from irate customers.

My phone has also been buzzing since the dinner with nonstop calls and texts from Karie and Viv. I blocked Viv's number a year ago, so she started using her mom's phone to bug me. I wish I could block Karie too, but occasionally she contacts me about Mom's hospital bills.

"What's wrong with that thing?" Tolyan says with a dark scowl at my vibrating phone. "Is it broken?"

"No. Just a lot of calls from people I'd rather avoid."

"It's annoying."

"Sorry." Our desks are close, and he's probably fed up after over a week of this.

When it buzzes again, he snatches it up. "Call this number again, I'll bury you, face first."

"Who the *fuck* is this—!" Viv's screech is so loud, I can hear it clearly from my desk.

"An assistant."

A pause. She probably didn't expect that. "Put my sister on the line! I know that bitch is there."

Tolyan stares lazily into the middle distance. "Of course. Who may I say is calling?"

"Vivienne Webber! Do you know who my daddy—"

"Tofu brain." He hangs up. "Why do you put up with this?" he asks me.

You have no idea. But he seems genuinely curious as he waits for a response. Probably nobody dares to raise their voice to him. Not unless they're full of liquid courage.

Since I can't tell him the truth, I paste on a smile. "Family. Can't kill them, can't live without them."

"Family is like a dog that hasn't been housebroken. Train them until they behave." He turns back to his laptop. For the hundredth time, I wonder what it is that he does all day. He says he organizes files, but nothing stored on the cloud requires that kind of full-time attention.

My phone shakes again. An impatient sigh wells, and I reach for it, about to turn it off. The text preview on the screen stops me.

—Adam: Hey! You free for lunch?

We haven't talked in a while, not since I messaged him that I was fine after the SportsBrews fiasco. I've been busy, and so has he. Huxley & Webber keeps its associates busy, determined to get its money's worth and more.

I smile a little as I type my response.

—Me: Yeah, sure. Around noon?

—Adam: Should be fine. Meet you at Tomate? I can make a reservation.

It's a popular Italian restaurant, specializing in pizza and pasta, about four blocks from the Pryce Family Foundation. He and I went there all the time until he started to get busy at work and Mom became sick.

—Me: Sure. See you there.

As soon as I send that, a new text pops up.

—Huxley: Can we do lunch today?

116

I bite my lip at the five short words. I wish I could hear his voice to gauge if he's still upset. But regardless, I'm a little bit torn. If I hadn't just said yes to Adam, I'd agree to meet Huxley. He's had some time to cool off, and we need to discuss our next step.

Besides, I'm dying of curiosity and anxiety over what he's been stewing about and what he plans to say. I know this won't be a friendly social outing.

—Me: Sorry. I already have a date.

—Huxley: A date?

Why does it feel like he disapproves? He and I don't have the kind of relationship where he gets to act possessive.

—Me: A LUNCH date. Just made it before you texted me. How about tomorrow at one?

—Huxley: Fine.

—Me: Okay. I'll go to your office.

—Huxley: No need. My assistant will send details.

Viv calls again, and I turn my phone off. Nothing's that urgent, and work calls are routed to the black phone on my desk anyway. Plus, she used up a year's worth of my patience when she slept with Peter.

At noon, I'm at Tomate. The place is already packed, but Adam managed to score a booth. Probably flashed his killer smile—people can't say no to that boyish grin.

He's in a khaki-colored suit a shade darker than his hair. Probably not going to the courthouse. He prefers a black suit for that. Claims it makes him look older and more serious. The gentle slope of his jaw and shining light-green eyes knock ten years off his true age. Most think he's "barely a kid" and too unseasoned. But if you start talking to him, it doesn't take long to realize he's brilliant.

"Hey," I say, giving him a hug. "Long time no see."

He gives me a good squeeze back. "Too much work. I swear, we live to work."

I laugh and take a seat opposite him. "Our bosses don't pay us to sit in the office and do nothing. And even if they did, I wouldn't want to. I'm making a meaningful impact in people's lives."

The foundation has built and operated schools in parts of the world where getting an education is generally a privilege reserved for the wealthy. It gives financial and logistical support to families with children receiving cancer treatment. Tens of thousands of battered women and children come to the shelters the foundation funds to be safe. Every Thanksgiving and Christmas, hundreds of thousands of turkeys and presents are handed out, so poverty won't be the reason a family is deprived of the holidays. The minute details of making all this become a reality aren't always fun, but the sense of pride and seeing what I can to do to help others make it all worth it in the end.

I'm blessed to have a job that not only gives me money but makes me feel fulfilled.

"So am I by making sure my clients' asses are fully covered," Adam jokes. "Think how I'm freeing up the courts, saving tax dollars."

"When your lucky numbers pan out, you'll be able to retire and be the guy who hires lawyers to CYA," I respond dreamily. He likes to buy exactly one lottery ticket every Sunday. Says he wants to test his luck, and it's the only hobby he can indulge in, since he never has much time.

I'm certain what little downtime he has, he wants to spend with his boyfriend. I met him last year at a deli. That poor man was harassed by an ex who refused to accept that the relationship was over, and Adam told the abuser to stay away from his boyfriend, all possessive and protective.

When the waiter comes by, I ask for a cheese pizza and ginger ale—they're about the only things I can stomach right now. Adam orders the meat special and a Coke and gives me a look. "What's with the plain cheese pizza?"

"Just craving it today. Change is good." And I need a good, smooth opening to tell him about the baby. Adam will be shocked, but I hope he'll support me. I feel guilty that I've been too stunned and overwhelmed to fully appreciate the life in my womb since I saw those two lines on the pregnancy tests. This baby's conception might've been accidental, but my love for it isn't.

"By the way…" Adam clears his throat and seems to grind to a conversational halt.

"What?"

"Okay, so, uh… Is it true you're getting married?"

"Where did you hear that?"

"Andreas mentioned it last week during a break. Said his granddaughter was engaged, and I thought he meant Viv, but then he said it was you."

"Oh. Well...yeah. I'm sorry I didn't tell you." I didn't say anything to Adam before because it felt weird to lie to my best friend after I agreed to a fake engagement with Huxley. Then since the dinner, I've been processing it. To be honest, I thought Huxley would've found a way to call it off by now. He said he didn't want to disappoint Emma, but he doesn't strike me as the type to go along with something that isn't part of his plan.

Not only that, he doesn't believe the baby is his. I'll never forget that expression of skepticism on his face. At least once the paternity test is done, he won't be able to hold that against me or the baby. Still, my heart is heavy because paternity alone won't be enough to make him care for the child. Just look at Nelson.

I sigh. The entire arrangement between me and Huxley has turned into a complete mess. I should've given it more thought before agreeing to it. Not only did we create a baby who might be hated by its father, but I'm going to have to lie to Adam. He might feel awkward, since my situation involves all his bosses in some way or other.

Feeling like a shitty friend, I place my left hand on the table so he can see it. "I—"

Adam lets out a shaky breath. "So it's really true?"

I nod, glancing away from him. "It sort of happened that way."

"I didn't even know you were dating anybody after Peter." His voice cracks with mild rebuke. He's probably worried that I'm on a rebound I'll regret.

"I wasn't. Not really. I mean... I met Huxley a while back. Like two years ago," I say, glad and relieved I can finally offer some honest answers. "He was the guy who drove me to the ER when Mom collapsed. Then I ran into him again at SportsBrew, the night I realized Peter was cheating on me with Viv, and we just hit it off. The rest is history." A helpless shrug. *Please let this be enough of an explanation...!*

Our pizzas and drinks arrive. I nibble on a slice, hoping the inquisition is over. I'd rather talk about something more exciting, like the latest legal brief he's been working on.

Adam doesn't touch his food. A sign that he's upset. His mood starts to affect mine, and my appetite wanes. I put the pizza down.

"That was, like, weeks ago." Hurt, anxiety and anger twist over his normally friendly face.

"Yeah. About...two months?" I venture a guess, then sigh. "I'm sorry, Adam. I should've said something." What kind of crappy friend am I to keep him in the dark for weeks? Even if he's been busy and I've been overwhelmed with everything going on, I should've at least texted him.

"This is way too fast. Are you sure about marrying this guy?"

"It was love at first sight." Kind of ridiculous to claim that now, when Huxley is furious enough to maybe strangle me the next time we see each other.

"Bullshit. You aren't like that."

"Like what?" I laugh softly. "Worthy of love at first sight?"

"No, of course you're *worthy*. You are. But you're too rational, and you have responsibilities you take very seriously. He might've fallen for you at first sight, but vice versa? No way. You'd never fall for a guy you barely know, or trust him."

"Well... I guess I trust him," I say with a forced smile.

Adam's eyes grow intense. "Does he love you and cherish you the way you deserve?"

I should lie and say yes, but the sincere worry in his eyes makes it stick in my throat. So I take a sip of ginger ale, trying to buy myself time.

Of course, Adam isn't fooled. "See? You know deep inside he won't be good to you."

There's no need to reach deep inside. Huxley told me how he felt.

"Are you trapped because of the baby?"

I blink. "How did you know? About the baby, I mean." *Is there anything he* doesn't *know?*

"Andreas mentioned he was going to be a great-grandfather soon." Adam runs his fingers through his sandy hair. "But I still can't imagine why you'd shackle yourself to a man you have no feelings for. You should be with someone who makes you happy." He stares at nothing for a moment as he shakes his head slightly, then his jaw firms. "If it's about your father giving you a hard time about the pregnancy, I'll do it."

Huh? "Do what?"

"Marry you. We've known each other for so long. If you need someone to raise the baby with, I'll do it. I promise I'll make you happy for the rest of our lives. I'll be the most devoted father and husband ever."

"Um…" I stop. *What am I supposed to say to this?* If he didn't look so earnest, I might laugh, thinking he was just kidding. "Nobody's going to believe we're getting married. Not for real. Besides, I need a rich husband."

His face falls. "Is it because—"

"Adam." I can't let him continue saying things he doesn't mean, making promises he can't keep, out of concern for me. Once he has time to really think things through, he'll regret this moment, and I don't want our friendship to be ruined just for a gesture that will ultimately turn out to be meaningless. Just knowing that somebody puts me first is amazing, but marrying me would require him to deny his true self and happiness. I care about him too much to let him do that to himself.

I paste on a bright smile. "Thank you for the offer, and I couldn't love you more for caring so deeply about me. But you know how things have been for me and how much I need money. And now, I got my wish." Nelson and Karie will definitely use my marriage as an excuse to quit paying for Mom's care, claiming I have a husband to share the burden. My head already hurts at the fight that'll happen when they realize Huxley won't be paying. However, Adam doesn't need to know that level of sordid detail. He'd try to help, but he doesn't make enough, not when he has an exorbitant student loan. "On top of that, he's young and handsome. The perfect trifecta." I keep my voice light to reassure him.

He reaches for my hand. "But—"

Suddenly there is movement next to the table and a fork strikes down like a hawk diving for prey. Adam and I snatch our hands away. My heart jumps to my throat, pulses painfully. The three prongs, vibrating from the force, dig into the wooden table where Adam's hand was just an instant earlier.

"Jesus, what the *fuck*?" Adam says.

"Whoever you are, you don't touch my fiancée," comes Huxley's steely voice.

Fury blazes in the icy depths of his eyes. He looks even more enraged than he did at the dinner. My mouth dries.

A large, warm hand wraps around my shoulder, and the subtle smoky and spicy scent envelops me as Huxley presses a firm kiss on my cheek, his eyes on Adam. "Hello, my love."

19

HUXLEY

WOMEN OFTEN LOVE me for my money and my connections. So it shouldn't be a shock to hear Grace say as much. I should appreciate that she's being honest, albeit behind my back. After all, I promised myself to give her a chance, not absolve her for everything she's done. Her behavior makes my path clear, and I can give her the same taste of public humiliation, helplessness and manipulation she's heaped on me without any niggling doubts that I'm being unfair.

What I *don't* appreciate is a guy sharing her table and attention. He eyes her like a stray dog desperate for a loving home. How dare he reach for her like he has the right to touch her? *And how dare she let him?*

I'm not a particularly religious man, but some divine entity must be looking out for me to make me crave pizza today. Otherwise, I would've never heard the true intentions from her own lips, and I wouldn't have caught this...display.

I couldn't love you more.

But you know how things have been for me and how much I need money.

Of course. How is she going to go back to budgeting and give up the joy of burning through twenty-five grand a month?

I've definitely been played. All because she looked at me with innocent eyes, and she and I had some amazing sex. *When did I start letting my dick dictate my decisions?* Disgust at myself flows through my veins like acid, followed by fury. She must've been laughing at me the entire time. She had to have been thrilled when she found out she was pregnant, so I couldn't just dump her without looking like a callous asshole.

If only Emma hadn't come to the dinner...

Even her presence there now feels like a part of a plot to put me in checkmate.

"You're her fiancé?" Adam looks me up and down with a small sneer on his face. He's trying to hide it, but resentment and jealousy seethe in his insolent gaze.

"Yes. Reach for her again, and you'll lose your hand."

"Huxley, he's a friend," Grace says.

Her attempt at clarification only fuels my temper. Just because they have some history doesn't mean I have to put up with him panting after my woman. Or her declaring her love for him. "Really? Do friends look at friends like they want to fuck their brains out?"

Adam turns bright red, looking flustered and embarrassed. Guess he never had the guts to tell her how he felt. Loser.

"What are you? A medieval thug?" he demands.

I shoot him a soulless smile. "Just a man keeping a stray off his property."

Grace gasps. "I'm not your property!" The guy gets redder.

"Grace, when a rich man acquires a pretty young wife, he's buying an exclusive property, not to be shared with anybody else. If you don't understand that, I can take other measures."

"Like what? Calling it off?"

Frankly, I wish that were an option. But I'm not going to disappoint and upset Emma because of Grace's machinations. Plus, if I must marry a Webber, Grace is the more tolerable evil. Vivienne would be worse— just as insufferable, stupid on top of it, unable to control herself even in public. Somebody like her would behave like a wild animal in private. "Like a spanking and a chastity belt."

Grace's jaw drops.

Adam jumps to his feet. "You asshole!" He pulls his arm back.

Anticipation and adrenaline pump through me. *Go ahead. Throw the first punch.*

Grace leaps between us. "*Stop it!* What's *wrong* with you? *Both* of you?"

"He can't talk to you like that!" The volume of Adam's voice attracts attention.

"But you can turn this conversation into a public spectacle," I sneer.

He notices the eyes on us and compresses his lips. "Sorry," he says to Grace.

"It's okay, Adam."

Her soft forgiveness stirs the dark beast of temper inside me. "*My fiancée* and I are going to have a private conversation."

"I don't have much time," she says. "My lunch break's going to end soon."

"It won't take long if you'll just do as I tell you without arguing." I grind out the words. Defiance flickers in her face, and I put a finger on her mouth. "Or we can just do it here in front of everyone. Your choice."

She pushes the finger away. "We can go now."

"Good." I throw a few bills on the table and give Adam a sidelong glance. "My fiancée doesn't eat meals another man paid for."

THE 4D AGENCY is mostly empty—almost everyone is out for lunch. Madison's at her desk, and she rises to her feet when I stalk toward my office. She notes my hand wrapped around Grace's wrist, then turns her attention back to me.

"Huxley, do you need—"

"Hold my calls," I say as I pull Grace inside my office and slam the door shut.

"What horrific bug crawled up your ass and died?" Grace demands, yanking her arm out of my grasp.

"Did you expect me to be kind and sweet when you tell another man you love him? And *in public?*"

She stares at me. "He's a *friend!* Like, since forever! And he wanted to help."

I snort. "Help himself to my fiancée, more like. No more men, Grace. I will not have you cheat on me, emotionally or physically. I want your everything. It isn't such a high price to pay to marry into money."

She clenches her hands, her eyes glittering. "Oh, okay. And does this little rule go both ways? I'd hate to be pitied because you can't quit eye-fucking other women or get an STD because you can't keep your dick in your pants."

"Obviously." I don't want to be another Ted Lasker. "I'm not a scheming hypocrite, unlike some people I could name."

She glares at me like she'd love to wrap her hands around my neck and squeeze.

I continue, "You'll behave like a proper fiancée, then a proper wife. And you'll stay away from him. No talking or meeting."

"Like I said already, he's a *friend*. F-R-I-E-N-D. Friend."

"Then get a new *friend*. A female one. That's the least you can do for *getting a rich husband*."

"Are you offering to buy me a friend?" she says sarcastically.

"I'll ruin him first, *then* buy you a friend. One who doesn't look like she'd love nothing more than bend you over the edge of a bed!"

Her face scrunches. "You're disgusting. And for your information, Adam is *gay*."

I bark out a laugh. "If he's gay, I'm a Pomeranian."

"I can't believe you!" She throws her hands up. "Just because *you* can't be friends with the opposite sex doesn't mean I can't. Not every man wants to sleep with me."

"Then why do they look at you that way?"

"What way?" She looks genuinely confused. A damn good actress is what she is, I remind myself.

"Like they want to fuck you on the spot!" I seethe. I'm being jealous, and it's difficult to deal with when I've never experienced this particular emotion before. I hate it that she comes in a package so pretty I can't let my guard down without jeopardizing my sanity. Does she want me to acknowledge out loud how she affects me? Fuck that. Over my dead body.

Grace puts her hands on her hips. "You are so"—she hunts for a word—"de*lus*ional! Oh my *God*! Why did I ever think—"

"I don't care what you think, Grace. You'll do as I say, or there will be consequences. As a matter of fact, I think it's time you moved in with me."

"Why? So you can keep an eye on me twenty-four seven?"

"Somebody needs to keep other men away."

She inhales audibly. Her jaw tenses so hard, I can almost hear it creak. "Why don't you go ahead and get me an ankle bracelet, too? It'll go nicely with that chastity belt."

"Great idea. Thanks for suggesting it. I'll have Madison get on that right now."

Her knuckles whiten. A vein throbs visibly in her neck, but the sight doesn't give me much satisfaction. To be honest, I don't know what would after that infuriating scene at the restaurant.

My eyes land on the prenup Bryce delivered. I throw it in her face. "If all your intentions are as pure as you claim, you won't have any problem signing this."

"What is it?"

"A prenup. To ensure you don't get a penny from me."

Disillusionment dims the light in her eyes, proving me right—she's been after me for my money. But there's no feeling of vindication—disillusionment of my own drips into my gut like poison. Perhaps I've secretly been hoping that Sebastian was right and she wasn't just another mercenary bitch.

"Are you going to require me to pay rent? Utilities?" Her voice couldn't be flatter.

"No. That would be ridiculous. Besides, you can't afford it." *Annoying.* It's like she somehow knows that I thought about charging her before deciding it was beneath me.

Her chest rises and falls rapidly as she glares at me. I notice how pretty her breasts look—recall how responsive they were that night—and I want to strangle myself. Finally, she grabs a pen from my desk and scrawls her name on the contract. "There. Satisfied?"

Not even a little. I don't know what will ever make me satisfied again. I hate her for disrupting my orderly and well-planned life. "Would've been more satisfied if I could have remained a bachelor—"

A commotion erupts from outside. Madison's raised voice comes through the closed door, although the words are unintelligible. Suddenly the door crashes open.

"When I say hold my calls, it means no interruptions!" I turn, ready to eviscerate the intruder.

It's Karie. Madison, breathing hard and with a few strands out of place from her normally impeccable updo, is holding her arm and trying to pull her back. Karie, meanwhile, tries to bat Madison's hands away.

"Get your paws off me!" Karie says, struggling to escape. "Do you know how much this dress cost?"

"A poor man's kidney?" Grace says under her breath.

I bite my lip to hide a sudden grin at the unexpected sass. It's irritating that her unexpected sense of humor continues to amuse me. "It's fine, Madison. Let her go."

Madison does so and takes a couple of steps back to let me deal with the problem.

I put on one of my least welcoming faces. "What the hell is going on?"

"Mrs. Webber showed up without an appointment and insisted on seeing you." Madison sounds calm, like she hasn't had a minor scuffle.

"Why would I need an appointment?" Karie turns to me. "Tell your help that I'm your mother-in-law!"

Grace looks away, closing her eyes in embarrassment. My jaw grows tight. "You're not. What do you want? You have ten seconds."

Karie huffs. "I've been trying to reach you and Grace, but couldn't."

"I blocked you." I wanted to do more, but the other measures I was contemplating are illegal. "Five seconds."

Her smug smile falters, but she recovers. "I want to be in charge of the wedding, but Catalina says there are plenty of wedding planners in the city. It's ludicrous! Tell her that you want me to do it. I'm entitled to the honor."

The honor? This woman didn't show an iota of kindness or warmth toward Grace at the dinner. Although she tried to hide it, she was angry, like somebody reached into her closet and absconded with her favorite Hermes handbag. Grandmother probably rejected her offer because Karie's likely to botch the job, either through incompetence or out of sheer spite. If she's anything like her biological daughter, she's petty and nasty enough to do just that.

"I agree with my grandmother." I let my gaze rake over the dress she seems to love so much. "I'm not letting a woman with the taste of a back-alley whore take charge of my wedding."

The makeup can't hide the flush creeping up her neck. "How *dare* you talk to me like that?"

"Easily. I open my mouth and form the words."

Grace lets out a choked sound, then covers her mouth.

Karie's chest is now heaving with rage. "I am the *mother* of the *bride!*"

"In what way? Grace didn't pop out of your vagina. You didn't raise her. And I can't give you credit for being a good mother based on how Mick and Viv turned out."

Her mouth opens and closes a few times. It happens when you get hit in the solar plexus with the truth.

"Then who's going to plan the wedding? *Her?*" She points a manicured finger at Grace.

"No, Grace is busy with her career," I say.

"What career? Making coffee for her boss?"

"You wouldn't understand, since the only thing you've done in your life is spend other people's money."

Karie is speechless. Her silence is truly golden.

I continue, "Thankfully, I have Madison, who always knows exactly what I want. Now that we're clear on the matter—and your ten seconds have long since expired—get the fuck out of my office. Or I'll have security toss you out on your bony ass."

20

GRACE

My STOMACH CHURNS with unease as I pull in at Nelson's house. It was satisfying to see Huxley deal with Karie this afternoon. He didn't pull any punches with me, but he didn't pull any with her either, thank God. If he'd been deferential to her, the marriage would become even more intolerable.

Not that there are any signs our union is going to be peaceful. I mean... Yes, what I said to Adam could have sounded bad, if you didn't know the context. But Huxley didn't have to fly off the handle without giving me a chance to explain. Or worse, reject the truth that Adam and I are just friends because he's just too damn proud and stubborn to admit he's wrong.

And that prenup! He acted like it was going to devastate me, but it only made me sad. *What have I done to give such a terrible impression of myself?* I've never treated him unfairly, but he views everything about me in the worst possible light.

I signed it to avoid wasting time and energy. I don't need his money. The document won't change my financial circumstances in any way. I'll continue to work and contribute to Mom's care. Nelson and Karie will continue to write their monthly checks. If they try to punt the responsibility to Huxley, I'll tell them I'll run to Andreas, although his assistant might block me from seeing him. He's a busy man, and he rarely has time for anybody, unless they can afford his exorbitant rate. It's exhausting to have to constantly fight for what I've been promised, but that's what happens when you're the lowest of everyone's priorities. If I threaten the reputation of the family, Andreas might spare three minutes, though... I think.

Before I left the 4D Agency, Huxley said I'd better be packed by eight. What does he think I am? A dog that jumps at the snap of his fingers?

Besides, even if I wanted to go along with him to avoid another argument, I can't. Not today. Karie was waiting outside his office. "We need to talk," she said.

"I'm busy," I told her brusquely, trying not to show satisfaction at how she'd been treated just moments earlier.

"Too busy to discuss your mom's bills?"

I stopped, and a smirk twisted her mouth.

"That's what I thought. Come over after work or we'll have a problem."

Now that I'm here... I exhale. Whatever Karie plans to do is going to be ugly. She understands she can't bend Huxley to her will, which means she's going to go through me. If Huxley and I weren't in the situation we are in, I might consider asking him for help, but I doubt he'll show me any mercy. He only got nasty with her because she interrupted him. I'll be lucky if he doesn't side with her just to make me miserable.

I walk inside and see not only Karie, but Nelson and Viv in the living room, seated in armchairs designed to look like thrones. Nelson must've left the office early for the occasion. No sign of the housekeeper—likely dismissed early so no outsider will witness the scene to come. The notion spikes my stress, and a fresh wave of acid sloshes in my belly.

"Call it off!" Viv demands.

"Good evening, Viv. You look lovely too." Since there's only a footstool, I remain standing, rather than crouching at their feet. The furniture setup is a silent reminder of my place in this family.

Viv slams her fist on the arm of her chair. "Call it *off*! You don't deserve him! You conniving bitch! You aren't really pregnant, are you?"

I put a hand over my belly. "You want to place a bet?"

She hesitates, suddenly uncertain. "Like you have anything worth wagering!" she finally says.

"You're right. I don't have any *thing*...except my mother's love."

Smug contempt crosses Viv's face. "Your mother's love? You wish—"

"That's enough!" Karie says.

Viv shuts up, which is weird. Normally she would argue and whine that she should be able to "exercise her constitutional right to free speech."

But before I can ponder on the odd reaction, Karie says, "You owe me an apology, Grace."

"For what?"

"For the way Huxley treated me."

She insisted on seeing me for *this*? "He's an adult. Ask him."

"Is this how you show gratitude for our sacrifice?"

"What sacrifice?" I ask, truly lost.

"We *have* been paying for Winona's treatment. It isn't cheap."

"Trying to set an example of generosity for you," says Nelson.

The words are suffocating. It always comes to this. *Be grateful because we are paying for your mother's care. Do as we say because we are paying for your mother's care. Don't you love your mother? Do you want her dead?* I look at Karie. "Not for free."

"Don't talk to your mother that way," Nelson says.

"She's not my mother. And never will be." I clench my hands to hide the tremor of anger.

He shakes his head, his mouth tight. "You're a disgrace. I expected you to be a better girl. We taught you better than this!"

"Oh, you taught me." All the pent-up rage explodes. "And whose example should I have followed? *Yours*? So you want me to bang somebody and then abandon the child? Or Karie, who used my mother's medical bills to force me into taking the LSAT for Viv so she could fraudulently get into Harvard Law? You've never shown me a single admirable quality, and I'd rather lick shit off the floor of a horse stall than become anything like either of you. Oh, and by the way, please *don't* come to my wedding. It'd be too embarrassing. *For me.*"

"How dare you!" Nelson shouts.

"Who's going to walk you down the aisle?" Karie manages. She's furious, but also concerned about the family image. It's everything to her.

"I'll think of someone. And you can bet it'll be someone who doesn't always put me down, or threaten to deny my mother medical care she needs. A homeless crack addict would be better than either of you. You've never been my family, not in any way that truly matters."

Nelson jumps to his feet and lunges forward. He raises his meaty hand.

Shock grips me in a tight vise—I can't move. Fire explodes in my face, and my head snaps to the side. I blink to clear my dimming vision. Coppery warmth fills my mouth, and the inside of my cheek stings.

He's never gotten physically violent before. He tries to act like he's above that and silently urges Mick to do his dirty work. Guess I hit too close to the mark and it was intolerable when he couldn't think of anything clever to rebut me.

"Get out, you ungrateful cunt!"

Nelson's vicious shout shatters the shocked stupor. I stare at him blankly for a moment, my face throbbing.

"You deserved that." Karie's tone is smooth and calm, but a satisfied smirk gives her away. "Next time, show some respect."

Behind her, Viv is grinning. And probably praying the bruise will still be visible at the wedding.

My brain numb, I seize the chance to leave without saying a word. My hands shake as I fumble for my fob, then climb into my car. The drive home passes like a fever dream, but somehow I find myself back in front of my condo complex.

Still on autopilot, I park the car and step out. My knees feel weak. I shouldn't be so stunned or upset. Nelson and his family have always hated me. They're just worried at the possibility that they might not be able to control and abuse me like they used to. They're probably terrified Huxley will learn what they've done to me over the years, especially after the way he showed nothing but contempt for Karie this afternoon.

Will they escalate this violence toward me? I wish there was something I could do. But if I report the incident to the police, nothing will happen. Nelson's a lawyer, and his son is the DA. Besides, even if the police are sympathetic, Nelson and Karie will withhold payments for Mom's bills in retaliation. Who knows when I'll be able to see Andreas and beg for his intervention? By then, it might be too late, and I'd truly end up killing the only family I have.

It's just a slap—a bruise and a little blood in my mouth. Both will heal. When Mom gets well enough to be discharged, I won't have to put up with Nelson or any of his family anymore.

"Where have you been?"

I freeze. Huxley appears out of a Bugatti parked two spots away. I quickly step into the building's shadow. I don't want him to notice what happened, because if he acts like nothing's wrong, it'll be humiliating and painful. There's a sliver of hope in my heart that maybe...just maybe Huxley won't be so cruel and uncaring after the way he stood up for me earlier against Karie. But the fear that he might turn his back on me is greater.

At the same time, if he notices and says something... Well, that could be embarrassing. I hate the irrational shame I feel over what Nelson has done. He's the bad guy, not me!

I try for a steady tone of voice. "What are you doing here?"

"I told you to pack your things. It's already after nine."

"Karie and I had some things to discuss at her house."

He comes closer. I shift deeper into the dark.

He reaches out and takes hold of my chin. His eyes glitter dangerously in the dark, and I swallow as trepidation clenches around my gut.

"Who did this to you?" His voice is low, but as icily cold as I've ever heard.

"What?" I say shakily. He couldn't possibly have seen my face...

"This bruise. Who did it?"

I push his hand away. "It's none of your business."

"We're engaged. That means you're mine now. And when somebody touches what's mine, it becomes my business." He pulls me closer to the streetlight.

I look away, unable to bear the judgment. His breathing roughens. He raises his hand, and I flinch. An expletive. My stomach twists.

His finger is oddly gentle as it brushes my throbbing cheek.

Inexplicable tears spring to my eyes. I blink rapidly. It'd be too foolish to cry and show weakness. In my experience, showing weaknesses is begging for abuse. I'm not giving anybody that power over me.

"A woman wouldn't be strong enough to hurt you this badly." He narrows his eyes. He's probably mentally going over all the people in my life he's aware of. His gaze burns into mine. "So not Karie. Or Vivienne. Who was it?"

I keep mum, looking down at my hands. Why does he care so much about who did it? It isn't like he can do anything to Nelson. The Huxleys' and the Webbers' business interests override everything.

"Fine," he spits out between clenched teeth. "We'll figure this out together."

21

HUXLEY

RAGE CHURNS AND BURNS. I grip the steering wheel with more force than necessary, imagining it's the neck of whoever touched Grace. She stares out the window as I drive to Nelson's house. She feigns nonchalance, but tension radiates from her. Her acting like she's afraid of me—that I'm just as bad as the man who hit her—stokes my fury further.

But could it really be her family? They're giving her a generous monthly allowance. Why do that if they hate her? Or is the payment to get her to shut up about the abuse, assuming it's an ongoing thing?

I consider the idea, but ultimately reject it. She has too much pride and sass to stay silent over money. And she has a job. It doesn't pay twenty-five K a month, but it's enough to maintain her dignity. Besides, wouldn't somebody at her office have noticed bruises by now?

I want to ask, but doubt she'll tell me anything. She didn't tell me who did this to her. What does she think I'm going to do? Join them? She flinched when I tried to turn her face so I could examine the injury.

She's my fiancée, my future wife. It's my responsibility to teach anybody who dares to touch her a lesson they'll never forget.

My plan to have her move in is pushed aside to deal with whoever had the nerve to mark her. It's more important—and far more urgent.

I pull into the Webbers' driveway. Nelson's home is ostentatious and way above his means. But his family is like that in every respect. Big egos with nothing to back them up.

I climb out and the open the passenger-side door. "Let's go."

Grace looks away, her chin tight.

"I can stand here all night."

Eventually she steps out, not meeting my gaze. She stays rooted to the spot. I put a hand on her elbow and bring her forward. I ring the doorbell, and Grace turns around, shifting until she's standing behind me in the dark. Fine tremors rack her. I hate that someone put this fear into her, and that I wasn't there to do anything about it.

Three beats later the door opens, revealing Karie, still in that ridiculous, overpriced dress that might look good if she were thirty years younger. Her eyebrows jump an inch—or try to, but her over-Botoxed forehead doesn't allow much freedom of movement. The corners of her mouth turn down. No cosmetic surgery can hide the deep, unhappy ugliness she holds inside.

She quickly schools her expression. "Are you here to apologize for your shameful behavior?" she demands haughtily.

"No."

"Then you aren't welcome." She glares at me, but blanches as soon as she notices Grace.

"I see you understand the reason for this visit." I grab Grace's hand and walk past Karie into the house.

"What do you mean? It has nothing to do with us!" Karie says hurriedly. She doesn't seem to realize her reaction has given her away. She shows no shock at Grace's swollen cheek, which by this point does look a bit shocking.

I stride to the living room. Nelson is in the middle of pouring himself a whiskey. But when he notices me, he flinches, spilling the alcohol. "Oh, shit."

Vivienne starts toward me until she notices I'm not alone. "Why is *she* back here?"

"Viv!" Karie hisses.

I scan the room. "Where's Mick?" The asshole could be hiding like the gutless coward that he is.

"He's not here. Busy at work." Nelson licks his lips. "Why?"

I pull Grace forward, gently but firmly. "Who did this to her?"

Karie lets out a shaky breath. "How are we supposed to know?"

Vivienne glances at Nelson, who turns his glass with listless fingers.

"No explanation whatsoever for the injury?" I say, my tone growing increasingly icy. "She was fine just this afternoon. And I doubt anybody at the Pryce Family Foundation did this to her. Then she came here." I look at each of them in turn, my eyes coming to rest on Nelson. "So. Who was it?"

He clears his throat. "She's a clumsy girl."

I cock an eyebrow.

"She probably ran into a wall." Avoiding my gaze, he opens and closes his right hand.

You. A fiery need to get justice for my woman erupts. I leap the distance, grab the back of his head and smash it against the wall hard enough to make the liquor cabinet shake.

"Augh!" he screams.

I smash his face into the wall again. Just because I feel like it, and he deserves to suffer.

He garbles another word that sounds like *fuck*, but it's hard to tell with the blood gushing from his nose.

I let go. He crumples to the floor. Karie rushes to him, then glares up at me. "You asshole!"

Vivienne starts crying hysterically. Grace just stares, her mouth slightly parted. I put a finger underneath her chin and lift it up, closing her mouth. I put my arm around her.

"Gonna sue yer ass," Nelson mumbles. "This is a fuckin' lawsuit."

Like I give a damn. I let my gaze sweep over the trio of Webbers. "Touch my woman again, and I'll end you."

22

GRACE

BACK IN HUXLEY'S CAR, my emotions feel settled, and I'm no longer operating on autopilot. I don't know how this kind of calm is possible after seeing such explosive violence. Huxley appears so civilized and suave that it's just incongruent that he was capable of ramming Nelson's face into a wall.

Twice.

"He only hit me once," I say as Huxley maneuvers his car on the road.

"The second one was for my satisfaction."

I mull that over for a moment. "Okay. And do you feel satisfied?"

His eyes flick to my face. A small muscle twitches in his jaw. "Not really. I should've hit him a few times as well."

There must be something wrong with me that a comforting warmth settles in my belly. He just admitted he was capable of more violence than he's shown. He also swore he hates me for "tricking" him. It's entirely possible that he could get mad enough at me to do some physical damage.

But for some reason, I'm not afraid of him. I just don't think he's going to lay a hand on me in anger.

He makes a left turn at the second intersection.

"You have to go the other way to get to my place."

"We aren't going to your place; we're going to mine. I told you you're moving in with me tonight."

"I didn't agree to that. And I don't think it's a good idea, anyway." Despite the way he sided with me against Nelson and his family, Huxley has a way of slipping under my skin, undermining my control and plans. Not to mention, every time he's around the place we're in feels small, like his presence takes up all the space. My skin tightens, and nerves sizzle. I can't afford to make mistakes—Mom's life rides on my decisions—but I become reckless around him.

"We can agree to disagree," he says.

The unyielding tone of his voice indicates the discussion is over. I should argue, but sudden exhaustion weighs me down. It's past my bedtime, and I've had too many emotional upheavals today.

Once we're married, we'll need to live together. So does it really matter when I move in with him? Also, Peter is refusing to replace my bed, and I'm getting tired of sleeping on the sofa.

Life is a series of battles. I need to pick the ones I fight and the ones I let go. This isn't one worth fighting. "Okay," I sigh. "Can we stop by my place so I can pack some stuff? It won't take long."

A beat. "You aren't going to argue?"

I laugh a little at how suspicious he sounds. "What's the point? If I don't move in today, I will later. It isn't like *you're* going to move in with *me*."

"No. Your place is too small. And there's no helipad."

I pause for a moment. It's surreal I'm going to marry a man who owns a freakin' helicopter, when I'm just grateful my car still runs okay. "Yeah. Exactly. What would you do with your helicopter? I'm not totally unreasonable," I say numbly. The sigh I let out is heavy with weariness.

"You're tired."

"Yes. It's been a long day."

A beat. "Is it the baby?"

Well, that's a surprise. I didn't think he would bring up the pregnancy after he was so upset earlier. "Maybe. I don't know. I've never been pregnant before. But even if I weren't, today's been full of upheavals." Dealing with Nelson and his family is always draining.

His mouth tightens, his eyes on the road. "I sent in the sample," he says.

I think for a moment. *The DNA sample.* "Thank you. I'll let you know as soon as I hear back from the lab."

"You're certain it's mine." It's not a question.

"I haven't slept with anybody else but you since that night," I say frankly.

"Your ex?"

"We hadn't been intimate for a few weeks. He was busy *working*." I close my eyes briefly, feel the car moving us through the night. "'Working' being a euphemism for riding my half-sister."

Huxley's jaw muscles relax a little as he continues straight down the road.

"Hey, you gotta make a U-turn," I say.

"No need to pack anything tonight. There are things for you at my place."

"Ew. I'm not using your ex's things." It'd be just as gross as using the bed Peter and Viv screwed on.

"I've never let a woman live with me."

My belly flutters, but I push the sensation down before my heart can start believing I'm special. He probably didn't want anybody touching his helicopter, and is likely upset now that he's forced to live with a wife he doesn't want. "How would you know what a woman needs?" It's impossible to imagine him buying feminine products.

"Madison took care of it."

"Madison?"

"My assistant."

I remember her. The carefully put-together blonde guarding his office. She gave me a look full of curiosity but shifted to a hint of judgment when she realized who I was. Call it a woman's intuition. Enduring Nelson and his family has honed my instincts when it comes to things like this. She doesn't approve of me, and I don't think she and I will get along very well.

"She's going to help plan the wedding, too," he adds.

"I guess that's better than Karie 'helping,'" I say, remembering the scene in his office.

He grunts.

Since he's feeling a bit sympathetic about my injury, this would be a good time to set some expectations. I need every advantage in dealing with him. "Look, Huxley. Things between us are strained, but I don't want to live with a lot of tension at home. I hope we can agree to be kind and courteous to each other."

The car stops at the light. He gives me a long look. My nerves start to fray as I wonder if what I'm asking for is too much for him to accept. It's possible he's decided to turn my life into hell. Or just be an impossible dick to live with.

He finally turns back to the road. "We can."

I let out the breath I've been holding. "Thank you."

23

HUXLEY

By THE TIME I pull into the garage, Grace is breathing evenly, her head resting limply against the window. She exhales softly through those perfect lips, but the bloody crust in the corner reminds me what she suffered earlier.

Fucking asshole.

I should've slammed Nelson's face into the wall until they were both completely flat, then kicked him until his ribs collapsed. I've never felt a fury this intense, like burning claws ripping into my gut.

I shut the car off and regard Grace, hating it that she has this effect on me. *How is it that I sometimes forget what a manipulative bitch she is?* She trapped me—and the baby inside her is the death knell to my bachelorhood, and more importantly, the freedom to choose my own wife.

Shoving aside conflicting emotions, I reach over to shake her awake, then stop. She's sleeping soundly, and there's no point disturbing her.

I hope we can agree to be kind and courteous to each other.

With a sigh, I climb out, open the door on her side and pull her into my arms, holding her like a princess.

Just what the hell is wrong with me? The proper course of action would be to tell her to walk inside herself. Her legs aren't broken.

She sighs and nestles close, her warmth and softness arousing a protective instinct I don't know I had.

Grace Lain is a danger to my emotional equilibrium.

Still, I don't force her to walk. I carry her inside to the master bedroom suite and lay her on the enormous California king. She looks so small and delicate on the cool gray sheets. I take off my jacket and drape it over the back of an armchair. She shifts a little, as though seeking a comfortable position.

I pull her up, then reach underneath her top and undo the clasp of her bra. She lets out a relieved breath and leans into me until her unbound breasts are crushed against my arm. The contact sends my blood sizzling. Lust crackles across my skin, and I grit my teeth. I'm not the type to take advantage of a recently abused and exhausted woman. Not to mention pregnant. Regardless of how much I loathe the situation between us, Grace merits consideration for her condition, and the baby deserves the best I can provide.

Reciting the Bill of Rights to distract myself, I change her into a nightshirt that is among the things Madison sent to the house. Then the housekeeper, of course, put everything into the closet in her usual orderly fashion.

Done. I step back, willing my body to settle down. Grace turns her head, showing the injured cheek. It's going to swell and hurt like hell if I don't do something about it. A pack of ice would help, but that would disturb her.

What are my options? I stand thinking for a moment, then rummage through the medicine cabinet. There must be something...

Bingo.

I pull out a tin of ointment that Griffin gave me. Apparently it works wonders for bruises, as well as joint and ligament pain. He special-orders it from an elderly pharmacist in Thailand for its non-greasy texture and lack of scent.

I go back to the bed and carefully spread the thick, translucent white cream on Grace's cheek. My effort pays off—she doesn't move at all.

With her entire demeanor relaxed, she looks even younger than she is. Her features are so delicate. Nelson's meaty paw shouldn't have been anywhere near her.

My phone buzzes from my jacket pocket. Annoyed, I snatch it up and see that I've missed ten calls from Mom. Concern pushes away mild exasperation. If she's calling like that, it's urgent.

I go into the walk-in closet and close the door to avoid disturbing Grace. "Yes?"

"What have you done?"

"A lot of things. Can you be more specific?" I ask, giving her a break, since she sounds frazzled.

"Nelson is trying to make me take over a case, a shitty one he's bound to lose."

"So?"

"The client is guilty as hell, and Nelson shouldn't have taken the case. But he's an idiot and the client is apparently a friend from college. Frat brothers." She sounds like she wants to murder someone.

On a different day, I might be more sympathetic. But right now, I have no patience for the Huxley & Webber drama. Not my circus, not my monkeys. "Just say no. Problem solved."

"I can't. He says the reason I have to take it over is because you 'brutalized' his face. He has to go to court tomorrow, but he's saying he can't go looking like this."

My phone buzzes and a photo of Nelson pops up. His eye is swollen shut already. Black and red mottle his forehead, cheek and jaw. A corner of one lip looks torn, although it's difficult to tell.

Should have slammed him harder. Then kicked him until he learned his lesson, so running to my mother would never occur to him.

"It appears that he must have accidently rammed his face into the wall a couple of times," I say with a hint of regret.

"Was your hand on him at that time?" she demands, her tone all lawyerly and suspicious.

"Not on his face, no. Just his hair."

"Huxley!"

I tug at my tie, undoing it, then unbutton the vest and shrug out of it.

"You're going to apologize and smooth his ruffled feathers."

"If I see him now, I'll finish what I started. And break his ribs to boot."

"Hux—"

"Hold on a minute." I step out quietly and snap a shot of Grace's face, then send it to Mom.

"What the...?" Mom's gasp rings in my ear as I return to the closet. "What have you done?"

"*Mother!*"

"Nelson did this?"

A beat of silence. "You think *I* did it?"

"You were upset with her. Don't think you fooled anybody. Even Emma was worried."

Damn it. Not Emma. "Nelson did it. I don't hit women unless they physically attack me. And usually not even then."

Mom sighs. "Are you pressing charges? A civil lawsuit?"

"I'll have to discuss it with her when she wakes up."

"Let me know."

"Why? You going to take her case?"

"She's going to be my daughter-in-law, so—"

"Don't even think about it. You're too tight with the Webbers."

"Meaning what?"

"Meaning I'm being smart. I don't trust you to destroy him the way I want to." I lay it on thick. Whenever I tell her she can't be trusted to do something, she goes overboard to prove me wrong.

"You gotta be kidding," she mutters. "I'll deal with Nelson." She hangs up.

I strip down to my boxer shorts, then head out to the bedroom. My phone buzzes again. What now?

—Emmett: Is it true you beat the shit out of Nelson?

What the fuck? He went crying to my brothers, too?

—Me: I wouldn't characterize it exactly that way. If I'd really beaten the shit out of him, he'd be too busy being hospitalized to complain to anyone.

I text that and slide gently under the sheets to avoid disturbing Grace. I paid an arm and a leg for this mattress, but the movement still might jostle her.

—Noah: What's going on?

—Emmett: Grant and I were having dinner with Andreas Webber, and he got a call from Nelson's wife. She was so hysterical, Grant and I could actually hear the conversation.

–Grant: It sounded like Hux broke something. On Nelson.

–Sebastian: I thought you were upset with Grace, not Nelson.

–Nicholas: He's too civilized to resort to violence.

I thought the same until I saw Grace's face.

–Grant: Why would Nelson's wife accuse you like that though?

–Me: Maybe because I gave him a taste of his own medicine.

–Griffin: HE HIT YOU??????

His outrage is palpable through the text. Busy as Griffin might be with his academic career and triplets, he will find time to beat the shit out of anybody who touches one of us. He's vicious, probably chews rusty nails daily to toughen up. And he's always been grumpy—not even marrying the sunniest woman on earth has improved his disposition.

–Me: Not me, Grace. So I hit him back.

–Sebastian: What a piece of shit!

–Grant: Only once?

I can already see the next line before he sends it: *What's wrong with you?*

–Me: Twice.

–Emmett: Should've broken his hand.

–Nicholas: Both hands.

–Noah: I thought you hated her.

My irritation flares at the reminder. I know I hate her, and I reacted uncharacteristically, like I did two years ago in the rain. But seeing her get abused snapped something inside. The way she makes my protective instinct go overboard is perplexing and unsettling. Still, I felt what I felt—period.

–Me: Yes, but just because I hate her doesn't mean he gets to touch what's mine.

–Grant: What's mine, huh?

–Emmett: Did you rip your shirt and pound your chest, too?

–Me: Fuck you.

–Sebastian: Did you break anything when you hit Nelson?

–Me: No. I didn't actually hit him, per se.

—Nicholas: What did you do?

—Me: Kind of made his face collide with a wall a couple of times.

—Noah: That's all?

—Noah: Told you Huxley hated her.

—Me: Shut up, Noah.

That asshole is trying to get me to admit something I'd rather not. He's probably trying to get revenge for how I made fun of him for his inability to get croissants from his baker babe.

—Sebastian: When Karl hit Luce, I broke his ribs.

Competitive, as usual. I narrow my eyes.

—Me: It was Griff's kick that did it.

—Noah: If Hux wanted to break Nelson in half, he could do it pretty easily. But he didn't. Like I said, he hates her. Doesn't care that much.

Noah's wrong. My eyes slide to Grace, and I flex my hand around the phone. I care *too* damn much, and that's the problem.

24

GRACE

THE QUIET SOUND of running water tickles my ears. I pull the sheets over my head, shifting. The bedding is incredibly soft, better than what you might find in a luxury hotel.

What...?

I don't have anything this nice in my bedroom. The temperature is slightly cooler than I'd like, too. And the bed smells like... *Huxley?*

I jackknife up, blinking hard in the dimly lit room. *What the hell?* I don't remember entering his home. The last thing I recall is our making a pact to be nice to each other.

I look down at myself. I'm in a long pink and purple nightshirt. My bra is gone, which explains why I was comfortable. *Did I take it off...or did he?* Just what happened after we agreed to be pleasant?

Definitely no sex, I decide. My thong is still in place, but maybe he pulled it to the side and then put it back...

Okay, *no.* I'm not the least bit sensitive down there. And as mad as Huxley is at me, I don't think he'd stoop to taking a woman who was practically comatose.

I can't believe I passed out and remember nothing. Who knew that nurturing a new life and getting knocked around would be so tiring? Thankfully, my face doesn't hurt much. Although it felt like hell last night, Nelson's slap probably lacked sufficient force. Not because he was holding back, but because he just isn't that strong after decades of lawyering.

I look around. This bedroom is as large as my condo. The bed is a massive California king with a sleek modern headrest against a wall fully covered with a smoked mirror. My purse is on the dove-gray bed bench. A couple of plush leather armchairs occupy a sitting area with a round mahogany table. Double doors to my left are ajar, revealing a walk-in closet with a tall island.

The sound of water stops. My mouth dries at the prospect of facing Huxley when I have no clue what happened last night after we arrived here. A moment later, he walks out of the en suite bathroom with nothing but a fluffy white towel around his hips. Although we had sex, I haven't seen him looking so casual and relaxed before. His body is solid, lean muscle covering his tall frame. It flexes as he moves. A droplet of water on his chest glides down to his deeply ridged abs. Although I can't see the movement anymore, my eyes drop anyway. Heat prickles my skin.

Oh geez. I thought only men get excited in the morning.

"Good, you're up," he says casually. "I was about to wake you."

"Um. Yeah." I clear my throat. "Why am I here?"

He gives me a look. "How many times do we have to go over this? You agreed to move in."

"Yes, but I don't remember agreeing to share your bed."

"In case you're wondering, nothing happened." His eyes bore into mine.

From the way they glitter darkly, he has to know I've been checking him out and getting turned on. A hormonal urge to throw caution to the wind and jump him battles with an absurd impulse to hide under the covers.

"My clothes…" I say, more to stop myself from doing something stupid than out of genuine curiosity. "Did you remove them?"

"Yes. It isn't like I haven't seen you naked before. When I take you, you'll remember it." His promise slides over me as erotically as the water droplet on his body.

My cheeks flame. "But the bed..." I need to take control of this conversation.

"Where did you think my would-be wife would sleep?"

"Um..." My gaze darts between him, me and the heavenly mattress under me.

"Exactly. My bed." He enters the closet, the doors wide open.

"There's a big difference between sharing a house and sharing a bed," I say.

"I wouldn't bring you here just to put you in another room."

"Who's going to know?"

"My housekeeper," he says over his shoulder, then drops the towel.

A hand over my mouth to contain a sound, I stare at the most beautifully sculpted male ass I've ever seen. A corner of his mouth twists with a hint of smug arrogance, but I can't *not* stare. I totally missed out that night.

"Your things are in here," he says.

"Thanks," I choke out. He starts to pick out a suit—

Oh, shit! Today's a work day and I need to get ready.

I jump up, head to the shower and close the door. This bathroom is larger than my entire bedroom, with a double vanity, separate shower and a huge Jacuzzi tub for two. The wall opposite the vanity is a smoked mirror, like the one next to the bed. But there's a regular mirror over the sinks, so I use that to—

What the hell?

My cheek is swollen, the corner of my mouth cut. Concealer should be able to cover the discoloration somewhat, but there's no way to hide the injury. Now that I look at the aftermath of what Nelson did, my face throbs dully. I'm glad Huxley didn't mention it. I wouldn't be comfortable getting into it with him first thing in the morning without coffee or a moment to figure out what to do.

I head to the toilet. The lid rises, blue lights illuminating the bowl. I give it a skeptical stare as it says something cheerful in a foreign language. It starts to spray a thin mist of...water?...inside the toilet bowl.

"Um... Hello? Good morning? Can you switch to English?"

The toilet doesn't respond—but the lights remain on. *O-kay*. I wonder if I should check with Huxley to see if it's all right to use the conversational commode, but my bladder says there's no time. As soon as I sit down on the seat—which is pleasantly heated—it starts playing music and making gurgling water noises.

I cover my face. *Why me?* It's too early in the morning to deal with this. When I'm done, I stand up and look around to see how to flush the thing, but the lid auto-lowers and the toilet flushes itself.

Shaking my head, I step into the shower stall, which, thankfully, does not talk. Seven separate jets sluice me down with heavenly hot water. *Holy cow.* I sigh with bliss. It's the kind of luxury I've only read about, but never thought to experience. The body soap and shampoo are from some fancy spa in France, and they smell vaguely like forest and spring with a hint of spice—Huxley's scent.

Recalling how outlandishly possessive he was yesterday at my lunch with Adam, I wonder if this is his way of marking me with his scent, like an animal. If he were a cat, he'd probably rub himself all over me to keep the other toms away.

You need coffee and food, girl. Low blood sugar and no caffeine make you think of silly things.

True enough. I didn't get a chance to have dinner last night, and suddenly I'm famished. I thank my lucky stars Dr. Silverman said it was okay to have a small cup of coffee each day. Apparently some doctors are stricter.

I dry my hair, then wrap a huge towel around myself and step gingerly out of the bathroom. Huxley is nowhere to be found. My shoulders sag a little—with disappointment? Relief? Who knows?

The walk-in closet is as big as the bathroom. The island in the middle is full of expensive-looking watches and cuff links. Guess Huxley takes his watches seriously.

Half the space has been left empty for me. A couple of dresses with tags hang on my side. I press my lips together. Everything is overwhelmingly pink. Even the bras and thongs look like they've been dipped in Pepto Bismol. Madison must really love pink. Not me—bubblegum pink is Vivienne's favorite color. She already wants to steal everything from me, and if I have anything pink, she'll covet it even more and make my life hell. Besides, the particular shade Madison picked out isn't flattering for my coloring.

But there are no other options, so I put them on. My black shoes don't match, while the pink stilettos Madison bought pinch my toes and heels terribly.

It's just one day—who cares? I decide, and leave the bedroom with my purse. The hall is long and wide, with a few oil paintings hanging on the shaded side. The morning sun slants over a smooth hardwood floor that smells faintly of beeswax and leads to a winding carpeted staircase straight out of *Gone with the Wind*. An enormous chandelier hangs from the high ceiling, each piece of crystal fracturing the sunbeams from the skylight.

The place positively drips opulent affluence, but there's an elegance to the interior that speaks of old money and luxurious comfort. It's quite different from Nelson and Karie's home, where every square inch glitters, tirelessly reminding everyone how important and wealthy its occupants are.

The delicious aroma of coffee leads me to the right...where I hit a huge eat-in kitchen. As I enter, I blurt, "Your toilet talks!"

"Of course. Just one of its many charming features," Huxley says over his coffee.

"Charming? Why do you need a toilet that talks and makes noises when you're doing your business?"

"Because it's Japanese," he says, like that explains everything.

I give up. Obviously I'm not going to understand. Coffee probably won't help, either.

A woman in her fifties unplugs a waffle iron, turns around and blinks once at the sight of me. "My Lord," she says, then glances at Huxley.

He lowers his cup of coffee and raises a hand defensively. "Wasn't me."

"You should see the other guy," I say quickly.

Huxley lets out a short laugh, and she chuckles softly. A small gap between her front teeth makes her look like a mischievous teenager. She pours me a cup of coffee.

"Here's your morning pick-me-up," she says.

"You must be a goddess. I'm Grace."

She laughs again. "Tilda. Nice to meet you."

I smile. "A pleasure."

"I'm the housekeeper. The way it works is, you tell me what you want, and I make it happen. Since the lord of the manor here didn't see fit to inform me in advance that there would be an overnight guest"—she raises an eyebrow while Huxley stares into the distance—"I've made you a Belgian waffle." She pulls a plate off a heater and slides it over to me. "He said it was your favorite."

I'm surprised he remembered. "It is. Thank you." I add a generous amount of syrup and whipped cream and start eating.

Tilda says she needs to check on the gardener and a few other things and leaves. I have a feeling she just wanted to give us some privacy.

Huxley munches on his bacon and studies me, his eyes narrow. "Didn't Madison buy any comfortable clothes for you?"

"This is good enough," I say between bites. She probably did the best she could, given very little info. No knowledge of my personal preferences or size.

"Good enough? For what?"

"Work."

His jaw tightens. "Call in sick."

"No. I'm not hiding just because Nelson's a jerk." I'm not using up my PTO because of him. That's set aside for visiting Mom on her birthday or—God forbid—an emergency.

"That isn't why I'm telling you to call in sick. What are you going to say to people when they ask what happened?" Huxley's gaze drops to my cheek, a hint of worry fleeting over his face.

This unexpected concern makes me want to squirm, especially since I'm not sure exactly what to make of it. Has he decided that I wasn't complicit in our families' machinations after all? Or is this just part of our agreement to be courteous to each other? His expression betrays nothing, so I pretend I didn't see the care in his eyes. "I don't know," I say lightly. "I'll think of something."

"Like the truth?" he asks, raising an eyebrow.

A shrug. "Maybe I ran into a wall." My phone has been silent. Although I blocked Viv and Mick, Nelson and Karie could easily reach me and threaten to hurt Mom to vent their anger and humiliation. After all, as long as Mom is at Johns Hopkins, I'm more or less helpless against their abuse.

Huxley's mouth tightens so much it resembles a hyphen. "Leave work early if necessary. You don't need to put up with whispers and speculation."

"But I *do* need the hours and the money."

"One of the perks of marrying a billionaire like you've always dreamed of is that you don't really need to work." He gestures carelessly at his home. "You already have a free roof over your head, free food in your belly. You don't have to kill yourself to make some spending money."

I say nothing. He wouldn't understand. And his face scrunches like he's just realized he said something he didn't mean to.

I can imagine. After hearing me talk to Adam about wanting to marry a rich man, Huxley refused to let me explain and swore I wouldn't get to touch a penny of his money.

I sigh. "Can you give me a ride to my office?"

"Not yet." He picks up a tin and opens the lid, revealing white goo inside.

"What's that?"

"For your face. It should help with the swelling and pain. I put some on your cheek last night, too."

Now I *really* don't know what to make of his unexpected consideration. He's confusing me by being nice and then nasty, back and forth. But I don't have the courage to tell him to stick to one track— what if it's the nasty track?

He dips his fingers into the tin and spreads it over my cheek. His touch is tender, as though he can't bear to hurt me. Being cared for reminds me of happy times with my mom, and my heart aches. If I'd found a man who loves me, would my life be like this all the time? Full of gentle affection and feeling safe?

"You should press charges," he says suddenly. "If not criminal, then civil."

"Can't afford it."

He snorts. "You're marrying into the Huxley family."

"And he's a Webber."

"Fine. I'll ask John Highsmith to take your case."

I stare at him. I've heard of Highsmith. One of the nastiest lawyers in the state. Nobody gets away with messing with his clients. Andreas often speaks of him with admiration...or exasperation, depending on whether he has to face him in court or not.

"I'll pay for his services," Huxley adds, apparently mistaking my silence for concern about the cost.

"I appreciate that. But I need the twenty-five thousand bucks a month from Nelson and Karie, so...I can't."

Huxley's eyebrows snap together. "Is your dignity worth only twenty-five K?"

I let out a hollow laugh. "Easy for a billionaire to sneer at twenty-five thousand. But it's not the money itself. My mother is absolutely worth sacrificing my dignity for. My dignity, and pretty much anything else as well."

He frowns. "Your mother?"

"I told you she was okay when we ran into each other again because I didn't want to go into the whole sad story. But she isn't doing well." I stare at the pool of maple syrup on my plate. Things would be *so much better* if she weren't ill. I wish she and I could have Belgian waffles and laugh over silly stuff like we used to.

I swallow a familiar lump and raise my eyes to meet Huxley's. My voice is surprisingly calm and steady. "She's been in a coma for the last two years. After a few months at Ronald Reagan, they moved her to Johns Hopkins so she could get treated by Dr. Blum. He's the world authority on neurological damage and cerebral infarctions. But he doesn't work for free, obviously. I'm paying what I can, and whatever I can't shoulder, Nelson and Karie take on. That's what the twenty-five thousand is for. I don't see any of it. It's sent directly to the hospital."

"Nelson and Karie?" Huxley makes a skeptical noise. "Why would they offer to do that?"

"They didn't, believe me. Andreas made them."

"I see." Huxley closes the lid on the tin with a soft metallic *chuff.* "Well, you needn't run to them for money anymore."

It takes me a moment to understand. "Are you offering to pay my mom's medical bills?"

"Of course." His gaze is cool and decisive as he looks at me.

"But...what about the prenup?"

"The prenup stands. But I can't let your mother die over mere money. Nor will I let you subjugate yourself to abuse for it."

"Thank you for the sentiment, but I don't think you really understand what's involved. The doctor is hopeful, but there's no guarantee when—or even *if*—she's going to wake up. And you can't stop paying even if you get tired of it, or if we happen to have a fight and you get pissed off at something I said."

He stares at me like I just slapped him. "Do you think I'd let your mother die over that measly sum? Or because we had an argument?"

"Huxley... I honestly don't know. Sometimes you're so nice, I feel like I can trust you. But then, sometimes...you aren't." I pause for a moment, debating between full honesty and pretty lies.

Huxley's expression is intent. He keeps his mouth flat and meets my gaze, his eyes unwavering.

I finally opt for full honesty, while choosing my words. "I'd like to think that you are a good and honorable man, but I thought the same about Nelson—only to be proven very, *very* wrong. He seduced my mom, who is much younger than him. He didn't disclose the fact that he was married."

Disgust twists Huxley's face.

"It kills him that he has to be responsible for her care. Karie too, for that matter. I understand why she resents it so much, but I can't understand how Nelson can be so cold and heartless toward a woman he must've felt something for to sleep with."

I close my eyes and shake my head as the familiar anger surges. I indulge it for a moment, then push it aside. It isn't helpful to dwell on it, not when Huxley's waiting for me to continue.

"Maybe he's just a sociopath, and Mom got unlucky," I say softly. "I don't know. It isn't like he can't spare the money. But to him, her life just isn't worth saving. Not unless his father forces him." I look directly at Huxley. "And if you ever decide to change your mind, who's going to force you?"

Shock flares in his gaze. I'm not sure why. Maybe he still can't fathom how a mere twenty-five thousand can mean so much. Or maybe he's stunned at the possibility of being forced to spend a penny on a would-be wife he never wanted. Regardless, I want to reassure him I'd never depend on him for something this important. "You don't listen to anyone much. Not your grandmother or your mother. The only person whose opinion seems to matter to you is Emma, but she doesn't know who I am, and she might not care what happens to my mom."

The more I speak, the darker the frown on his face.

"So I want you to understand, Huxley. It's a huge gamble for me. I can wager my own wellbeing, but not my mother's. She's the only family I have."

25

GRACE

I've definitely offended Huxley.

He didn't say anything after I turned down his offer, but tension was pouring from him, to the point where I could barely breathe in the car. I'm not happy to have hurt his feelings, but risking my mother's life simply isn't an option.

"Thank you," I tell him. "I'll Uber to my place and grab my car."

"It isn't necessary. I'll send you a car and have yours brought to the house." His tone is gravelly, his jaw tight.

An instant refusal springs to my lips, but I swallow it. It's not worth an argument. "Okay. Thanks."

I take the elevator up to the Pryce Family Foundation. The place is bustling with energy already. Charitable work is more expensive and labor-intensive than people imagine. That's why so many NGOs waste their resources, even without meaning to.

"Tell me the wall is broken."

I blink at Tolyan's curt greeting—or was that even supposed to be a greeting? It's hard to tell with him. "Good morning. What do you mean?"

He points to my cheek. "That. You 'ran into a wall,' obviously. And the wall better not still be standing."

"It is...sort of."

He drops his eyes to my ring. "What good is a man who can't avenge his woman?"

"The wall got bloodied."

He grunts. "You put down a dog when it attacks people for no reason. You should blow up walls that bruise people as well."

I say nothing, unsure if he's joking. It's impossible to tell with him, since he always speak in that flat, inflectionless way.

"You need coffee?"

Wow. I must look terrible for him to offer. He's never been this solicitous before.

Elizabeth steps out of the elevator, takes one look at my face and rushes over. "Oh my God, *Grace*. Are you all right? Do you need a safe place?"

"No. I'm fine," I say.

"Who did this to you?"

I press my lips together and lower my eyes for a moment, too embarrassed to admit it was my father, and annoyed with myself for feeling ashamed about the incident when I didn't do anything wrong.

She glances at Tolyan. He shrugs. "She says the wall is bloody."

She puts a gentle hand on my shoulder. "If you need anything, *you tell me*, okay? I don't care what time it is or where you are. You *will* call me."

I nod, warmth prickling my eyes. "Thank you."

She goes into her office, followed by Tolyan. For a fleeting second, I'm tempted to ask if the foundation can help with my mother's medical bills. The organization has a division that assists with bills for critical care. But just as quickly as the urge pops into my head, I push it away. The fund isn't infinite, and too many people don't have the luxury of an asshole father who can shoulder the burden. Elizabeth is the sweetest, so she'd find a way to help me...which would mean that I'd be taking the money away from somebody who desperately needs it.

About half an hour before my lunch break, I get a text from the OB-GYN, confirming my appointment on Friday. I tap the corner of my phone for a moment. Should I ask Huxley if he can join me? It's his baby too, and Dr. Silverman said we should be able to hear the heartbeat now.

I put a hand over my still-flat belly. It's so strange to think there's a life inside. The last time I went, there wasn't anything except some black-and-white dots and lines on the sonogram monitor. A heartbeat seems like such a massive milestone.

Huxley was upset when I told him about the baby, but surely by now he's come to accept its existence. He should get to experience the miracle of each developmental stage.

–Me: I have an appointment with OB-GYN this Friday at 3. Want to join me? We should be able to hear the heartbeat for the first time.

–Huxley: I'm going to be in London for a few weeks starting tomorrow, so I'll have to pass.

I start to type that I could make a recording of the baby's heartbeat for him, but the next message stops me cold.

–Huxley: My schedule is always tight, and I don't have time to waste on unimportant matters.

The text feels like a punch to the solar plexus. Pain steals my breath away, and I bite back a soft whimper. *How can words hurt so much?* Not even Nelson's cruelty was this agonizing.

Maybe it's because my hopes for the baby seem doomed. When I was growing up, I wondered why I didn't have a father. Mom told me he was just away and busy, but he loved me very much. I made cards for him every Father's Day, Christmas and his birthday, even though some of the nasty kids in school mocked me for making cards for a nonexistent parent. Then when I finally got to meet him, he was unbelievably cold and abrupt. I realized I was nothing more than an unfortunate inconvenience to him, and I felt small and unwanted. Without my mom's love and support, it would've been even more devastating.

I don't want my child to go through the same gut-wrenching experience. It deserves better. Huxley's kindness since Nelson's attack made me think for a moment that maybe we could have a pleasant life together, and he could be a good father for our baby.

I stare at the screen, rereading his response. I don't know which hurts more—Nelson's slap or Huxley's cold-heartedness. Maybe they just hurt in different ways.

My phone buzzes with a call from an unknown contact. I pick it up in case it's about the changed venue. "The Pryce Family Foundation. Grace Lain speaking."

"Madison Chilton, Huxley's assistant. He asked me to help you with the wedding." Her voice is as smooth and polished as marble—and just as coolly impersonal.

"Yes, he did," I say, recalling the scene in his office.

"I'm texting you a few wedding invitation designs. Can you tell me which is your favorite?"

My phone vibrates, and I check the three she sent. She must be extremely partial to pink, because the first one is *overwhelmingly* pink. The second one is gray, which I'm not crazy about because it looks drab and dreary. The third one is a mix of sleek black and white with pink and blue accents, and something about it feels off to me, even though I can't quite say why.

"Has Huxley seen these?" He has excellent taste in his house décor and clothes. Assuming he didn't pay for professional help with them, he might be able to articulate what needs to change.

"Yes. Which is why I'm sharing them with you to get your sign-off on one of them. The date is set for three weeks from now."

"That soon?" He hasn't said a word about it. Not only that, he's going to be out of country for a few weeks. Did he intentionally do this to ensure he had as little involvement as possible?

"He thought it'd be best if the ceremony took place before you started showing."

"I see." But I really don't. Is he trying to be considerate, or does he consider the wedding ceremony a chore to be done with as soon as possible? If he hadn't responded the way he did to my message, I'd probably be thinking the former, but now it's impossible to be certain. "Is he going to be able to be part of the planning at all? I heard that he's going to London."

"I doubt it. He's going to be extremely busy, even with me there."

"You're going, too?"

"Of course. I accompany him on business trips. It's my job to make sure every aspect of his life runs smoothly." A hint of smug satisfaction and superiority. I can almost hear the unspoken *Unlike you.* "There's no need of his I can't meet."

A hint of something sexual simmers underneath her words. The idea of him in London with Madison makes my heart jump into my throat, my gut burn. The trip is work related, but she's gorgeous and they'll be spending weeks together at a hotel. He's about to be shackled to a woman he doesn't want—and a baby he can't be bothered with. What are the odds that he's going to be faithful?

I'm not merely jealous. I don't trust him, either. The courtesy and respect we promised each other during the ride back home yesterday seem so flimsy, they might as well not be there at all. His reactions to the appointment and the upcoming ceremony show me his true intentions.

I take a breath and modulate my tone. "Did he say anything about the third choice?"

"Do you like that one?" She sounds a little surprised.

"I'm not sure..."

"If it helps, the theme of the wedding is Amazing Grace."

"Amazing Grace?" *What does that mean?* Do people have themes for their wedding these days? A commitment to love and a better future together isn't enough...?

"Yes." She clears her throat. "If Huxley didn't put it into so many words, it's a double entendre—for you and the future of your marriage."

He isn't even hiding how he really feels. I hate the hint of pity in Madison's voice, especially because there's also a tinge of schadenfreude. She enjoys putting me down with impunity because her boss doesn't show me respect. But what have I done to earn *her* enmity? I'm already too emotionally overwrought to have a productive conversation. There's also part of me that's slightly apprehensive— what if Huxley sides with her? I'll look even more ridiculous. "That's what Huxley wants?"

"Yes."

"Fine. Then the third one should do. The black should be onyx, absolutely no other shade."

"I'll make a note."

I hang up without another word, grab my purse and leave for lunch. The two painful interactions have killed my appetite, but my baby shouldn't starve just because Huxley and *Madison* are jerks. It's irritating I forgot to pack a lunch, though; eating out isn't cheap, but so many things have happened in the last twelve hours that it slipped my mind.

Tolyan watches me gather my things. "Want me to come with you?" His eyes flick to my cheek.

"No. But thank you anyway." I walk out and step into the crowded elevator. *A sandwich. But not anything with tuna or broccoli, like Huxley said,* I decide pettily. Ham and turkey with a slice of Swiss and two strips of crispy bacon should do nicely.

When the elevator reaches the lobby, I'm first out of the car. I head to the main entrance, my steps brisk. A rough hand grabs my arm.

"Hey, bitch! You ignoring me?"

I glare up at Mick. What's he doing here? He's always too worried about his public image to make a scene. "Of course. Why do you think I blocked you?"

His face turns bright red. "You ungrateful cunt. I'm pressing charges."

"For what?"

"For assaulting my father!" he hisses, shaking me by the arm.

"You think *I* smashed Nelson's face? Don't you see what he did to me?" I tilt my face so Mick can make note of my injuries.

If he notices, he doesn't show it. His nostrils flare, and his focus is on the injustice done to his family. "Don't think you're going to avoid jail time. Nobody from Huxley & Webber is going to defend you, and you can't afford a lawyer good enough to stop what I'm about to unleash on you!"

I try to pull away, but his grip only tightens. "Let go of me before I press charges against you!"

"*I'm* the DA, not you!" he sneers.

"Let go of my fiancée," comes Huxley's cold voice.

Mick stiffens, but his bravado doesn't fade. "Stay out of this! I'm on official government business."

"Seriously?" Huxley cocks his eyebrow. "You, by yourself,

manhandling my fiancée in public? Official government business? Let's see just how *official* this becomes when I file suit against the city on her behalf." The words roll out casually, but his eyes are hard. They glitter like they did right before he slammed Nelson's face into the wall.

Mick lets go. He's always been a coward who bares his teeth against anybody weaker than him but tucks tail when someone stronger is around.

"Good. Now—if you and your family continue to harass people around me, I'm going to have to do something to show the world what kind of man Nelson really is."

"He's an honorable man!" Mick blusters.

"Who hits his daughter."

"She asked for—"

"Shh!" Huxley raises a finger. "Think very carefully before you complete that sentence. She is the future Mrs. Huxley Lasker."

A vein in Mick's neck throbs. The Adam's apple bobs, and his eyes dart between Huxley, me, then back to Huxley. "You're going to pay for this!"

"Come collect anytime."

"Asshole!" Mick says, then stalks off. He keeps his arms slightly spread, as though the gesture can hide his defeat.

"Are you okay?" Huxley asks, his gaze dropping to my arm.

"I'm fine."

He raises an eyebrow. "You shouldn't use that tone if you want me to believe you."

I look up at his gorgeous face. The concern in his eyes. He's so hot and cold—telling me he's too busy to care about our baby, then making it clear our marriage is doomed before it can start, only to rush to my defense against Mick. My emotions ping-pong, leaving me unsettled and confused.

Still. Even if he's hot and cold, I'm not. "Thank you for the help."

"It was nothing."

"What are you doing here?"

"Checking up on you." His eyes drop to my still-swollen cheek.

"You're confusing me."

A ghost of smile dashes across his handsome face. "Consideration shouldn't be cause for confusion. Unless you have plans, let's have lunch together."

A refusal is on the tip of my tongue. I want to eat alone and lick my emotional wounds. But he's here—taking time out of his *busy* schedule —and when am I going to have a chance to talk to him about my doubts before the wedding?

"Okay. You pick the restaurant."

26

HUXLEY

CONTRARY TO HER telling me to pick the restaurant, Grace apparently doesn't really want me to choose, because when I suggest Mexican, she purses her lips. Korean gets a frown. She shoots down French and Italian. Finally, I suggest a sandwich shop and she says yes.

If this is her being hormonal over pregnancy, it isn't too terrible. I've had worse with not-pregnant women unable to go along even after telling me I could make the decision.

Grace grabs some kind of club sandwich with bacon. She declines chips and gets the largest-sized iced tea. I order a roast beef with extra horseradish. Chips and Coke, of course. She doesn't say anything except "Thank you" when I pay for the lunch. Either she's peeved about something I did, or her emotions are all over the place because of the pregnancy. At least she's able to eat normally, unlike Lucie. Sebastian was going crazy until they discovered she can stomach key lime pie.

And the baby in Grace's womb is behaving and not giving her issues —another blessing. Although I haven't received the paternity test results yet, I have a gut feeling that the child is mine. And my instincts are rarely off—at least when my mind isn't clouded with rage and a sense of betrayal.

We take a small table, and Grace unwraps her food. "Have you seen the themes for the wedding?" she says finally, then bites into her sandwich.

I nod. Madison showed me some ideas she worked on. As expected, she did an excellent job, even though I scoffed that "Saving Grace" would be more suitable than "Here comes the bride."

"And you're okay with the final choice?" Grace's carefully smooth tone can't hide the razors underneath.

"I'm okay with whatever." Is she upset because she didn't have any direct input from the start? I thought she would appreciate the help, since she can't count on Karie.

Perhaps I should clarify some things about the ceremony. "I'm not going to spend any more time and energy on this than I have to. It's your wedding." *There.* That should improve her disposition. All women dream of weddings, make plans for them and obsess over the details. I take several big gulps of Coke to wash down the sandwich, and wait for her to smile gladly.

Grace's expression turns stony.

Of course. I should add one more thing. "You can continue to use Madison. She's efficient and knows what will please me if you want my input but don't want to bother me."

"You don't want to be involved?" Her voice is slightly shaky.

What's that about? My sisters-in-law didn't really care that much about my brothers' input, did they? I can't remember, since I only showed up for the ceremonies. Then an idea finally hits me. "Did Karie call you and refuse to pay for the wedding?" I snort. That entire family is so predictable and pathetic. "Don't worry. I'm paying, and you'll get a proper wedding, just the kind you've been dreaming of."

Instead of smiling with delight, Grace gives me a strange look. "How about the baby?"

"What about it?" *What's with the abrupt change in topic?* She could've at least said thank you. I generally don't care if people give me credit or not, but I want her to smile at me and call me awesome. My stomach twists sharply. What the hell? I'm acting like a teenager in throes of his first love. Ugh, no. *More dignity, less ridiculousness,* I lecture myself, and keep my expression unreadable.

"It's your responsibility, too."

"I know. I'll provide everything the baby needs. You don't have to worry about that." I reiterate my commitment, but I'm sure I've already made it clear I won't shirk my duties on that front.

She continues to stare at me like she can't process this. What did I say that was so weird?

I add, "I'll be in London for three weeks. It's unavoidable." I've been putting this trip off for a while, and now I have to go or else. The timing isn't ideal, but I've made arrangements for Grace. "You'll get security to ensure that there won't be a repeat of the Nelson incident."

Instead of being touched, she looks vaguely annoyed. "You mean somebody to spy on me and report my every move?"

"Of course not. It's for your own safety."

"No, thank you."

I ignore her intransigence. "This is non-negotiable. But don't worry, they'll be unobtrusive."

"Sure, like a chastity belt," she mutters.

"What?" My irritation mounts over her refusal to accept my considerate gesture at face value.

"Nothing. But when you're back in town, I don't want them anymore."

Calm down. She's pregnant and hormonal. "Fine."

She expels a breath. "Is that all?"

"Madison's coming with me. So there may be some delay due to the time difference, but she can still coordinate with you."

Something volatile and dangerous crosses Grace's face. "Are you sleeping with her?" The question is like a crack of a gunshot. Shocking and enraging. *What the hell kind of gears turn in her little head?*

Her questioning my honor is infuriating. I haven't been able to quit thinking about her, and felt like an asshole for getting an erection last night, lying next to her, given her physical and emotional state. The need didn't go away in the morning, and I've been trying to be a gentleman, only to be accused of betraying her?

"No. Don't be absurd," I bite out.

She tilts her chin stubbornly. "But you're with her all the time."

"No, *she* is with *me*. Not the other way around. Because she's my assistant. It's her job."

Grace shakes her head. Her thoughts are transparent on her face: *So what? I don't believe you.*

"Are you kidding? You're moody because you think I'm screwing my assistant?"

Grace stares at me like a mule refusing to move. "What if I am?"

"If you are, you're being absurd."

"Fine. Make me believe you. Put Madison somewhere else in the company."

The blatant display of jealousy stirs an inexplicable euphoria, but the possibility that she's trying to control the way I run my agency dampens it. It reminds me of my grandmother's sneaky scheme to wrest ownership of the business from me.

There's only one way to show Grace how ridiculous she's being. I toss the paper napkin over my tray, stand up and wrap my hand around her wrist.

"What are you doing?" she says.

"I'm going to fuck this nonsense out of you."

THE AYLSTER RESIDENCE is close and convenient. And the perfect place to remind Grace of the chemistry we had. Does she think that happens all the time with everyone?

I pull her into the room. The door shuts with a click.

She glares at me. "Is this what you use for your rendezvous with her?"

Her question throws another bucket of gas on the fire inside me. "If I were screwing my assistant—*which I'm not*—I wouldn't have to bother with a hotel. I'd do it in the office!"

Her cheeks flush, but the sharp glitter in her eyes doesn't diminish. The plain skepticism fuels more than just my rage. My overheated blood pools into my cock, and I want to screw her until she accepts that I'm not the kind of man who sees nothing wrong with fucking multiple women at the same time. Just because I'm forced to marry her doesn't mean I'm going to abandon my sense of right and wrong. *I am not my father.*

Digging my hand into the silk of her hair, I kiss her, careful not to reinjure her mouth. She slaps at my shoulders, then bites my lip. The copper tang fuses with the sweet taste of hers. Perversely, it only strips a layer of civilized restraint from me.

Her breathing grows uneven. Her slim fingers thread in my hair and clench it, but she doesn't push me away. She seems torn about something, and I lick the cut on my lip, then run my tongue over her mouth, earning a small tremor from her.

"Kiss me with all the rage and fire you feel," I demand. "Kiss me like you own me."

Her eyes flick up at me. "Are you really mine?"

Jealousy burns in their blue depths, and I'm gratified. "You'd better hope so. Because I'm about to fuck you like I own you."

"You don't own me any more than I own you," she counters, her voice raspy.

"We'll see about that. That ring is the mark of my ownership."

Pushing her to the bed, I press my mouth over her neck, suck and nibble the thin, sensitive skin there. Her pulse beats erratically against my lips and tongue, betraying her reaction. She tightens her fingers in my hair possessively and a soft whimper vibrates through her chest.

I grip the sides of her dress and rip it open, the buttons in front flying across the room. Grace gasps. "What am I going to wear?"

"Who cares?" I whisper darkly as I push down the bra and cup her breast.

The hardened nipple presses against my palm, and her back arches as I brush my thumb over the sensitive tip. Her body is incredibly responsive, sensual shivers running through it at my slightest touch. A lovely shade of rose colors her from head to toe, and the fragrance the body wash she used this morning—*my* body wash—intensifies, smelling sweeter than it does on me, mixing with her feminine aroma.

My mouth waters, and I pull a nipple into my mouth. She cries out softly, twisting into me, pressing her body upward. Her grip grows tighter and more desperate. She always clings like she can never be sure if she can count on a satisfying climax.

My girl, you'll always get multiple orgasms that rock you to the core.

I let go of the nipple and suck on the other one. Her legs move restlessly over the sheet. She rubs her inner thighs against my pelvis, showing what she wants.

I nip and suck her breast until she's softly malleable, but it isn't enough. I want her complete surrender. Her acceptance of her place in my life and a promise never to doubt my honor.

Her breathing hitches. She's close, small tremors racing through her. I pull back.

"No!" she cries.

"Patience." I kick off my shoes and rip off my suit, cursing softly under my breath at my tailor for placing so many damn buttons on my clothes. She watches, her eyes avid and greedy. Her earlier skepticism has dissipated, replaced by need and desire. But this is temporary. She has to look at me like this all the time, not just in the throes of lust.

When I'm fully naked, I loop my finger under the thin string over her pelvis. She doesn't show any signs of pregnancy, but the knowledge there's a life growing in her womb gives me a sense of excitement and awe. I lay endless kisses over her belly—over our child. Showing her that she won't be alone in raising it.

She gasps, her stomach fluttering. She opens her legs, and I snap the string, ripping the flimsy thong. Her scent is stronger, all female arousal, juicy and delicious. She's visibly wet, and I smile with satisfaction.

"Huxley..." she begs.

"My pretty, pretty girl," I purr. "So open, so wet for me."

She tilts her hips.

I run the flat of my tongue over her wetness. Her fingers twist the sheets, her back arching. Breath catches in her throat as she throws her head back. It's as though her body is suspended, waiting in breathless anticipation. I pull her flesh apart to reveal the swollen clit, and run the tip of my tongue over the quivering nub. She cries out, chokes out my name.

"If you're really mine, too, prove it," she pants.

I pull her delicate flesh into my mouth, use my tongue and teeth to make her feel good. She grows impossibly wet, the slickness like hot honey. She grinds her hips against my face. Fuck I love it when she's blatantly carnal. A huge wave of lust crests over me, and precum drips from the tip of my cock. The tension in her body is almost at the critical point, and I stop.

"No," she begs. "Please, Huxley, please."

"Oh, not yet, my Grace. You haven't earned it yet."

The pleasure-dazed look on her face is so tempting, I want to say fuck it. But I refuse to veer from my course of action, especially when I'm going to be away for three weeks. I won't have my fiancée imagining me in bed with my assistant.

I push her up on her knees and position myself behind her, so she's leaning against my chest, her ass resting in my lap. The door to the walk-in closet is open, showing our reflection in the mirror inside.

"Look," I say.

She blinks, then squints at the mirror. Her face flushes bright red. "My God."

"You see this cock?" I glide my dick between her legs until she can see the tip and the glinting silver ball. She shivers, biting her lip. "Feel how hard it is?"

"Yes."

"I've been like this since I met you. I think about you, and I want to take you." I move my cock along her folds, making sure to bump into her clit, squeezing a helpless sound from her throat.

Her eyelids start to drift lower, and I stop. She digs her nails into my forearms in protest.

"Don't close your eyes. Watch," I command.

I take my fingers and spread her open, so she can see better in the reflection. My cock pushes into her dripping pussy, inch by agonizing inch. My balls tingle, and my spine prickles with the need to pound into her. But I don't want to be rough when she's with our child.

"See how well you take my cock," I order her as my shaft drives deeper into her. Her thighs shake, and she puts her hands on my hips for better balance. She's so hot, and the sensation of her slickness directly on my dick without anything between us pushes my blood to the boiling point.

"Huxley..."

"This body was made for me." I run my hand over her chest, caress her plump breasts, down to her belly and lower until two fingers rest over her clit, then press with just enough force to push her higher, but not over the edge.

Even more wetness drips along my cock. I maintain eye contact in the mirror and pull back, showing her my dripping shaft, its veins pulsing.

"Oh my God." Her eyes glaze.

"You're mine, Grace. And I'm yours. No other man can fill this pussy, and no other pussy can take my cock."

"Huxley..."

"Say it," I order her.

She moans, but won't repeat what I said. She rocks her body, trying to take the pleasure I'm denying her. I tilt my hips so she can't get the right angle, but I stroke her clit, teasing her.

"Please. Huxley, please!"

"Say it." I rub slightly faster, making her arch into my touch and grind into my finger, move up and down my cock. I pinch her nipple and tug. All the delicious sensation, but none of it enough to satiate. She moves harder and faster. But everything she's doing is as futile as someone drinking seawater to quench their thirst.

The sight of her taking my cock drives me to a fever pitch, and my instinct screams at me to push her down and fuck her hard and fast until she screams my name. But I rein the impulse in. Lust isn't in the driver's seat. I am.

A strong tremor racks her sweat-misted body. A sob tears from her chest; her breasts shiver. Tension grips her, but she can't go over the edge. Her pussy tightens around my cock, and sweat pops out along my hairline. I grit my teeth, fighting my baser instinct.

She's biting her lip in the reflection. I smack her ass, urging her to say the words before my control breaks. A breath shudders out of her, the tight inner muscles gripping my dick. I slap the other cheek, earning a soft moan. My jaw clenches as I struggle to hold on. But seeing the red handprint on the baby-smooth skin only fuels my desire.

"No other cock can take my pussy," she sobs just as I'm about to say fuck it. "And no other pussy can take your cock. Oh my God, *please*."

Elation sears through me, and I grip her hips and pound into her, finding and hitting the spot that drives her wild.

She screams her orgasm at the first thrust, then again as more powerful and relentless orgasms break over her. I watch her reflection, her bare breasts bobbing with each drive, her eyes glassy and mouth slack with bliss. I kiss her neck hard enough to leave a mark.

Her voice goes hoarse, and she collapses in a boneless heap as I empty myself inside her in a violent climax that wrings everything from me. Air saws in and out of her, rough and uneven. I wrap my arms around her, spooning her, then press a firm kiss to the base of her neck.

When I can breathe more evenly, I instruct the concierge to bring an emerald-green Dior dress from the boutique on the second level of the hotel. Pink isn't Grace's best color. She squirms a little, turning to face me, her beautiful face soft with the pleasure I've given her. I kiss her hard.

"Now. Forget that nonsense in your head, and be a good girl until I get back."

27

GRACE

FORGET that nonsense in your head, he says. *Be a good girl until I get back,* he says.

Yeah, easy for Huxley to say when he's foisted that godawful assistant of his on me to deal with. I tell Madison her help isn't necessary, but she insists on staying on like a louse in a dirty head of hair, saying Huxley would hate to leave me on my own without anybody to help.

She's wrong, of course. He'd love nothing more than to leave me on my own. He wants me to ditch Nelson and his family's money and put myself at his mercy, and end my friendship with Adam because he can't handle the fact that I have a friend with a penis. At least the security he hired isn't overly obnoxious. But that isn't saying much.

I can't afford to refuse the financial help from Nelson and Karie yet, and there's no reason to abandon Adam just because Huxley's being weird. It's unbelievable how Huxley and I have the most amazing chemistry in bed, but outside of it, we're completely incompatible. Unfortunately, we spend more time outside of bed. Unless we figure out a way to live a more harmonious life together, it seems like things will only get worse.

Just then, the paternity test from the lab lands on my phone. It confirms the baby is Huxley's, obviously. I forward it to him in case the lab hasn't sent him the results directly. At least my baby will be spared the heartache of being denied by his father.

–Huxley: The lab just sent me the report too.

–Me: Is that all you have to say?

–Huxley: No. I was an asshole earlier. Shouldn't have said what I did, and I'm sorry. Even before the report arrived, I suspected the baby was mine.

Oh, thank God. The apology soothes the anxiety I've been harboring about the baby's future.

–Me: When were you going to tell me?

–Huxley: I was going to talk to you about it when I got back in town. Gotta go. I have to wrap up this meeting and a few other things.

–Me: Okay. Thanks for the apology. Hope you have a productive evening.

I end our exchange on a friendly note. If he feels this way, surely he'll be a better father than Nelson. But an internal voice cautions me to be realistic. He still hasn't said a word about the OB-GYN appointment. Of course, coming to that wouldn't make him a good father, but it still hurts that he wants to minimize his involvement.

If he felt that the baby was his, why didn't he say something about seeing Dr. Silverman? Even if he couldn't come while he's in London, he could've shown *something*—concern, curiosity...even excitement at the possibility of hearing the baby's heartbeat.

I stew over Huxley's confusing reaction for the rest of the morning, but can't figure out how he *truly* feels. I call Adam during my lunch break to apologize for Huxley's behavior.

"Ah, don't worry about it." Adam is gracious as usual. "It was nothing. But are you okay?" His voice turns soft with concern.

"Yeah, I think so." I put a hand over my belly. *I have to be okay and stay strong for the baby's sake.* It can't really count on anyone but me.

He hesitates. "So. Are we still friends?"

"Of course." I force a bright smile, hoping it reaches my voice. "Why wouldn't we be?"

"Well, you know. Sometimes when people think a friend is in the way of a romantic relationship, they dump the friend."

My heart softens. He must've been worried after that horribly possessive display from Huxley. "Adam, I would never do that to you. You've been my best friend ever since I came to L.A." He stayed even when I couldn't afford to go out like I used to.

A pause. "Okay. I'm glad."

"Are we good?" As the question slips from my lips, my eyes land on the desktop calendar with a red circle around today. The OB-GYN appointment. Huxley can't go because of his business trip. But if he hadn't been so callous when I asked him if he wanted to come with me —or if he had mentioned something about the appointment after the paternity test result landed on his phone—my heart might not feel so heavy.

"Of course. But are you sure you're okay? You sighed seven times."

I blink. "I did?"

"Yeah."

I bite back an eighth sigh. I guess I'm more upset about going alone to the upcoming appointment than I thought.

"What's wrong? Come on. You can tell me."

"Well..." I clear my throat, doing my best not to sigh again. "My respect for my mom seems to grow each day. I don't know how she had me on her own. It must've taken so much courage."

"But you have your husband." Adam sounds a little choked up. Despite his sharky legal mind, he can get really sentimental. "And you have me. You aren't alone."

"He won't go to the OB-GYN appointments with me. I told him we could hear baby's heartbeat for the first time, but he wasn't interested. Too busy to be bothered. And now he's in London."

"I'll go with you," Adam says instantly.

"Aren't you busy?"

"So? You're my friend, and this is important to you. I'll make the time."

"But it's today at three."

"Okay. I can take work home."

A little lump clogs my throat, and tears spring to my eyes. "You're the *best* best friend, Adam."

"I know." His sigh sounds a little wistful. "Don't forget, I'll always be here for you."

~

DR. SILVERMAN'S office is on the third floor of a sleek high-rise. She apparently moved, and Elizabeth told me the new location is much more convenient if you're coming from the foundation. The office décor is soothing, with lots of sage and light yellow. Books for children line the lower shelves, while pamphlets and titles for women's health occupy the upper ones. There are posters for regular pap smears and breast cancer screenings on the walls, and several hand sanitizer dispensers on the tables and reception counter.

The reception area is empty except for a couple of women and the receptionist. It's apparently Dr. Silverman's philosophy to not keep patients waiting for long. Adam isn't there when I arrive. Mild disappointment unfurls, but I shouldn't be upset. Although he's always been there for me, I've never imposed on him without any notice before. It's possible he got caught up in something.

I put a hand over my belly. *It doesn't matter.* I'm here alone, which I expected ever since Huxley sent that curt text, sounding annoyed that he might have to waste precious time on something as inconsequential as a baby.

The receptionist welcomes me with a smile and directs me to the examination room, where the doctor is already waiting. Silver glints in her otherwise dark bob, but instead of making her appear older, it makes her look experienced and authoritative.

"How are you feeling?" she asks after some pleasantries.

"Fine, actually. No morning sickness or anything."

"Excellent. No mood swings?" she says.

"Maybe a little? I don't know." I let out a hollow, overwhelmed laugh. "There are so many things happening right now with my job, the wedding... Everything." *My baby's father doesn't really seem to care about any of it, regardless of what he says. Actions count more than words. I just want to hide somewhere and cry for a while.* Except I'm hardly ever left alone. Huxley moved me into his house and put a team of guards on me, and Tilda is *always* around. She said Huxley asked her to stay with me until he returns. *What a lucky girl you are to have such a solicitous fiancé!* the glint in her eyes said. But I know better. He probably wants to make sure I don't do anything he won't like, such as inviting Adam over.

The only positive thing about being at Huxley's place is that Nelson and his family can't just come over and harass me. Mick tucked tail and slunk away, but he doesn't have the patience to lie low for long. His ego demands he gets the outcome he "deserves," and that means he's going to put me in what he deems to be my place.

Dr. Silverman's face softens with sympathy. "You have a lot going on, including all the hormones surging and your body changing. Don't be so hard on yourself. You're doing the best you can, given the circumstances. And don't be afraid to ask for help, or take time off to get sufficient rest. A lot of women simply don't ask because they're afraid of imposing, but if we don't ask, nobody's going to know to offer. That includes the baby's father."

I nod, not bothering to share that I *did* ask, and Huxley made it clear he was only interested in providing monetary support for the life in my womb. "I understand."

She asks a few more questions, makes notes. She records my weight and blood pressure. Then she has me lie down for the ultrasound.

The black-and-white image is still a big mystery to me, but she has no problem pinpointing the baby or measuring its length. "Here it is. It's about the size of a large blueberry. Isn't it adorable?"

I blink at it, a feeling of awe replacing my blue mood. The fetus is tiny on the screen, but even smaller in reality. How it will become a baby I can hold in my arms in a few months is a miracle.

She turns to smile at me. "Ready to hear the heartbeat?"

I nod with a grin.

"Want to record it? I can send it to you so you can forward it to your fiancé, parents, grandparents and anybody else who might be interested."

Dr. Silverman's offer breaks my heart. Huxley won't bother listening, and Nelson and Andreas won't be interested, either. But my mother... Hearing her grandchild's heartbeat might help her recover faster. I pray the miraculous life growing inside my belly will help Mom wake up.

"Sure. My mom would love that." I smile wanly.

"Okay." Dr. Silverman taps a couple of buttons on her equipment control. "This helps us hear the heartbeat," she explains as she puts a wand over my belly.

Suddenly the rapid whooshing sound fills the room. "Oh my God," I say, a hand over my mouth. My eyes grow hot with tears as an inexplicable surge of emotion takes my breath away.

The door to the room suddenly opens. "What did I miss?" Adam appears, his hair slightly disheveled and tie askew.

"Adam!" I say, then start laughing with joy that he came as he steps forward and holds my outstretched hand. I didn't realize until now how much I wanted someone who cares to share this moment with. Although Mom will hear the recording later, it won't be the same with her being so far away and unable to hug, laugh and cry with me. "You're here."

"Sorry I'm late. The deposition ran later than I expected." He takes my hand and keeps holding it as he pulls a chair over and sits down.

The doctor looks pleased as she watches us. "Perfect. You're just in time. Hear that? That's the heartbeat."

"First time hearing it," I add.

"Wow! A strong baby." Adam smiles, looking at me.

"I know."

Dr. Silverman lets us listen for a few more moments, then she turns to him. "I'm glad you could be part of this. It's important for the father to start bonding with the baby as early as possible."

The tips of Adam's ears turn red. He runs a hand down his face as he glances at me.

"He's just a good friend," I explain softly. "He offered to be here because my fiancé is out of the country." *The baby isn't on his priority list.*

Sympathy crosses Dr. Silverman's face. "I see. Well. I just sent you the recording, so..."

"Thank you." I hope a forced smile can hide the burning sensation in my gut. Right now, I couldn't hate Huxley more for making my baby an object of pity.

28

GRACE

—HUXLEY: Madison knows what she's doing. Let her handle everything, and you just relax. Go get a facial or massage or whatever a bride-to-be does to make herself feel happy and beautiful.

A facial? Or a massage? If Huxley were here right now, I'd strangle him. I texted him that his infernal assistant was impossible, and *this is what he texts back?*

I can't decide if he's being patronizing or actually believes that Madison shits golden chocolate unicorns. Regardless, it's painfully obvious that I'm not going to get any help from him in keeping her in her place.

Since I have to wrap up the projections for the upcoming fundraiser by the end of the day, I shift my attention back to the spreadsheet on my computer. Fuming at an absentee fiancé isn't going to help.

Elizabeth walks in an hour later than usual with Tolyan in tow. I start to smile and say hello, then freeze. Andreas is with them.

He's in a bespoke three-piece suit, looking as imposing as ever. I haven't spoken to him since the disastrous dinner. He's probably seen Nelson's bruised face. Or maybe not, given how busy he is.

Andreas walks over to my desk. "Can we talk for a moment?" he says, his voice modulated and smooth.

I point at myself in shock. "Me?"

His high forehead creases and he nods curtly.

"I guess...?" I bite my lip. "Um. Do you want to go to a conference room?" Maybe this is a sensitive matter. Like somebody hiring him to sue me, although his time seems too valuable to be wasted on informing me of this in person.

He checks his watch. "No need." His keen eyes roam over my face. "I had breakfast with Elizabeth to discuss some legal matters and wanted to come up here to see how you're doing."

Should've known he was too busy to come here just to see me in person. "I'm doing...um...great?"

Andreas frowns. "It shouldn't be a question."

"I'm doing great," I state again, making sure to keep my voice level. "Unambiguously so."

"And the wedding? It's getting done?"

Ah. Now I see. He's trying to get me to reconcile with Nelson. Appearances matter. Andreas will totally want Nelson to walk me down the aisle at the ceremony because that's the "proper" thing to do. "Yes. It's going fantastic," I lie. I'm afraid if I tell him how much I can't stand Madison, he might volunteer Karie to help me. "You don't have to worry about anything," I add. "Huxley's paying for it."

The furrows between his eyebrows deepen. "Why? It should be your family."

"Huxley volunteered. Guess it's part and parcel of true love." I paste on a smile.

"Ridiculous." Andreas's tone is almost scoffing. "Have the bills sent to my accountant. The family will do its duty."

"Of course." I don't bother to argue. I'm not going to win, not against somebody like Andreas. Once he sets his mind on something, he doesn't change.

"Good. I have to get going, but if you need anything, you know how to reach me."

I nod and add more wattage to my smile. He doesn't mean I should reach *him*. He means his assistant. "Have a great day. It was nice seeing you."

He leaves without a response. My phone buzzes with an alert.

Barely suppressed annoyance shivers through me as I glare at Madison's latest text, heavily hinting for me to agree to the color scheme. I'd rather have a courthouse wedding than this. Huxley is in advertising, so maybe he is seeing some superior aesthetic to the color scheme he wants, but do we have to have a monochromatic ceremony? If he wants black and white, he could just ask the photographers to make him a set of black-and-white photos.

—Me: I'm not really sure about the white chrysanthemums. Pink roses and peonies are prettier.

—Madison: Chrysanthemums are the flowers of the emperor.

—Me: What emperor?

—Madison: Of Japan.

My jaw drops, then I close it and start grinding my teeth. Ever since the OB-GYN appointment, everything from Madison just grates. If it hadn't been for Dr. Blum sending me a positive update on Mom's condition, I might scream and throw the phone out the window in frustration.

According to his email, Mom's fingers twitched when she heard the baby's heartbeat. I wish I could've been there to hold her hand and tell her myself that it's her grandchild. He told me the nurse assistant assigned to my mother is fantastic, playing my voice recording for my mom every day and reading her books and the news so she won't feel alone in silence.

I forcibly turn my attention back to the greatest current annoyance of my life.

—Me: If I wanted to be surrounded by the symbol of the Japanese imperial household, I would've married the Emperor of Japan! I'm marrying an American who has no ties to Japan!

—Madison: His aunt is Japanese.

—Me: And you know what? My great-great-great-great-grandfather was the King of England! So I think I should be able to have roses, don't you?

—Madison: You're being unreasonable. Huxley is paying for everything.

—Me: No. Andreas Webber is paying. He is my grandfather, in case you didn't know.

Thank you, Andreas, for stopping by this morning to tell me you'd pay.

–Madison: I'll see what I can do.

My knuckles are white, and my hands shake. Every time she says that, she discards my wishes and does whatever she claims Huxley wants. And if I text him again, he's going to tell me to get "another facial," like that'll make me happy. If I get too many wrinkles for my age, it'll be because I scowl every time I have to speak to Madison!

–Madison: By the way, you sure you don't need assistance with the gown?

Why? So you can put me in a nun's outfit or something else that I'm going to find objectionable? She says everything she's conveying is what Huxley wants. And when I text him, he says something along the lines of "Let Madison handle it—that's her job."

This must be his revenge for being forced to marry me. But has he ever asked himself who picked me as his fake fiancée in the first place? How was I supposed to know I was one of the Webber marriage candidates? He never told me the details. I never had any reason to disclose that Nelson Webber was my father, or that because he's such a world-class dickhead I never changed my name to reflect his parentage.

–Me: No. Grooms never get a say on the wedding gown.

–Madison: I see. BTW, Huxley wants to know how your face is doing.

Every time I think Madison is being difficult just for the sake of being difficult and blaming Huxley for everything, she asks me something like this. It throws me off because I can sort of imagine him wondering, not because he's worried about how I'll look on the big day, but because he genuinely cares.

But if he's concerned, he could just text me himself. Like when he told me to treat myself to a facial. But no—he keeps going through Madison, who constantly rubs me the wrong way. She and I didn't get off on the right foot, and I'm convinced at this point that we'll never see eye to eye on anything.

Since I'm feeling irritated at the insistence on having white chrysanthemums at the venue rather than the pink roses I prefer, I send a curt response.

–Me: It'll be fine by the wedding.

The swelling is gone, and there aren't any marks on my skin. Huxley's whitish goo worked its miracle.

—Me: I gotta go to a meeting, so can't talk more today.

That's a lie, but I can't handle more of her right now.

—Madison: But we only have a couple of weeks left. Not even.

—Me: Maybe Huxley shouldn't have picked the date he did, then. It isn't my problem if you have to work overtime. In case you forgot, I'm pregnant with his baby, and I need my rest.

I then put my phone face down on the desk. I've used up all my patience for the day.

"Hey, there you are!"

Peter.

My face scrunches. *Is the universe kidding me?* I stare at my laptop and start typing. If I concentrate on writing the projection Elizabeth needs today, he might walk right past me without noticing. For all I know, he's just discovered charitable donations are tax deductible and wants to minimize liability.

But today isn't my lucky day. Peter stops in front of my desk. I continue to type, but he doesn't get the hint.

For some moments, my world is my computer monitor with a backdrop of Peter's stupid burgundy pinstripe suit. Finally, he clears his throat. "Grace, we need to talk."

I take my time finishing my sentence, then look up. "Hello, Peter. What are you doing here?" I ask in my most professional voice. I don't believe in bringing personal drama to work.

But if I did, I would dance at how awful he looks. His usually crisp shirt is slightly wrinkled, and the dark circles around his eyes could rival a crying clown's.

Peter sniffs, then clears his throat again. "Life has gotten impossible since you made me homeless."

I shoot him a fake frown-smile. "I don't remember doing that."

"Oh, come on. You kicked me out even though you knew I'd moved in with you and had no place to go."

Revisionist, thy name is Peter. "I think the real problem was you cheating on me and then expecting me to let you continue to live at my place. For free."

He doesn't address the points that don't work to his advantage. "Sleeping at the office isn't doing it for me. It hurts my back."

"Your lower back? Just above the hips?"

Peter looks surprised, and then a bit gratified. "Yes! Right there in the old lumbar region."

"Well, there are plenty of ways to loosen *that* up. For example, you could have sex with my sister again."

He ignores my sarcasm—he must be really desperate. "I'll give you two hundred bucks to sublet your place."

"Ex*cuuuu*se me?"

"I'll only be there to shower and sleep. Two hundred is more than generous."

Madison, and now Peter. Is there a *doormat* tattoo on my forehead that everyone can see but me? "Well, tempting as that offer is, I don't believe my fiancé would like you sleeping there."

"Fiancé?" An incredulous snort. "You aren't engaged."

"Because I'm not good enough for a man to marry, right?"

He shrugs. "Like I said."

I give him a thin smile. "Here you go."

I hand him one of the invitations. He looks at it but doesn't take it. So I push it into his chest.

"Fiiiiine." A smirk appears on his lips as he opens the envelope. "You know, you don't have to marry the first guy you can find just to prove me wrong. Have some standards, Grace." His tone says *he* is the standard I should aspire to.

I must've been blind and deaf to ever think he was worth dating.

He finally pulls out the invitation and opens it. Red blooms on his cheeks. "What the *fuck*? You're marrying Huxley Lasker?"

"Oh, good. You've heard of him."

"No way! He could do so much better than you."

Well. Huxley certainly didn't want to marry me. Not that I'll share that information with Peter. "And yet here we are. Love is blind." I paste on the most saccharine, lovesick expression I can manage.

"Love?"

"Mm-hmm." I lift my left hand and wriggle my ring finger so he can see the giant rock. "I hear a man's love is proportionate to the size of the diamond."

He takes in the sight and turns even redder. Hopefully he's remembering all the shitty things he said, ostensibly to remind me of my place: a nice, sweet girl who is oblivious to what her boyfriend is up to, and even if she's aware, knows better than to say anything, lest she be tossed aside like garbage.

But shame isn't an emotion Peter feels. If he did, he wouldn't have slept with Vivienne.

"Have some respect," he says stiffly. "Stop trying to make yourself look better by showing me a fake wedding invitation and fake diamond. There's no way he would go for a girl like you."

"I understand your skepticism. The idea that *you* managed to date a girl good enough for a man like Huxley—even for a little while—must be difficult to wrap your mind around. But you're welcome to come to the ceremony and see for yourself."

He snorts. "If you're *really* marrying a billionaire like him, why are you insisting I pay for your bed and sheets?"

"Because you soiled them. You break it, you buy it."

"Just launder them!"

"I don't think so. I'm not reusing sheets and a mattress that have been soiled with the fluids of another woman and a cheating piece of sewage scum like you."

"You're such a bitch! Ask your rich fiancé for the money!"

"Just as soon as you tell me why he should pay for your screwup." I give him an expectant look.

"I'm not giving you a penny!"

"Hey," comes an impatient voice, "if you're too poor to donate to the charity, why don't you get out of my way?"

I turn to look at the new visitor, who seems average in every way—height, weight and looks. Nobody would find him memorable, except for an exceptionally high forehead and flaming orange hair. He is far better dressed than Peter. Although he's just in a button-down shirt and slacks, the material is expensive and well tailored.

"Who the fuck are you?" Peter demands.

"Joey," Mr. Orange Hair says with his chest puffed out. "And you are...?" He looks Peter up and down with slight distaste, as though he were a used dildo at a garage sale.

"Peter Olivier." Pushing the jacket back, my ex puts a hand on his hip and juts his chin like an MMA fighter before a match, then use his height to look down on his opponent. "I'm a lawyer."

Joey scoffs. "Oh, one of those two-hundred-thousand-dollar-a-year rent-a-dicks? Pathetic." He makes a shooing gesture. "Get lost before I sic a better and bigger lawyer on you."

"I work at Huxley & Webber." Peter drops the name like a nuke.

"Excellent. In that case, Jeremiah Huxley won't need to hunt you down like a dog to sue your ass."

Peter immediately flinches, blood draining from his face. He often told me one of the scariest lawyers he's ever met is Jeremiah Huxley.

"Now get lost unless you want me to permanently fuck you up."

Peter blanches and, with a final venomous glance at me, turns and leaves.

"Loser," Joey mutters with a smirk.

"Totally." I smile at him. "Thank you."

"Eh, all in a day's work. I just hate people who think they're better than they are." He beams at me. "So! You must be Grace Lain."

"Yes. Um... Do I know you?" I say it as pleasantly as I can. He mentioned something about donating to the charity, so he might be a donor, although I don't remember anyone named Joey. Or with that hair.

"I'm *the* Joey. Joey Martin." He pauses and regards me expectantly.

"Ah, of course. I see." *Who is this guy?* I smile, hoping I don't look as awkward as I feel.

"I'm here for the invitation. Ted hasn't received it."

Why does this man keep acting like I should know who he's talking about? "Ted...?"

"Ted Lasker? The greatest movie producer of all time? Huxley's father?" He cocks an eyebrow. "*The* Ted Lasker? Don't tell me you didn't know."

"Ah... Actually, Huxley never told me." Now I sound as awkward as I feel. Great.

"Huxley, Huxley, Huxley." Joey shakes his head. "Well, now you know. So. The invitation?"

"Um. Yes, of course." I give him one of the last five I have left.

"*Thank* you." Exhaling with joy, he presses the invitation against his heart. "I was worried it might've gotten lost in the mail. USPS is incredibly unreliable when they're handling important mail for Ted, you know."

"I'm sorry to hear that, but he could've just shown up. Nobody would've turned him away at the ceremony."

Joey forces a laugh. "Ha ha. Yes, well. Ideally not, but... In any case, he wants to frame this. After all, it's the first one he's actually received."

"Aren't Huxley's brothers already married? Did all of their invitations get lost in mail?"

"Probably. Like I said, USPS is terribly unreliable." He waves a hand.

I press my lips together. I've never had the postal service lose a piece of my mail, but maybe somebody's stealing Ted's. The man is super famous. It's possible he has a stalker or two.

"Anyway, now that we've gotten that out of the way, have you thought about doing a non-traditional wedding?"

Beyond having "Amazing Grace" as the theme? "I'm not sure. The ceremony is going to be pretty non-traditional as it is without adding more to it."

He leans closer, lowering his voice to a conspiratorial whisper. "But haven't you ever wanted to be a star?"

"A star?" Don't tell me he's suggesting I should pick "The Star-Spangled Banner" as the wedding's theme. Although... It might not be any more ridiculous than "Amazing Grace."

"A *star*," Joey repeats, like he's offering a small child a donut. "And all you would have to do is let Ted walk you down the aisle."

I finally understand what he's offering. "Oh. Well, um, please thank Ted for me, but I'm not interested in being an actress."

"This isn't an offer to cast you in a movie. Ted's *presence* is what would make you a star."

"Ah." *That's some ego.*

"So?"

"Um..." I was planning to walk alone, but...

"Ted has always wanted to walk a girl down the aisle, but what with fathering seven boys..." Joey lets out a dejected sigh.

I nod slowly. "Right."

"His sons can be impossible to reason with."

No kidding. Look at Huxley.

"Especially Griffin," Joey adds, probably to avoid badmouthing my groom. "He's really violent. The worst of the lot. You'll want to stay away from that asshole. I bet you he kicks his wife and kids. And his students. He's an econ professor, you know. Probably got tenured by beating the crap out of the president of the university."

I try to picture a staid professor, wearing a jacket with elbow patches, beating up another faculty member—and fail. "I see. Well, thanks for the warning. So. I take it your boss couldn't walk Griffin's bride down the aisle...?"

He snaps his fingers. "Now you've got it. So. Your answer?"

Despite his casual smile, the intensity in his eyes builds. This is really important to him. Honestly, I don't see why I should turn it down when it's just such a small thing Ted is asking for, and it doesn't cost me anything. An added bonus is that it's going to be a fabulous figurative slap in the face for Nelson. He hasn't apologized for hitting me, and I haven't forgiven him. And Andreas didn't ask us to reconcile, either.

I smile. "Why not? I'd love it."

"Perfect!" Squealing, Joey gazes at me like I've single-handedly cured erectile dysfunction. "You're a gift from God. When I saw a picture of you, I just knew you'd be reasonable. You're too beautiful not to be perfect like that. Anyway, if you need anything—*anything at all*—you call me." He hands me a thick black card. It says JOEY in gold and has ten digits underneath. "It's my *personal* number. Fewer than a hundred people have it. Sweetheart, you won't regret this. I will be the gateway to all your dreams and desires."

29

HUXLEY

—EMMETT: Where are you? I thought we were going to have our final Huxley-as-a-bachelor dinner?

—Me: Stuck at the airport.

—Grant: Maybe he thinks it'll be boring?

—Noah: We can't do strippers. I'm keeping my eyes faithful for Bobbi.

I snort. Normally, Noah's absurdity would make me laugh, but right now, tension has me wound too tight.

—Sebastian: Huxley wouldn't skip it for a lack of strippers.

—Griffin: The traffic in L.A. is shit today. Hux, can we order and start eating? I haven't had lunch, and I'm ready to eat these goddamn plates.

—Noah: Jesus, eat the bread, you sociopath.

—Me: I'm in London. Heathrow.

—Nicholas: London?! What are you doing in London? The wedding is tomorrow!

—Me: I know.

Another set of group texts arrives, this time from my cousins.

—Bryce: Dude, you gonna get here?

—Ares: TFs are getting anxious.

Of course the elders are worried. They are terrified that I might not show after all. I'm that big of an asshole to them.

If the bride weren't Grace, I might actually leave them hanging. But for reasons I don't want to delve too deeply into, I don't want to humiliate her like that in public. She and I didn't have the best start, but she seemed sincere when she spoke of her mother, and I...

I let out a long breath, half affectionate, half exhausted. The plain fact is I wish she were here. If she didn't take her job so seriously, I might've asked her to take some vacation days and come with me to London and shop while I was working. Hopefully, she splurged on facials and pedicures and...stuff. Amy and Lucie swear by that crap every time they're stressed.

—Me: I'm in London.

—Ares: Doing what? London's not that interesting.

—Bryce: No stripper is worth it, cuz!

—Josh: If you miss the wedding, your mother's going to disembowel you. Unless Grandma gets there first.

My wrathful gaze swings to Madison, who's already biting her lip. "Well?" I demand.

"I'm really sorry. But we can't take off until we receive permission to land."

"I don't care what's missing. I want the jet in the air or you're going to put me on the next flight to Los Angeles that will ensure I arrive in time for the wedding."

"I'm trying."

"I don't pay you to try. I pay you to accomplish your tasks."

Madison's snafu with the paperwork is infuriating. And shocking as well—she's never failed me before. Regardless, it's unacceptable. It's her job to double-check all my flight schedules and paperwork to make sure my jet can take me wherever I need to be at whenever I need to go. If she's no longer capable of doing her job, I can always get a new assistant. No one at the agency is irreplaceable.

My phone buzzes.

—Grace: Are you sure about having no dress rehearsal whatsoever?

Her annoyance is palpable. She thinks my being in London and unavailable is a sign that I'm snubbing her. But this trip was unavoidable. The 4D Agency is opening a new office in London, and my presence is needed to finalize the deal. Even in the digital age, some things have to be done in person.

On top of that, I hired Bryce to create a medical trust to pay for Grace's mother's care, and had to videoconference with him to go over the details during my little free time. But I wanted to get it done before I returned to the States.

Grace said she didn't want to rely on me because she's afraid I might change my mind or use it to control her. The idea is insulting, but then, we don't have faith in each other yet. The trust will ensure that she isn't taking the money for herself. Twenty-five grand a month is a lot for Nelson, and not sustainable indefinitely. The man likes to live lavishly, and he spends money as quickly as it comes in on his vacation homes, cars, clothes and watches. Mom often says he's lucky that he'll be able to do his own bankruptcy filing when it becomes necessary.

–Me: Right now, I'm stuck in London, so I can't.

–Grace: Amazing Grace indeed. There might not even be a ceremony.

–Me: Don't worry. I'll be there.

–Grace: I'm warning you—I won't be left at the altar. I'm going to marry the first bachelor I spot.

Jealousy sticks a flaming sword into my gut. Madison told me Grace invited her guy friend.

–Me: Like Adam?

–Grace: Yes. Or maybe your father.

–Me: Ugh. The image. And believe me, he's not the marrying type.

–Grace: Well, he seems to care more about this wedding than you do. So he wouldn't be a terrible backup if you don't show.

I shake my head. Dad is already thrilled he got invited to the wedding. Madison apologized, saying it happened even though she warned Grace to not invite him. By the time Madison found out, it was too late.

Should've told Grace myself before leaving. That way she would have understood how detrimental inviting Dad to the ceremony would be. The man is going to make everything about himself. Jesus, even the sun revolves around him in his worldview.

Although I initially wanted him to attend just to embarrass my family, Grace deserves a dignified ceremony.

—Me: What did I say about filling your head with nonsense?

—Grace: Excuse me, but you aren't back in the country yet! Is that nonsense? And don't forget that YOU picked this date, not me! And YOU chose to go to London! How hard is it to get a flight back home? It isn't like you're in Siberia!

She sounds sort of cute and funny when she's angry like this. Reminds me vaguely of an outraged hamster a high school girlfriend used to have. Every time you picked her up by the scruff, she would squeak and start waving her paws as though to hit you.

A reluctant smile tugs at my mouth.

—Me: I promise I'll be there. Now stop stressing. It isn't good for the baby.

I turn to Madison, because Grace has a good point. I shouldn't have picked a date so close to my return date from my London trip. But Madison was worried that if the ceremony took place too late, Grace would show, which would limit her gown options.

This isn't how I wanted to get married. I shouldn't care about the desires of my unwanted bride. But taking away gown options from Grace when ultimately it takes two to create a baby made me approve the date. I want to continue to cling to my anger that she got pregnant on purpose, but she couldn't have planned it. It was my condom and my sperm.

"I don't care if I have to sit inside a lavatory," I say to Madison. "You will get me on a flight to L.A. in the next hour or you're fired."

30

HUXLEY

PERHAPS IT'S the threat of termination or just sheer luck. Magically, the paperwork is in order—and my jet takes off.

I take a nap, then shower and freshen up. There's barely enough time to reach the orangery for the ceremony once we land. Thank God I brought my tuxedo just in case. I put it on and slick my hair back.

"You look perfect," Madison says with a small smile. "Allow me." She reaches over and adjusts the tie. "Better."

"Thanks."

"I'm sorry about the snafu."

I nod. "Don't let it happen again."

She pales a little. If she thought I'd say it was fine, she thought wrong. Her screwup bothers me more than I expected. I'm being manipulated into marrying a Webber to cement the families' alliance. Normally, I'd do anything to stop the scheme. I might not have been so anxious to depart London if the woman I was being forced to wed was Vivienne.

For some reason I haven't been able to sort out yet, I don't want to leave Grace by herself at the altar. Perhaps having seen the hollow pain in her eyes when Nelson hit her affected me more than I realized. But I

196

don't ever want her to feel that bone-deep humiliation again, not in front of that godawful family of hers.

Once the plane touches down, I drive straight to the orangery. As I merge onto the highway, my phone alerts me to newly arrived texts.

–Grant: You ever gonna get here? Less than 2 hours left!

–Noah: Do you think Grace is armed?

–Nicholas: I wouldn't blame her if she tried to shoot Hux. She wouldn't even go to jail. One female juror, and *bam*! Not guilty.

I roll my eyes.

–Me: There will be no jury nullification. I'm in LA now. Already driving.

–Emmett: Don't drive and text!

–Me: I'm dictating.

–Grant: I don't believe you. You haven't made any errors.

–Me: Jealousy is such an ugly emotion.

–Griffin: Forget dictation errors! The real problem is that Dad got here with Joey, and now I can't find him anywhere.

Fuck. My hand tightens around the steering wheel. *What's Dad up to now?* I should've been there hours ago to keep on eye on things, especially him and Joey! Fucking Madison.

–Grant: Jesus, this wedding is doomed.

–Noah: So what? Hux never wanted to marry her.

–Me: That doesn't mean I'll jilt her.

–Noah: Why? Somebody blackmailing you?

The question makes me pause, since I haven't been able to figure out the why yet. So I go for the first answer that pops to my head.

–Me: No. Emma's attending.

My brothers don't say anything. They know how I feel about Emmett's mom—and that she's my moral compass. I'm grateful Emma never sided with my family when it came to my career choices. She's always encouraged me to spread my wings and soar to the heights of my dreams.

–Griffin: It's hard, living up to another person's standards.

–Me: If we all lived up to yours, we'd be living in caves and grunting to communicate.

–Griffin: Fuck you.

I chuckle despite the tension of the last forty-two hours. Griffin hates it that his mother expects him to live up to her standards—beautiful, fit and accessible. She almost always has a crisis when she's between boyfriends—who are generally at least thirty years younger—and demands Griffin make everything better for her.

As I pull into the venue, I blink at all the black and white decorations. White, I understand. But don't women like to pick something other than black for weddings?

I climb out, and Emmett notices and rushes over. "Finally! Sebastian said he'd kill you if he couldn't hand off your custom rings personally. Apparently, Lucie's really looking forward to seeing the designs, and he hasn't shown 'em to her yet."

"So Seb came through with the hardware. Good."

"Did you really tell him they needed to be kept secret until you guys exchanged the rings?"

I nod. "What's up with these colors?"

Emmett shrugs. "Got me. Your bride must love black and white. At least it's pretty...?"

"More like inoffensive."

We walk into the place. Mountains of white chrysanthemums are everywhere. They're nice enough, but not the kind of flowers I expected. Grace seems like a rose and daisy kind of girl.

"Is this supposed to be a wedding or a funeral?" Aunt Akiko comes over. She's in a brilliant red and cream kimono, which she takes out only when she feels the occasion is special enough to warrant it.

"A wedding," I respond.

She nods. "Do white chrysanthemums mean love in America?" She blinks up at me.

"I wouldn't know." I wish I could ask Grace what she was thinking.

"Well. They're going to start soon. At least the soprano looks competent." She gestures vaguely at the direction of a singer in a pale blue dress.

"Looks that way." Madison handled hiring the staff, so the singer will probably be okay.

I barely have time to say hello to the guests as I walk to the altar to wait for Grace. Emmett and Ares stand with me as my groomsmen. The others are unhappy, but with Grace not having any bridesmaids, it would be ridiculous to have all of them with me.

A quick scan of the audience doesn't reveal where Dad is. Nelson, however, is badly bruised again. During one of the calls to set up the medical trust, Bryce said Nelson got carjacked. He didn't resist—too chickenshit, of course—but the masked thug punched his face a few times before driving away with the Mercedes, which was found the next day. WALLS MUST BEHAVE, all caps, was spray-painted on the burned husk of the car. The police have no idea who did it—there was no surveillance footage or witnesses. The security camera in the garage was apparently out of service.

Next to him, Karie stares straight ahead, her eyes refusing to focus on anything. Mick sits with his lips tight, and Vivienne sobs carefully into her handkerchief so she doesn't ruin her makeup. When she realizes I'm looking at her, she lifts her head and mouths, *It's not too late. I'm here.*

She must've smoked something before coming. It *is* too late, precisely because she's here. Can't uninvite her now without making a scene.

Mom looks alert. Uncle Prescott leans over and says something to Aunt Akiko, who nods with her eyes wide. Catalina is smiling—probably feeling triumphant—and Andreas checks his watch.

Still no Dad...

Emma and Rachel are one row behind Catalina, and the former gives me a small wave and smile. She's probably the most genuinely happy person at the wedding because she has no clue what's *really* going on and wants the best for me. Rachel's with some boy-toy arm candy who barely looks eighteen. Guess she got rid of the last "love of her life," who managed to stay with her for, like, two months. None of my other brothers' mothers have come. Grant's mom hates my mother. Nicholas's mom can never keep her commitments, so nobody expects her to be anywhere she says she'll be, except possibly at Dad's birthday parties. Noah's mom is a hermit, and Sebastian's in Paris again.

What the hell? Adam is sitting on the bride's side—all stoic but vibrating with misery. It's as though he's been asked to sit in one of

Griff's econometrics classes without an Excel spreadsheet. Why did anybody think it was a good idea to invite him?

Actually... Grace considers him a friend, and she wants to test her limits. My initial irritation slowly fades. He can enjoy watching me make Grace legally mine...and then go back to his undoubtedly tiny apartment and cry.

Finally, I see Joey—hard to miss that shock of orange. But there's *still* no sign of Dad.

Weird. He wouldn't miss this for the world. I scan the audience again, wondering where he could've gone. Suddenly suspicious, I look up at the sky with narrowed eyes. But—nothing. Guess he isn't going to attempt to parachute into the ceremony. He tried to attend Grant's wedding from a helicopter, blaring Wagner's "Ride of the Valkyries" at full volume.

Grace appears at the end of the aisle, her arm linked with...

Dad's.

Gasps rise from the guests. Her dress is classic, with a long train and a poofy skirt made with layers and layers of chiffon. Diamantés sparkle on her fitted bodice, which she would not have been able to wear if she were showing. A finger-length veil blows softly in the breeze.

And the entire thing is *jet black.*

Both my eyebrows rise. Is this a figurative flip of the bird because I made a joke to Madison about the theme of the wedding being "Amazing Grace," and Grace found out about it?

I certainly didn't expect her to run with it and make it her own, but the black wedding gown is surprisingly chic. I like the way she wears it with confident audacity. A reluctant admiration begins to swirl in my gut, along with a hint of heat that has to do with more elemental needs.

I missed her while I was away in London. The realization is a little unnerving. She's just a scheming manipulator. But my libido doesn't care, and it bothers me that I'm putting physical attraction above character.

If your father hit you, you would want to find a way to escape.

That doesn't give her immunity. Not after she fucked me over so spectacularly. Still, retribution is far, far from my mind as I gaze at her.

Tears glint from Dad's eyes, and he dabs at them. If you didn't know better, you'd think he was the actual father of the bride. Meanwhile, Nelson turns red. Or at least his black-and-blue complexion is turning more purplish as he glares at Grace and Dad.

For once, Dad's penchant for being a self-centered asshole is paying off. I don't have to hear it from Joey or Grace to know that he asked to walk her down the aisle. He always wants to be the star of any event, and this is the closest to stardom at a wedding he can get without actually getting married himself. This public snub of Nelson is the proverbial cherry on the sundae.

The soprano starts singing "Amazing Grace." Grace starts her march, her steps leisurely and nonchalant. *Atta girl.*

My brothers and cousins glance at each other, while Andreas and Catalina squeeze their eyes shut, much to my satisfaction. My sisters-in-law seem frozen in shock. Aunt Akiko is staring at Grace like this is the most wonderful wedding ever. Dad doesn't seem fazed at all, and Joey is busy recording the moment on his phone.

I smirk. Yep. This is definitely Grace telling me what she thinks about the theme I mentioned to Madison. My bride's defiance is amusing, and I respect her for having a spine and this much chutzpah.

When Grace and Dad reach me, he hands her to me and says, "Be good to my girl or else."

I give him a look. "You're *my* father, not hers."

"Not anymore. I walked her down the aisle, and now she's mine."

For God's sake. "Go away, Dad. You're making the officiant wait."

"Fine." He tugs on the lapels of his tux, gives the audience a wave and struts off.

The officiant is a judge who's a good friend of Grandmother's. He begins, not showing any reaction to this highly unorthodox wedding.

"This is the best omen for our life together," I whisper to Grace, my eyes trained straight ahead.

"I did what you wanted. Didn't Madison tell you?"

"She tells me everything." Actually, she overshared the details of the wedding, including how much everything cost. I eventually had to tell her I don't care about the money. Even if Andreas hadn't offered to pay, I wouldn't care how much Grace decided to spend. It isn't that much to give her the wedding of her dreams.

"I'm sure."

What's up with the sarcasm? Grace is getting the ceremony she wanted and has made a public statement about her feelings. Shouldn't she be satisfied?

The officiant is looking at me expectantly. I chafe at the idea of reading a line in someone's script like a puppet. A perverse urge to say, "I don't," is on the tip of my tongue until I glance in Grace's direction. She's pale, her hands tight around the bouquet.

She's nervous. She expects me to do something to turn her into the butt of a joke.

Suddenly the subversive urge dies. I say, "I do," with the solemnity the occasion requires.

Her grip on the bouquet relaxes. "I do," Grace says softly when it's her turn.

We exchange the rings. The specially designed wedding band has three stones—one pearl, one clear diamond and then a third stone, pink for her and blue for me. They represent the new life we've created, and she and I, bound as family. The placement of the stones and setting make these rings unique and interesting, more than mere bands.

The officiant rambles a bit more about our wonderfully bright future and then intones, "You may kiss the bride."

I lift the veil over her head. She looks up at me. Her eyes are unreadable, but they shine beautifully under the gorgeous California sun. Although she made the wedding as funereal as possible, her makeup is perfectly done, highlighting her high cheekbones, wide eyes and soft lips.

"Wife," I whisper, then claim her mouth.

On cue, the waterworks start, accompanied by a loud wail. "It's obvious Huxley and Grace aren't meant to be! They married to a funeral song! She's in black! She wants Huxley to *diiiiie!*"

The smile on Grace's face doesn't falter. But the moment is shattered.

My arm around Grace, I turn to Vivienne, who's now crying in earnest, not caring that her makeup is a mess. Karie is looking the other way, refusing to police her out-of-control child. *Who the hell invited these parasites again?*

"'Amazing Grace' is what many couples in Japan use for their wedding, and I always wanted an international wedding, which Grace lovingly agreed to with an open mind." My voice carries over the guests.

Grace's startled gaze bores into my cheek. I look at her and nod. *Yeah, it's true.*

I continue: "And black wedding gowns are considered ultra-chic in some elite circles in Asia. So stop insulting my wife and this beautiful ceremony with your narrow-minded bigotry. But then, I might be expecting too much from a woman who thinks almond chicken is authentically Chinese."

Grace chokes back a small laugh. "You're making it hard for me to hold on to my grudge and hate you," she whispers.

I want to ask what reason she has to be upset with me, but a loud shriek interrupts me.

"You're so *mean*!" Vivienne cries harder. Andreas glares at her like he'd love nothing more than to strangle her, and Mick notices and pokes her in the side. "Why are you hurting me?" she screams.

Dad's eyes flare. *Oh shit.* He's never found a drama he didn't love—or want to be at the center of. He runs up to us, arms spread, and hugs Grace hard. "Ignore the commotion, honey. It doesn't concern you. You have me—Daddy Teddy."

Daddy Teddy? Ugh. No.

He isn't finished. He puts his hands on Grace's shoulders. "I predict that you will end up with a baby who can sing like an angel. I always wanted one of those. Ideally a girl. Girls are more fun. Welcome to the family, my love! And you can ignore that crying bitch! Jesus, I've seen fourth-rate porn actresses who can turn on the waterworks better than that."

31

GRACE

The wedding is overwhelming. I'm actually shocked the ceremony happened at all. When Andreas said Huxley's plane still hadn't landed three hours before the starting time, I thought he was going to have his revenge by not showing at all, thereby humiliating me in front of everyone. Viv would've pointed and laughed hysterically with joy, and Karie would've smiled that smarmy, simpering smirk she always uses when she doesn't want to seem overtly pleased.

But Huxley came. And he defended the questionable choices for the wedding and my gown, making it clear to everyone it's actually quite fashionable to have "Amazing Grace" and a black gown.

He's a very intelligent man. He has to know why I picked black. And yet he defended me.

Why did he change his stance? I can't reconcile the heartless man who told me our marriage might as well be a funeral and doesn't care about our baby with the man who took revenge on Nelson for me and made that perfect public statement to everyone.

Have I married a Jekyll and Hyde? And am I ever going to be able to tell which one I'm dealing with?

The reception is even more overwhelming. On paper, it looked fine. Order this and that. Make special arrangements for certain guests with food restrictions and allergies. Seat people here and there. Oh, and learn to waltz, because that's going to be the first dance. Of course, Madison should've told me as soon as she found out rather than waiting until the week before, but overall the planning wasn't that bad.

The actual event is insane. Toast after toast, glasses are raised. The music, the dancing, the constant press of people—it's all simply too much. And then there's the emotional rollercoaster I've been riding, all the way from fretting over the possibility that Huxley might not show to the shock of Viv's outburst. These sorts of ups and downs are not what I'm used to. Not coming so quickly one after another, anyway.

Still, I manage to paste on a smile and fake being a happy bride. At least I've been spared morning sickness so far. It'd be a sight if I threw up in the middle of all this chaos.

Suddenly, it's time for Huxley and me to have our first dance as a married couple. *Oh crap.* How do you waltz again? One-two-three... and...? The steps I practiced every night have disappeared from my memory. Panic surges, and I feel like a kid who's blanking out on every word she memorized for a spelling bee.

"Breathe," Huxley says as he leads me to the floor.

I inhale, trying to control the anxious flutter in my gut. He doesn't smell like a man who was flying until three, four hours ago. His woodsy soap reminds me of the pine forest Mom and I visited on our last vacation together in Flagstaff, and it calms the agitation in my belly.

"I'm nervous." I lick my dry lips.

His eyes drop briefly to my mouth before rising again. "It's just a simple waltz."

"Easy for you to say. You undoubtedly know how to waltz. You were probably born waltzing. I've barely had a week to master this."

"Shouldn't have procrastinated. Anyway, don't worry. Follow my lead, and nobody'll know if you mess up."

I look at him, disbelieving.

A corner of his mouth quirks. "I promise. Just relax and leave it to me." He puts a large, firm hand on my back. Despite my nerves, the warmth sends a spark of excitement along my spine.

The music starts, the strains from string instruments rising. My pulse races, anxiety and sexual anticipation mingling. He's a man of large physical appetites, and he's going to want me in his bed tonight.

"Breathe," he says again.

I realize I've been holding my breath all this time. No wonder I felt worse and worse.

He waits for me to exhale, then gently moves to the beat. "You're doing very well. You think I was born waltzing? *You* were born to waltz." He waggles his eyebrows exaggeratedly.

I laugh a little. He does a fancy twirl and dip, making my heart jump. "See?" He smiles.

I nod and smile back, even though I'm not sure about his motivations. He might be making an effort because he knows it was unfair to expect me to master the dance in a week, and he doesn't want to look bad out here on the floor. On the other hand, I can't deny that he's being considerate, and even though it might not be entirely for my benefit, I feel myself softening toward him.

When our dance is over, I realize a lot of people have been recording it with their phones. Then more dances—with Ted and Andreas—and so many people I've never met on Huxley's side of the family—mainly his brothers and their wives—come over to hug me and welcome me into the family. If they know the real story behind our marriage, they don't show it. And Griffin, the brother Joey had a lot to say about, doesn't look like a typical genteel academician. He has a dark, don't-fuck-with-me expression. But he hugs me politely and grunts, "Welcome to the family," without displaying any violent tendencies.

Sebastian's wife Lucie stares at my ring intently. "Interesting. I love the pearl and the diamonds. These stones are each very unique."

"They are?" I glance down. The pearl is obvious, but the diamonds look about the same.

"This one is slightly pink, although it's difficult to tell. And this one in the center is clear. Excellent cut. Sebastian has some of the best designers." Lucie sounds half proud and half jealous.

When she notices my curious scrutiny, she smiles. "I'm the CEO at Peery Diamonds, and Seb is the CEO at Sebastian Jewelry. Friendly rivals."

"Were you always friendly?" I ask, slightly amused.

She laughs. "No. We had a rocky period, but we made it work. We're good now."

Emma comes over to chat with us, too. "I'm so happy for you both." She smiles, her eyes warm. "The ceremony was unique, but so typically Huxley. I would've been disappointed if he'd done a traditional wedding because that's just not him. I'm glad he found a woman who understands and accepts that side of him."

"Thank you," I say with an easy grin of my own. She has a way of putting people at ease and sliding in little compliments. "I'm so glad you came. Huxley told me you were one of the most amazing people he knows."

"He did?" She laughs softly. "He's always so kind."

"Not kind. Honest," he says.

Elizabeth hugs me, and her husband Dominic wishes us well. "I always knew you'd buck tradition, and I love it!" she says with a huge grin.

Joey appears and takes a selfie with me. "Amazing, right?" he says with a wistful sigh. "Just the way Ted walked you down like that. It's a dream come true, Grace. A dream come true."

Beside me, Huxley sighs.

"I'm sure," I say, smiling a little at Joey's absurdity. But he seems to mean well.

"Still got my number, right?" he asks.

I nod.

"Don't lose it. Like I said, you need that if you want your dreams to come true. I'm the fairy godmother you didn't know you had."

Huxley tilts his head down to me. "Didn't Griffin already come over to introduce himself? I wonder why he's coming back?"

I turn to look, but don't see Griffin in the crowd. When I turn back, Joey has vanished.

Huxley shrugs in response to my questioning look. "Maybe an upset stomach?"

Unfortunately, I can't avoid my so-called family forever. If it had been left up to me, I would've made sure they never came anywhere near me or the wedding. But Madison said it'd look terrible if I didn't have "family" attend the ceremony to wish me and Huxley well. And apparently Huxley signed off on the idea.

Still, it's unfair that their presence makes me want to hide at my own wedding. The tight set of his jaw shows how displeased Nelson is. He would've preferred to marry Viv off, but he has to act like he's fine with this turn of events. Andreas is watching, and he won't forgive Nelson if he does anything that damages the alliance between the families.

Not only that, he doesn't have the courage to approach me when Huxley's around. He waits until Emma pulls my new husband aside for a moment. *What a coward.*

"Well, you've certainly outdone yourself, marrying into the Huxleys," he says stiffly. Next to him, Karie chugs down a glass of champagne as though she's washing away a bad taste in her mouth.

"Parasite, that's what you are," Viv says, finally having gotten over her crying fit. Her eyes are bloodshot.

"Scientists say that about fifty-five to sixty percent of a human body is made of water. You must be down to about forty percent by now," I tell her.

She started sobbing the moment Huxley kissed me. After Ted called her "that crying bitch," she wailed even louder until everyone moved to the reception.

"How about no more twenty-five thousand dollars for you, huh? You ingrate!" Viv spits.

My throat tightens, and I clench my hands, shaking with resentment and anger. It's always about my mom's bill. If that's how she's going to be, I can strike back too. After all, admitting to Harvard Law that I took her LSAT means they'll be rescinding their offer.

Before I can issue my threat, Huxley's arm wraps around me. "Like she needs money from you people. What's the point of having a rich husband if she has to grovel for a measly twenty-five grand from a bunch of tight-fisted assholes?"

I pinch his arm surreptitiously, signaling him to stop talking. I already told him why I couldn't accept his money.

But Huxley doesn't take back his words.

Nelson and Karie pale. They don't know that Huxley isn't fond of me. As far as they're concerned, not holding those bills over my head is going to free me from their control, and they can't have that. What if I told everyone the kind of abuse I've suffered at their hands? What if I told people that Karie forced me to take the LSAT for Viv?

"There's no reason to get vulgar over *money*," Nelson says, as though he couldn't care less about the stuff. "We'll continue to pay for her expenses, of course."

"You will not. *I* provide for my wife." Huxley's voice is firm. It brooks no argument.

I can almost believe he means it, even though I know better. His father must've taught him acting.

"She's our daughter!" Karie protests.

I snort softly. *Their daughter? Since when?* I was an embarrassment to Nelson, and an abomination to Karie. To Mick and Viv, just someone to abuse and take their anger out on. They treated their housekeepers with more decency.

Huxley scoffs openly. "Is she? Before she was Grace Lain, and now Mrs. Huxley Lasker. She was never a Webber. How's your face feeling, by the way? I heard you had another unfortunate incident involving your car."

Nelson shakes. He can't believe Huxley won't show him even a smidgeon of respect. I'm just stunned that Huxley has defended me. Again. *Am I dealing with the nice Huxley today?*

"Nobody's allowed to insult my wife," my new husband declares. "How you treat her is a reflection on me, so you *will* treat her with respect and dignity. Understood?"

If Huxley and I didn't have an unpleasant history, I'd probably be overcome with joy. But I know too well how unpredictable his moods can be. It'd be foolish to assign too much significance to his behavior right now.

Time to set things straight so I don't end up being at Huxley's mercy over Mom's bills... "Huxley, they've been paying all this time, so if they want to continue—"

Nelson and Karie nod eagerly, but Huxley's cool voice cuts me off. "Don't cover for them, sweetheart. They won't be a part of your life in any way."

"You have no right to separate a family," Nelson says shakily.

"In case you missed it, *I'm* her family now. And I've set up a medical trust fund for my wife."

I stare at Huxley. *A trust fund?* Since when did I get this fund from him? Didn't he make me sign a prenup so I wouldn't even have lunch money if I didn't work?

He continues, enunciating clearly: "She doesn't need you anymore."

I reel at the abrupt announcement. I try to grasp what it means. Is Huxley promising to pay for my mom's care until she opens her eyes? What about the rehab she'll probably need once she wakes up? It feels both surreal and scary to imagine that I may never have to beg from Nelson and Karie again because control is shifting to my husband.

Viv glares at me, her eyes flashing with jealousy. She's so simple and transparent. She's thinking about all the shopping she could've done if she'd married Huxley and gotten a hold of a trust fund. Frustration brings a fresh wave of tears to her eyes.

I tug at Huxley's hand.

He looks down at my smaller and slimmer fingers around his, his brow furrowed.

I lick my dry lips. "Can I talk to you for a second?"

32

GRACE

I PULL Huxley to the room set aside for me to change and do my makeup and hair. I shut the door and lock it behind us. "What did you mean by a trust?" My voice shakes. Actually, my whole body is trembling as I wait for his response.

"Exactly what I said. I had Bryce set it up with my accountant. It'll automatically pay your mother's bills. Twenty-five thousand to Johns Hopkins each month. The payments will continue until they become unnecessary."

"But what about when she wakes up and needs therapy at some place other than Johns Hopkins?"

"Also covered by the trust. Like I said, it's for *all* your mother's medical care."

My mind whirls, trying to process what he's done. At first glance, it seems incredibly generous, but part of me is deeply afraid. Nothing this good comes my way without ripping away something just as good or better. I understood what I was giving up with Nelson and Karie—just my dignity and bit of autonomy. But what am I losing with Huxley? Is it something I can part with?

"On what conditions?" I can barely get the question out. "Do you need me to do anything?"

He frowns in confusion. "What do you mean?"

"There must be something you want in return." I take a deep breath. "I need to know what that something is."

"Oh. Well, yes, there is one thing."

Here it comes. "What?"

"I want you not to worry about how much your mother's care costs."

That's...*it?* I stand there stupidly, blinking.

"When I thought Nelson was giving you twenty-five thousand dollars a month in spending allowance, I disapproved. It seemed ridiculously extravagant, given that he doesn't make the kind of money to support you in such a way. I assumed you were difficult—greedy, even—and demanded the money from him. I had no idea he was using your mother's life to control you." He lets out a heavy, impatient sigh. "Jesus, he let his entire family push you around. But you're my wife now. Of all the things you could be worried about, the ability to afford your mother's care shouldn't even be on the list. I have a reputation for being a dick, but I'm not *that* big of a dick. No money could be spent better than in saving your mother's life."

Can it really be true? I blink away tears. Nobody's ever put their money where their mouth was, showed me my mother's life was indeed valuable.

"It doesn't matter if we fight, or you piss me off or...whatever. This trust will guarantee that your mother is always taken care of. It's out of my control, and legally irrevocable."

I fan my tear-heated face, then dab at my eyes to prevent my eyeliner from smearing. "I don't even know what to say." My voice is shaky with a suppressed sob. The heavy burden on my shoulders is gone, and I didn't realize until now how difficult the struggle to save my mom's life was for me. I did it because I love her, but that doesn't mean it was easy.

A buoyant sensation fills me, and I cry-laugh, looking at Huxley's handsome face through the tears. "I'm... Oh my God. *Thank you.*" I hug him. "I don't even know what to say other than that, and that feels inadequate to express how much this means to me."

"It's nothing." He hugs me back, placing warm arms around me. "A small wedding gift."

"Not small." I shake my head. "It's huge. Life changing. Life*saving*. I seriously don't know how to thank you."

A corner of his mouth quirks up in a smile, but there's a hint of discomfiture. Is he embarrassed by my praise? "Money should be spent well." He kisses the tears at the edges of my eyes. "Your mother's life is worth it."

All the unease and unhappiness of the last three weeks melt away. We didn't get off on the right foot, and we seem to communicate badly at times and say petty things. But when it really counts, he shows he cares.

What does it matter that the wedding decoration and color scheme are more suited for a funeral than a wedding? *My husband just made sure Mom will be okay.* Genuine hope for the future starts to bloom in my fluttering heart.

33

HUXLEY

GRACE SEEMS bright and carefree as we have another dance and mingle with the guests. The responsibility and financial burden of the hospital bills must've been suffocating, even though she never let on. She shouldered it with love and hope for her mother's full recovery. Although I swore my wife wouldn't get a penny from me, setting up the trust feels right. Who should she turn to if not her husband? Adam? Ha! I feel satisfaction at being her provider, giving her what that loser can't.

He acted like the wedding was killing him. I have no patience or sympathy for a man who has no balls to go after what he wants. He left without saying anything to Grace, his shoulders slumped. Still, what could he complain about? He got to drown his grief in some of the most expensive top-shelf liquor around.

We head home, leaving the staff to take care of the cleanup. No honeymoon has been planned, since I wasn't in the mood before and Grace never asked. But perhaps we can do something. Hit Florence or Japan. Aunt Akiko offered to recommend some of the most beautiful places in Japan, ones most foreigners don't know about. "So romantic, too! You'll love it. Even though you met your wife in an arranged marriage, with proper effort, you can have a good life together. People still do those in Japan and live very happily. And lots of people in history didn't even get to meet their spouses before marriage."

She probably added the last part to show that I did better than those people. At least I got to see my bride before the actual wedding. Still, the sentiment is sweet, and I too hope that my marriage isn't a complete disaster. My home is my sanctuary, and should be without drama or emotional upheaval. I have enough of that at work, dealing with difficult and demanding clients.

"Is this the car you drove when we first met? On that rainy day?" Grace asks, touching the seat with her hand. If the silk and train around her were traditional white, she'd look like a cream puff.

My cream puff.

"Yes." Because I'm feeling just a bit sentimental and mellow, I add, "I like this car. Even if I didn't, I couldn't get rid of the vehicle where I did my first good deed."

She laughs softly. "I doubt that. You can be surprisingly generous." Her eyes shine as she looks at me.

"It's nothing," I say gruffly.

"Maybe to you. Remember—what you call nothing is something that could change everything for someone else. If you hadn't given me that ride, I don't know what I would've done. If you hadn't created the trust, I'd be at Nelson and his family's mercy for..." She shrugs. "I don't know. A long time."

"He's nothing to you. He's not your family, he's not even your father, not in any way that counts. If he or his family ever bother you, just let me know." I've never had a high opinion of Nelson or Karie, but now it really couldn't go any lower. On the other hand, sometimes people surprise me. Nelson and Karie might take out a shovel.

When we reach our home, I exit and the door on her side rises. I go around the car and extend my arm. "Wife."

She lays her small, delicate hand on my palm. With a grin, I pick her up, one arm under her shoulders and the other under her knees. She yelps, then puts an armlock on my neck.

I laugh. "Relax. I'm not going to drop you."

"Aren't I heavy?"

"You kidding? You're like a cream puff."

"A cream puff, huh? Even though my dress is black?" Her eyes twinkle.

"Okay... A chocolate cream puff."

She laughs. "So we won't make the Internet news for being that couple who threw out his back and broke her hip?"

"Never."

"Man. I always wanted to be famous." She flutters her eyelashes.

I laugh. "Fame is overrated, but if you want it, I can arrange something."

"Like what? Call Joey the Fairy Godmother I Didn't Know I Had?"

"Please." A small shudder runs through him. "I can do a thousand times better."

She's all curiosity now. "Okay, impress me. What are you going to do to make me famous?"

"Outdoor sex comes to mind."

"*What?*"

"I mean, if you want me to throw out my back and break your hip, we might as well have some fun while we're at it..."

She lets out a shriek of laughter, the blue of her eyes brightening a shade or two. Her body is warm and soft against me, and the light, citrusy perfume she was wearing earlier has faded, leaving only the mouthwatering fragrance of her feminine scent behind.

I really missed this woman in the last three weeks. Not just her body but her humor and pluck. And the amazing way she handled my father so that he actually behaved like a somewhat normal human being at the wedding, despite my misgivings.

My skin hot and prickling, I kiss her, our lips touching softly as I carry her across the threshold, up the winding stairs, to our bedroom. My tongue flicks out and licks the seam of her mouth, only to have hers come out to do the same, her hand now cradling my cheek. She strokes my skin tenderly, her eyes full of gratitude and affection.

It's nice...but not enough. I want her eyes to burn with lust as well.

I place her on the bed and deepen the kiss. She plunges her fingers into my hair, holding me tight as she returns my kiss with open carnality. I run my hands along her bare arms, feel goosebumps against my fingertips. She shivers and sighs.

"I know it sounds weird, given that we've had some rocky moments...but I think I missed you," she whispers against my mouth, which still tingles with the taste of her.

I put my forehead on hers. "I won't be gone for so long again, not for a while." I press a dozen kisses on her face. "I missed you, too."

A small smile curves her mouth. I trace the line with my tongue and—

My home security system beeps twice, a signal that somebody is at the gates.

Who the hell could it be? My brothers know better than to plan a gag gift or prank on my wedding night. And Joey values his life too much to disturb me right now.

Probably some idiot who's at the wrong house. I claim Grace's mouth again—

The system beeps again. *Damn it.*

"Isn't that a visitor?" she says.

"Fuck 'em. Nothing's more important than this." I go back to kissing my wife.

Her phone starts ringing, and she pushes me away gently. "I'm sorry, but I have to take this."

"Let them leave a voice—"

"It might be about my mom." She tries to smile, but falters. Anxiety cools the heat in her eyes.

I hold her hand as she picks up her phone. A small frown creases the skin between her eyebrows.

"What is it?"

"It's Adam."

What the fuck? The bastard's transparent attempt to screw with me amplifies my frustration. "Ignore it."

"It might be important. He wouldn't call me this late if it weren't."

"He's trying to cock-block me."

She gives me an *are you serious* look. "That is just beyond ludicrous."

"Fine," I grind out, realizing she isn't going to give in. "We'll see who's right."

She answers the phone, putting Adam on speaker, as though that will prove me wrong. I sit behind her, wrap my arm around her belly, place kisses along the sensitive skin on the side of her neck, then suck, just the way she likes.

Her breathing hitches. She clears her throat. "Adam, is everything okay? It's so late."

"Am I interrupting anything?" he says, his words slightly slurred.

"It's our wedding night. What do you think?" I demand, cupping her breasts.

The line goes silent. Perhaps he got the hint and hung up.

Grace bites her lip, then bats at my hand, but I shake my head. "You said he isn't trying to cock-block me. Prove it," I whisper into her ear, then nip the earlobe so she knows I'm serious.

Air shivers in her lungs. I lick the spot I nipped. She trembles with need and digs her fingers into my wrists, trying to fight for control. I pull down the bodice of her gown and flick my fingers across her beaded nipples. Her back arches; her ass subtly grinds into me. She feels amazing against my hard cock. It's been so long.

"I'm at your house," says Adam.

Grace stops with a gasp. Rage shoots to the top of my skull.

"The one owned by that man, I mean," he adds.

"What the *fuck*?" I thunder.

The bastard ignores me and talks to her again. "I have to talk to you. Now. My Uber left, so I can't go home."

"Unless you want to hear my wife screaming my name as she comes, stop calling." I kill the call and plunder her mouth. Jealousy is an ugly beast that rides me as I plunge my tongue into her mouth, like I'm fucking it. But what the hell? How's a man supposed to be calm when another man who obviously covets his wife shows up on their wedding night?

Her phone rings again. And again. The security system beeps over and over. I ignore them, but Grace grows too tense. Every time I stoke her fire, the phone and security system going off throw a bucket of water on it.

Finally, it's too much. "I'm going to murder that son of a bitch!" I grind out, pulling away from her to beat the absolute *shit* out of this guy.

She wraps both arms around my waist, momentarily preventing me from getting up off the bed. "Huxley, stop. Please. Give me five minutes to deal with Adam," she says in a small, half embarrassed half cajoling voice. "And we can do whatever you want afterward."

34

HUXLEY

I HEAD to the foyer with Grace, who straightens her dress to look presentable. I shed my wrinkled tux jacket and pull the cuff links out of my sleeves so that I can roll them up.

"He's taking too long to get here from the gates," I grouse. "It's getting docked from his five minutes."

She just hugs herself and shivers. I pull her toward me and put my arm around her, lending her my warmth. "What's wrong?"

"It's just... Something feels off. Adam wouldn't be like this if it wasn't important. What if Mom's doctor contacted him?"

"Why would he do that?"

"Adam is listed as an emergency contact. In case Nelson or I are unavailable."

I grudgingly admit that that's reasonable. Still, the fact that Adam has that connection with her and could use it to get her to see him regardless of the time of day is infuriating. I'm going to replace him with myself on the contact list.

Finally, Adam shows up. His suit is wrinkled, the tie pulled down to mid-chest and half undone. Red rims his bloodshot eyes, and he smells like alcohol. *Helped yourself generously to my liquor, didn't you?* His hair stands up like a bird's nest after a hurricane. There's a grayish-green tinge to his already substandard complexion. If he throws up, I'm going to call the police and bill him for the cleanup.

"What happened to you?" Grace's voice is all sympathy and concern.

She makes a move to go to him, but I tighten my arm around her. She isn't touching that rabid shit. Look at him. He's diseased. Unhinged. Possibly both.

"I tried to be open-minded. Really. Be happy for you," Adam says, somehow managing to stand upright.

"Thank you," Grace says awkwardly.

"But... You married a violent man."

Is this fucker serious?

He continues, "Are you really okay?"

I start to step forward to give him a demonstration of just how violent a man I can be, but Grace leans into me. "I'm more than okay, Adam. Huxley has been very good to me."

Her words soothe my temper somewhat.

"But what about Nelson—"

"He slapped me first. My husband did what he had to do."

"You're alone in the world because of your mother's bills! Is he"— Adam points at me—"using them to control you?"

"No." Grace sounds pained, and maybe a little bit embarrassed and exasperated. "Adam, please. You're drunk and don't know what you're saying."

"Hear that? Now get out," I say.

He turns to me, his gaze burning with grievance.

I mentally shrug. The world is unfair, and he should blame himself for not doing everything in his power to protect and woo Grace before. The only reason he's angry is because he had no capacity to do so and wants to blame somebody else for his failure.

"You don't deserve her," he spits out finally. "She's too special for someone like you."

I shoot him a cool, triumphant smile. "Yet I have her in my home and in my bed. It's my ring on her finger. She bears my name. She is Mrs. Huxley Lasker, and she will be the mother of my child."

He turns red as I speak, but then smirks when I mention the baby.

"Who cares about all that stupid shit?" He laughs unsteadily. "A ring. That doesn't make her yours."

"You dare covet my wife?"

"And your child?" he continues, sneering. "The doctor thought it was mine." Another laugh.

"What doctor?" I frown.

"Her OB-GYN. Didn't you know? *I* was the one who held her hand when she went in for her appointment. *I* heard the baby's heartbeat for the first time with her, shared that special moment with her. Not you, Mister Woman-Owner."

Grace tenses next to me. It's all the confirmation I need.

"Tell him, GG," Adam says, his insolent eyes on mine.

GG? The nickname is like gas on the fire.

"Adam, you need to go," Grace says. "Now."

I add nothing, since he doesn't belong in our discussion.

"Why? Because you still cling to the hope that he can be good to you?"

"You're going to be embarrassed tomorrow when you sober up. Just go," she says, her voice tight.

He gives her sad puppy-dog eyes. He must use that expression to his advantage to get what he wants. "Fine. But only because you're upset." He turns around.

"Show your face around my wife again, and I'll break it."

"Yeah, yeah. I'd make a better father for that baby than you'll ever be," he says over his shoulder, then stumbles down the long driveway toward the main gates.

I slam the door shut and pull Grace into the living room. She expels a frustrated breath. Is she upset I found out how little she thinks of me? I was working my ass off and setting up the trust for her mother's care, while she was seeing her doctor and sharing one of the most important moments of the pregnancy with another man.

What else did she share with him? Not her body—he would've thrown that in my face. But just because she didn't let him get between her legs doesn't mean she hasn't cheated on me emotionally.

I never understood crimes of passion. But right at the moment I'd happily strangle both of them.

"I can't believe you took that asshole with you to hear the baby's heartbeat!" My finger shakes with rage as I point in the direction of the gates.

"You were in London."

"But *him*? You couldn't have asked someone else?"

"He offered because you weren't here. How is that my fault? Or his?" she says.

"Because you're my wife. The baby in your womb is my baby."

Her chin sets in a stubborn line. I liked her feistiness before, but not right now. She has no idea how close I am to the breaking point. "I wasn't your wife back then."

"We had an agreement! And you were wearing my damn ring."

"You said you were too busy!"

I feel like my head will explode at her accusatory tone. "You never gave me a chance!" She never told me. Never said a word about what happened at the appointment. If it hadn't been for Adam, I might've never found out my baby has heartbeat now. "I would've made time!"

"How? Would you have flown back home just for the appointment and then flown back to London?" Her tone says what I'm saying is nonsensical absurdity.

Except... That's exactly what I would've done, I realize. "Meetings can be rearranged. I can lose a few hours' sleep if I have to. But a milestone like the one that asshole got to witness only happens once. I want to be present for every big moment. The child won't just grow up in material comfort. It will grow up knowing it's important. That Daddy —*me*—has its back."

"Then why did you say you were busy?"

Are we back to this, really? "Because I *was* busy. I'm always busy. I have to make an effort to free up time. It is *your* responsibility to tell me these things as my wife and the mother of my child."

"You're impossible!" she shouts.

"And you keep forgetting that every inch of you is *mine, and mine alone*."

She glares at me, her eyes brilliant with furious tears. "Go fuck yourself."

"How about I fuck you senseless instead? And fill you with my cum every time you forget who you belong to?"

Shock registers on her face, but before she can say another word, I crush my mouth against hers. The kiss isn't gentle and playful like before. It's raw, with teeth, to give her just enough pain to punish her.

She doesn't take it lying down. She bites back, sharp enough to draw a bit of blood from my tender flesh. The feisty reaction drives me crazy, even more determined to tame her, show her who owns her everything.

If she meant to drive me insane with jealousy, she's succeeded. I rip the zipper down her dress and yank it down her body, revealing her plump breasts. She crosses her arms to hide them, but I lower her wrists and hold them behind her with one hand.

Her chest shudders as air saws in and out of her. The pulse in her neck flutters wildly, and fire flares in her eyes—she's turned on and angry at the same time.

I keep my eyes on hers. "My tits. Mine to touch." My hand closes over one. The soft weight feels amazing, and I knead it, my thumb coming close but not touching the puckered nipple. Her cheeks grow rosy with heat, and she bites her lip, trying to contain a whimper. I angle her wrists so her back arches further, pushing her breasts toward me. "Mine to taste." I close my mouth over it, sucking hard.

A soft moan tears from her. Her knees buckle, and I push her against the cool floor-to-ceiling window facing the dark garden. She throws her head back, resting it on the glass and thrusting her breast into my face.

Satisfaction glimmers, but it isn't enough. I push the dress lower until it's puddled around her feet and she's in nothing but a garter belt and stockings, just like the first time we slept together. I turn her around, so her tits are pressed against the window, then push my hand between her and the cool glass and run my finger along her folds. They're scorching and dripping. Her hot breath fogs the window.

"Do you think he's still out there, watching?" I whisper into her ear.

She shudders, a flare of panic in her eyes. "You wouldn't..."

"Why? You think I'm too possessive to let him see it?"

"Aren't you?"

She's right. Every glass pane in the house in specially treated to prevent anybody outside from seeing what's happening inside. Her bare breasts might be pressed against the glass, but nobody can see them.

But instead of telling her that, I dip two fingers into her slick depths and move them until I find the bump that makes her feel extra good. She squeezes her eyes shut, every cell in her body tense.

"If he sees your pussy's taking in my fingers, you think he'll give up?" My words break over the pulse in her neck.

"Huxley, he's not into me that way."

"Hah. You think."

"We shouldn't—"

"We will. You said we could do whatever I wanted. This is what I want."

I release her pinned wrists, and she spreads her fingers over the glass as though to find purchase. I knead her sweet ass as I finger-fuck her and tease her clit with a butterfly-soft touch.

Soon she's moving to the tempo I set, pleasure winding through her. "Does he know what a greedy slut you are for me? That you only take your husband's cock?"

She rests the back of her skull on my shoulder as she pushes against the glass, grinds against my hands. I cup a breast and tease the tip. A soft scream. She's so damn responsive.

To *my* touch. To *my* hands. To *my* cock.

I undo my pants. Let my throbbing dick spring out. The tip is already slick. I hunger for her, and it still enrages me that she's open to seeing Adam again.

Tapping the insides of her ankles, I spread her open. "Stick your ass out like a good girl for me. Show me how hungry you are for your husband."

Expelling a shaky breath, she obeys.

"Pump your fingers into your pussy."

"Huxley..." she gasps.

"Do it."

She pushes two fingers into herself. I watch them disappear then move in and out. She's trying to reach the spot I can, get the fullness I've given her. She can't achieve either on her own, but it's enough to keep her on the edge, frustrating her. She sobs softly. "Oh my God. I can't."

"What do you need in your pussy, wife?"

She shakes her head, and the motion makes her breasts swing. I pinch the nipples, tugging them. She arches her back, pushing her ass against my erection. A fine sheen of sweat glints on her beautiful body, and I kiss the lovely slope of her shoulders and back.

"Who do you belong to?"

"You," she says in a breathless whisper.

I rub the tip of my cock against the opening of her pussy, then glide forward until the ring grazes against her swollen clit, earning a gratifying shiver from her. "Say it again."

"You," my wife chokes out. "I belong to you."

"Don't you ever forget it." I drive into her, feel her muscles spasm around my thickness. She lets out a strangled cry, her head thrown back, exposing her vulnerable neck to my touch. I wrap my hand around it, feel her veins pulsing with life and need.

She convulses after only a few pumps. I thrust into her with more speed and power, making her whole body shake. My fingers dig into the sweet curve of her pelvis, and I cup her breast, teasing the pointed tip. She twists her head back, and I kiss her deep and hard, our tongues tangling.

Only one word pounds in my head as I pick up the tempo: *mine, mine, mine.*

And she whimpers, our mouths pulling apart. "Yes, yes, yes," she chants to the beat of the word in my head. Or maybe I'm saying it out loud. Impossible to tell with blood roaring in my ears, pleasure tingling at the base of my spine, then pooling in my cock. It thickens and hardens further inside her, and she spasms around me, gripping me hard.

My control snaps. I drive into her one last time and shoot my cum into her, just like I promised. She goes boneless in my arms, resting her back against my chest and struggling to breathe. But the possessive, jealous beast inside me isn't satisfied. Not really. It's chafing that there's a better way to mark her mine.

Warm fluid trickles down our legs, and I dip my fingers into it. Then I stand her up straight and write MINE down the front of her torso. The writing shows even in the dark window.

Better.

Then I spin her around, capture her mouth and start all over again.

35

GRACE
AM I IN BED?

I BLINK in the dimly lit bedroom. The last thing I remember about last night is climaxing until I lost count and nearly passing out on the kitchen counter. Huxley was insatiable and determined to make a point, as though sex could make everything better.

Granted, I love having sex with him. He's amazing in bed...or in front of a window. He does things that make me lose my mind—a way of mastering my body that's as addictive as heroin. When he said Adam could be watching us, it made me tremble with trepidation and anticipation.

But—great as it is—sex doesn't solve any of the other issues between me and Huxley: his resentment and his hot-and-cold reactions. He doesn't get to act hurt and ignored after texting what he texted about the doctor's appointment. He doesn't get to make a declaration that he'll be present for our baby, which left me speechless and dumbfounded. Annoyance surges that he flung it at me last night the way he did. It was a beautiful and honorable sentiment, the kind that would've brought me relief and even joy if he just hadn't delivered it like that.

Still, it's a new day. I don't want to argue or fight, and what Adam did was clearly out of bounds. I don't know why he had to provoke

Huxley on our wedding night. If I didn't know better, I'd think he was purposely trying to hurt me. Huxley didn't deserve that sort of confrontation, not after being so generous and kind to me.

Be the bigger person. Offer an olive branch.

To find the recording of the baby's heartbeat, I reach for my phone. Several texts fill my screen.

—Adam: GG, I'm so sorry. Did I say anything stupid last night?

—Adam: Are you okay?

—Adam: Did he take it out on you?

—Adam: Please. I have to know. I'm so sorry.

I heave a long, heavy sigh. My first instinct is to say it was fine—but it wasn't. What he did wasn't just inappropriate, it could've irreparably damaged Huxley's and my relationship. This is no love match with a strong foundation. Huxley is a proud man who's upset at being stuck in a situation he never wanted to be in. Although I make my own money and no longer have to beg anybody to pay for Mom's care, it's painfully obvious that Huxley is the one with more power in our marriage. If he wants to, he can make my life very unpleasant, regardless of any resistance I might put up along the way. He might even try to take the baby away. The prenup means nothing because all the court needs to do is look at me and him. He's from a powerful family, well connected and wealthy. I'm the opposite.

It'd be so easy for him to convince the world he's the better option, and that I'm just a gold digger, hoping for a big payday.

—Me: I'm fine. He didn't take things out on me, if you mean physical violence.

Adam doesn't seem to get the subtle rebuke in my allusion to the words he used last night because he only responds, *Thank God!* I tighten my jaw.

—Me: I think it would be best if you refrained from coming over or doing things that would upset Huxley.

—Adam: Is that your wish or his?

—Me: Mine. He's my husband and the father of my baby, Adam. He didn't deserve to be treated like that on our wedding night. It was uncalled for.

—Adam: I was drunk.

—Me: Yes, that was obvious. I'm disappointed that you drank until you lost control of yourself.

—Adam: Again, I'm sorry.

I don't respond. There's nothing more to say, since neither forgiveness nor continued anger is an acceptable response.

Despite the night of debauchery, I'm surprisingly clean—there's none of the stuff Huxley smeared all over me and my own fluids. After a quick shower, I dry my hair, put on a simple T-shirt and shorts and head downstairs.

He's in the kitchen, enjoying his coffee. There's no hint of last night anywhere. *Did Tilda clean up?* Probably best not to ask.

Huxley pours me a small cup of coffee and slides it over.

"Good morning," I murmur.

"Good morning." His voice doesn't reveal anything. "Want some breakfast?"

"Yes. Please."

He shovels a mountain of scrambled eggs and bacon onto my plate. "Here."

"Thanks." I pick up a fork, then hesitate. *It's going to be awkward no matter what. Might as well get it over with.* "Adam texted that he's sorry."

"Did he now." Huxley's tone says he'd love nothing more than to take the apology and use it for proctological purposes on Adam's ass.

"I asked him to keep his distance for a while. What he did wasn't cool. He crossed a line he shouldn't have."

Huxley's expression softens. "Does this mean you realize I was right and he won't be your friend anymore?"

"Um..." Give this man an inch, he's ready to take the whole continent. "No. He's still a friend."

The muscles in his jaw twitch as his expression turns stony. "A friend who keeps crossing the line."

"Not keeps. Once. Besides, he's a true friend." I nibble on a strip of bacon. "When Mom became sick and things got tough, a lot of my friends sort of drifted away. They offered sympathy, and they hoped Mom would get better and all that. A couple sent cards. But ultimately, I wasn't that much fun to be around when I was constantly stressed about Mom."

Contempt for them flashes in Huxley's eyes. "You also had a lot of bills to juggle. Being fun for your 'friends' wasn't your priority."

"No, it wasn't." I give him a wan smile. "Anyway, I realized I couldn't depend on any of them, except for Adam. He stood by me and made sure I was okay. So he's not someone I can just end a relationship with. I want to give him another chance. Maybe two or three chances. I hope you understand."

There's an internal struggle happening inside Huxley. "I don't want to."

"You said I was yours last night," I say calmly. Huxley seems determined to be judgmental about me and Adam. But I don't want to get emotional and waste this opportunity to set things straight. "And you're my husband. Why does it matter that somebody else is my friend? He's not the one I'm sleeping with. I've never slept with him. I'm never *going* to sleep with him. He's *just* a *friend*." I pause to take another bite of the eggs. "Plus, like I said, he's gay."

"Yeah, sure," Huxley grumbles, but the tension in his shoulders eases. "No more of him acting like he's the father of my baby."

"He won't. I was just distraught, and he offered to go with me a few hours before the appointment because I didn't want to go alone." I pull out my phone and place it on the counter. "I know you missed it live. So it may not be the same, but do you still want to hear the baby's heartbeat? The doctor recorded it."

His eyes flick to the phone, then at me. Surprise and pleasure brighten them. *Maybe he* can *be a good father to our child, regardless of how it came about.*

I hit the button in the center, and the rapid whooshing sound comes out. Emotions swell again as I lay my hand over my belly. I will never get used to hearing my baby's heartbeat.

Huxley's eyes soften, and a gentle grin tugs at his mouth. "Is it supposed to be that fast?" His voice is raspy with affection, surprise... and a tinge of concern.

"Yes. The baby's healthy. The doc said it's maybe the size of a blueberry." Smiling, I demonstrate with my thumb and index finger. "Actually, probably a little bigger now." I make the gap wider.

"I want to go with you when you go next time. Who's your OB-GYN, by the way?"

"Dr. Silverman. Elizabeth—my boss—referred me. She's really good."

Huxley nods. "I've heard the same. Two of my sisters-in-law have had babies, and a third is pregnant."

"Do you need me to consult with you about your schedule before I set up the next appointment?"

"No. Just send the info to Madison so she can add it to my calendar."

He's so agreeable and attentive. Totally different from how he was when I texted him. He might've been under a lot of pressure because of the trip to London. He almost missed the wedding too, because the business there was so hectic.

Do not pick at the situation. I'm lucky that he's trying to be the kind of father I dreamed my baby could have.

36

HUXLEY

GRACE and I have a lazy Sunday. Although her refusal to completely cut Adam out of her life is disappointing, I accept she's compromised as much as she can. Still, *how can she not see that he's into her?* He doesn't even try to hide it. What kind of friend barges into a friend's house on her wedding night, knowing exactly what he's going to be interrupting? I'd bet a billion dollars Adam did it on purpose.

Bastard.

Grace and I spoon on the largest sofa, cuddling as a couple on TV fight. The guy supposedly cheated on the girl and—of course—got caught.

"Why do guys cheat?" Grace shakes her head. "They always get found out."

I run my fingers through the silky strands of her hair. She smells amazing. Like my shampoo, but better. "They think they're smarter than everyone, especially their significant others. If they respected their partners, they wouldn't cheat."

"Isn't that just sad?"

"You thinking of your ex?"

"And Viv." She makes a displeased sound deep in her throat. "They were doing it *at my place*, too."

"Idiots." What moron would trade Grace for Vivienne? Might as well swap a Bugatti for a Ford Pinto. And speaking of nice stuff... "I got a present for you."

"You did?" She blinks.

"Technically, it's for the baby," I clarify, in case she becomes disappointed I didn't bring any jewelry for her.

"Isn't it a bit too early to start buying baby stuff?" she teases.

"Yeah, but I saw it on display and had to have it. You'll love it. Lemme see... Where is it?" Madison should've had it delivered during the ceremony. She took care of my bags and paperwork after we landed.

Then I see it—the most perfect stroller in the discreet corner between the kitchen and the living room. The design is very British, and it caught my eye when I was passing by a high-end baby goods store.

Casually I get up, then roll it toward Grace. A broad smile splits my face. "Ta-da!"

Her eyes widen; her jaw goes slack.

"Shiny and chic." I grin. "What do you think? Nice, right?"

"Uh. Yeah. The design's really, um...European?" She stares at it for a moment, reaches out to touch the body, then stops. "Is it made of brass?"

"No." I laugh. "What would we do with a brass stroller? No, it's rose gold. Eighteen karat. Good stuff."

The skin between her eyebrows tightens, and her jaw slackens some more. She starts to say something a few times, then finally manages in a slightly screechy tone: "*You bought a gold-plated stroller?*"

"Well, yeah, it's, you know, gold." I spread my arms. "But it isn't about the *metal*. Don't you think it's cool?"

"It's gorgeous, but *gold-plated*? Didn't they have a normal-people stroller? You know, made with, like, plastic or something, maybe?"

"But then it wouldn't have caught my eye. Why would I buy anything that doesn't scream my name? Or in this case, my wife's name."

She looks at me like I'm speaking Greek. "Oh my God!" Her tone says I'm insane. "How much did you pay for it?"

"I don't know. Madison probably has the receipt somewhere—"

"You—don't—know?"

I shake my head.

"I don't believe you." She pulls out her phone and starts typing. "Holy *shit*! Over *sixty thousand dollars*?!"

I shrug. "Yeah, somewhere around there, maybe." Or maybe not. "If it's that important, I can ask Madison to check. Honestly, I wasn't paying attention to the price. I just thought about how cute and stylish you would look pushing this with our baby in it."

Her cheeks flush with a combination of shock, appreciation, disbelief and joy. She covers her mouth with her hands. "I don't know what to make of you."

"I know, I'm complex. But I can explain me to you. Generous husband. Amazing baby daddy. A man you should please. Maybe the man you should put Adam on hold for..."

She laughs, then snorts when I mention Adam. She approaches the stroller slowly, like it's the Holy Grail, gingerly touches the handle and pushes it a bit.

Grace looks even prettier than I imagined. The gift could've cost a million bucks, and it would've been more than worth it to see my wife like this.

"Wow," she breathes softly.

"It even *feels* golden, doesn't it?"

"It's...incredible. I don't know what to say." She laughs.

Her joy is so contagious, and I can't help but smile. "I told you—just a 'thank you' will suffice."

"Thank you." She hops over and loops her arms around my neck, surprising me, and plants a kiss on my lips. As she pulls back, I tunnel my fingers into her hair and pull to me again for a proper kiss.

My phone buzzes. I ignore it and deepen the kiss instead. Hormones are surging, and I want to take my wife to bed again.

The phone keeps on vibrating. It's not work—I told everyone I wasn't answering anything this weekend. Reluctantly letting her go for a second, I glance at the screen to see if it's anything urgent.

–Noah: Nobody said Vivienne Webber was on crack.

–Sebastian: Jesus... somebody needs to stop her.

–Griffin: Need help?

–Me: What did she do?

–Noah: She made a post on an anonymous site that's basically a knockoff of Reddit's Am I the Asshole yesterday morning. It didn't get much attention, but now that she updated it with a link to your wedding, it's gone viral.

What the fuck?

–Grant: Why do people care so much about the wedding? No offense, Hux, but it was just a wedding.

–Griffin: He's Ted Lasker's last remaining bachelor son. Or was.

–Noah: She's claiming Grace stole you from her.

–Sebastian: You didn't tell us you were engaged to Vivienne before.

My jaw tenses so hard, I feel like a molar will crack.

–Me: Because I wasn't. What's that idiot bitch saying?

Noah sends the link. The post is long and rambling. Most of it is garbage. *How in the world did she get accepted to Harvard Law?* Money? Blowing a few deans? She must suck like a riptide.

I'm 28F, and I have a sister who is really into everything I like. It's been very hard to survive her because my mental health isn't the best, and she knows that and uses it to exploit and control me. There's something really disconcerting about being manipulated into doing things I'd rather not because she made me. Nobody around me believes me because she always puts on a nice mask for the world, but that doesn't mean I don't suffer. The mental anguish is unbearable, and it probably makes my anxiety out of control and lowers my self-esteem. I think she hates me because she doesn't think I deserve anything nice in the world. She thinks a girl who's prone to panic attacks and insecurity should stay in the background while she shines.

Then one day I met and fell in love with this guy. He's only about a few years older than me, but much more successful and worldly than I could ever hope to be. He's so sweet and kind too. When he holds my hand and says my name, I feel like he's the one.

Unfortunately, I made the mistake of mentioning him to her. When my sister saw him, she decided he's too good for me. She got him drunk, seduced him, claimed she's pregnant with his baby. He's a good, responsible man so he did the right thing, but it really hurts, especially when she forced me to come to her wedding to wish them well or else.

He was mine first. I cried at the wedding, but she called me stupid and bad-mannered to cry. I feel so helpless, and the whole situation is deeply triggering because my sister also has more of our parents' love and care. I want to cut her out of my life, but she says I'm being selfish to do that, especially when there's baby shower and things like that I should plan and attend as the auntie.

Am I the bad guy here?

What the hell kind of fiction is this? She even added a photo of Grace and me from the wedding, although our faces are hard to see from the angle. But it won't take long for people to figure out whom she's talking about.

There are tons of comments. The top one doxes Grace, attaching a recent photo and revealing her name, previous address and where she works. Given the weird tics in the writing, it's most likely Vivienne posting as somebody else, thinking that will shield her. She doesn't have my home address to post. Or maybe she's scared to go that far. But it doesn't matter, because even the most rudimentary online search will reveal Grace is married to me.

Then Vivienne's sock puppet account starts talking shit about Grace, me and our baby. Apparently, the child is doomed to be "fucked up" because it's going to be raised by people like "that man-stealing ho" and a "blind dumbass who can't tell a good woman from bad." Others pile on, each comment growing viler. Don't these people realize they're talking about an innocent unborn baby here? It's like being behind a keyboard has completely zapped their decency and filter.

A savage throbbing starts in my head. People can attack me. I can handle it. But they aren't allowed to bully my wife or our baby.

Another anonymous comment says, *I know the sisters in real life. Grace is truly awful, one of the worst people I've ever met. We moved in together before she realized the OP was dating Huxley Lasker. So she kicked me out to pursue her sister's man, leaving me homeless. It's been two months, and I'm still unhoused. I have no money for furniture or anything since I gave everything away before moving in with her. With the economy and the rent being what it is, I don't know when I'll be able to get a place.*

This must be Grace's ex, that scumbag lawyer who cheated on her—conveniently leaving out the fact that he makes plenty enough money to get an apartment if he weren't so fucking cheap.

My hand clenches around my phone. The weasel doesn't have the balls to throw the first rock at Grace. But he's "brave" enough to comment anonymously to fan the flames someone else started.

Vivienne has crossed the fucking line. Nobody attacks my wife and our baby and gets away with it.

—Nicholas: What nonsense is this? Does anybody really think they could get Huxley drunk and take advantage of him?

—Sebastian: Vivienne Webber does.

—Griffin: Are you going to kick her ass? If so, I'll give you some pointers.

—Me: No. I'm going to murder her then throw her body where there's no Internet or mobile network.

Even as I send my response, my mind whirs, trying to think of a satisfying way to destroy her. Along with Grace's asshole ex.

"Why the frown? What are you looking at?" Grace asks.

I sigh. "You're not going to like it." Normally, I wouldn't show her such ridiculous gossip, but it's going viral, and she needs to be ready, especially with her identity exposed. "Here."

She takes my phone and reads. Her frown grows deeper and darker until she's cursing softly under her breath and sits up forcefully. "Are they *kidding*? They cheated on *me*! And Peter moved in all of a sudden one day without telling me. How could they say things like this? It's so shameless." She bristles and lets out a gasp. "Did Viv just dox me *and say crap about our baby*?" Her eyes glisten with unshed tears. She is the strongest woman I know, but no expectant mother would remain unaffected, seeing such viciousness said about the precious life in her womb.

I loathe seeing my wife in pain. "Yes."

"How am I going to stop them?" she says hoarsely, gesturing at my phone helplessly.

"You?" I frown. "Why do you think it's just you?"

"What?"

I pat her back. "You don't think I'll just sit by after this, do you?"

"Are you going to try to take this down?"

"No." I shake my head. "That would only fuel the fire and get people to post screencaps. Once something's posted online, it's forever. You need to cut the loss and make a mitigation plan."

"Such as?"

"Defamation lawsuits. They'll learn that spreading lies that damage our reputation is expensive."

"Our reputation?" Grace blinks in confusion. "You look like a good guy. I'm the horrible, gold-digging baby-mama ho."

I snort. "I sound like an idiot who can't hold his liquor. Besides, I wasn't drunk that night at the Aylster. I was very sober when I was with you. We had sex because we wanted to, and it was amazing, and that's that."

Grace smiles, as I intended. Vivienne isn't worth getting upset over.

"Our baby will not be fucked up, especially since we will keep Auntie Cunty away." I put a protective hand over her belly. "We're going to keep it safe."

She nods, placing a hand over mine. "Thank you. Please feel free to do whatever you want to those two. But I don't want to sue. I want to get even my own way." Her eyes glint evilly.

I smile, loving it that she is already formulating a plan to fight back. This is utterly adorable. Did I think she was like an angry hamster? She's more like a kitten getting ready to pounce. "Go for it."

"I will. But how do I make what I'm about to do go viral? I've never done anything like this, but everyone should hear about it."

"Why don't you ask for help from people you know?"

She purses her lips in confusion. It's both frustrating and endearing.

"Me—your husband. All your brothers- and sisters-in-law. Your mother-in-law, although honestly, she's only good at suing people." I hesitate for a second. *Ah, what the hell.* "And your father-in-law, who knows how to stage a great scene."

"I don't want to impose on anyone."

"How do you know they're going to think that it's an imposition? My brothers sound pretty pissed about what Vivienne did. And I'll bet you their wives aren't amused, either." I show her some of the texts.

Her eyelids flutter as she reads what's on the screen. "I thought they didn't like me, but were just pretending to be friendly for appearances' sake," she says slowly, as though the notion is too alien to readily accept. "Don't they know the full story behind our marriage?"

What does that have to do with her asking for help when she needs it? Then it slowly dawns on me. When she needed help the most, she was treated badly—or used. Her own father refused to show kindness to her when she was desperate to save her mother. Although Andreas tries, the man is just too busy to make sure she is all right. Most likely after her mother became hospitalized, Grace only had herself to rely on. Others couldn't be trusted to watch her back. She even refused my help until I created a trust so I couldn't yank it away from her on a whim.

Sympathy and a protective urge well up. Nobody should feel alone to the point that they're afraid to ask for help. I wish I could go back in time—the day she learned her mother would be moved to Johns Hopkins—and offer to help with her mother's care so she wouldn't have had to beg Nelson.

"You're my wife, Grace. Whatever you need is yours. All you have to do is say it."

"Even if I ask to borrow that black AmEx you keep in your wallet?" Mischief bubbles in her voice. She doesn't realize the effect my understanding of her past has created on me. She could make me furious enough to pop a vein, but I will never be able to deny her.

I shrug, careful not to project anything that could be misinterpreted as pity. Pity is not for a woman who's kept her sense of humor and gumption despite all the shit thrown at her. Admiration is.

"I take it you have something specific in mind?"

"Oh, yes. Very specific." She starts nodding to herself. "Unmistakably specific."

"As long as I get a front-row seat."

"Thank you. I'll pay you back."

"Consider it a wedding present."

Surprise fleets over her pretty face. "You already gave me a present."

I kiss her. "I take care of what's mine, wife."

37

GRACE

W HEN I RETURN TO WORK, nobody tries to throw eggs or rotten tomatoes at me. So yay for a win?

But that doesn't mean there's no harassment. Some people with no lives have discovered my Instagram account—or maybe Viv let it slip using another anonymous account she created just to egg them on— and currently my inbox is full of people yelling at me for being a "horrible human being who doesn't deserve to live."

Why do so many people phrase it as "don't deserve to live," as though that's somehow nicer than saying "deserve to die"? But apparently, I am underserving of life according to a bunch of strangers online. And so is my baby because it's just a "tool to steal her sister's man."

Well, I refuse to give them any power over me. It's not like I *have* to check Instagram or anything. But the rabid mob behavior is unacceptable. Someone more fragile, or at the end of their rope, might feel compelled to take a drastically harmful measure.

They also say I shouldn't continue to work at the Pryce Family Foundation because a horrible human being like me shouldn't be in a position of power over the most vulnerable segment of the population. Of course, they have no idea what I do at the foundation. I never meet the people we help. I just organize fundraisers so we can raise money to assist. As a matter of fact, most of people I deal with are vendors and venue people and donors, who are far wealthier and more influential than me.

Several people in the office greet me, congratulate me on the marriage and ooh and aah over my ring without mentioning the gossip. They probably know me too well to believe the garbage online. Furthermore, it's Elizabeth's policy to not discuss or address unfounded rumors that don't concern our mission. Her stance is "Rumors do not advance our goals. They hinder us by sapping our mental energy and focus."

"If you need a guy who knows a guy, let me know," Tolyan says, his voice as flat as usual. But a glint in his eye seems to indicate he's joking. He needs to work on his delivery—not that I'll tell him that, since he can get scary when he's annoyed.

"Yeah? You know somebody who doesn't mind effing up a girl?" I tease.

"I might. Just because somebody lacks a penis doesn't mean she should avoid accountability."

"I'll...keep that in mind. Thanks."

I check my email. Another venue came through, so the art auction can continue as scheduled. Of course, we'll need to move a lot of items from the old place to the new, but the contract from the previous hall specified they'd cover the cost incurred in a situation like this.

At eleven thirty a.m. I get a text from Joey.

–Joey: So all Ted has to do is show up at noon?

My belly jitters a little. I can't believe Joey not only responded last night but offered to do what he could. Although he promised to do me a favor, in my experience people often become too busy when asked.

–Me: Yes. With his friends and entourage.

–Joey: And be himself?

–Me: Yes. Don't let me down, Oh Fairy Godmother I didn't know I had.

–Joey: You know what? I think I like you. Don't worry. Your wish and all that.

I cover my mouth to suppress a little squeak. Huxley said I was foolish to involve Joey and Ted, but I want them there if possible. Ted's fame will ensure what I'm about to do will get the attention it deserves. Viv used the details of my wedding to make her post go viral. I can do the same with the people at my wedding, although I'm not asking anyone but Ted and Joey. Huxley said I should ask his brothers instead, but I'm too nervous to bug them. Plus, none of them are as famous as Ted Lasker.

Then I close my laptop, gather my purse and drive to Huxley & Webber.

The law firm occupies seven stories of a thirty-six-story building. It has a huge marbled lobby with a high ceiling and incredible acoustics. Andreas told me never to say anything I wanted to keep secret in the lobby because every sound carries and echoes.

But now, it's perfect for my needs. Viv and Peter turned me into an online spectacle. They're about to get a taste of their own medicine.

A security person in a dark navy uniform comes over, his round head shinier than the polished marble floor of the lobby. "Miss...?"

"Mrs. Huxley Lasker," I say smoothly. A big, warm hand rests on the small of my back, and I smile. Huxley has arrived just in time, like he said he would.

"Hello, wife." He kisses my cheek.

"Hello." I turn to the security, who is eying Huxley with surprise. "Jeremiah Huxley should've given you instructions."

"She did," the man says.

Jeremiah didn't get upset when I contacted her about the post. She merely cackled with glee. "How much do you want to squeeze out of these two? Name the number. No matter how big, I'll make them pay."

She deflated when I told her I just want a massive screen and surround-sound system set up in the lobby, the cost charged to me. "I'm not billing you for such a trivial amount. But listen, my dear. Speeches and explanations are boring. You want a victory in the courtroom, striking them where it hurts the most. Always hit below the belt, make them drop to their knees and beg for mercy—which you'll show none of, of course. Enemies are to be eviscerated, not to be given a second chance to return and take another swing at you."

I raised my eyebrows. She wasn't just talking about Viv and Peter—this was life advice. "Oh, this is going to hurt. I promise."

She tsked. "It better, or I'll be sorely disappointed in you and take the matter into my own hands. Nobody messes with a Huxley and gets away with it." Her tone was brusque and businesslike, but the sentiment was anything but.

I smiled, feeling like a general who just received a huge, unexpected reinforcement and support from HQ. "Thank you, Jeremiah."

"You may call me Mother. Don't forget—*pietas et unitas*," she said, and hung up.

"Do you have everything?" Huxley asks, scanning the lobby.

"Yes."

"I'm looking forward to this, although I feel like I already got a big present."

I cock my head curiously. "When?"

"When you called yourself Mrs. Huxley Lasker."

"Well, obviously. That's who I am now." I keep my tone prim, but my lips twitch with a smile.

He kisses my temple, pulling me close. "Look, if this doesn't work out, it's okay. I'm still going to get them."

"Get in line. Your mother offered, too. Something about hitting below the belt and making them drop to their knees."

He chuckles. "That's Mom. But I have my own personal revenge planned."

"You do?"

"See the people there?" He tilts his head. "That's the crew I use for filming commercials. Half of them are going to livestream this, while the other half are going to record it for posting online everywhere. Since they decided to take it online, why not?"

I blink up at him. "That's brilliant." I hug him.

He wraps his arms around me. "I know."

I laugh at his arrogance, then decide it's not arrogance if he can back it up.

Murmurs rise when the doors open and Ted and Joey walk in, surrounded by their entourage of thirty or so, consisting of bodyguards and...whoever follows famous Hollywood people around. Ted is in a button-down shirt and slacks, a stylish cream fedora on his head. The hat would look over-the-top on any man who can't strut à la Ted. He could teach a peacock a thing or two.

Joey, meanwhile, is in a movie-poster T-shirt—one of Ted's—and dark slacks. His hair is practically vertical; he probably ran his fingers through it one too many times, and now it looks like an orange flame.

"My daughter!" Ted announces dramatically as he spreads his arms open and hugs me. He air-kisses both my cheeks. "So. I heard you wanted me?"

"Yes," I say, laughing.

"You don't know how much it delights me to hear it. I really should've had seven girls, rather than seven boys."

Huxley shakes his head. "And you would've made at least seven therapists very wealthy."

"Wealthy? They would've become impoverished because there wouldn't be any need for *me* to see them!"

When it was just me and Huxley, people were glancing at us surreptitiously—they've likely seen Viv's ridiculous post with over a thousand comments. But now that Ted is in the group, people openly stare and pull out their phones. Many linger, rather than leaving. Some are probably gathering the courage to approach the man.

The huge contemporary clock embedded in the wall facing the main street chimes noon. Lawyers and other professionals start to trickle out of the elevators for lunch.

Showtime. I go to the security desk and insert a USB stick into the AV system control, then hit play.

The screen comes on. A man and woman roll around in my old bedroom, their clothes strewn around them. In the upper-left corner is a nightstand with a framed photo of me and Mom on it. It's obvious the room doesn't belong to the couple.

The guy's pale ass is moving in a frenzy of thrusting.

"Oh fuck, Viv." Peter's grunt comes through the speakers. The audio on the camera in my bedroom is topnotch, just like the seller claimed.

More in the audience pull out their phone. Some are texting, some are filming. *Go for it.*

"Just a little more," Viv says. She twists her neck, and the movement reveals her face for the camera. A few gasps rise from the crowd.

Guess some people are recognizing her as Nelson Webber's daughter—and my sister.

"Damn it, just shut up." Peter lets out a loud moan. "Fuck, that was good."

"Yeah." Viv's voice is a bit too even. She didn't come. Not even bothering to fake it.

Not that Peter notices. "You're the best, babe," he breathes out. "Jesus, just amazing." Then he flips over. His now-spent cock would've flopped on the screen like a dead goldfish, except for a small eggplant emoji I put over it. The public doesn't deserve the punishment of seeing it.

"Oh shoot!" a woman in the lobby says.

"Whoa, that's a small dick!" Ted exclaims. "Did you see how that eggplant icon was enough to cover it? Who the hell makes a sex tape with a dick that small?"

"Somebody with no shame," Huxley responds.

Titters fill the lobby. I try not to laugh.

"I know," Viv says on the screen.

"So much better than Grace," Peter agrees.

A sneer twists Huxley's face. Ted shakes his head.

"She's a cheap whore, just like her mom. A man like you knows quality."

"No shit. And deserves it, too."

Viv's giggle fills the lobby. "I know. Hey, do you think she's going to cry if she finds out?"

"About what? Us?"

"Yeah."

"Probably. I mean, it isn't like she's got many options. Just look at her."

"True. She's the kind of girl you fuck, not marry."

Peter sure loved to throw that line at me, and it wasn't even his own original thought. How unsurprising.

"Who the fuck does that marshmallow dick think he is?" Ted thunders, his face reddening as though somebody called *his* penis small.

"A guy Grace fucked, but didn't marry," Huxley's succinct response follows. His eyes hit me. "You never told me he was awful in bed as well as out of it."

I give him a look. "You didn't ask."

"You know my dad likes you," Viv says. "I can see a bright future ahead of you."

"You're the best." Peter kisses her.

And the screen cuts to him in the bed, alone, looking up at a person. The angle's such that you can't see it's me he's addressing.

"Get off your ass and get lost before I call the cops for trespassing. Don't ever come back."

I cross my arms. It's still strange to hear myself on the speakers. Huxley puts a hand on my shoulder.

"Nope. I should get to live here until I find a new apartment," Peter says.

"*What?*"

"Wow," Huxley says.

"I moved out," Peter says over the speakers.

"When? Why?"

"Last month. I thought it made sense for me to live here with you. Saves money. I sold my old couches and TV for a decent price."

"So his dick is small, and his bank account is smaller?" Huxley says loudly.

"Just so we're on the same Kafkaesque page... You decided to move in here without telling me because you're too cheap to pay rent for your own apartment?" the me on screen demands.

"Not cheap. Smart."

"Broke!" Ted says. "What kind of a cheap ass does this? Grace, my daughter, you should've dated better men. Like me. I would've never moved in with you, and I certainly never would've fucked a girl as ugly as that Viv Webber. At least I'd have the decency to invite you if I was going to expand my female horizons, assuming I found a chick hot enough to be worthy of us. I would've never left you out, and my dick is bigger. Which is important. A dick like that?" He gestures at the screen. "You might as well be using a baby's thumb. Am I right?"

"Absolutely, boss," Joey says with a bright smile.

Huxley curses under his breath. I stare mutely, unable to decide if Ted is saying things to pile humiliation on to Peter or if this is just how he is.

"Thank you...?" I say finally, since he's taken time out of his busy day to come by and help this scene go viral.

"Dad, you were doing so great until thirty seconds ago," Huxley grinds out.

"Eh." Ted waves his hand. "Joey, put the whole video on my accounts, whatever they are. Make sure my online acolytes know how *I* feel, because that's important."

Did he just call his followers *acolytes*?

"Really, this is just sad. I thought lawyers were supposed to be more dignified. I've seen porn stars with more modesty." He checks his watch. "I feel like I have to do something now."

"You have a meeting with Ryder Reed," Joey says, mentioning one of the hottest Hollywood stars.

Ted snaps his fingers. "Oh yeah, Ryder. Let's go, then." He hugs and air-kisses me again. "I'm so glad I was able to visit. You did all right there, but if you ever need tips on camera angles or lighting, you come talk to Daddy Teddy."

"I will."

"And you know what? I'll get you Ryder's autograph. Consider it an early birthday present."

I smile, unable to bring myself to tell him my birthday was four months ago. The man is all over the place, but at least he tries. I might be setting the bar low, but after Nelson, Ted looks like the father I've always wanted.

He leaves, causing a flurry of activity as his bodyguards clear a path and Joey says, "Make way, make way!"

Meanwhile, the porn video loops and starts back up, just in case anybody missed the good part from before. I can't have that.

There is the sound of rapid footsteps—and Peter is suddenly rushing toward me, his face red. There's something that looks like white foam around his mouth. Is he frothing? The sight is both amusing and pathetic.

"What the fuck is wrong with you?" he screams. Huxley steps

forward, his palm out. Peter runs into the palm and glares at Huxley. "Who the fuck—"

"If you have something to say to my wife, say it with respect."

"You can't tell me what to do."

Huxley cocks an eyebrow.

A moan fills the lobby. Guess Peter in the recording just came. "Turn that shit off!" He gestures at the screen.

I blink innocently. "Why? I just wanted everyone to know the truth after what Viv and you did to me. A picture is worth a thousand words. I figure this vid's worth about five million."

"At least," Huxley says. "The first showing was livestreamed, and more videos will go up. My father's accounts have over sixty million followers combined, and he might even ask Ryder Reed to mention it just because."

"You can't record that without my permission! That's illegal! Violation of my privacy! Not to mention, I never signed a release!" Peter's scream is so loud, everyone can hear it. And nobody is leaving. This might be the most exciting office gossip of the century for these high-priced lawyers.

"You can't expect privacy when you screwed my half-sister in my bedroom!"

He freezes, unable to continue. He looks like an intellectually challenged amoeba. After a couple of seconds, he recovers. "That doesn't mean you can damage my reputation." He jabs his finger in my face, almost touching my nose. "I'm suing your ass, bitch—"

Huxley's fist shoots out in a lightning-quick jab, and Peter's head snaps back. He falls on his ass and covers his mouth. "Augh!"

"Told you to speak respectfully to my wife."

"Gonna sue yer ass!" Peter cries.

"I'd say that you have a promising career in porn, but your dick is too small, so maybe not."

Peter pushes himself up. His lips are busted, and tears glisten in his eyes, for God's sake. Huxley didn't hit him that hard. I've seen what he can do to a man's face when he's really intent on damaging the other party. Peter starts toward the elevator bank, but notices a huge crowd of people pointing and whispering. He falters, his cheeks flaming. He spins around and runs toward the parking lot. That's his motto: bluster, and if that doesn't work, run. He's going to hop in his car and drive away. Then later claim something like he had to be alone with his thoughts, as though they're worth anything.

"That was satisfying." I look up at Huxley. "Thank you."

"You're welcome. Thanks for letting me be part of this." Then he lets out a dark laugh that hints that the tap to Peter's face isn't all that's amusing him.

38

HUXLEY

–Emma: If I were you, I'd never cross your wife.

I have to laugh.

–Me: You taught me better than that.

My brothers' reactions are more exuberant as usual.

–Noah: Mad respect, bro.

–Nicholas: Respect for Grace. I don't think it was Huxley's doing.

–Me: Correct.

–Noah: Damn. I think I love her. Not as much as Bobbi, obviously, but she's good.

–Sebastian: But the license plates? That doesn't seem like a Grace thing.

–Me: Nope. You're right.

–Noah: Aw, man! How come you never invite me to the good stuff?

–Me: Grace decided who could be there.

–Emmett: I'm hurt she asked Dad but not us. Did we do something?

–Grant: Griffin probably scared her.

–Griffin: Shut your mouth, Grant. Women are never scared of me. They love my face.

True enough. Griffin has the prettiest face out of us, thanks to his model mom.

—Noah: Do you know some snakes fake looking harmless to put their prey at ease?

My shoulders shake at the texts that come from my brothers. It didn't take more than forty-eight hours before the incident in the lobby went viral. Now it's Vivienne and Peter who look like absolute assholes. Liars always lie, thinking they're smarter than everyone else. But how could Vivienne and Peter think they're smarter than my wife?

—Bryce: Your wife is vicious. Love it!

—Ares: Go Grace! I always hated that weasel Peter.

—Josh: You're just happy it embarrassed Nelson.

—Ares: He's another weasel. But a partner weasel. One of these days I'm gonna fuck him up.

—Bryce: Geez. That's so properly lawyerly of you.

—Me: What's wrong with fucking up Nelson?

—Josh: Stop encouraging him!

Then texts from my sisters-in-law arrive.

—Lucie: You didn't tell me you married a complete kickass!

—Bobbi: We're not worthy.

—Amy: I almost peed in my pants. Nobody got much work done at GrantEm because everyone was too busy watching the livestream and talking about it!

I raise my eyebrows. GrantEm is the VC firm Emmett and Grant founded. Everyone there lives to work. For them to take even a little office time off means Grace's revenge was on point.

—Me: I'm glad my wife impressed you.

—Sierra: It was crime against womankind that she had to sleep with a man with a dick like that. I'd send her some of our products, but then maybe she doesn't need them, now that she has you.

Sierra is the CEO at a very popular and profitable adult toy company.

—Aspen: I dunno... Huxley wasn't exactly on time for his wedding. And he left her alone for...how many weeks was it?

—Me: You're being unfair. It was a business trip.

—Aspen: Which your assistant should've managed better for you to avoid stressing your bride. Grace basically holed herself up in a room, and I felt bad. Grant told me your assistant is good at her job, but if she were, she wouldn't have let a schedule snafu like that happen.

–Lucie: Yeah, true. If I were you, I'd have a talk with her to avoid any issues.

I go still at her gently worded warning. Her previous assistant seemed capable...until Lucie audited her work. Madison has never given me a reason to doubt her competence. My projects were never sabotaged, none of our ideas and portfolios leaked due to her carelessness. I should give her another chance. True, her screwup in London caused me stress, but ultimately I made it to the wedding in time.

My phone pings again.

–Grace: Was the license plate thing you?

I grin. Guess she saw the other video, too.

–Me: What if it was?

–Grace: You're brilliant!

–Me: Told you I had something planned.

–Grace: Brilliantly evilly planned. L84ANAL!!! Hahaha. I'm dead. :laughing-emoji:

I let out a soft chuckle. Her happiness is infectious even through texts. Although I plan to sue Peter and Vivienne for defamation, Grace deserved something with quicker gratification. So I swapped his license plates with the L84ANAL ones. His driving like a bat with its head cut off to get away from Huxley & Webber lent quite a bit of credence to the whole thing. And, of course, I had a couple of people follow him and get footage of that as well.

–Grace: It's awesome that he didn't notice at all! And a whole bunch of people posted about it, and it made the lobby video go even more viral.

–Me: Vivienne and Peter aren't the only ones who can make something viral. :shrug-emoji:

–Grace: When are you getting home today?

–Me: About seven? Why?

–Grace: If I told you, it wouldn't be a surprise.

Anticipation courses through me. I plow through everything on my agenda, including a meeting in the afternoon on the new creatives for an up-and-coming cosmetics company and a call with an overanxious client. At six thirty I step out of the office and lock the door behind me.

"Heading home?" Madison says with a professional smile.

"Yes. Have a good evening."

"You too. By the way, tell your wife I enjoyed the videos she made."

I look at her for a moment. The guileless smile and clear eyes. There's no way she purposely created the mess in London. She just made a mistake. I shouldn't let what Lucie said color how I treat Madison. It wouldn't be fair.

When I step inside the house, I'm hit with an incredible aroma of herbs and tomato sauce. Tilda must've made Italian.

I head into the kitchen to filch a taste, but find Grace in an apron stirring a simmering pot. She looks adorable with her hair twisted into a messy topknot, a pair of white earbuds in, nodding and swaying to a tune only she can hear. She dips a bit of sauce out with the wooden spoon and licks her finger, then smiles. "Oh yeah, baby. So good."

I wrap my arm around her and kiss her. Taste a hint of tomato. "Mmm. You're right. So good."

She laughs. "Hey. I didn't know you'd be here already!" She pulls the earbuds out and puts them in their case.

"Just a little early." The clock on the wall says it's ten till. "Traffic was light, for once."

"Then let me get the pasta going."

"Is there anything I can help with? I can't cook, but I can bring you" —my eyes fall on pasta—"the spaghetti."

Her eyes sparkle. "Not necessary. I got it. Why don't you just go relax? Or maybe get a glass of wine if you want?"

"What are you making?"

"Pasta pescatore." She throws the pasta into a pot of boiling water and hits the timer.

I head to the massive wine cooler and bring out a chilled bottle of Chateau d'Esclans Garrus, which should be perfect for a seafood pasta. The rosé is aromatic with a hint of glazed pears and berries and tastes like vintage champagne sans the bubbles. I uncork it, pour a glass for myself and serve a cold, fizzy white pear cider for Grace. It's naturally sweet with a refreshing finish and nothing to upset her taste buds. She hasn't shown any signs of morning sickness so far, but I don't want to risk triggering it.

She clinks her glass against mine then hesitates for a second, like she isn't sure what to toast to. A small laugh bubbles from her throat, her cheeks turning pink. "To a great husband," she says softly, a little breathless and a little shy. A hint of disbelief and pleasure shimmering in her glowing eyes says she can't believe our marriage has become so much more pleasant than either of us expected.

To be honest, I often wonder how I ended up being so soft with her, given how angry I was. But even when I remind myself of the disastrous dinner at Grandma's house, I can't cling to the anger long enough. Grace has a magical ability to chip away at my hardened defenses, even though she's really just a cream puff.

"To my beautiful wife of many talents."

Her flush deepens, the sparkles in her eyes growing brighter. "Thanks." She takes a sip of the cider, then her eyes go round. "Oh, wow."

"Like it?" I say, enjoying her reaction. It's fun to spoil my wife. She shows appreciation over the smallest things.

"Love it. Where did you get it?"

"Nieve. I ordered a couple of cases when you got pregnant."

"Thank you. This is amazing. I could sip it all day long."

She puts the glass down and drizzles balsamic vinegar and olive oil on slices of fresh mozzarella, tomatoes and basil. The timer goes off, so she drains the pasta and starts tossing everything together in a big bowl, then divides the portions into two smaller bowls. And with a final flourish, she pulls garlic bread from the oven and lays it out on a long rectangular plate.

"Voilà!" She spreads her arms with a wide smile. "A simple pasta dinner. I hope you like it."

I grin at her infectious mood. "I love it."

We take everything to the dining table. I pull out a chair for her, then take my seat.

"So what's the occasion?" When a woman cooks, it's for a reason. Maybe she saw something that caught her eye and has to have it.

My wife doesn't have the things that women buy that are pretty but aren't really useful or necessary, like stylish shoes or hundreds of purses or watches and jewelry. Her car is old, and she doesn't have any jewelry except for the engagement ring and wedding band. Her clothes are classy but not trendy.

Anticipation starts to swell at the idea of buying her something pretty—and maybe not even really useful or necessary, but just because she wants it. Actually, I should also get her a Maybach. It would be more comfortable than her old Corolla, and she deserves a better car anyway. She's pregnant, and she's my wife. I make a mental note to place an order.

"Nothing special." She shrugs shyly. "Just wanted thank you for your help."

Her softly spoken words make me pause in surprise.

She continues, "I could've still fought back, but you made it easier. Knowing that somebody is on my side just...gave me a strength and confidence that I haven't felt in so long." Her eyes glow in the light. "I never thought I'd feel it again after Mom was hospitalized. So. Thank you."

She looks at me like I'm a superhero sent to earth just to save her. Something hot, sweet and slightly uncomfortable swells in my chest. I didn't do anything exceptional. Any man would have done the same for his spouse.

"As I said, you're my wife, Grace. You will not stand alone against the world."

She nods, her eyes suddenly bright with a sheen of tears. I squeeze her hand.

"You're so good with words. No wonder you're in advertising." She lets out an awkward laugh and blinks fast to get rid of the tears. "Go ahead. Take a bite," she says after clearing her throat.

I start with my favorite—the pasta. The spaghetti is cooked to perfection, and the sauce has the right balance of acidity and richness. The thinly sliced calamari, which would have ended up rubbery if prepared by a lesser cook, is juicy and tender. If she ever gets tired of working for the foundation, she could open an Italian restaurant and make a killing. "This is amazing," I say.

"Thanks. It's Mom's recipe. She taught me. She's the best cook."

Grace flushes. "Of course, it would've been better if I hadn't forgotten the parsley."

"Didn't Tilda shop for you?"

"Nope. I couldn't have her do it and use your money when I'm trying to thank you, could I?"

Or perhaps it was due to what I told her when I threw the prenup in her face. Thinking back on it, I feel like a jackass. She probably told Adam she needed to marry for money because of her mother's medical bills. I shouldn't have jumped to conclusions without knowing more about the situation.

She continues, "It puts me behind my savings goal, but you've been good to me. You deserve it more than that bastard Peter."

"You cooked for him, too?" I hope the bastard choked on it and nearly died.

"Yeah." She wrinkles her nose. "The day he got promoted. That's also when I found out what he really thought about me, which is why I was upset enough to not care about being frugal and went to another bar to have some drinks."

"Doesn't the Pryce Family Foundation pay you well?" The rumor is that they do, but then, things could be different in reality. Everyone has a public persona, including Elizabeth Pryce-Reed King.

"It does, but money is always tight. I need to send two thousand bucks to Johns Hopkins every month, so—"

"What? Why?"

"Nelson and Karie made me contribute. They thought I should have a hand in Mom's care." Frustration and contempt fleet in her gaze. "They probably thought if I had to pay that much, I wouldn't want to continue with her treatment. Mom's life doesn't mean anything to them, and they can't imagine it being significant to anybody else, either." She shakes her head, her mouth twisted.

"What a bunch of assholes." I should've rearranged Nelson's face permanently. What kind of heartless monsters try to force a woman into a situation where she might have to give up on her own mother because of money? "I can add the amount to the monthly bill."

"You sure? I don't mind paying. I've sort of figured out the budget."

"Obviously not, if buying some seafood puts you behind your

savings goal." I frown as another thought occurs to me. "Do you ever get to splurge on yourself? Just go out and have fun?"

She shakes her head. "I haven't done anything like that in a while, but it's okay." A seemingly nonchalant shrug. "When my friends drifted away after Mom got sick, I learned that they weren't real friends anyway, you know?"

"I can imagine." I squeeze her hand again. It's heartbreaking that friendships can be so fragile, and I hate it that she was made to feel even more alone because of the callous people around her. "Anyway, there's no deductible requirement to the trust, so let it take over the two thousand you've been paying. It's specifically set up to pay for *all* her medical care. You don't have to shoulder so much on your own anymore. You have a husband now."

Her mouth parts, and she hesitates for a bit, like she's surprised at the offer and unsure what to do about the unexpected gesture of goodwill. It makes my heart ache to realize she isn't used to receiving compassion from others. She's been walking a precipice all this time, carefully balancing everything despite all the crap that Nelson and other assholes threw at her. She couldn't be more courageous. I reach over and squeeze her hand, wanting her to know she doesn't have to take everything onto her delicate shoulders—it'll be my honor and privilege to carry them for her.

Finally, she gives me a tremulous smile, her eyes shimmering. "Thank you. That'll be a huge help."

"So what are you going to do with your extra money? No need to tighten your belt so much, is there?" I tease, trying to lighten the mood. She's too strong to want to show tears.

"Save up, then buy a house with a big yard so that Mom can have the flowers she loves so much when she's better and leaves the hospital." The words flow from her easily and automatically, like a child sharing a long-held dream.

What's wrong with this house? I don't expect Grace to put her mother in a nursing home after the latter's recovery, and there's no reason for her to buy a new place. The home we're in has four wings. Her mother can have one, and we could hire a few private nurses to help take care of her.

Grace continues before I can mention any of that. "Maybe someplace in Montana."

Shock sucker-punches me. *"Montana?"* It's so damn far from California, and she knows my business and family are here. Is there something for her in Montana? Am I even in this future she's spinning?

She blinks. Her eyes clear, as though she just came out of a trance. "Mom always wanted to go," she explains, shifting in her seat and pushing her pasta around with a fork. "I've never been, but she said it's really pretty. Lots of land and nature. You know, big sky and all that. I want her to be where she wants to be, surrounded by what she loves the most. Life is short."

No good argument comes forward. How do I protest such a simple desire for her to give her mother the life she wants? Even if she recovers, her health won't be the best. Will Grace want to spend most of her time with her mother in Montana? What about me? Our baby? Are we going to end up like my dad and the mothers? Co-parents, but never a true couple—a family—who live together, have shared memories?

The questions stick in my throat. What if she says she wants to live in Montana with her mom, and doesn't want to think about the rest? I didn't expect this to be her vision for the future. We never really talked about how our marriage would be except for the fact that we'd be civil to each other. But then I didn't think I'd end up caring so much about her.

"We haven't had a great time in L.A.," Grace adds almost defensively, glancing at me. "Meeting Nelson was her biggest mistake." The light in her eyes dims as she looks down.

I reach out and tuck a wayward strand of hair behind her ear, stroke her cool cheek, then tilt her chin up. My wife should never lower her head like there's something wrong with her existence. She is a gift I didn't know I would receive, and I almost ruined it by being a stubborn jerk before. "She would never think that. I'm sure she's disappointed that Nelson isn't a better man, but she can't regret meeting him. Without that meeting, she wouldn't have had you."

"How can you be so sure?" Her voice is shaky with a hint of uncertainty and guilt, like she has somehow convinced herself over the years that if it weren't for her, her mom could've had a better life.

"Because of the mothers my brothers and I have. Do they wish Ted was a better father? Oh, yes. Do they regret having us? Absolutely not. If they did, they would've aborted us. Ted gave them that option."

Joey said as much once when we were fighting. He shouted, "Your mothers should've aborted you when Ted gave them the chance! He offered to pay!"

I add, "Besides, how can she regret having you? You're the loveliest and most devoted daughter. I can't think of many women who would do as much as you did for their moms."

"She's my only family," Grace says.

"Not anymore," I remind her. *I deserve to be in the future you're dreaming.* "You're my wife. You have more family than you can imagine."

39

HUXLEY

GRACE GETS on her hands and knees in front of the coffee table. In the armchair behind her, I sit and appreciate the view of her luscious, peach-shaped ass in the air, the erotic curvature of spine and pelvis. My surging libido says she's hot and interested, but my brain says she's totally not thinking about sex right now as she inspects the table from various angles.

So make her interested, my hormones argue. *That coffee table's at just the right height. The brothers and their wives won't be arriving for a while. And if they get here early, make them wait outside.*

Yeah, no. I don't think that's going to earn me any brownie points. Grace has been anxious ever since I said they were coming over for dinner.

"What are you doing?" I say.

She doesn't bother to look at me. "Checking to see if there's any dust."

"Why?"

"Because your family's going to be here any second?"

"*Our* family," I correct her. "You're a Lasker, too."

"Yes, our family," she says vaguely to humor me. "This passes," she mutters. "Okay, now the lamps—"

"Do you think anyone's going to come here, get on their hands and knees and judge our coffee table?" I put a hand at her elbow and help her up. Her belly is getting more rounded, although when she wears a loose dress, like the one she's in right now, you can't really see the mini baby bump.

It's the crazy pregnancy hormones. Sex will cure it, my libido says as hot blood pools in my dick. I ignore my body's reaction to her nearness. She has a lushness now that wasn't there before, a sweeter scent. It's like she's a flower in full bloom, and my boner leaps up at every opportunity, hoping and praying.

"No. But it's the first time they're coming over." She twists her back.

"No, it's not." My libido is right about one thing: this entire endeavor is crazy. She's behaving as though she's planning to go through every room in the house to make sure every surface is spotless. There isn't enough time for that. However, even if there were, I wouldn't let her. The place is big enough to house the entire U.S. Olympic team. "They've been here before."

"Fine." She huffs. "First time I'm meeting them—"

"You met at the wedding."

"Stop being obtuse. I mean the first time *here*."

"So what? They're your family, too, Grace. Did you go through all this rigamarole when your mother visited? Or when your friends came by?"

"No," she says reluctantly.

"So don't do it now. If anyone disapproves of the housekeeping, I'll tell Tilda. That's her job, not yours. You are supposed to relax and enjoy the evening."

She laughs shakily. "Easy for you to say. You're their brother."

"And *you* are now their *sister*." I lead her to the dining room and hand her a glass of the bubbly cider. "They aren't coming over to stress you out. They're coming to spend time with you and get to know you better. To be a more cohesive family."

She sits down and takes a sip of the icy cider.

I go behind her chair and rub her tense shoulders, earning an appreciative sigh. "If you don't make an effort, families drift apart. So my brothers and I have always made sure to meet regularly. Mainly over meals because we have to eat, and it kills two birds with one stone. The Huxleys have the motto *pietas et unitas*—loyalty and unity. But I feel that more with my brothers and their wives than the Huxleys because I haven't spent enough time with them.

"The brothers and their wives want to be part of your life, want to bring you into the circle. You're their family just as much as me. So relax and smile. They'll love you."

40

GRACE

Maybe it's because Huxley is standing by my side the entire time—the solid feel of his arm around me, its comforting protective support. Or maybe it's the decisive way he said his family would love me.

The anxiety that's been plaguing me vanishes, and I find I can smile with ease when the first brother, Noah, arrives. He's a wildlife photographer, as well as a social media and carb addict, according to Huxley. He said Noah was lucky to marry the best baker in the county. And his wife, Bobbi, follows from behind. A pretty blonde with dark brown eyes, she towers over me, and has a lanky but ropey body that doesn't seem to be capable of storing carbs. She gives me the first hug, then Noah.

"We're the first, yeah!" he says.

"Only because you cut me off." Grant is one of the two financial geniuses in the family. His wife Aspen is a pretty redhead with a dancer's posture, spine straight, her limbs supple.

Noah shrugs. "You blinked."

"You should show more respect for the Bugatti." This from another brother. Emmett, the one whose mother Huxley respects and adores, and the other financial genius.

"Ignore the boys," Aspen says, hugging me. "It's good to see you again."

Emmett's wife Amy hugs me too. A blonde with no-nonsense eyes, she works for Grant at the financial firm. Huxley told me Emmett hates it that his wife has to work for Grant, who apparently makes her work too hard and too late. "You look so pretty! I love your dress."

"Thank you." I flush. "And yours is lovely, too. That blue really brings out your eyes."

"Some impression you're making," says Nicholas to the brothers. He's the nice, steady one, according to Huxley. And it turns out that I actually know his wife, sort of. Molly has a popular Instagram account on romance novels that I follow.

She gives the best squeeze, all soft and sweet. "I love your posts," I tell her. "You've recommended so many great books!"

Her eyes sparkle. "I'm so glad! We should compare notes later. And you should totally come over. Nicholas built me the most amazing library. You'll love spending time there."

"Hear, hear," Amy says. "That's where we go when we want to hang out and read."

"I'd love that." I smile, relieved—thrilled, even—at the genuine affection and warmth that Huxley's brothers and their wives are showing me.

Griffin appears in the foyer. He's in a casual T-shirt with a stain that's somewhere between yellow and green on his shoulder and faded jeans, although the outfit still doesn't make him look like the kind to beat up people for tenure. He must've noticed my stare. "The stain's old, and the shirt has been laundered so it shouldn't be too gross. I'd have worn something else, but this is the only clean shirt I have in the closet after the kids decided to drool and smear food on everything over the last four days." He sounds chagrined and slightly tired.

"It's my fault," his wife Sierra says, shoving her messy strawberry-blond hair out of her face. "I didn't feel well the last two days, and Griff's had to deal with the triplets on his own. They only want Mommy and Daddy, not their nanny."

The brothers and wives make a sympathetic noise. *Triplets!* I'm stunned at just being pregnant. How did she cope when she heard she was going to have three babies at once?

"We'll bring the kids next time," Sierra says. "We thought it might be less hectic without them. Plus, I really need some adult time. I love them to pieces, but oh my God! I'm not a red-haired pony!"

We laugh. The last to walk through the door is Sebastian. The CEO of Sebastian Jewelry and, according to Huxley, the biggest asshole in the group because he can't stand losing. But from the affectionate glint in Huxley's eyes, I figure Sebastian's cool in spite of his competitive streak.

He comes in with his wife Lucie, who is a six-foot blonde with ice-blue eyes. I've never admired somebody's jewelry before, but the stuff on her is amazing. Even to my casual eye, it looks priceless, sparkling like it has its own inner light. A string of rubies wrapped around her ankle is stunning, the color like fresh blood backlit by fire. Karie often puts on a lot of bling to display how wealthy she is—and it's as ostentatious as she can afford. But Lucie's pieces are balanced for elegance and beauty, giving off an air of casual affluence in the service of exceptional taste.

"You made it!" Bobbi says. "I brought a key lime pie!"

"You're the best." Lucie hugs her, then turns to me and hugs me too. "I'm going to hug everyone before I get moody. Pregnancy hormones are not being kind to me."

"You okay?" I say as we move toward the dining room.

"Oh my God. Mood swings and weird food cravings." Lucie sighs. "How about you? How are you holding up?"

"I'm doing surprisingly well," I say, feeling a little abashed and squirmy that I'm doing so much better than her. "No morning sickness or anything. Not too moody. But it's still early, so..."

"I'm happy for you," she says warmly. "Hopefully it stays easy."

"Pregnancy is different for every woman," Amy says, patting Lucie's shoulder affectionately.

"Perhaps so." Sebastian glowers at Lucie's belly. "If that baby doesn't start behaving, it's going to get a good spanking when it comes out."

"Yeah, right." Noah snorts. "If it's a girl, you're the one who's gonna be whipped." He makes a whip-cracking sound.

"I don't think so," Sebastian says. "I plan to be a stern disciplinarian."

From the way Huxley rolls his eyes and the other brothers shake their heads, everyone agrees with Noah.

Tilda and the staff set a massive spread of grilled beef, pork roast, chicken, Caesar salad, pasta, veggies sticks and lots of bread and salted butter before everyone's arrival. She didn't bother with desserts because Bobbi said she'd send some. We grab whatever we feel like eating and go to the table. Huxley puts down his plate and pulls out a chair for me. I notice all the brothers do the same for their wives. Lucie only has a slice of key lime pie and some celery.

"I want to tell you how much I admire what you've done. That revenge was inspired," Noah says, before biting into heavily buttered bread. "It's almost like you knew a guy who knew a guy! How did you get the recording of them in your bedroom? Do you have a stalker who films your house?"

Curious eyes turn on me. "No, thank God. I'm not that interesting."

Huxley makes a skeptical sound deep in his throat. "Don't underestimate yourself," he whispers.

Flushing and elbowing him teasingly, I cut the roast beef on my plate. "Viv has a habit of stealing my things and then denying that she did so, even though it's obvious that she did. So I got fed up and installed a camera in my bedroom without telling anybody. It only records if it detects motion or sound in the room. I sort of forgot about it because I'd been occupied with the wedding and the pregnancy. But when she decided to make me an online celebrity, I thought I'd return the favor. Peter getting caught in it is a bonus, since he helped her."

"Damn. That's *good*." Noah turns to his wife. "We should get one of those for our bedroom."

Bobbi stabs some lettuce. "No. You'd just watch the videos of us over and over again for your own entertainment."

"So? I might get lonely out on the veldt. With nothing but the wilderness around, shooting cheetahs. I might need something to comfort me."

Sebastian rolls his eyes. "If your precious cheetahs could, they'd get a restraining order against you."

"They don't even know I exist. Yes, I am just that smooth." Noah nods with deep self-satisfaction.

Next to him, Bobbi rolls her eyes, but a small smile on her lips says she's crazy about him. They lock gazes, and something illicit and unspoken passes between them. I look away, feeling an urge to blush.

"How about the license plates?" Sierra leans forward. "How did you manage that? Did you have a camera set up to capture it too? Maybe a drone?"

I shake my head. "I wish I could take the credit, but that was all Huxley."

"Damn." Emmett whistles.

"That's brilliant." Molly beams. "No wonder you work in advertising!"

Huxley preens. "Why, thank you. I'm glad *some*body recognizes where my talents lie."

"Your mom still saying you should join the firm?" Grant says before shoveling a piece of pork into his mouth and reaching for a glass of Merlot.

"Yes, of course."

"The woman doesn't give up." Griffin grunts. "The worst ones never do."

Huxley leans over. "He probably got a call from his mother asking him to be her date to some party in Barcelona."

"Barcelona? Like, in *Spain*?" I ask.

"Rachel doesn't care," Huxley whispers.

"I was disappointed that you didn't want me for some reinforcement," Emmett says to Huxley, dragging my attention back to the conversation.

"Me too." Sebastian grunts, then immediately pours more pear cider into his wife's now-empty glass. "Although I would've done better than everyone here. I don't let anybody fuck me over and get away with it. And if they touch one of us"—he makes a circle with his knife—"they just fucked with the wrong man." The knife stops, pointed at him.

"You think you can do better than that sex tape and L84ANAL?" Noah is skeptical.

"Hell yeah."

"I'll call you next time. Just to see if you can top it," Grant says with a glint in his eyes.

"You're just bitter because you lost the tennis match last weekend."

Grant bristles. "You cheated!" He pretends to look far beyond Sebastian's back. "'Wait... What's Aspen doing with Zack?'" His peeved gaze returns to Seb. "Really, asshole?"

"That's low," Griffin says, then chuckles.

"Were you losing until then?" Huxley asks. Sebastian declines to answer.

Aspen snorts. "I have told you a hundred times, Zack is just a friend," she says to Grant, half exasperated and half amused.

"Exactly. Have more faith in your wife, man." Sebastian shoots Grant a smug grin.

"Still an asshole," Grant mumbles.

Something pings on Noah's phone, and he immediately checks it, then starts scrolling. Bobbi tears a piece of croissant off for him, and he opens his mouth to accept it, his eyes still glued to the screen, then places a quick peck on her retreating fingers. The corners of his eyes crinkle, and she smiles.

"Oh, by the way, your ex resigned," Molly says as though she's just remembered.

"Where did you hear that?" I ask. I haven't followed what happened to Vivienne and Peter that closely.

"Jeremiah mentioned it when I saw her to discuss my lawsuit against my boss."

"Serves him right. He'll never work as a lawyer again. Who could respect him after that small-dick comment from Dad?" Huxley says with evil satisfaction.

"By the way, when is your boss going to jail?" Emmett says, then turns to me. "The guy sexually harassed and assaulted Molly. A bunch of other women, too."

"Wow. What a jerk. I hope he rots in jail forever," I say most sincerely.

Molly wrinkles her nose. "It's a civil suit, so no jail. He wants to settle in exchange for an NDA."

"Ha! Trying to buy your silence. Tell him to go suck it," Grant says.

"Jeremiah will."

"By the way, what does Dad have that I don't?" Noah says mournfully, finally looking up from his phone. "I still can't believe you wanted Dad as your backup for the revenge thing."

"Well, I didn't want to bother any of you," I explain, hating that he's unhappy.

"Still…" Griffin sounds disappointed. Actually, all the brothers look sort of disheartened.

"Next time—if there is a next time—everyone at this table will be first on my list. It's just that Ted's been really kind," I say.

"He isn't too terrible." Lucie bites into another slice of key lime pie. She still hasn't touched the celery sticks on her plate. *Maybe they're garnish…?* No, wait. She puts a glob of the pie on the celery and starts chewing. I have to look away.

"Jesus, that's criminal," Noah says, his face scrunching.

"That's an…interesting mixture of flavors, for sure," Amy says diplomatically.

"The combination is di*vine*. Try it." Lucie scoops up more green pie on the green celery stick and munches happily, completely immune to everyone else's reactions.

"It's the baby," Sebastian says defensively.

"Are you craving anything?" Huxley seems like he wants to will me into craving something bizarre, just so he can bring it to me and tell his brothers it's all cool, I'm just pregnant.

The question makes me blink and realize I haven't had any weird cravings. "Not at all. As a matter of fact, I feel great." I glance down at my plate with its decimated beef and mashed potatoes and the last bite of a roll. "I'm just glad I'm not hankering for tuna and broccoli like Jeremiah."

Grant makes a gagging noise. "Ugh. That's disgusting."

Sebastian's eyes slide to Huxley. "That explains some things."

"Bite me," Huxley mutters, but his eyes twinkle.

I marvel at the affection running through every interaction they have. It's nothing like the meals I was forced to share with Nelson and his family. Not only that, there's so much unspoken thoughtfulness. Huxley hands me more beef, probably because he noticed me gobbling it up. And Bobbi silently pushes the butter closer to me when I pick up a roll. I smile my thanks, and she grins back.

"Wonder what Grandma craved when she was pregnant with Dad," Noah muses out loud.

"Probably bleach," Emmett says.

"Don't be mean. Ted can be nice," Molly speaks up. "He is just a bit, you know…"

"Monomaniacal?"

"Egotistic?"

"Convinced of his own divinity?"

"No," Molly says, "Just a little…outlandish, that's all."

"It's only because you have a terrible father that you think he's acceptable," Nicholas says, then turns to me. "But you must have the worst to call Ted *kind*."

"The *worst*," Huxley says. "He's lucky I didn't kill him."

Sebastian considers. "True. If Roderick had touched Lucie, I would've killed him."

"And I would've been your alibi," Noah says gravely.

The rest of the brothers nod in agreement. They seem like an unbreakable spear and shield for each other—and that protection extends to their women as well. Huxley reaches and squeezes my hand. Abruptly I realize I'm now part of this tight-knit family. Shock shivers through me. I've been alone and defenseless for so long, it's difficult to process.

Still, I lean my head on his strong shoulder and take it all in, feeling lucky and also wishing my life could be like this forever, even though experience has taught me that good things rarely last.

41

GRACE

HUXLEY SENDS me a little bouquet of daisies the next day at the office, giving me a lift amid the foundation's typical morning bustle. The card reads:

A little something to bring a smile to your beautiful face.

–Your devoted husband

Is the message something he came up with, or one of the default options the florist offered? His current attitude is nothing like how harsh he was when he found out that I was Nelson's daughter. Has Huxley realized that I never meant to deceive him and now wants our marriage to work?

I noticed he's trying hard to include me in his family gatherings, too. His efforts have given me a sense of belonging I've missed since Mom became sick. My mind whispers things are just too good to be true. But don't I deserve something good after years of hardship?

Just enjoy it while it lasts.

True. Angsting won't make a difference.

My eyes return to the flowers. They're lovely. So is the sentiment. I pick up my phone and send him a photo of the bouquet.

—Me: Thank you. They're so pretty.

—Huxley: I would've preferred to see a shot of your smile.

He attaches a cartoon brown bear GIF that looks out from the screen soulfully with its forepaws clasped together. I laugh at the unexpectedly sweet response, then snap a selfie and send it to him.

—Huxley: Beautiful.

—Me: The flowers add to my desk.

—Huxley: And you add to my day.

I smile. When he's like this, I really want our marriage to work. I just wish I could be sure that it's on a solid foundation. That, despite the prenup, we will be together, so I don't feel like our future is hidden in some kind of fog.

—Me: I gotta go to a meeting. Talk to you later.

I confirm the final details of the art auction for next week. Everything's all set, all our hard work finally paying off. The proceeds will go to shelters, kitchens, mental health counseling and more for veterans. Elizabeth was horrified to see some recent studies on the bleak situation many veterans face, and she wants to help them get back on their feet and lead productive lives with dignity and pride.

She was a little nervous, since the foundation used to spend its energy on women and children, but she shouldn't have worried. So many people have promised to come. They know she'll use the funds wisely. She doesn't even draw a salary at the foundation, and puts her personal money into paying for a big chunk of employees' salaries and benefits. I asked her once what would happen if she ran out of personal money, but she told me there's plenty, and her financial advisor, Gavin Lloyd, is doing a fabulous job of getting her the return she needs to fund the foundation for as long as necessary.

As soon as I'm done with the checklist, an email from Dr. Blum hits my inbox. I open it immediately.

Your mother's progress is very good. Her fingers twitched when we played your baby's heartbeat. We start every morning that way, and let her know it's her grandbaby. I think it may be giving her the will to wake up. She isn't fully awake yet, but sometimes she taps once or twice with her index finger to indicate yes or no. However, her eyes are still closed. We aren't sure why, but we are now quite optimistic about recovery. I hope you are too. Here are some photos from last week. And she was very fond of the pink orchids you sent because the nurse said she thought she saw your mother smile.

As I read, I put a hand over my mouth. My eyes grow hot with tears, and they fall in rivulets. This is by the far the most positive note from Dr. Blum yet. My heart swells, and I read the email one more time, slowly, to make sure I didn't miss anything the first time.

Mom is making progress.

She will recover.

All the abuse I put up from Nelson and his family was worth it.

"What's wrong?" Tolyan asks, plucking a tissue from his desk and handing it to me with a small frown.

"Nothing. It's my mother. She's doing better." I dab my eyes, then blow my nose. "Excuse me. I need a moment." I stand and head to the elevator. The joy inside my heart is too big to contain, and I simply can't sit still.

What wouldn't I give to be able to fly to visit with Mom right now, but I can't leave with the auction happening so soon. Besides, I'm going to see her soon—her birthday is in a few weeks.

Maybe I'll ask HR if I can extend my time off, so I can spend more time with Mom this year. I'd love to read her the latest romance novels by her favorite authors, and tell her all the ridiculous things Huxley is buying for the baby, like that gold-plated stroller. And the bespoke silk onesies he ordered from his tailor in London!

The stroller was crazy enough, but the onesies are whole another level of madness. I told him as much, and he said, "They're really nice. Why shouldn't our baby have the best?"

She'll find it amusing. And outrageous. But it'll reassure her that I married a generous man, who won't make me or the baby suffer like

Nelson did with her. I'll pick out flowers myself and bring them to her every morning during my visit, too.

Suddenly I want to see Huxley. I want to share the news and thank him for taking over Mom's bills. When she wakes up, it'll be in no small part due to him. Plus, I can't forget him giving me a ride that rainy night two years ago.

It's almost like the universe sent him to help me when I was at my lowest. It sounds so whimsical and superstitious, but what else could it be? I used to think that nothing good happens in life without bad, but maybe that isn't true. Nelson and Karie's bad mojo drove all the positive energy my way.

When I exit out of the elevator to the garage, a figure steps out of the shadows. I yelp and place a hand over my racing heart. "Karie? What are you doing here?"

She's impeccably put together, as usual, although her dress is still too tight and revealing for her age. Her forehead and eyebrows don't move at all—a Botox-induced condition that's gotten worse over the years. "Why aren't you answering my calls and texts?"

"Because I blocked your number after the wedding."

"You *blocked* me?"

"Sure did. I figured, why subject myself to your insults and mistreatment now that my husband has set up a trust to pay for my mother's health care?"

Her expression turns stony. Guess that never occurred to her. She probably thought she would always lord it over me as long as Mom was at Johns Hopkins. After taking a moment to gather herself, she stiffens her spine. "You have to stop with this unjust harassment of Viv."

"Unjust harassment?" I cock an eyebrow.

"All those videos! How could you put fake stuff like that online? We all know the woman isn't her."

"Uh, I walked in on the two of them. In person. It was most definitely Viv."

"Says you."

"The videos show her face. Among other things."

"You faked them! And you'll apologize to her for what you've done!" Karie commands, full of confidence that I'll do as she asks.

I give her a cold look. "Or what?"

"Or—" She stops. She was going to throw Mom's bills in my face, except she just remembered Huxley is now paying for them, not Nelson.

"You know what? You're pathetic, Karie. Simply pathetic. Without money, you're nothing. Even with it, you're not much."

"At least I'm not a whore who slept with another woman's husband," she sneers.

Her words don't even hurt because they aren't true—and she knows it from the way her chin hardens stubbornly. "The same old, same old, huh? Well, creativity was never your strong suit." My back straight and chin up, I rest my hands on my hips. "I'll tell you who the real whores are. One, your disgusting swine of a husband, who seduced my mom, who was over ten years younger than him, without revealing he was married. Think that might make *him* a whore?"

"Nelson had—"

"Think carefully before you answer because it may reveal your misogyny. There's something really ugly about women who go after other women because they don't have the guts to go after the men who are the real culprits. Oh, and also, your precious Viv decided to sleep with Peter, knowing he was my boyfriend at that time. Then she had the audacity to claim that I stole Huxley from her."

"Because you did!"

"We all know that isn't true. If she'd ever slept with him, she would've revealed something about Huxley only somebody who'd been intimate with him would know." Viv never said a word about his piercing. "By the way, you know what's ironic?" I lean forward and smile. "If Viv hadn't stolen Peter, I would've never gone out to that bar that night. Wouldn't have spent the night with Huxley, which means I wouldn't have gotten pregnant with his baby, which means he wouldn't have picked me to be his bride. Guess that's just proof that karma exists."

Karie shakes, her knuckles white. If she thought she could get away with it, she might try to slap me. "You think you've won, but you haven't. You pathetic, ignorant child. You'll be sorry, but no amount of begging will earn you our forgiveness!"

"Ever thought about seeing a therapist? They might be able to prescribe you something to help you see reality more clearly," I say as I walk to my car.

Karie doesn't follow or make a scene, probably due to the security cameras. She wouldn't want me to do to her what I did to Viv.

That woman is delusional to think she has any influence over me now. If she'd shown me kindness when I was alone and without support, I might reconsider. After all, she does love her daughter very much.

Maybe a therapist would also help her understand you have to be good to get rewarded by karma. You always reap what you sow.

I mentally push Karie aside and focus on the amazing report from Dr. Blum. And how awesome it will be to share it with Huxley, so he knows that he's making a huge difference in my life—that he's saving my mother. Maybe we can grab some lunch. It's a little early, but I'm hopeful based on our much-improved interaction over the past few weeks.

Security at 4D lets me in after I show them my ID and sign in. My steps are light as I cross the lobby and walk out of the elevator toward Huxley's office.

Madison stands up from her desk and blocks my path by extending an arm in front of me. The move invades my personal space, and I get a whiff of her floral perfume, which instantly gives me a mild headache.

"Excuse me. You can't go in there."

"Is he in a meeting?" I ask. Maybe I should've texted before coming over.

"His schedule is full. He's a busy man, and people can't just barge into his office to see him without an appointment," she says with a marble-smooth voice. "He isn't at your beck and call."

Her proprietary attitude grates on my nerves like sandpaper. Who does she think she is to talk to me like this? "I never said he was. But he's also my husband, and it's almost lunchtime."

"He's my boss, and I know his schedule and what he has time and energy for." Her gaze sweeps over me as her lips twist into a barely perceptible smirk.

If she'd merely said Huxley was busy, I would've left without a word. But she's picking a fight, as though she has some claim on him. I won't tolerate that from his employees, no matter how long she's been at the company.

"Do you think just because he wanted our wedding theme to be 'Amazing Grace' that you get to disrespect me? I am his wife and the mother of his child." I put a hand over my belly. "He'll make time for me. And if he can't, *you* will find time for me in his schedule."

The smug superiority vanishes from her face. "You can't talk to me like that. I don't work for you."

"No. And you won't work for him for much longer if you keep up with that attitude."

I arch my eyebrow, and she glares at me then steps aside. I walk into his office, only to find it empty. Vague disappointment unfurls, deflating my buoyant heart. Even if I'd texted him, it wouldn't have mattered— his phone sits gleaming on his neatly organized desk.

"Where is he?" I ask.

"Obviously not in his office." Madison's tone is polite, but her eyes glint with smugness. Instead of telling me like she would if I were anybody but his wife, she's opting for passive aggression.

"So you don't know? What a fantastic assistant you are." I shoot her a disdainful smile. "Tell him I stopped by. You can manage that much, can't you?"

Then I turn and leave without waiting for a response. My previously bright mood has darkened. I grab a box of fancy Belgian chocolate on my way back to the office to soothe my annoyance. The indulgence feels good, especially since I haven't been able to buy what I want without worrying about money for so long.

Later that day, Huxley comes home, smelling like Madison's perfume.

42

GRACE

"Do I smell okay?" Huxley asks the next day over breakfast. He showered last night when I told him the scent on him gave me a headache. He seemed surprised that he smelled like anything except his body wash. He showered again this morning before joining me in the eat-in kitchen.

"Yes," I say. "Thank you."

He nods. "It might've been the cigar I had when Ares came by. I'll be more careful."

I smile without correcting him. I think back on the way Madison blocked me yesterday by raising her arm. At that time, it seemed like a casual gesture, but now that I think about it, she lifted her limb in such a way that her wrist would be in my nose.

She's playing a game. Viv's done it too, except with less finesse. Still, that doesn't mean I'm okay with it. Madison's attempt to place a wedge between me and Huxley makes the whole world seem bleak.

"By the way, I don't like Madison."

"Why? Did she do something?"

"She's rude. I don't like the way she speaks to me."

Huxley frowns. "I'll have a talk with her. She's been under a lot of pressure recently with one of our clients being difficult. When they become unreasonable, she has to run interference."

Tension tightens the muscles in my neck and shoulders. "I hate to put it this way, but her stress isn't my problem. Her attitude is. Did she tell you I stopped by yesterday?"

"Yes, she did, and I'm sorry I missed you. I stepped outside to clear my head after an irritating call with that same client. Seeing you would've been much better."

His soothing words mollify me a little. He gets up and rubs my shoulders, and I relax into his touch, enjoying the gentle strokes. "She also acts like she's so much closer to you than me."

"We work closely together, but she won't cross certain boundaries." His tone is firm.

I should let it go, but what happened yesterday and the tinge of her perfume on Huxley from last night still rub me raw. "Won't or can't?"

His hands pause on my shoulders. "Both. Don't you believe me?"

Pettiness doesn't suit me. Neither does clinging to unnecessary resentment and jealousy. It'll only tear me apart. But getting rid of my feelings is easier said than done. I drag air deeply into my lungs, then exhale, imagining all the toxicity from Madison leaving my soul. "I do, but that doesn't mean my trust extends to her as well."

"Like I said, I'll have a talk with her. And I'll get you an assistant of your own, so you won't have to deal with her directly. I should've thought to get you one earlier, somebody to manage all your doctor's appointments and so on, so you can rest when you're here at home."

"Huxley!" I gasp in shock. "I'm not telling you this to get you to hire me an assistant."

"But you must be really busy to not shop for new dresses and stuff."

"I don't want to buy maternity clothes so early, since I don't know how big I'm going to get." I'm not showing as much as I thought. When I texted Dr. Silverman, she said it was normal for first-time moms. "And just to be clear, I didn't contact Madison to have her buy me maternity stuff." As if I'd let someone like her near anything for my baby or pregnancy. After our interaction yesterday, I wouldn't put it past her to sprinkle chicken blood on the baby's pacifier or something.

Huxley pauses, then turns me to look at him. "I'm not talking about that. I'm talking about the art auction hosted by the Pryce Family Foundation."

I stare up at him, nonplussed.

"I'm going," he clarifies.

"Okay... But what does that have to do with my needing to go shopping?"

"You're going to be my plus-one."

"*Me?*" I squeak.

He laughs. "Yes. You're my wife. Who else would be on my arm if not you?"

I gasp. "Oh my God. You're right. I didn't think about that at all." I've never attended a fancy event like the auction. How much longer is it going to take before I get used to the kind of life my husband leads?

He hugs me. "Look. Why don't we shop for jewelry during your lunch break today?"

"Are we going to have enough time?"

"We can eat and shop at the same time. You seem partial to sandwiches. Ham and turkey with Swiss and bacon, right?"

I blink. That's the one I had when Huxley came by the foundation. "You remember everything."

"When it's important."

Hot pleasure sweeps over me. I launch myself at him, hugging him hard, and inhale the amazing scent of forest and spring and him.

He laughs. "I get a hug over remembering what you like on a sandwich?" He squeezes me. "I'll pick you up at a quarter till noon. We'll get you something pretty."

HUXLEY SHOWS up exactly at eleven forty-five at the Pryce Family Foundation and hands me a single bright red rose. "For my beautiful wife."

"Thank you," I say with a smile, feeling the weight of others' eyes as pleasure slowly swirls through me.

"Have fun!" Brenda, one of the assistants, says with a wave and wink.

"Thanks." I turn to Huxley. "So. Where are we going?"

"Sebastian Jewelry, unless you have another place in mind. Seb can be a dick, but he knows gemstones." There's a hint of affection.

"Did he pick out the stones for Lucie?"

"Yup. And believe me, it isn't easy to get something that meets with her approval. Not when it comes to jewelry. Hopefully you'll like something there."

I've never been inside Sebastian Jewelry's flagship store. But then, I never thought I'd be able to afford anything here. From the polished black marble to the textured wallpaper, from the soft, pleasant scent and piano melody in the air, the place exudes old-money elegance and affluence.

As soon as we step inside, a uniformed clerk locks the door and flips the sign over to say, *Closed.* Another one trots toward us, stopping when I lean toward Huxley to have a discreet moment.

"Wait... It's closed?" I whisper.

"To the public. Not to us."

"I don't understand."

"I rented the entire store."

My jaw slackens. "Can you *do* that?" I've only seen it happen in movies.

Huxley shrugs. "Why not? We're family."

Ooh. A special hookup! "Do we get a discount?" I whisper, barely able to suppress my excitement.

He gives me a slightly bemused look. "A discount?"

"You know. A friends and family discount?"

"With Seb?" A snort. "More likely a surcharge."

I gasp. "What?"

"Just kidding." Huxley laughs. "You're so funny about money. You know what the limit is?"

"No..." We didn't discuss a budget.

"This." He pulls out his black AmEx. "You can get whatever you want."

I narrow my eyes, then make a show of scanning the countless sparkling diamonds, emeralds, pearls, sapphires and rubies. "How about everything in the store?"

"Why not?" He turns to the clerk, who is waiting for our signal. "My wife wants everything."

"No!" I smack his shoulder lightly then look at the clerk. "He forgot his medication. Let me look what you have first."

The man smiles. "Certainly. My name is Jared Andersen. This way."

He leads us to a private room complete with a plush love seat and an armchair and a beautiful onyx table. Four trays full of various baubles await my perusal.

"You didn't have to rent the whole store if we were going to be in a private room anyway," I whisper.

"I might've done that if you were just my girlfriend. But you're my wife." He kisses my forehead.

I flush with pleasure at the solemn way he calls me his wife. A sense of belonging ripples through me again, and I lean my head on his shoulder, enjoying the warm solidity of his strong body. He threads his fingers through mine, and I feel like I can walk into any battle with this man by my side.

Another clerk comes forward and places a plate with a ham and turkey sandwich in front of me, along with the pear cider I've become addicted to. Huxley gets a roast beef and Coke.

"Take your time." Huxley's eyes barely flick in the direction of the trays.

"Mmm. Hard to decide. They're all pretty." I look closely at the emeralds while nibbling on the sandwich. The set has earrings and a necklace set in platinum. The square stones are a green so deep, they look like something out of a wild forest. Some associative switch gets thrown in my brain and I'm reminded of Huxley's scent. There's a hint of that annoying floral again, but it's much lighter compared to yesterday and doesn't give me a headache. Madison must've doused herself in perfume to leave some on my husband. I may never understand her motive behind provoking me, but she isn't going to ruin my lunch-slash-shopping date with Huxley.

I resolutely shift my focus back to the jewelry. The diamonds are pretty, too. So are the pearls—flawless, lustrous and large. Both are safer options, classic, and would go well with anything. But somehow my eyes return to the emeralds. Since Huxley wants me to buy a new dress for the auction, I want to get it in purple, since I already have two black dresses. But will green stones work with a purple dress? I narrow my eyes, trying to picture the combination in my head.

Go for the safe option. Diamonds and pearls are the easiest to mix and match.

But I don't want to be safe. I want to be adventurous for once, and not worry about repurposing what I have for later. *Hmmm.* Dilemmas, dilemmas... I can't believe I'm mentally stuck when Huxley already has his black card back out of his wallet. Must be years of living on the edge. I swallow the last bite of the sandwich, wondering which—

"My wife would like the emeralds," Huxley says to Jared.

I start and turn to him. "How...?"

"Easy. You looked at them twice, the second time for a very long time. You pursed your lips and got that faraway look in your eyes. Then you looked at the diamonds and the pearls, but couldn't quit staring at the emeralds, so why not get them?"

I flush, pleased and shy that he was watching so closely and understands me so well. "I was just thinking about matching them with whatever dress I might buy."

"Go for it. Emeralds are surprisingly versatile, at least when the stones are that saturated."

"He's right, Mrs. Lasker. These will go well with whatever ensemble you select for a special occasion."

I smile. "Thanks."

The man leaves with the black AmEx, and Huxley says, "Told you," with a warm smile.

"You sure did." I give him a quick kiss. "Thank you." Then I stand up. "Now that that's done, I have to use the ladies' room. Excuse me." A slim woman comes forward and takes me to a beautifully appointed bathroom with a stack of fluffy cotton towels and toilets that look like the one Huxley has from Japan. But not exactly the same—the ones here don't talk.

I read that as the baby grows in your womb, your bladder can't expand much and you have to hit the bathroom more often. But why am I experiencing that when the baby is still so tiny? I wash my hands and reapply my lipstick. In the mirror is a flushed woman whose eyes are shining with something too intense to be called mere affection. My belly flutters, like right before a rollercoaster is about to drop. Excitement and trepidation entwine around my heart. Somehow, despite our initial friction, I'm much more into Huxley than I ever imagined possible.

I finish up in the bathroom and head out to join my husband. Familiar voices come from the private room, and I shift so I can listen without people inside seeing me.

"Huxley, thank God I caught you," Madison says, breathing hard. "James is here, demanding to see you."

"For what? He isn't supposed to be in town until next week."

"I don't know. He's hysterical."

"Is he ever not?" Huxley mutters in disgust. "Is Miguel in to show him the files?"

"Miguel says he can't pull anything from the cloud, and he's apparently lost all his files...?" Madison makes a small, helpless noise in her throat. "IT is on it, but James says he has to talk to you or else."

"Let me wait for my wife first."

"He doesn't seem to have much patience," Madison adds.

"It's his fault for showing up without making an appointment." Huxley's words couldn't be more terse.

Guess Madison wasn't entirely lying when she said nobody sees Huxley without an appointment. But she didn't chase after him to let him know of my visit, either, unlike with this James fellow.

Pasting on an innocent smile, I step into the room, take my place next to Huxley and give him a kiss. My surreptitious glance at Madison shows her watching us with a stony expression. "Sorry to keep you waiting," I whisper.

"It's nothing." He strokes my back. "All good?"

"Yes."

"They're going to courier the set to the house," he says. "I hate to leave early, but I have a work emergency I can't get out of. Madison will give you a ride back to your office."

"I'd hate to impose. My office is in the opposite direction from yours. I can Uber," I say, not wanting to spend any more time than necessary with his assistant.

"Nonsense." He presses a kiss on my crown. "See you tonight."

I wave, then turn to Madison. "Guess it was quite the emergency." My tone is bland.

"Yes. With an *important* client." Her gaze is insolent as she regards me.

Couldn't have been that *important* if Huxley said he ought to wait, I think as I wait for her to make the next move. This James barging into the office might've been a coincidence, but her acting like it's a huge deal isn't. She wants to interrupt our date and make me feel as insignificant as possible. It might've worked if I hadn't developed such a thick skin, thanks to Karie and Viv.

Madison's phone pings. She glances at the screen and frowns a little. The creases vanish from her forehead as she answers. "I'm surprised you called me so quickly. Yes, of course I understand. Nobody would blame you for leaving." Her eyes slide in my direction, then rest on the diamonds. She nods a few times. "No. I suppose expecting a child you never wanted would make things less tenable. Don't worry. I'll take care of everything. Sure, H. See you soon."

She ends the call and turns to me with a smug expression. I want to claw her eyes out for talking about my baby like it's a bothersome burden, but that's the exact reaction she wants, so I cling to control. When Huxley said he'd talk with her, I thought he'd do so in the morning, when he arrived at the office. Guess he forgot.

She takes my elbow as though to help me up. She smells like the perfume from yesterday.

I pull away from her. The vile scent makes me want to puke in her face. "Nice perfume."

"It's my favorite. Huxley's too." She couldn't sound sweeter.

"Is that so?"

"I could send you a bottle..." She looks at me intently, a corner of her mouth curving in a taunt.

Amusement and irritation sweep over me. She thinks she's so clever, but she's an amateur compared to the kind of crap Karie and Viv often pulled on me. Her plan is so transparent. Figure out a way to get the scent on Huxley and then wait for the fireworks. Actually, she's probably curious as to whether I already exploded and when Huxley would become annoyed with me enough to argue and raise his voice. Or maybe she's curious if he brought me here to smooth my ruffled feathers.

Or... maybe she's hoping I'll lose my temper with her right now and make a scene bad enough to embarrass Huxley. All she has to do is keep that I-didn't-do-anything expression while I verbally berate her.

I maintain my bland façade. "I don't need a bottle to wear the perfume. The scent rubs off on me when Huxley takes me to bed."

She flinches, red suffusing her cheeks. "It doesn't bother you?"

"What? That you want to get fucked by my husband so bad you can't pretend to be a half-decent assistant around me?"

The red on her face turns ugly. Her jaw tightens, and a war wages across her face briefly as she debates her next move. "He and I could be sharing the scent the same way as you."

I smother a laugh. If she'd slept with Huxley, she wouldn't be talking about some perfume. She'd be rhapsodizing about how amazing his piercing feels. "Then why do you look so pinched? A well-fucked woman should be glowing."

She inhales sharply.

"I've tolerated you because my husband says you're a good assistant. If you want me to continue to tolerate you, you'd do well to stop trying to bait me."

"He never wanted you. He'll never like you. The prenup says the baby is his. He'll take it and leave you with nothing. Just because he can."

This jab hits home. In the heat of the moment, I signed the contract without checking it thoroughly, infuriated that he was treating me like some gold digger when he was the one who asked me to be his fake fiancée in the first place. But what if there's something about the baby? I didn't expect him to want it, since back then he was questioning the paternity.

I school myself to hide my reaction. Madison might not know what's in the prenup either, just making a wild guess, hoping it hurts. She won't be getting the satisfaction.

"Nobody crosses him and gets away with it," she adds. "And you entrapping him into a marriage he never wanted? You've crossed the Rubicon."

"I don't give a damn if I crossed the damn galaxy. I'm still his wife, and you're just an assistant with an overblown sense of self-importance."

She falters. *Bet this wasn't what she expected.* She wanted to see me get jealous, pout and stew in insecurity.

"He set up a special trust to pay for my mother's exorbitant medical bills." My eyes flick around the jewelry store before I add in a smooth, in-charge voice, "He rented out this entire place just to buy me something pretty for our next evening out as a couple. He wouldn't have spent a penny if he didn't care about me, and you know it. So keep your mouth shut and drive me to my office like a good little assistant."

DESPITE GETTING the best of Madison in our verbal smackdown, the interaction leaves a bad taste. The warm, effervescent sensation from spending part of my lunch break with Huxley is gone, replaced with irritation and annoyance that I was forced into an unacceptable position because of his continued leniency toward his assistant.

How can he not see she's been panting after him all these years? That she can barely control her hostility toward me now?

It's even more upsetting after his outrageous jealousy over Adam. My friend wasn't anywhere near as obnoxious as Madison. Not to mention, after I asked him for space, he's given it to me.

Now that I think about it, my rebuke to Adam was too harsh. Why should I give up my best friend because of Huxley's unreasonable feelings, when he can't respect my being upset with his obnoxious assistant?

I leave the office a little early, since I'm done with the day's tasks, and head straight home. Huxley gave me a copy of the prenup after I moved, and I shoved it in a drawer in my vanity and never looked at it again.

I read the document with more care this time, my emotions calmer than when I signed it. The agreement says I am not getting a penny of Huxley's money, now or ever, which is fine. It's his money, and I didn't do anything to help him build his fortune.

But there is a small subsection that says the baby's custody will belong solely to Huxley. Madison's words slide into my heart like hot blades. *She was right.*

How could I have missed this? Even if I was upset?

The possibility that Huxley would want to keep the baby didn't really cross my mind. He was furious when I told him about the pregnancy, and my experience with Nelson taught me that men don't want babies they have no emotional investment in. Karie is an important life partner from a proper family that could help Nelson, so the children he had with her mattered. But Mom was just a meaningless fling, and I was an inconvenience he wished had never existed.

But since then, Huxley's attitude has changed. He said that he cares about the baby and me, and he will be present for the life we've created. And his actions have backed that up. He brought home that outlandishly lavish stroller and ordered bespoke onesies. It wouldn't surprise me if hand-stitched baby booties arrived from Italy in the next few months.

I firmly believe what I told Madison. Men like Huxley don't spend money and time on people who don't matter. Our baby and I *are* on his list of priorities. I honestly don't think he's going to divorce me or do anything to hurt me or our child.

But did he feel that even when he had his lawyer draft the prenup? Probably not. He just wanted to take a baby he didn't want to torment me.

I slowly rub my throbbing temples. I shouldn't hold that against him, unless I see evidence that he still plans to do it. But I do hold him accountable for making me feel a chilling uncertainty about my future after he acted like he would like me to consider one with him in it, especially because it's his damned assistant who keeps trying to sow doubt.

He can't claim ignorance, because I already told him about Madison's problematic attitude and conduct. What will it take for him to see what a snake she is and how unfair he's being by indulging her? Frustration mounts as I fume, so I try some breathing exercises. Stress isn't good for the baby.

When Huxley asked me to keep my distance from Adam after the latter crossed the line, I did. My husband ought to show me the same courtesy.

I shove the prenup back into the drawer. He isn't a stupid man. Nor a hypocrite. But when it comes to Madison, he has a giant blind spot, whether out of habit or just the convenience of having a competent assistant.

Maybe I should give him a taste of the kind of disrespect I've been subjected to. After all, people gain better clarity when they're the one suffering.

43

HUXLEY

SOMETHING'S wrong with my wife.

She's been tense since the lunch at Sebastian Jewelry. I thought maybe it was due to my only getting her the emeralds—she might've wanted some diamonds, too—but that doesn't seem to be it. I told Jared to let my wife grab whatever she wanted before leaving.

I arrange for a spa and facial for her before we head to the art auction. Perhaps that will cheer her up. Then I recall how she asked me to start showering in the evening and surreptitiously sniff myself. I only smell the soap from the shower I took earlier. Have I started to smell, somehow? That's...weird. Nobody's ever complained.

"Why are you sniffing yourself?" Emmett asks.

"Just to see if I smell like anything," I say, puffing a cigar to decompress before the art auction.

Sebastian, Emmett, Grant, Nicholas and I are on a large patio, complete with tables and chairs, at the spa where our wives are getting dolled up. We're ready in our tuxedos, but of course the women are taking longer, running late as usual. The place operates in its own time zone because nothing ever ends on time. But Lucie and Molly love it, so here we all are. The things we do for our women.

At least the spa provides free liquor to waiting men.

"It's the cigar," Emmett says, sounding extra superior and all-knowing. "It probably makes her want to puke. Women are sensitive when they're pregnant."

"I don't smoke cigars at work."

"What?" Nicholas says.

"Grace has been asking me to shower every evening," I explain. "I think she's upset about something, but not sure what."

"You could just ask," Grant says.

I scowl. "I don't have to ask. She said she doesn't like the way I smell after work." She's also shown an exceptional interest in the kind of projects I'm managing, especially with Madison. If she'd shown any hint of being bored or tired with her employment at the foundation, I might think she wanted to work at 4D.

"If you'd bought her some extra jewelry on top of those emeralds, she wouldn't have noticed your old-man smell," Sebastian says.

"Right. Because that's what all women want," I say sarcastically.

"Some want books more," Nicholas says.

Seb sips his Dom. "Embed diamonds on the covers and she'll want them more."

"Amy loves diamonds, but she prefers to wear them," Emmett says. "But I really doubt Grace is upset over emeralds, unless they were small and cheap."

"Sebastian Jewelry doesn't do small and cheap," Seb says.

"Maybe she got upset because the shopping was cut short," I say, thinking out loud. "I should've driven her back to her office instead of Madison."

Grant winces. "You had *Madison* drive her?"

"Of course. Why?"

"Unless Grace is blind, she knows Madison has the hots for you."

Here we go again. "How many times do I have to say it? She does not. Even if she did, she's too professional to show it."

Emmett shakes his head. "You're blind when it comes to her. She looks at you like a guy she wants to screw."

"On the floor..." Nicholas says.

"Or the desk..." Grant says.

"Or that comfy couch you have in your office..." Sebastian suggests.

I wave them away, exasperated. "Don't be ridiculous. I already talked with Madison."

"This ought to be good," Emmett says, leaning forward.

"She said there's nothing, but promised to be more careful about her interactions with my wife. She also told me it's possible Grace is unhappy with her because she's been too busy to help Grace with managing her schedule."

Sebastian gives me a look. "You're an idiot."

Grant shrugs. "Just get a male assistant. Problem solved."

"Or get one as incompetent as Marjorie so nobody could ever believe you'd fall for her." Marjorie is Emmett's most worthless assistant. I don't know how he puts up with her, but he does. Probably too busy to hire a new one to replace her, since he has to do his work and half of hers.

"I'm not entertaining your ridiculous idea." I finish my cigar.

One of the receptionists sticks her head into the patio. "Thank you for your patience. The ladies are ready."

Soon the double doors open, and our women walk toward us. I start to step forward with a grin, then falter. The subtle makeup on Grace brings out the high cheekbones and the blue of her wide, expressive eyes. Her dark hair is curled and twisted into a soft updo with wisps framing her beautiful face. The deep royal-purple dress with a side slit wraps around her body like a lover's embrace, but the stones glittering from her ears and around her throat aren't emeralds. They're red garnets set in what appears to be silver.

Sebastian notices too and gives me a slight shake of his head. *Not my inventory.*

Of course not. The stones aren't the best, and the setting is okay, but not exceptional. You could purchase them from any mid-tier department store.

"Where are your emeralds?" I ask, without showing any signs of judgment. It's possible the garnets are from her mother, therefore sentimental and important to my wife.

"At home." Her gentle fingertips brush over the reddish stones. "I just thought these would be better today." The words are slow and measured. She flicks her eyes at my brothers and their wives, then presses her lips together. She wants to say more, but in private. Perhaps there's a story behind the jewelry that she only feels comfortable sharing with me.

I squeeze her hand tenderly to signal I get the underlying meaning: sentimental pieces. The initial disappointment wanes. I would've loved to see the jewelry I bought on her, but what does it matter? She's more breathtaking than I could've imagined for our first social gathering as a married couple.

I kiss her, careful not to smudge her cherry-red lipstick. "You look good enough to devour," I whisper into her ear.

"Maybe after the auction," she whispers back. "*If* you're good."

I laugh. "Is there something you want?"

She gives me a sidelong glance, her lashes lowered, her pretty mouth pursed in thought. "What if there is? Will you get it for me?"

"Of course. What's the point of having a rich husband if he can't get you what you want?"

She lifts her eyes, and there's a ghost of a smile on her lips. "Okay. I'll let you know."

FOR A CHARITY AUCTION, this event sure drips with money—the white-cloth-covered seats and tables, the glitzy, tuxedoed quartets and the liveried staff circulating around. Balanced on the staff's hands are trays laden with fancy canapes made with the finest cheese, caviar, cream and crackers, as well as flutes bubbling with priceless champagnes, both golden and rose.

But then, people won't open their pockets if they don't think the occasion is special enough. You have to make people *feel* wealthy in order for them to loosen the fists around their money.

I keep my hand at Grace's elbow as we walk further inside. Many of the guests here came to our wedding. Their avid gazes follow us; clearly they're curious how our marriage is going after such an unconventional ceremony. They want to decide if they should ingratiate themselves with Grace, or subtly snub her.

Grace meets their eyes with her chin held high, a small smile on her lips never faltering, like a queen facing down her subjects. My chest puffs with pride at how well she's handling herself.

Elizabeth comes over, dressed in a chic ivory dress and emeralds. She's one of a few in the city who set the fashion trends for the old-money elites. The sight of the green stones reminds of the stones I bought...but Grace left at home.

"Welcome. So good to see you. You look amazing! Both of you!" She hugs me and Grace, giving us air kisses. "Marriage suits you. And I love your necklace. So cute!"

"Thank you," Grace says. I wait, hoping she'll say more—maybe how it came from her mother, but she doesn't add anything.

"You did an amazing job," Elizabeth says before turning to me. "Your wife is a woman of tremendous talent. You should be proud."

"I am." I smile. Elizabeth never says anything negative, but she also doesn't give empty praise.

"Please enjoy yourselves, and I hope you find something you like tonight."

"I'm sure I will," I say.

She fleets away to greet another guest. I stop a waiter for a glass of ginger ale for Grace. As the man leaves, my eyes collide with...

What the hell? Is that *Adam*?

I squint. The sandy hair, the slightly gloomy look in his eyes—probably from losing the woman he wants to another man—and the pale complexion from spending endless hours in the office without any time off. *Yup, it's him.* He's in a tuxedo, his hair slicked back, sipping champagne. If his eyes weren't constantly scanning the crowd, and his foot weren't tapping the floor in anxiety, he might look like he fit in.

He abruptly turns and walks behind a crowd of men and women chatting and laughing. *What is he doing here?* He doesn't make enough to be let in. Not on the associate's salary he earns from Huxley & Webber.

I turn to speak to Grace...but she's gone.

44

GRACE

PULLING Huxley's head out of his butt is much easier said than done. I was going to tell him about the garnets when he asked me about the emeralds, but his brothers and their wives were around. It would've been too much drama to get into it in front of them, especially since they probably have no clue about my conflict with Madison. I prefer to keep that private between me and Huxley. After all, I only want him to realize Madison's not as innocent as she pretends, not embarrass him in front of his family.

He hasn't brought up the emeralds again, and he acts like nothing's wrong. I feel foolish as I stand in the ballroom with his hand at my elbow. How do I casually bring them up? After we're home, maybe?

I can ask him to help with the necklace clasp and segue into it, mentioning Adam gave me the garnets. Huxley definitely won't react well. Then I will—as calmly as possible—compare the way he feels to the way I've felt every time he's come home with a whiff of Madison's nauseating perfume over the last few days.

I asked him to shower each night, and he's done so without a word. But how could he not know he smells like his assistant when she must be rubbing herself all over him or something to leave her scent on him?

The only reason I haven't exploded already is that I trust that

Huxley isn't cheating. He not only declared I was his, but he was adamant that *he* was *mine*, too. And showed it to me in the rawest way possible.

Besides, if he were screwing Madison, he wouldn't be dumb enough to come home without taking a shower first to erase her scent or any makeup she might've left on his skin. But that doesn't mean it doesn't grate on my nerves. He's a smart man. How can he not realize what she's doing? Not even my verbal smackdown at Sebastian Jewelry has put a stop to her behavior. If it had, he wouldn't have come home smelling like her perfume in her transparent attempt to sow discord.

I don't want to come across as a nagging or whiny wife by continuing to bring up my issue with Madison when Huxley seems determined to keep his head stuck in the sand. But damn it, I *am* his wife—with certain rights and expectations.

After I give him the taste of what I've been feeling the last few days, I'll make my case that he should get rid of Madison—or at least not work with her so closely if she's too good to just dismiss outright. I deserve that much consideration from my husband.

Huxley goes to get me something to drink. Fortunately, I've made sure to have some nonalcoholic beverages at the auction.

There is a huge blue and green abstract painting to my left titled *Somewhere Between Dusk and Dawn*. In between the two colors is a sliver of fiery golden orange, and I love the contrast and the brush strokes that give the upper part a fluffy feel and the bottom part a rough, grassy appearance. The artist—Lynn—is the younger sister of the guitarist from the popular band Axelrod, and for some reason I thought her work would be grungy or something. I follow the wall, looking at some of her other paintings.

"You were looking at *Somewhere Between Dusk and Dawn* for a while. Want me to buy it for you?"

I turn around in surprise. "Adam!"

"Hey, GG. Long time no see."

I stare at him, take in the still-friendly eyes and bright smile that are without a hint of awkwardness or resentment. Happy relief tugs at my heart. What happened on the wedding night must've been just a drunk aberration. It's like the disagreement we had never happened, and he's still my good friend. "I missed you."

"Missed you too," he says softly. His downcast eyes make him look shy and boyish at the same time. "So I guess I'm forgiven?"

I give him a quick hug. "I was upset. But I didn't mean we shouldn't be friends anymore. I'm sorry if you thought that."

He sighs, patting my back, then lets go slowly.

"So..." I notice the well-fitted tuxedo on him. "Are you here with someone?" He's from a middle-class family, and he doesn't have the money to throw around at an auction like this. If he were a donor or somebody who might be invited to participate, his name would've been on the list I triple-checked over the last several days.

"Nope. Here on my own." He reaches out and holds my hand, the motion deliberate and gentle, as though he's afraid of frightening me. "I'm not poor anymore," he blurts out. The tips of his ears turn red.

"What?"

"GG, I finally won!"

"Won what?" But as soon as the question is out of my mouth, I know.

"The lottery! Five hundred million dollars."

I stop for a second, trying to process and figure out if he's joking. But his expression remains sober. My jaw drops. "Are you *serious*? Oh my *God*! That's amazing! I've never met somebody who's won the lottery before. Congratulations!" I hug him, thrilled at his good fortune. He's one of the nicest people in the world, and he deserves this kind of karmic reward.

"Thank you."

"Wow." I cover my mouth with my hands. I always thought Adam buying lottery tickets was amusing and interesting—that someone as rational as he is would spend money on something so unlikely—but he beat the odds to be one out of hundreds of millions. "Xander must be over the moon," I say.

Adam frowns. "Xander?"

"Oh. Aren't you guys still dating?" Then I realize I haven't seen Xander in almost a year.

Adam looks at me like I just told him a Martian spaceship just landed in the middle of Los Angeles. "*Dating*? He's not my boyfriend."

"But... Remember when his ex got really weird and aggressive? You got in his face and told him to get lost because Xander was with you now."

"Well, *Xander's* gay, yeah. But I was just helping him out. His ex is a little crazy, and Xan was worried. But he and I are just good friends." When I continue to stare, he adds, "GG, I'm not gay."

I just blink. And my mind starts to whisper, *Huxley was right, Huxley was right, Huxley was right.*

A frown still on his face, Adam continues, "You only married that man because of your mother's medical bills. Well, now I can take care of you and your mother, all that," he says earnestly. "Everything I have will be yours."

My heart jumps to my throat at the bright fervor in his gaze. He can't possibly be saying what I think he's saying—

He reaches out and takes my hand. "Divorce Huxley Lasker and marry me. I've always loved you, GG. You're the only one for me."

His proposal and declaration hit me like wrecking balls, one after another. They must've dislodged a gear in my head, because nothing's turning.

"You never cared for him, did you?" Adam asks earnestly. He tightens his grip on my hand, as though to squeeze out an answer. "You shouldn't be with a guy you can't stand. I'll be good to you and raise your baby like it was mine."

I open my mouth, but nothing comes out. Instead, my face overheats, and I realize tears are gathering in my eyes. They're composed of something between sorrow, regret, pain and affection. I love Adam, but it isn't romantic love. Marrying him would be like marrying a brother. Adam is a great guy and deserves a woman who can love him and wants to make him as happy as he makes her. "I—"

"Five hundred million is a *lot* of money, even after taxes." He says it faster, with more force, as though afraid of rejection and its implication on our friendship. "You'll never lack for anything. I swear. I'll buy you another necklace, much better than the one you're wearing."

"Adam." My voice cracks as I struggle to find the right words. I don't want to hurt him, but I don't know what to do or say. Helplessness overwhelms me, and I wish I could stop time and take a moment to think and pull myself together. "I'm so touched—"

"Five hundred million after taxes would be less than two hundred, not enough to attract a trophy wife as pretty as Grace," cuts in Huxley's frigid voice.

Shit. I blink away the tears and turn to him. But he isn't looking at me. His entire focus is on Adam, his feet shoulder width apart and jaw tight. Every line in his body vibrates with barely leashed violence. Once he's finished with Adam, he'll deal with me.

I wanted Huxley to feel the kind of anger Madison aroused in me. But not like this. The focus needs to be about our relationship—not a proposal from a third party that pushes Huxley beyond reason.

"Maybe in your shallow world." Adam tilts his chin, not to be cowed. "But GG values more than money in a man, and let's face it— that's all that you can offer."

Huxley's mouth twists into an ugly line. "You've come sniffing around my wife one too many times. I can only tolerate your insolence for so long. Do you think winning the lottery makes you somebody?" He scoffs. "You'll always be a loser with no balls. You know deep down that you have nothing to offer Grace, which is why you bought *lotto tickets*. For fuck's sake, how pathetic do you have to be?"

He suddenly grabs my necklace with both hands, pulls hard until the silver chain snaps and throws it on the floor. I gasp in shock. The red stones scatter like dull pennies.

"My wife doesn't wear jewelry from another man. The best you can hope to offer is a cheap necklace—or another like it. No amount of money is going to change that."

Adam turns white, then suddenly blood rushes to his face right before he lunges at Huxley, swinging his fists. Huxley shifts to evade the attack, then knees him in the belly. Gasping, Adam clutches his stomach and collapses.

"Stop it! Both of you!" I cry out, stepping closer to the two men. They aren't just creating a scene—they're ruining the charity auction.

Instead of quitting, Adam lunges up, swinging blindly.

"Careful!" Huxley shouts, pulling me back just in time.

Adam's fist arcs right past my belly. My heart leaps to my throat. A billion beats a minute thunder in my head. I wrap my hands around myself protectively, fear gushing through me. My knees shake, then give out as what could've happened if Huxley had been even a second too slow flashes through my mind. He pulls me tight, holding me and putting his body between me and Adam to shield the baby.

"Are you all right?" Concern and fury vibrate through his taut voice.

I nod, still too jittery to speak.

"Oh my God..." Adam says unsteadily, his face turning ghostly white. "I'm so sorry."

"If you're sorry, get the fuck out of our lives," Huxley grinds out.

Adam's eyes flick to me. Maybe he's looking for my forgiveness or reassurance. But I'm too shaken to figure out which, and I'm not okay with the way he threw the first punch at Huxley, even if my husband did taunt him. Adam is a lawyer. Surely he could've figured out some way to respond without resorting to violence.

When I say nothing, something in his gaze dies a little. Then he walks away, cutting through the rising murmurs around us.

Huxley holds me tighter. Then he says, "We need to talk."

45

GRACE

"WHAT THE HELL WAS THAT ABOUT?" Huxley demands as soon as we're in one of the private rooms set aside for guests who might need to rest. "'Divorce him and marry me. I've always loved you, GG. You're the only one for me. You never cared for Huxley Lasker, did you?'" he sneers. "What a *touching* display of affection. How would you have responded to him if I hadn't been there?"

The rein on his temper is gone. I do my best to keep my cool even though frustration burns in my chest so hard, it's painful to draw in air. I only wanted to show how irritating and upsetting it is to have my concerns not taken seriously enough. Instead, Adam proposed and created an unnecessary drama for me to handle. "It wasn't me, just him," I say in a calm enough voice.

The veins in Huxley's forehead visibly pulse. "Don't treat me like an idiot, Grace. You planned this auction. You knew he was going to be here."

"I was just as shocked as you were at seeing him. There are other people putting the auction together at the foundation. He could've gotten an invitation through one of them."

"*Riiiiight.* That's why you were conveniently wearing his jewelry." Huxley's eyes burn with rage as they rake over me.

"I only wore it to show you how infuriating it is to have you ignore me!"

"I *ignored* you?" He glares at me like I just backhanded him. "I bought you emeralds specifically to match your dress! *You* encouraged him by putting on the garnets!"

There's no talking to him. He's so hung up on the jewelry, like that's the sole problem between us. Old bitterness boils over. "Just the way you encourage Madison by brushing away my concerns!"

"I didn't encourage her!" he shoots back. "I spoke to her more than once, and she promised to address your concerns."

Is he kidding me? "Then why does she insist on being rude to me? Or challenging me? Or implying that she's having an inappropriate relationship with you?"

"What?" He just looks dumbfounded. How ridiculous. If he'd spoken to her, he would know the big parts of her transgressions. Him playing dumb only stokes my anger.

If he's going to act innocent, I'm going to list everything she's done that's pissed me off, including the ones I never told him about because they seemed so small and petty. Maybe one of them will jostle his memory or make him realize how horrible his vaunted assistant is.

"When she insisted you wanted 'Amazing Grace' to be the theme of our wedding—"

"*She* told *you*?"

I ignore his outburst and continue, "—I thought, *Okay, he's upset over the situation, so I'll just go along with it.* When she told me it was *your* wish to have white chrysanthemums rather than the roses I wanted because chrysanthemums symbolize the Emperor of Japan, I also went along because you said you were busy in London and I didn't want to argue."

He looks at me like I just sprouted a cucumber out of my forehead. "I *was* busy, but why would I want anything to do with the Emperor of Japan?"

I shrug. "Beats me. Maybe because your aunt is Asian? You would have to ask your precious, perfect Madison."

His eyes narrow at my sarcastic tone, but I'm past caring. The rational, calm speeches I've prepared are mentally ripped into pieces and thrown up in the air. All that's left behind is seething resentment and fury at the utter disrespect I've received.

"Then she wanted to advise me on what to wear to the wedding. So I told her to stay the hell away because no way in hell I was letting her put me in a literal potato sack, saying it was what *you* really wanted. Then I picked a black dress because it seemed fitting, given how you wanted to rub it in my face that this marriage wasn't going to last."

"Grace—"

I lift a finger. *"I'm not finished.* That isn't all that she did. She then refused to let me see you when I went over around lunch break on the day you sent me daisies. She said you were too busy and important, and a mere wife wasn't entitled to your time, unless I made an appointment first."

"What the fuck?"

"Then she made sure I would smell her perfume, and you came home that night wearing the same scent. Tell me: what was I supposed to think at that point?"

46

HUXLEY

THE QUESTION SLAPS ME. *I smelled like what?*

My instinct kicks in, saying that isn't the important part. "I didn't cheat on you."

"What would you think if I came home from work smelling like another man?" Grace's voice shakes with pent-up anger and frustration.

I'd lose it. Demand to know why she has another man's scent all over her. Suspect that even if she hadn't slept with him, she probably did something she shouldn't have. But nothing happened with Madison. I worked, then came home. End of story. "I didn't sleep with Madison," I say firmly, a hint of plea in my tone, needing her to believe me. "The only woman in my life since that night at the Aylster has been you."

Grace makes a neutral sound in her throat. "On the day when you had to rush back to the office because she interrupted our time at Sebastian Jewelry, she got a call from someone. She said to the caller that she understood expecting a child he never wanted could make things difficult and that she would take care of everything."

Does Grace think *I* called Madison to say shit about her and our baby? I'm both sad and pissed off that I haven't done enough to earn her trust and she jumped to the worst conclusion possible. "I didn't call her after I left Sebastian Jewelry."

"Maybe so. But she called the person 'H.' Like Huxley."

"It could've been Harold or Henry." I toss out two of the clients we've worked with, but my explanation sounds feeble, even to my own ears.

"Then she offered to send me a bottle of her perfume. Her favorite, she said. And yours, too."

Just what the hell has Madison been doing behind my back? She doesn't even wear perfume! "I don't give a shit about women's perfume, unless it's on you."

Grace continues as though she hasn't heard me. "I told her it wasn't necessary, since the scent rubs on me when you take me to bed. You should've seen her face."

Under any other circumstances, I might laugh at her comeback. But I've been set up by the one person I never thought would betray me.

Fucking Madison.

How dare she backstab me? She's undermined all my efforts to show Grace we could have a future together. When I spoke to her about Grace's disapproval, she immediately apologized, acting innocent and claiming miscommunication. I believed her. I thought perhaps Grace and Madison didn't get along due to some incompatibility in their personalities. Grace is rational and gentle, with an ability to laugh no matter how absurd and difficult her circumstances are. Meanwhile, Madison is driven, somewhat impatient and loathes imperfection or delays.

But this isn't mere miscommunication or personality conflict. The examples Grace brings up are too specific. People who lie or exaggerate opt for generalities.

Abruptly I realize it was Madison who always responded to my talk regarding Grace's concern with sweeping statements. My stomach sinks. *Shit.* How could I have not noticed sooner?

"But then you know what she said?" Grace continues. "She told me you and she could be sharing the scent the same way."

Grace's words are like gasoline over an already-raging fire. "That bitch. Grace, I swear—"

She raises a hand to stop me. "Maybe she couldn't stand being goaded. She also added you never wanted me and you'll never like me.

You'll take my baby from me and leave me with nothing just because you can. 'Nobody crosses him and gets away with it. And you entrapping him into a marriage he never wanted? You've crossed the Rubicon,' is what she said. Precisely, *exactly* what she said."

I'm going to murder her. "Grace, I would never do such a thing—"

"I wasn't sure what to believe—"

"I told you I'll be a good father to our baby. What kind of monster deprives it of its mother? Not even mine did that!"

Grace's blue eyes darken with old pain and anger. "I don't know. Maybe the kind who told me not to bother him when I texted him about the OB-GYN to hear the baby's heartbeat because he was too busy with more important things?"

"What?" I stiffen at the unfairness of her statement. "I've never done that. You never texted me about an appointment. I had to hear about it from that fucking Adam!" Despite my intentions, my voice rises. Even back then when I was upset with her, I wouldn't have been so callous about the baby. Whether it was conceived in love or not, whether it was planned or not, it deserves the best I can provide.

"I can't believe you forgot what you said."

"*I didn't say it.* I would never say that. Grace—"

She pulls out her phone and scrolls around then gives it to me. "Read it."

I do, and can't believe my eyes. *My phone had to have been hacked,* I think, but except for the appointment response, all the other texts are ones I sent. "I don't know what happened," I say hoarsely. "But it wasn't me. I promise."

Perhaps the desperation in my plea sounds genuine to my wife. Her expression softens a bit. "You told me Madison is a good assistant and under a lot of pressure and stress. Then why is she expending so much energy on putting a wedge between us?"

All my brothers' and cousins' teasing that Madison has the hots for me pop into my head. As do memories of me confidently rebuffing them because I thought they were just giving me shit over nothing.

It's true she's been the best assistant I've ever had. She always knows what I want without my having to spell it out. The only real mistake she made was the paperwork snafu in London, which almost made me miss my wedding...

Or was it really a mistake?

"I didn't get into the specifics of her argument with me at the jewelry store because I know you didn't sleep with her, contrary to what she tried to make me believe. If you were sleeping with her, you would've been more careful." Grace sighs wearily. "I'd prefer that she not work at your agency, but I also understand that you don't want to lose a good employee who's been with you for a long time. I can compromise and wouldn't mind if she didn't work so closely with you. But then you kept coming home smelling like her perfume, which started to piss me off more and more."

Jesus. Then it hits me—why Grace asked me to shower the last several evenings. And why she asked me about what I was working on, specifically with Madison.

"I didn't want to sound like a nagging, suspicious wife, especially when you said you'd speak to Madison about my concerns. My acting annoyingly paranoid is exactly what she would want, because that would cause cracks that might become more serious in our marriage. But I still couldn't understand just what you were doing together during the day to come home smelling like that." Pain fleets through her beautiful eyes. "Whether you're sleeping with her or not isn't important. I shouldn't have to tolerate it. I'm your wife, Huxley."

She looks at me, and I feel like a knife is digging into my gut. "No, you shouldn't." I take her hand and rest my forehead on the back of it. Gratitude, relief and fury whirl through me, one after the other. I swallow an odd lump in my throat at her generosity and forgiveness. "I'm sorry you had to bear that, and thank you for your faith in me."

I kiss the soft skin on the back of her hand, then each of her knuckles. Then I raise my head and reach for my phone.

–Me: I need you at the auction immediately. Come to the Presidential Suite when you arrive. The concierge should give you a key.

Then I send an instruction to the IT team at the agency and ask the concierge to let my assistant up when she arrives. "Do you need anything?" I ask Grace. "Something to drink, maybe?"

She thinks for a moment. "I'm a little hungry. I haven't really eaten anything since lunch. Maybe some pear cider and chocolate cake?"

I frown at her choice. "Shouldn't you get something more nutritious if you haven't had any real food since lunch?"

"If you insist that I pair my cake with celery sticks, I'm leaving you."

Despite the tension in my gut, I chuckle. I realize no matter the circumstances or what kind of mood I'm in, Grace has the ability to make me laugh. I wouldn't have slept with her that first time if she hadn't been able to brighten my shitty evening with humor.

I ask for a slice of double chocolate lava cake and a couple bottles of the pear cider. When the order arrives, she takes a forkful of cake to her mouth and closes her eyes. "This is life. I almost feel human again."

"After just one bite?"

"It's the superpower of chocolate."

Knocks. The door opens before I can answer, and Madison walks in, her strappy stilettos hitting the floor. Her unbound hair curls around her shoulders, her eye makeup smoky and lips cherry red. The dress she has on is cut low, but the skirt reaches two inches above her knees. Not exactly professional, but not something I can find fault with if she says she was out with friends.

She comes to a halt when she notices Grace. Then she looks at me, smiles and comes forward until she stands one and a half steps away from my side. "Good evening, Huxley. And you too, Grace. You both look very nice," Madison says, all professional and proper.

I sniff, trying to get a whiff of her perfume, but all I can smell is soap and some generic fragrance from her cosmetics and lotion. Is my nose that insensitive? Just to be sure, I sniff again and cock my head. Grace takes another big bite of her cake, then raises her eyebrows at me and shrugs. I guess she's not smelling it either.

Then it hits me. *The perfume campaign we've been working on.* The client sent us boxes of the new perfume to "help inspire us," and many of the female staff used it, saying how lovely and floral it was. I personally don't care for it that much—not my kind of fragrance—but I never said anything, since my nose became numb to it soon enough and I quit noticing.

Madison was one of the women in the office who fell in love with it, and she sprayed it around her desk more or less every day when I walked by. Was it so she could plant a seed of doubt into my wife's heart? If Grace hadn't had faith in me, she would've tormented herself thinking I was cheating on her. After all, it isn't as though she has a better role model in life to believe otherwise.

"Is there anything I can do for you, Huxley?" Madison's voice is smooth, but uncertainty flickers in her gaze.

"You're terminated, effective immediately," I state flatly. I feel the weight of my wife's surprised gaze on my face. "Collect your things on Monday. You're locked out of the agency network, so don't even think about grabbing anything there."

"What?" Madison takes a stunned step back, then stiffens. "Why are you doing this?"

"I've warned you more than once, but you've overstepped your boundaries."

She clenches her hands. "I didn't do anything!" She is speaking to me, but her glittering eyes are on Grace, who calmly polishes off her chocolate cake. Madison doesn't seem to realize her reaction has betrayed her guilt.

"Didn't you? Spraying me with your 'favorite perfume' isn't your latest bullshit?"

A sickly pallor replaces the color in Madison's face. She understands I'm too calm to be trusted. "I overheard you talking to Bryce!"

I give her a look. "Just to be clear—are you admitting to eavesdropping on a conversation with my attorney held in my office, behind closed doors?"

She flinches, obviously realizing her error. "I just wanted to understand you better so I could do a good job. Come on. We've known each other for so long. Longer than her."

"It's only because we've been working together for so long that you were able to fool me, undermine my marriage and hurt my wife." I despise her for abusing my trust.

"You aren't going to give me a chance to explain?" It's comical how aggrieved she sounds.

"I don't give traitors a chance to take another swing at my wife." The possibility of Madison coming after me doesn't bother me, but the notion that she might attack my wife? All bets are off.

Madison takes a step toward me, her arms coming up. "Huxley—"

"Come any closer and I'll have security throw you out."

Her already-pale face turns even more bloodless. She sways a little. I hope she doesn't faint. She might crack her head open on the oak table behind her, and housekeeping will be annoyed if they have to get a bloodstain out of the ivory carpet.

"Get out," I snap.

She turns to Grace beseechingly, but my wife is too busy quenching her thirst with the bubbling cider. If she weren't pregnant, she would be chugging down a flute of Dom.

Defeat finally enters Madison's gaze as it dawns on her there will be no mercy from Grace, either. She stumbles out, the door closing with a click behind her.

"So. She never gets to make excuses?" Grace says. "Try to tell her side of the story, so you can verify who's being honest and who's overreacting or whatever?"

"Trust should be repaid with trust. You trusted that I didn't betray you with Madison despite all the signs that could have pointed to that. Also, I figured out why I smelled like the perfume and didn't notice."

"I'm all ears."

I tell her about the campaign the agency is working on. "She took advantage of the situation, and I cannot forgive that."

"You aren't going to sue her or anything, are you?" Grace looks slightly anxious. "I just don't want her around us, not punished excessively."

"If she leaves quietly, I won't do anything." I almost wish Madison *would* make a fuss, but she knows me well enough to realize my next step wouldn't just leave her jobless, but professionally ruined. I hold Grace, smell the chocolate on her breath. "Is there anything else you want to tell me? Any doubts? No matter how small, I'd like to know."

"Well." She clears her throat, resting her head on my shoulder. "The prenup said the baby belongs to you and you only." Her hand drops to her slightly rounded belly.

"It's the custody arrangement in case we get divorced," I explain, wincing inwardly and wishing I hadn't been such a dick back then. "When I had Bryce draft it, I was so angry, I put that in there to hurt you. But now...it's a moot point."

She smiles. "So we're on the same page about staying together?"

"We are. But when your mother wakes up..." I pause and try to think of an elegant way to word it, so I don't come across as though I'm urging her to abandon her mother or withhold what her mother deserves. "Am I still part of your future?"

Grace shifts, turning around to look at me. "Of course."

"But Montana—"

She stops me with a quick kiss. "Okay, let me tell you about Montana. I've held on to that same vision for forever, even before Mom became sick. She loves nature, and I always felt like she might be happier away from here. I'm sorry if I made you feel like you weren't included in my future. I never really considered revising my idea for my life because it just felt so...automatic, almost out of reflex. I want to—"

I put a finger over her mouth, not wanting her to say anything in the moment that she'll regret later. "You shouldn't come up with something on the spot just to soothe my anxiety without giving it the consideration and time you need. I can't be happy without you, but I also can't be happy if you aren't happy. So you take your time. I can wait."

47

HUXLEY

WHAT I HATE most in life is doing the right thing, only to have it kick me in the teeth. I almost wish I hadn't stopped Grace when she opened her mouth to speak last weekend. Then I'd at least know what her first, unfiltered impulse might've been.

Now she's thinking. She hasn't given me a single hint as to where her thoughts are headed, and I can't ask because I told her I'd wait. Who would've thought my patience was so limited?

But I don't dare rush her. Our future is a serious matter, and requires serious consideration.

"Your coffee, and the documents you asked for." Claude, my new assistant, places a cup of fresh java and the old posters and spreads from The Origin campaigns spanning two decades. The new client apparently doesn't believe in digital copies, only paper.

"Thanks."

He smiles and returns to the desk that used to be occupied by Madison. Claude is young and without a lot of experience, but that works to his advantage, since he doesn't have any bad habits from previous employment. I can train and mold him into the perfect assistant. The kid works hard and he's smart. If he shows creative talent, I might later move him to another division. Madison would've had the same opportunity to advance if she hadn't said she didn't have a single creative bone in her body.

My phone rings with a call from my accountant. *What's this about?* He never calls unless it's important.

"Hello, Earl," I say.

"Good afternoon, Huxley." His mild voice is almost a cliché for a proper professor or accountant. He always greets me with good morning or good afternoon, even though whatever he's about to say is going to turn the day into a shit-fest. "I'm calling because I've observed some, ah, irregularities with the trust you set up for your mother-in-law's care at Johns Hopkins."

I sit up straight, a tight knot in my gut. The care Grace's mother's getting at Johns Hopkins is too important. "What irregularities?"

"The invoices are suspect. The address and the invoice numbers seem off. I noticed because my own mother-in-law was also at Johns Hopkins for a stroke."

"So? Call and fix them," I say, irritated that he spiked my anxiety for nothing.

"That's the thing. Every time I call the number on the invoice, it sends me to voicemail, saying everyone's busy. And nobody ever gets back to me, even though I've left detailed messages each time. So I finally called the main number I got off their website. Guess what? There's no patient under the name of Winona Lain."

"*What?*" The moment stretches as my heartbeat accelerates. *What the hell...* Did Nelson take Winona out of the hospital and install her elsewhere? No, that doesn't make sense. Grace would've known. "Are they sure?"

"That's what I asked. I told the young lady on the phone she must be mistaken, because I have outstanding invoices for a patient named Winona Lain." He lets out a long, slow breath. "But she said as far as their computer records show, the last time Dr. Blum saw Winona was a year ago."

48

GRACE

AFTER THE LONG AFTERNOON MEETING, I finally get a little break to check emails. There. I smile when the latest update from Dr. Blum pops up.

I'm happy to report that your mother has made some amazing progress! She is showing interest every time we play the baby's heartbeat, and when we asked her if she knew who it was, she tapped her finger once. Then when we asked her if she knows it's your baby, she tapped her finger once, again! It's a miracle! Then just this morning, she opened her eyes briefly.

I cover my face, stifling a gasp. She hasn't opened her eyes in two years!

She wasn't conscious for long, but her pupils responded to light. Everyone was thrilled, but I'm sorry to say we forgot to record the moment in our excitement. Next time.

There's no next time about it! I'm flying to Baltimore next week for her birthday, so she won't be alone. Last year, even though she couldn't do anything, I held her hand and talked to her.

Will she open her eyes? Maybe listen to me and blink and tap my palm for a little communication?

Oh, wait! I should ask Huxley if he can go with me. When I wasn't sure if our marriage would last, I was hesitant, but now... I lay a hand over my heart, nearly bursting with enthusiasm. It's sort of last minute, so he might not be able to get away, but if he can, Mom would love to meet her son-in-law. *Ooh, I can also put her hand on my belly.* It's getting more rounded now, although it looks more like a little paunch than an actual baby belly the way I imagined. Maybe the baby will move for the first time when Mom touches my stomach. Wouldn't that be amazing?

Hope and excitement bubble in my veins. I can't imagine a future brighter than this. Huxley asked me to think about my future really carefully, but I already know what it is. I'm just waiting to tell him over the weekend at a beautiful restaurant with candlelight and delicious food. Elizabeth says Éternité is fabulous and romantic, and even I've heard of it. Karie always wanted to go, including the time Viv got her acceptance letter to Harvard Law, but they could never get a table due to the endless waitlist. All Elizabeth had to do was send a text, and voilà, she got me a reservation. "A cousin of mine owns it," she said with a mischievous wink.

When I get home, Huxley is already in the kitchen. "You're back early," I say, going up to him for a kiss.

"Mmm-hmm." He kisses me, but the frown on his face stays. I rub the spot gently to make him stop, but the frown only worsens.

"What's wrong?" I ask. "Did something happen at your office? The new assistant not working out?" Huxley got a male assistant after firing Madison. I know he specifically hired a male assistant for me, even though I told him he should hire whoever was the best. Just because an assistant is female doesn't mean she'll be as awful as Madison, but he shook his head. He isn't leaving anything to chance.

"My assistant is fine," Huxley says.

"I'm glad, then." I kiss his furrowed spot, then pour myself a glass of cold water. "I have fabulous news. But first, how busy are you next week?"

"Why?"

"I'm going to visit Mom. I do it every year on her birthday, and I'd love it if you could join me. I'm dying for her to meet you. Dr. Blum was so optimistic. He said she even opened her eyes!" I beam at my husband, bursting with elation and eager to celebrate this amazing milestone with him.

But instead of smiling, he gives me the strangest look. Not regret that he's too busy to go. More like...

His eyes are downcast, his mouth flat. He clenches and unclenches his hands. A muscle in his jaw twitches erratically. *Isn't he glad Mom is improving? Isn't he proud of the fact that he made it happen?*

The smile on my face slips as the happiness glowing inside me dims. "Why are you upset? Are you...bothered by Mom's progress?" My voice shakes.

"No!" Horror crosses his face. "Never. It's nothing like that."

"Then why do you look so miserable? Did something happen? Are we going bankrupt?" I try to joke, hoping he isn't distressed about Dr. Blum's report for some reason.

"I've been trying to find a good way to say this, but..." Huxley exhales roughly.

My mouth dries as icy fear pushes out the joy and twists my gut. "What is it? You're scaring me."

"Your mother isn't at Johns Hopkins." He couldn't sound more pained.

"What?"

"That's what my accountant said. He told me he tried to pay the invoices, but something was wrong. So he called the hospital, and they told him she's not a patient."

"That can't be right. I get updates and photos every week from Dr. Blum, and he's a real doctor there. I spoke to him the last time I went to see her." I rack my brain for more reasons Huxley's accountant could be mistaken. "And I've been sending two thousand dollars to the place every month. If Mom wasn't there, why would they take my money?"

Confusion clouds Huxley's expression. "You send money directly to them?"

"Yes. I use their online payment portal, and the money gets taken out. My bank statements show they're for Johns Hopkins."

Huxley's eyes narrow in thought. "Text the doctor and tell him you're visiting next week."

I do, using the number I have for him. It doesn't take long before I get a response.

–Dr. Blum: I don't think that's a good idea.

A cold knot forms in my gut. My fingers shake as I type my response.

–Me: Why not?

–Dr. Blum: Your sudden presence could have a negative effect.

Fear—sour and metallic—coats my mouth. What is he talking about? He's the one who told me to send voice memos and so on for Mom, saying they would help. How could my being there in person be worse than her listening to recordings only?

–Me: How so?

Three dots appear and disappear on the screen. Apprehension tightens its icy hand around my neck. I breathe in carefully, feeling like I'm about to throw up. My hands turn clammy as the seconds tick by.

Finally, a response arrives.

–Dr. Blum: She's used to auditory sensations. Her brain is learning to process olfactory now. It's a very delicate process, and you don't want to overload her.

–Me: But you said she opened her eyes.

–Dr. Blum: Yes. But that doesn't mean she's ready to see you in person. Not yet, anyway.

–Dr. Blum: Or we may risk her shutting down again. We don't want to do that, do we?

–Me: I don't understand. After my last visit, you said you wished I could afford to be with her more so she could get direct interaction with me and recover faster.

Nothing. Not even three dots.

No, no, no.

I call. It goes to voicemail. I try again, but he doesn't pick up.

Terror and denial slice my heart into pieces. The air seems so thin now, and my vision dims. I hear something shatter.

"Grace!" Huxley's warm hands wrap around my arms. "Breathe, baby. Breathe." His eyes focus on mine as he pulls back and makes an exaggerated motion of dragging in air. Numbly, I follow suit. "Good. Now, out." He sags his shoulders and lets the air out. I do the same. "Again. Don't pass out on me." He pulls me gently. "Careful. There are glass shards on the floor."

I glance down. Somebody must've dropped a glass. "I don't understand. Nelson wouldn't have moved my mom without telling me first. Or if not me, at least Andreas, who ordered him to pay for the care."

Huxley dips his head and looks into my eyes. "I know you're upset, but give me twenty-four hours to look into this. The woman in the hospital billing department who my accountant talked to is young and only started working a couple of months ago. She might've made a mistake, or maybe doesn't know how to look up where your mom was moved to. But they're three hours ahead of us, so you have to give me a little time to work on this, okay?"

"I don't believe that the billing department lady doesn't know."

"Well, it's a possibility that we should check. Now, listen. You feel chilled." Huxley runs his hands over my arms. "Why don't I start a hot bath for you? It might make you feel better. And please—let me take care of this. I've already hired people to look into it as quickly as possible."

His eyes cloud with worry—and a tinge of guilt. He's withholding something. But what? Something worse than the possibility that Dr. Blum might've been lying to me all this time? That Mom isn't doing as well as I thought? That the damn hospital might've misplaced her like an unoccupied bed they forgot about until now?

"What are you not telling me?" I rasp, wanting to give him a chance.

"Nothing." His answer is too prompt. He parks me on a stool. "Don't move until I come back. I'll start the bath and clean up the floor, okay?"

I nod because that's what he wants.

He disappears upstairs, to the master bath.

I grab my car fob and walk out, glass be damned.

49

GRACE

I STOP my car with a loud screech in front of Nelson's house. I barge in, slamming the door into the wall with a bang.

"Nelson! Karie!" I shout as my long strides carry me further inside.

"What the fuck?" Mick says from above. He and Karie are standing at the top of the staircase.

There they are. I take the steps until I reach them.

Karie looks down at me like a queen would a peasant. "Are you here to apologize and take back what you did?"

I ignore the asinine question. "Where's my mother?"

"Why are you asking us? She's at Johns Hopkins, unless your husband did something with her," Karie says stiffly, tilting her chin high.

I clench my hands so I don't give in to the urge to strangle her. That wouldn't get me the answer I need. "She's *not* at Johns Hopkins. Huxley's people can't locate her." I add the little lie to prevent Karie from continuing to play dumb.

"They're probably stupid and blind." Mick snorts.

"Dr. Blum won't respond anymore either." My voice trembles with fear and fury.

"Maybe he got tired of your nagging and paranoia. Just look at you," Mick says, a little too gleefully. His smirk says he definitely knows something. But my gut says it's Karie who's controlling the situation. Her children always take their cues from her. If she won't talk, Mick won't, either.

"I'll ask again: where is my mother? What have you done with her?" I do my best to keep my voice calm despite rising hysteria. Losing my cool won't solve anything. Karie and Mick are like snakes, and they'll exploit any weakness they see.

"I didn't do anything. Nothing happened to her," Karie sneers.

"Then why can't Huxley's people locate her at Johns Hopkins?" My tone grows loud as panic suffocates me. Just what did they do to Mom? How could I have been so stupid to trust that Nelson and Karie would do the right thing?

"His incompetence isn't my problem."

"Care to repeat that to his face?" I say.

Karie shuts up. Mick bristles. It must hurt his pride that he can't just flip the bird at my husband.

"I'm going to visit her on her birthday next week, Karie."

An *oh fuck* panic cracks her mask. "Aren't you too busy ruining Viv's life to make a trip like that?" she says, trying to deflect my attention from Mom's whereabouts.

But that only confirms my suspicions. Did Karie do something to Mom as revenge? Even though Huxley's trust took over the bills, the staff at Johns Hopkins dealt with Nelson and Karie all this time. I take a step forward, my unblinking eyes on Karie. "What did you do? Please just tell me. It doesn't have to get ugly. But it will if you persist in lying. Don't think I won't do whatever I have to in order to find out the truth."

"Nothing!" Karie shouts with more force than required.

"For fuck's sake, don't be so melodramatic. Mom didn't do anything. Your slutty mother just died." Mick chuckles.

The words hit like punches to my gut. I grit my teeth as I struggle to process. He can't possibly mean it. His laughter is proof enough, because what kind of monster laughs over the death of a person? He must be saying shit because he's pissed off. He always acts impulsively. "Shut up! Stop lying." It's more a plea than a rebuke.

Karie sighs. "It's true. She died the day before you took the LSAT. We got a call from the hospital."

Shock freezes me. My pulse thumps in my head, muffling the sounds from the outside world. *She died... She died...* The words explode like grenades and shred me like shrapnel. Mick would lie for shits and giggles. Karie... She does everything with calculation.

Mom... *Oh my God, Mom!*

"Hush." Karie slaps Mick's arm as he keeps on sniggering.

"But it's so funny! Look at her face!" He points, his whole being practically glowing with delight. "She's crying now!" He doubles over in hilarity.

I ignore him. My pain demands I get answers. "And you didn't tell me she died?" I whisper as hot tears soak my cheeks.

Karie shrugs. "What good would it have done? She was already gone. It would've affected your focus while taking the exam."

Every vein in my head throbs. I put a hand at my pounding temple. "You didn't tell me so I could score better on the LSAT for Viv?"

"Yes. It was the smartest thing to do."

The smartest thing... The words echo in my head. Mom's death ranked below a stupid fucking LSAT. Why... Why did I ever agree to take the test for Viv? Yes, Karie demanded I do so if I wanted Nelson and her financial help to continue, but it was all for nothing. No, worse than nothing. I'm being punished for doing something unethical and vile. Mom died alone with nobody by her side because I took the easy way out.

I struggle to figure out some way I could've changed the outcome back then. And I hate myself for not being able to think of something because it feels like letting Mom down. Hell, I already let her down. More fresh tears roll down my face. "But later... Why didn't you tell me Mom passed away?"

Karie snorts. "So you could behave like an out-of-control animal? You weren't obedient and good when you thought your mother was at our mercy. How would you have been if you learned she was dead?"

"All this was for *control?*" My voice cracks further.

"What else? If you'd been a good girl, it wouldn't have been necessary."

"A good girl who takes a test for her sister to sneak into law school, right?"

Karie's face remains stony. Not even a flicker of shame.

"Would you have told me Mom died the day before the LSAT if I'd been 'good'?"

"No. But I might've told you afterward."

So it was my fault...because I couldn't keep my mouth shut or let Nelson and his family walk all over me. *Mom... I never got to say goodbye.* "What happened to her? Where is she now?"

Karie smirks. "Don't worry, we aren't heartless, despite what you told your husband. We cremated her—"

A sob breaks through my hand over my mouth.

"—and scattered her ashes in Baltimore, near the hospital."

My heart pumps with such pain that it feels like it's going to burst any second. I make a fist and push it against my chest, hoping it will lessen the agony, but the anguish only intensifies. "You psycho bitch!" I pant. "Why would you do that to her? Why would you tie her to the fucking hospital where she was lying helpless, alone and dying? What kind of monster are you?"

"Shut up, you ungrateful bitch!" Mick shouts. "Who the fuck are you to talk to my mom that way?"

"Who the fuck are you to cremate my mom? Or scatter her ashes near the hospital? You weren't her family! You were her haters!" Abruptly, wrath rages through me, overwhelming the grief. They aren't getting away with this. I won't let them. I point my shaking finger at them. "I'm going to make you pay for this!"

"You dare threaten us?"

"Oh, it's much more than a threat. It's a promise!"

"You little...!"

Mick takes a step forward, and suddenly pain explodes in my cheek, my vision going bright then dark. My body tilts from the impact. My foot slips. I reach out to grab the railing, but my hand is too slick with sweat.

I tumble and roll. Instinctively I wrap my arms around my belly. The edges of the stairs cut into me, but my body barely registers the pain as the world spins.

Finally I stop, my back on the chilly marble floor. I think I heard Huxley scream my name from somewhere as something warm and thick trickles from between my legs and pools around me.

50

HUXLEY

"How is she?" Emmett says as he rushes toward the waiting area with Amy. They're both in their office clothes. They probably cut their workdays short—nobody has weekends at GrantEm. Grant follows soon after. Aspen's already here, having arrived from their home.

I tilt my head, resting the back of my skull against the cool concrete wall behind me. I squeeze my eyes closed, but the vision of Grace lying in her own blood continues to haunt me. "I don't know." My voice is hollow, rough with fear and uncertainty. "They're still checking her out."

I pray the doc will hurry up and come out and tell me what's happening to Grace and the baby. At the same time, I don't ever want him to come out unless the news is going to be positive.

She can't lose the baby after discovering how inhumanely her mother was ripped from her. She never got a chance to say her farewells, to get the closure she deserved back then. If anything happened to the baby... She's one of the strongest women I know, but she might not be able to bear the heartache. And I will be helpless to shield her from the pain.

"Jesus," Sebastian whispers as he arrives with Lucie, who

immediately covers her mouth in horror. "Is that all...?" He wipes a hand across his jaw, gesturing at me.

I look down at the red stain all over my shirt and pants. On my hands, between my fingers and around the wedding band. As awful as I look, Grace looked far worse at the bottom of the Webbers' stairs, a sheet of crimson spreading around her. I picked her up, felt the hot blood soaking me, each fresh drip sending terror through me until my knees shook.

Mick opened and closed his mouth; Karie just stared. Before they could offer some bullshit excuse, I left with my wife. *Have to take care of her and the baby.* I stiffened my legs and spine, taking long strides and placing her in my Bugatti. *Have to stay strong for my family.*

"Fuck." Noah thrusts his fingers into his hair. "Let's get you a change of clothes."

I shake my head. "Can't. I have to wait for Grace."

"Then how about we just clean you up a little? You don't want to scare her when she wakes up," Molly says gently, then brings several wet towels.

"Thanks." I take the towels, but merely hold them. Cleaning up seems so frivolous. What if Grace doesn't wake up? She lost so much blood. I wish I hadn't studied law. If I'd studied medicine, I could be more use to her now.

"What happened?" Sierra asks.

"I think her mom died." I manage to push the words out through my numb mouth.

"Oh no." Bobbi's face softens with sympathy.

"It gets worse. It looks like her mother died about a year ago, and Nelson and Karie kept it from her." Karie and Mick didn't say anything, but I could piece together that much based on what Earl told me and what Grace murmured while half-conscious. She cried out, "Mom, Mom... I'm so sorry," while tears fell from her eyes.

When confronted, instead of doing the right thing, they undoubtedly dug in their heels. Mick thinks he's slick, but I saw him hit her at the top of the stairs.

Suddenly my terror morphs into sheer rage. Do they think what I did to Nelson was brutal? Wait until I get my hands on Mick. I'm going to kill that motherfucker.

"What the fuck?" Nicholas mutters in disgust. "What kind of assholes do that?"

I shake my head, incapable of any sort of clarity on that point. As the seconds tick by, even more dread and self-recrimination pulse through me until I want to rip my hair out and bury my face in my hands. I should've known she wouldn't be able to just sit tight while I confirmed the details. After Earl dropped his bombshell, it didn't seem right to tell her about her mom until I had all the facts. I would have waited until my investigators had looked into the matter before telling her about Winona if she hadn't asked me to go see her mother in Baltimore. Lying to her face, saying that I'd love to, would have been an appalling betrayal when I already knew that she would never see her mother again.

Earl said he found out that her mother's body was given to a couple who claimed to be her family. The hospital believed them, since they were the people paying her bills every month. They said the body had been cremated, but beyond that, they didn't know.

Mother arrives with Grandmother. The former looks terrible, her red mouth set in a tight line, her eyes flashing with murderous fury. Grandmother shakes, not from age—the old bat is healthier than most people thirty years younger—but with barely suppressed rage. Uncle Prescott and his wife join us. My cousins show up, too. They don't show any reaction to the blood on me except to press their lips together. Aunt Akiko turns deathly pale. She's probably remembering her miscarriage. She lost her only baby at the end of her first trimester and never became pregnant again.

Ares gives me a light pat on the back—which to him is equivalent to a full-body hug, because he hates touching or being touched. Josh squeezes my shoulder.

Bryce lets out a rough breath. "What did the doc say?"

"Dunno yet."

"Where is Nelson?" Grandma's tone says he should be here.

I shake my head. "Don't know. Don't care." It's good he isn't here, because I might kill him.

"What happened?" Mom asks.

The idea of recounting what Grace had to go through again makes me want to vomit. Seb fills them in.

"What?" Mother's sharp voice cuts through the air. "Grace's mother passed away a year ago, and those weasels never told her?"

"Oh, that poor child." Aunt Akiko's face crumbles.

Just then the doctor comes out, dark circles around his sunken eyes giving him the appearance of gloom and doom. But the small smile on his lips gives me hope.

"My wife...?" I ask hoarsely. The air around us stills as my family hold their collective breaths.

"She's suffered a slight concussion and a hairline fracture in her left forearm, but other than that she's fine. She just needs to rest and take things easy."

"Thank God," I whisper, burying my face in my hands.

Small sighs rise around me, the tension visibly easing.

"And the baby?" Aunt Akiko asks shakily.

I clench my hands, pressing the fists against my brow. *Jesus, say it's fine, say it's fine, say it's fine.*

"The baby is fine as well."

I lift my head. "Thank you, doctor."

He nods once. "Just doing my job. Dr. Silverman will be coming in the morning, as requested."

"Can I see Grace now?" I ask.

"And me," Grandmother says.

"Only one person at a time, no more than three visitors a day and ten minutes each. She's sleeping right now. She'll be sleeping until the morning. She's going to need plenty of rest. Absolutely no stress or upsetting her. No physical exertion, either."

I nod, then carefully open the door and step inside her room in the private wing at the hospital. The Huxleys donated a huge sum of money to construct this part of the wing—reserved for oncology and wealthy and famous clients who require discretion.

The room is beautifully decorated with sunny yellow walls and fresh sunflowers in giant vases. My wife lies on a huge bed, needles in the back of her right hand for a couple of IV drips.

I walk quietly toward her. *She's fine, my ass.* Instead of protecting her head, she wrapped her arms around her belly. Little cuts and scrapes mar her face, especially on the high points of her cheeks and forehead. Her little freckles look exceptionally dark against the ghostly pallor of her skin.

Tenderly I hold the hands that shielded our baby from harm, and kiss the bruised and scraped knuckles. She doesn't stir. Her breathing is so quiet and gentle, I have to put my ear over her chest for a sign that she's alive—and with me.

The doctor said she would sleep through the night. She did her part. It's time I do mine.

51

HUXLEY

I RETURN HOME to shower and change. The clothes remain stiff from Grace's blood. I throw them into a bag to be burned. The shirt used to be my favorite, but not anymore. I'll never get the image of the coppery stain out of my head. Or how quickly the blood flowed out of her.

I almost lost her. I won't be making the same mistake again.

When I reach Nelson's mansion, I'm fully clothed in a black three-piece bespoke suit and carrying the slim onyx cane every Huxley gets when we are born. The platinum knob has the coat of arms of the Huxleys, each wolf's eye set off with a pigeon's-blood ruby. On the side of the cane glints PIETAS ET UNITAS etched in silver. I've rarely pulled it out of its case in the closet, but then the world hasn't really given me a reason to...until now.

Despite the late hour, every window in Nelson's home blazes with light. Andreas's Maybach crouches on the dark driveway like a wounded beast. My jaw tightens. The bastard never came to the hospital. Grace is his granddaughter, too.

I open the door and step inside. There's no staff around, but then, Nelson and Karie seem to believe that as long as they show their true colors selectively, their reputation will remain intact.

As I get closer to the living room, I can hear raised voices. I slow my pace to hear what they plan to do to cover their ass.

"You have to help me!" Nelson's plea has a tinge of desperation.

"How? You've shamed me, Nelson Emmanuel Webber. I couldn't join the Huxleys. I had to wait around the corner like some stalker and eavesdrop on the doctor informing them of Grace's condition!" Andreas thunders. "How am I going to face Catalina? No, no, forget her. How am I going to face Jeremiah on Monday when I go into the office? Or Prescott? How about Ares and the rest?"

"Why should you be worried? You didn't do anything," Karie says. "Grace just slipped."

"*Slipped?*" Andreas says. "That's not what I heard. Your idiot son pushed her!"

"I was just shooing a fly," Mick says.

"Can you testify to that under oath, inside a courtroom?" Andreas demands.

"Wait, what do you mean?" Karie says.

"Do you honestly think the Huxleys will let this go? They *live* their family motto!" I can tell from the tone of voice that Andreas is seething.

"But Huxley Lasker doesn't want to be part of his family! Look how he refused to join the firm," Nelson points out.

"He still has the Huxley cane! And no matter how she grouses in public, Catalina adores that boy, and Grace as well, because *she is now a Huxley through marriage!* You amoral, self-centered *imbeciles!*"

"It's just my word against hers," Mick scoffs. "And who's more credible? I'm the DA."

I've heard enough. "Ah yes. Credibility." I walk into the room, twirling my cane casually.

Mick brims with smug defiance, and Nelson and Karie are wary. But Andreas takes in the sight of my cane, and his Adam's apple bobs as he pales. He knows what this means, despite my outwardly calm mien.

"How is Grace doing? I wanted to stop by, but I've been busy at work," Nelson says quickly.

"A bit late to ask, isn't it?" My eyes slide over to Andreas, and the corners of my lips lift. "All that fuss to cement our family ties, only to destroy them. What a waste, eh?"

Andreas and Nelson frown, the former in trepidation, the latter likely wondering how he's going to pull his family out of this mess.

"Huxley." Karie gives me her typical fake smile. "I don't know what you think happened—"

"I saw what happened, Karie. I carried my wife out, remember?"

She shuts up.

"So you saw her slip," Mick says shamelessly.

"Did she slip?" The rage in my heart no longer burns. It's so arctic now, even my skull feels frigid. "Let's go see where it happened. It might jog my memory."

Mick hesitates.

"You're the DA, right? Isn't that what you do when you have a witness whose details seem a bit muddled?" I ask with a honeyed smile.

He smiles back in relief. "Of course."

He and I go to the long staircase.

"Here." He gestures. "Better?"

I look down. The floor has been wiped clean, leaving nothing but sparkling marble. They might've been able to clean up the blood, but not their crime against my wife.

"Hmm. Why don't we go up to where she slipped?" I say.

"Yeah, sure." He and I walk together.

I count each step. *One... Two... Three...*

And with each number, my mind conjures the image of my wife's delicate body hitting the edges, her skin tearing, more and more bruises appearing until a bone in her forearm fractures. The icy anger in my chest swells until it feels like my heart will burst with wrath.

The doctor said she was lucky. The one who's really lucky is Mick, because if she'd been permanently injured, I would've broken his neck.

We reach the top of the stairs. Twenty steps total. I inhale deeply, rein in the fury. It's not time yet.

"Just between you and me," Mick begins, lowering his voice conspiratorially, "I know you never wanted the baby. So. It's like an at-home abortion." He sniffs. "You're welcome."

Oh, you motherfucker. "Mick." I clap my hand on his shoulder. "It's only an abortion if the baby is unwanted. Otherwise, it's murder."

Shock flares in his beady eyes. "Don't tell me you want the thing!

You had to marry Grace rather than Viv because of that clump of cells. That 'baby' was just an indiscretion, nothing more, just like Grace was an indiscretion my father wishes he could erase."

I cast my gaze at a spot behind him. "Ooh, a fly!"

"What?" He turns his head.

I shove him, putting a foot out to catch his ankle—and let go of the reins on my rage.

"Fuck! Ack!" Mick screams as he tumbles down the stairs. I watch him cover his head as he rolls and spins down the steps. How unfair that he gets to avoid a concussion when my wife got one protecting our child?

I stroll down. I thought watching him suffer like Grace had might be satisfying, but it isn't. He's bigger and stronger. Doesn't look like anything is broken. He isn't even lying in his own blood.

"Fucking asshole!" he yells from the bottom of the stairs.

Definitely nothing broken. I swing my cane.

He raises his arm, screaming even before the cane connects with a loud *thwack*.

What a pussy. This fucking weasel dared to touch my wife and hurt her.

I swing again and again, counting in my head. I'm a fair man. I won't strike more than twenty times—one for each step.

"Oh my God! Stop it! You're going to kill him!" Karie screams.

"Stop! I'll do anything!" Nelson pleads.

But neither of them is brave enough to come forward and physically shield their son with their own body.

Eight... Nine... There is a *crack*, and I feel the bones in his forearm go.

"Mom! Dad! Do something!" Mick screams, spittle dripping from his mouth.

"Mommy and Daddy aren't coming to your rescue, Mick," I taunt him darkly.

"Fuck! Augh!" He pulls his head down, trying to make himself as small a target as possible. He's probably hoping I'll tire myself out.

I'm not even winded. I've chased down balls playing tennis with Sebastian, who doesn't believe in friendly competition, just winning. Smacking a more or less immobile target is piece of cake. "What's the matter, scumbag? I'm just erasing your parents' *indiscretion*. I'm sure the entire family wishes you'd never been born."

"This is battery!" he shouts. "I'll press charges. Your ass is going to jail!"

"Do it." Another smack.

"No one's gonna protect you," he tries to threaten, but the slobbery delivery ruins the impact.

"I don't need anybody's protection. I can protect myself. Can you?" I hit him again. Something else—not my cane—cracks.

Mick screams in pain. The cocky insolence in his usually smarmy face shatters as he realizes his parents aren't going to put themselves in danger for him. He looks to Andreas, who turns away in disgust.

"I'm going to make sure you pay for what you've done. And I'm going to sue you until you have nothing left to your name."

"Who's gonna do it?" He can barely get the words out.

I straighten. I'm at fifteen, but if I hit him more, he might just die. That won't do. I'll save the five for later.

"I can think of a few people. But if nobody will take the case..." I flash him my friendliest smile. "Congratulations! You'll have done something none of my family was able to do. I'll pass the bar and deal with you myself."

52

HUXLEY

GRACE LOOKS SO small and delicate on the hospital bed. The doc said she would be awake after a good night's sleep, but it's been four days. He looked utterly flustered when I demanded answers. Dr. Silverman could only tell me the baby is fine, nothing more, but she's an obstetrician. More specialists examined my wife, but they couldn't say what was wrong either.

"Maybe the concussion is more serious than we initially thought," was the only explanation offered.

"Are you kidding me? Didn't you do enough tests to make sure?" I snarled. Intellectually I understand alienating the doctors isn't the best course of action, but I have no patience for their incompetence. The possibility that Grace might not wake up is petrifying. I've never felt a terror this dark, not even when I landed wrong during that half-pipe stunt that left me in a coma for a few days.

My brothers and their wives have come by. So have my cousins. Mom merely looked at me and Grace with an inscrutable expression, but Uncle Prescott told me there's been a bloodbath at the firm.

"Nelson's done. But if Jeremiah doesn't fuck him up enough to satisfy me, I plan to finish the job." His tone said there wouldn't be anything left for me once The Fogeys were done with him.

Ares was less calm. "You're hiring John Highsmith to go after Nelson, Vivienne and Mick? What the hell, man?" He sounded like I'd just backstabbed him.

"Nelson is a junior partner at the firm," I said. Besides, John hates Nelson. Apparently, it's a personal grudge that goes back a few years.

"So? I can still mess him up. And if it's not enough to give you satisfaction, I'll call you uncle for the rest of my life. *Pietas et unitas,* cousin. We were a legal powerhouse before the Webbers, and we'll continue to be a powerhouse after them."

"He's right," Josh said glumly. Although he wasn't as expressive as Ares, he didn't exactly hide how he felt either. "If you can't trust your own flesh and blood to have your back, who can you trust?"

"Fine," I told them. "Go ahead and run 'em through the shredder."

Their eyes glinted. "Awesome," Josh replied.

I might've joined the frenzy to rip Nelson apart, but my entire focus right now is on my wife, who still hasn't opened her eyes. Every second that passes with her lying on those white sheets singes a sliver off my heart.

How could she have borne this uncertainty and fear for two years after her mother collapsed? Even being right next to Grace isn't enough to alleviate my anxiety. How did she function with her mother all the way off in Baltimore, three time zones away? I don't think I'll be able to go on if Grace doesn't wake up, and I have to send her somewhere far away. She is so much stronger and more resilient than I could ever be.

I sit by the bed and hold her small hand in mine. But it doesn't seem enough, so I link our fingers and rest my cheek against her knuckles.

"Come on, Grace. Open your eyes, baby. You can beat this. Don't let Mick and Karie get away with it." Fear spikes, and suddenly my pleas turn into a threat. "If you *don't* wake up, I'm going to drop my plans for revenge against them, and they'll walk away scot-free." My voice cracks a little with desperation. "You don't want that, do you?"

"No..."

I lift my head, then blink, unsure if it was my imagination or if she really spoke. Her eyelids flutter like little butterflies. Air catches in my throat, forming a hot lump. I don't dare exhale, too scared that if I breathe wrong, I might jinx the moment. She finally opens her eyes. They're slightly glassy, then gradually clear and focus on me.

"The baby?" she asks, trembling with trepidation.

Relief shudders through me—she's not only awake, but I can tell her the good news. "It's fine," I manage to choke out, then blink hard to clear the hot tears gathering in my eyes. My wife needs me to be strong. "You protected our child. Thank you."

She pulls her hand from mine, then strokes my cheek. "You haven't been sleeping well? You look exhausted."

"You were in a coma for four days."

Her eyebrows arch. "That long?"

I nod. "You scared the shit out of me at Nelson's house...and now this."

"I'm sorry. But you didn't really mean it when you said you'd let Mick and Karie go, did you?" Her jaw tightens. "I can never forgive them. His smug face... Her smirk when she spoke of my mom..."

I gather her hand, clasp it in both of mine, then kiss her fingertips. "You don't have to worry. I won't forgive them. Nobody in my family will, either. They're done."

"I know you asked me to wait, but I just couldn't. The idea that my mom might've died alone and I knew nothing about it... I can't believe she's been gone all this time, but Dr. Blum kept sending me emails telling me how well she was doing, giving me false hope." Tears pool in her eyes.

"It was an impersonator. The real doctor was horrified when I contacted him." And he plans to pursue legal action.

"Did you figure out who did it? Was it Karie?"

I shake my head. "Vivienne." She was so scared of being found out that she almost peed her pants. Apparently, nobody told her a burner phone wasn't going to be enough to shield her identity.

Grace gives a long, tired sigh. "I never did anything to her. Why does she hate me so much? Why is she so cruel?"

"Because she's a horrible human being."

"Is it because Karie hated my mom?" Grace looks at me, desperate to understand. It breaks my heart that she's still subconsciously looking for some excuse for Nelson and his family despite claiming she doesn't like them. She probably doesn't want to believe her own biological father and his family could be so heartless.

I shake my head. "If Viv were a good person, that wouldn't have been enough to make her behave like that. Some people are just..." No word seems adequate. "...awful. There's no reason."

Grace lets out a shaky breath. "I never got to say goodbye. I never thought I'd have to. The doctor's updates were always so upbeat. I sent everything he asked for, anything that might help with her treatment. All the audio recordings I made. The flowers. Nothing reached her. It was just entertainment for Viv." Grief, pain and fury ravage her pale face.

I suppress the rage seething in my belly and hold her tightly, since this moment is for her to grieve and try to find a bit of consolation.

"Is she the one who took my money, too?" she asks.

I close my eyes for a moment, wishing I had better news. "Yes. She created a fake payment site, and you basically deposited two thousand dollars a month into her account." The urge to beat Vivienne the way I did her brother was overwhelming when I saw the report. She's lucky she doesn't have a penis—otherwise, I would've put her in the hospital.

"We can get her for that, can't we? Even if her pretending to be Dr. Blum isn't a crime?"

"Yes. Impersonating a medical professional, identity theft, fraud, unjust enrichment—the list goes on and on. And Dr. Blum said he'd file suit. Ares is taking the case, pro bono. He's dying to destroy Vivienne for you."

"Thank you." She wipes her tears. "Your family's been so kind."

"Not my family. *Our* family, Grace." I hold her tighter.

More tears fall from my wife's wounded eyes, soaking my shirt and sending a searing ache all the way to my heart. "I just wish I'd known sooner. At least early enough that I could've taken the ashes. Karie told me they cremated her and scattered her ashes in Baltimore near Johns Hopkins. Why would anybody do that? Why would anybody think Mom would want to be in a place where she was confined by illness? Karie said they didn't want to tell me Mom passed because it was the day before I was supposed to take the LSAT for Viv."

"What?"

Grace's face crumbles. "Karie threatened to withhold payment for Mom's bills if I refused, and instead of doing the right thing, I said okay. I just feel like I'm being punished. If I'd said no, they wouldn't have had a reason to not tell me. Then at least Mom's ashes wouldn't be scattered all over Baltimore. There aren't any of her favorite flowers or the green fields she loves—loved so much."

Hearing her blame herself for others' wrongdoings shreds my heart. I wish we'd met earlier. I wish I'd been kinder. Perhaps gone with her to the emergency room two years ago. Called and checked up on her periodically to offer to help so she wouldn't have been blackmailed. Or ended up devastated like this.

"I don't even know what all the sacrifice was for," she says, choking on her tears. "Mom said good things happen to people who try hard and do their best, but…"

I run a soothing hand over her back as more of her tears soak my shirt. "I know it sounds whimsical, but I think your mother sent you to me that night two years ago."

Grace tilts her face to look at me, her cheeks glistening.

"You said she never woke up. But she might've known you'd need somebody by your side. Do you know I wouldn't have been where I was that night if it hadn't been for a family dinner I was forced to attend? Normally I'm too much of an asshole to give a ride to some girl who looks like a drowned rat. But that day, somehow I felt compelled to make an exception and be nice. Then I ran into you at the bar over a year later. There are nearly four million people in Los Angeles. What are the chances that we'd run into each other again when we didn't know each other's names or remember how we looked? What are the chances I would have still kept your number and called you? And there's the baby. I'm fanatical about birth control, but here we are. What are the chances that all these things happening to one couple?" I wipe the tears from her face. "Probably billions to one, Grace. If this isn't fate, I don't know what is." I kiss away the sorrow and desolation in her eyes. "I was destined to find you and love you."

She expels a tremulous breath. A fresh wave of tears falls from her puffy, red-rimmed eyes. Her nose is pink, and her cheeks are flushed. And she will always be the most beautiful woman in the world.

"This baby"—I put a protective hand over her belly—"and I will be your family, Grace. We won't be able to replace your mother—nobody could—but you'll never be alone. I promise."

"How can you? No one knows when it's their time," she whispers.

"I'll quit the cigars and alcohol. Exercise more. Cut back on the bacon. I'll make sure I outlive you."

A ghost of a smile passes over her teary face. "But then you'll be alone."

"Only for a little bit. I don't think destiny would be cruel enough to keep us apart for long." I kiss her. "I love you, Grace Lasker, my miracle, my fate."

"I love you too," she whispers fiercely, crying harder.

I hold my wife while she lets everything out in tears.

53

GRACE

"I want to go home." My voice is hoarse and rough as I tell Huxley. *How long did I cry?* No idea, but I feel completely wrung out. No regrets, though—something feels lighter and cleaner in my heart.

Part of me will always grieve for my mother—the lonely death and having her ashes callously abandoned in Baltimore. Karie said she scattered the ashes, but I know better.

When Huxley spoke of how we managed to meet and come together despite the odds, it feels like some being out there is watching over me. I lost Mom, but gained Huxley and our baby. I scan the hospital room, the countless bouquets and get-well balloons and teddy bears, coming to rest on a couple of giant fruit baskets with a note saying, *You just get better while we avenge you.*

I have brothers- and sisters- and cousins-in-law who care. Jeremiah and Ted try their best to act as surrogate parents as well. The latter is quite unhappy that he's in Nice to meet with some distributors and new faces he'd love to cast in his next film, rather than in L.A. "You just tell that husband of yours what you need, and if he doesn't deliver quick enough, let me know. I'll spank his ass for being unworthy of my daughter."

"I will," I tell him with a little smile.

After the doctor clears me to be discharged, I change, then Huxley pushes my wheelchair. I feel a bit ridiculous since my legs are working fine, but apparently it's hospital policy.

He stops in the lobby. "Wait while I get the car from the lot."

"We can walk together."

"It's too far away. I don't want you to overexert yourself." He frowns like he's worried I might break.

Although part of me wants to reassure him I'm fine, seeing me bloody and unconscious gave him quite a scare. So I nod and say, "Okay. I'll wait."

"I'll be back soon. Don't go anywhere."

"I won't. I promise."

I watch him walk through the crowd, then past the automatic doors. When he vanishes behind a couple of trees, I pull out my phone to check messages. I have so many, some from people at work, some from Huxley's brothers and their wives. Actually...*my* brothers and sisters. It sounds a little strange, but feels good at the same time. Everyone is worried about me, wishes me well.

–Griffin: Next time Hux wants to beat someone like Mick up, tell him to take me with him. I can do a better job.

–Sebastian: Seriously. I think Huxley only cracked one rib.

–Griffin: I would've broken at least four.

–Noah: Amateur. I would've done six.

–Emmett: Push him off a cliff. Problem solved.

–Grant: What kind of asshole shoves a pregnant woman down a flight of stairs?

–Nicholas: What kind of asshole shoves any woman down a flight of stairs?

I smile. I can't believe that in addition to my husband, I have six tall, broad-shouldered brothers to keep me safe.

–Bobbi: If you crave anything, lemme know!

–Lucie: There's nothing she can't bake.

–Amy: I can make a mean casserole!

–Aspen: Don't you have to work?

–Amy: I can take some time off.

–Molly: If you need something to read, I'm your girl.

—Sierra: Or if you just need somebody to talk to or cheer you up... Me me me! Pick me!

Then there's more.

—Bryce: If you need anything message me.

—Josh: I don't sleep, so you can text me any time you need something.

—Ares: Nelson's a dead man.

—Bryce: Ares means that. You don't have to worry about a thing.

I laugh a little at how everyone expresses their support and love in their own way. Maybe Huxley is right—this is fate.

"There you are! I was afraid I'd missed you when the nurse said you were discharged."

I stiffen at the sound of Nelson's somewhat breathless voice. His suit is crisp, and his hair is carefully coiffed, but a closer look reveals tense lines fanning from his slightly bloodshot eyes. He keeps rubbing the back of his neck—a tell that he's anxious. I start to look away.

"Grace, you have to stop your crazy husband."

"My crazy husband?" I cock an eyebrow.

"He's trying to destroy Mick and Viv."

"So?"

"So?" he blusters. "They're your siblings."

"No, they aren't. They're bullies."

Nelson puffs out an impatient breath. "What happened was regrettable. But Mick didn't mean to push that hard. You're still young and healthy. You can always have more babies."

It's almost unbelievable. *He has no idea what my condition is.* He couldn't be bothered to check up on me and the baby, but he has the energy to chase me down to demand my forgiveness on his children's behalf.

If nothing else had cemented my disgust for him, this would have done it. "I might—after this one, if Huxley and I decide to have another."

Nelson frowns, his mouth tight. "So...you didn't lose it?"

"I never said I did."

"Then why are you being so difficult and vindictive?"

"Well, let's see. Just for starters, you don't think there's anything wrong with Mick pushing me down a flight of stairs?"

"It was just a friendly little shove. It isn't his problem that your balance is so poor."

"And I suppose it was just a *friendly* prank when Viv pretended to be Dr. Blum and stole two thousand dollars a month from me."

"Jesus, it's always about money with you. Fine. I'll pay it back," he says dismissively.

Contempt curls my mouth. Nelson will never understand it wasn't about the money, but what it represented—hope for Mom's recovery. Just thinking about what he and his family did to her makes me want to hurt him. "Get lost and never show your face again. You're dead to me."

"I'm your father!"

"You were my sperm donor. You were never my family. He is." I point at Huxley in the Bugatti that just pulled in.

Nelson notices, then blanches. "Fucking psycho," he mutters, then walks off as quickly as he can without appearing like he's running away.

"Some father, leaving his daughter to a 'fucking psycho'!" I keep my voice loud enough for him to hear, but he doesn't turn back or slow down.

I climb into the car.

"Everything okay?" Huxley studies me. "You look a little tense."

"I'm fine." I give him a reassuring smile. "I just saw a little cockroach and had to shoo it away."

He gives me a look. "A cockroach? Inside the hospital?"

"Yeah, but it's gone now. Doubt it'll come back." I smile. "Come on. Let's go home."

54

HUXLEY

INVITING WARMTH. Lovely softness. A sweet scent.

The intoxicating femininity that is my wife slowly seeps into me. Still drowsy with lingering sleep, I wrap my arms around her protectively. My cock is already hard, and her nearness makes it swell further. My hand instinctively closes around a mound that's grown plumper in pregnancy.

I lay kisses along the back of her neck, the need to make her feel good guiding me. Dr. Silverman cleared Grace for sex yesterday. What kind of husband would I be if I failed to pamper my wife in bed?

The negligent kind. "You awake?" I whisper.

"Uh-uh." Her reply is somewhere between a mewl and whine.

A teasing smile on her lips, she turns and nestles closer. Her head rests in the crook between my neck and shoulder, a soft purr coming from her throat.

Is that how it is?

Grinning, I knead her breast, dragging the pad of my thumb back and forth across the hardened nipple. Her breathing grows choppy. She arches into my touch like a kitten basking in tender strokes. Love and the need to satisfy her unfurl. She still has her eyes closed, although her eyelids flutter.

"You keep on sleeping and enjoy," I say, then pull the other nipple into my mouth and suck gently. I don't mind indulging her when she's caught somewhere between sleep and desire. It'll be fun to coax her awake, have her join me in lust.

Her breath catches. She digs her fingers into my hair, holding me against her bosom. She's so sensitive. I slip a hand between her soft thighs. Her slickness drenches me, making my blood boil.

Her eyes remain closed, as though she hasn't been fully pulled out of sleep. I move my finger along her soaking folds, teasing the opening of her pussy and swollen clit.

Finally her mouth falls open, expelling a pent-up breath. Her tits tremble, her areolas rosy. She rocks her hips, chasing an orgasm. She's so beautiful when she's honest in pleasure. I continue to stroke her, but without increasing the pressure like she wants me to.

I want to hear her say my name. I want her to open her eyes, look at me and beg.

After a few more moments, it happens. "Huxley," she says with a shaky sigh. She lifts her eyelids. Her passion-glazed gaze meeting mine sends an electric spark down my spine until my cockhead bumps against my taut belly. Her fingers dig into my shoulders. "Please."

The plea is barely audible, but hearing it snaps my control.

Enough screwing around. I spread her thighs. She inhales sharply, tilts her pelvis. "Yes, yes." The soft chant is like a siren's call to my already libido-addled mind.

She reaches for my cock, but I move away. Confusion clouds her gorgeous eyes briefly. Flashing her a wicked grin, I run the flat of my tongue along her wetness.

A cry tears from her throat. She tunnels her fingers into my hair. My mouth closes over her, and I devour her, licking and sucking, using my tongue to torment her. She bucks her hips, shamelessly urging me. Her naked need drives me wild.

She whimpers my name, her voice full of love, trust and need. Her muscles tighten and quiver, the movements of her pelvis jerkier and faster as I plunge two fingers deep inside her and suck on her clit.

She screams my name, her fingers tightening in my hair. I lap her up, easing her down from her peak.

Instead of sighing and sinking into the soft mattress, she sits up and flips me over. With a wicked and determined look in her eye, she straddles me in a reverse cowgirl, giving me a view of her gorgeous ass, then makes her way down.

"Look at this guy," she purrs, then wraps her hand around my shaft.

Jesus. Her touch is like a lightning strike, making my vision go white. It's been a while, and I've never been more turned on.

I feel her warm breath over the cockhead. Precum flows freely from the tip. All the lava-hot blood in my body seems to pool in my dick.

"Grace..." I whisper. I didn't wake her up to make me feel good, but I still say her name like a plea.

Soft laughter bubbles from her, full of satisfaction and need. Her hot tongue swipes the tip, and my pelvis jerks.

She pulls the head, piercing and all into her mouth. Another sexy laugh—and the vibration sends hot quivers all over my body. As she slowly moves her mouth along my shaft, I knead her gorgeous ass, then pull her close to me so I can lap her up again.

She moans around my cock, and sharp pleasure races through me. Desperately clinging to control, I shallowly fuck her mouth. I can't stop my hips from moving—I'm but a man wild for his wife. Her juices drip down her thighs. Feeling her grow wetter with my cock in her mouth makes me nearly lose control. I eat her up, not wanting to miss a drop of her sweetness. She grinds against my mouth, digging her fingers into my thighs. I try to pace us, but it's impossible with pleasure pounding into me in endless waves.

She convulses first, arching her back as she climaxes. My cock muffles her scream, and I can't hold on anymore. I come, emptying myself, and breathing like the space between her legs contains the last air on Earth. I can't remember the last time I came this hard.

Grace is like pliant goo on top of me. Her warm hair pools over my legs. I start to gather her close, wanting to hold her and enjoy the moment.

"That was amazing," she murmurs as she slips out of my grasp and leaves our bed.

"What are you doing?" I ask with a frown. "It's barely seven."

She walks toward the bathroom. "I know. Time to get ready for work. We're already late."

"Come back to bed." I stretch. "I still have two more weeks off."

"Well, then *you* can stay home. I'm going in to the office," she says over a shoulder.

"Wait." I sit up. "There's no point to my vacation if you're going to work!"

"But I thought you were exhausted." She's all innocence.

"I'm not exhausted. I took a month off to be with you." Everyone at the office looked at me like I'd lost my head when I announced my month-long vacation. I've never taken so much personal time.

"You mean to hover over me. Don't think I don't know." She slips into the bathroom. I follow, and she starts brushing her teeth.

"I'm not hovering." I wrap my arms around her from behind and bury my face in her neck. Her scent is stronger in the morning, all sweet and alluring. "How about we stay home and have sex? We can go through every position in *Kama Sutra*."

"Nope. I can't even open the fridge without you acting like I'm about to break my arm."

"Because you were hurt." I start to brush my teeth too, since I want to kiss her properly.

"I'm not spending the next two weeks doing nothing but having sex."

"We'll eat and sleep too, in between sex."

Rolling her eyes, she shakes her head, although her mouth twitches with a suppressed laugh. "I'm not made of porcelain. I'm making a speedy recovery. Even Dr. Hamilton was shocked."

I cast around for some excuse to get her to change her mind. "We haven't had a honeymoon."

"Seriously? You just want to spend the next two weeks at home, having sex, and call it a honeymoon?" She presses a hand over her chest. "Be still, my heart."

That shuts me up. *She's right, damn it.* Never argue with your wife without caffeine.

She rinses her mouth. "Let's compromise. We'll both go to work, and I'll stop by your office for a nice lunch. How about that?"

I rinse mine as well. "How about we both *don't* go to work, enjoy lots of morning orgasms and then have brunch around eleven? I know a great place."

Turning toward me, she grows serious. "Huxley, a routine is good for me. Plus, I like my job. It gives me happiness and fulfillment. I don't think it's good for me to sit at home all day until the due date. Okay?"

It's unfair, but when my wife flutters her lashes so prettily, I can't say no. "Okay. But we are going to have lunch together."

She beams. "Deal. I'll pick you up myself."

EVERYONE AT WORK looks at me like a deer in the headlights when I stride out of the elevator.

"Is everything okay? Aren't you out until the end of the month?" Claude says.

"Yes, but plans change. I have a lunch date, so adjust my schedule accordingly."

He follows me into my office with the day's agenda of meetings, marking the ones I should consider attending.

"Make sure the creative meeting at ten is finished by eleven thirty," I tell him. Then I send a bouquet of pink roses to my wife's office, the flowers she wanted to have at our wedding but couldn't because of Madison.

My former secretary still hasn't found a new job, based on gossip I've overheard in the staff breakroom. There are questions as to why she was fired so suddenly. Although I haven't said a word, everyone suspects it must've been something awful, since people know how much I depended on and trusted her. I purposely keep my mouth shut about it, even when headhunters and other executives ask. Whatever they imagine is going to be far worse than the truth. That's why most of the campaigns we do aren't overt. They are designed to engage the imagination, lead people's minds where we want them to go. It's harder, but much more effective.

My phone buzzes in the middle of the meeting. Since my wife's texts are the only exception to the "do not disturb" mode—I'm not ever repeating the situation where somebody answers her texts behind my back—I glance at the screen.

–Grace: Thank you! They're so lovely! :smiling-emoji:

I smile.

–Me: Happy first day back at work.

I turn my attention back to the presentation. "That pink isn't quite right. You want something lighter and softer, but not overly pastel. A hint of pearlescent, and the music should be at a slightly faster tempo to give it a more energetic feel. Otherwise, it's too lethargic. I'd fall asleep."

Chuck takes notes, his pencil scratching the yellow legal pad he carries everywhere.

"Any questions or concerns?" I say.

"Nope." Chuck and the others shake their heads. They're in charge of the vodka popsicle campaign. Ah, the fun things we push. They're too sweet for my taste, but they provide a good kick, perfect for a hot summer day or night when you need a little break.

"Great job, everyone." I leave the meeting, checking the time. Grace said she'd come to the 4D office, and I want to pick her up and take her to the new French restaurant that opened last month. It's getting great reviews, which say it has the best chocolate lava cake in the city. It would be hilarious to ask the server to bring it with celery sticks. Whatever expression she makes is going to be cute, I think with a smile.

An elevator opens with a soft chime. Just as I'm about to step in, Nelson jumps out and grabs my arm. "You!"

My face twists with disgust. "What are you doing here?"

A slightly wrinkled suit hangs on his frame. His cheeks have sunken a bit more since the last time I saw him. Dark circles take up half his face, and there are new lines ravaging his forehead and cheeks. "You have to stop them."

Them?

"Everyone at the firm's out to get me."

"The firm. You mean Huxley & Webber—which I'm not a part of."

"Come on! They're only after me because of you! They're trying to force me out."

I fake a shocked gasp. "And Andreas won't save you? Or how about your brother Bill? Aren't you two close?"

Resentment seethes in Nelson's gaze. "They aren't doing shit for me. They're too busy covering their own asses."

"You mean they won't shield your immoral behavior." I shoot him a look full of contempt. "I'll never forgive you for depriving Grace the opportunity to get the closure she deserved with her mother. Scattering the ashes around Baltimore... What kind of dick does that? No matter how you felt about the woman, she was the mother of your child. She deserved better. So did Grace."

"Wait, wait! If I give you the urn with her ashes, will you help me?"

"What?"

"Look, Huxley. Son." He puts his hands on my shoulders with the most paternal expression he can muster. "There's been a misunderstanding, I'm afraid."

I arch an eyebrow. This is going to be good.

"Nobody scattered the ashes, oh no. They were merely *misplaced*, but thankfully found."

My ass, they were misplaced. "Then why didn't you and your wife give them to Grace?"

"Well." Nelson licks his lips. "I thought it might be too distressing for her. I mean... She's always been a competitive child. She might have felt upset or thought it unfair that she didn't have a mom when Viv and Mick did. But if you can make my, ah, work issues go away, perhaps we can arrange for the ashes to be transferred to her. I'd hate to deprive her of a chance to properly grieve and say goodbye. Everyone needs closure, after all."

Does he think I'm stupid? He kept the ashes—assuming they really are Grace's mother's ashes, and not something he scooped out of someone's fireplace—as insurance in case Grace found out the truth and wouldn't stay quiet. I really should've shoved his face into the wall more than twice. "How do I know the ashes are really her mother? It isn't like we can run a DNA test."

"A perfectly logical question." He reaches into his coat pocket and pulls out some paper. "This is proof of the chain of custody for Winona's ashes. I hired another lawyer to do it, so you know I'm not lying."

I look it over. Nelson has been very thorough. Guess he was more worried than he let on about Grace's reaction to her mother's death.

"Why don't we call it even after you hand me the ashes and ask for forgiveness? That's the least of what you owe."

The tension in his face eases for the first time since he exited the elevator. *He thinks the deal is done.* "Must we assign blame and fault? We *are* family."

"I'm afraid Catalina won't back down without an apology. And you know how my mother is."

His expression sours before he catches himself. "Fine. Then I'm—"

"I'd like the ashes first. It's been a year."

"Of course. The urn is in my trunk."

I gesture for Claude to approach, then turn back to Nelson. "Can you give your fob to my assistant so he can bring it up?" I'm not budging on this. If I don't act now, Nelson will find a way to avoid giving me the ashes because he knows giving them up means giving up any final hold he has over Grace.

"It's a black Lexus." He rattles off the plate number. "Underground parking level two."

"Got it." Claude leaves.

"So. How about you make that call to your mother?"

"My assistant isn't back yet."

Nelson clears his throat. "Could we move to your office? Have some coffee, perhaps?"

You expect me to serve you coffee? "I need to go out soon."

Nelson rolls his weight on the balls of his feet as we wait, shifting back and forth to burn off nervous energy. His eyes scan the office, but my employees are too discreet to stare blatantly. They'll gossip afterward in the breakroom.

An elevator door opens. Grace steps out, followed by Claude, who is holding a huge white urn. She's wearing a brilliant smile, which fades when she spots her father.

"What are you doing here?" she asks.

"What are *you* doing here?" he says, stiffening.

"I'm here to have lunch with my husband." She comes over, loops her arm around mine and gives me a kiss, which I return with a grin.

"You got it?" I ask Claude, since he seems to be struggling a bit. The kid has a pencil neck and even thinner arms.

"Yup." He huffs. "This thing is *heavy*."

Grace looks at him with mild curiosity.

"My new assistant, Claude. Claude, my wife Grace."

"Hello." His greeting is polite and friendly. "Nice to meet you."

She smiles warmly. "Likewise. I'd offer to shake hands, but yours seem occupied."

"Please put that in my office," I say to Claude, who disappears.

"Now. What about that phone call?" Nelson says.

"I haven't heard an apology yet."

Nelson's face twists. His pride won't let him admit he's in the wrong.

"A sincere mea culpa isn't such a high price to pay for keeping a partnership at Huxley & Webber," I point out.

"No," he agrees reluctantly. "Look, Grace. I'm sorry for all the misunderstanding—"

"On your knees," I say.

"What?" Red suffuses his cheeks.

"How can it be sincere if you just say some meaningless words about misunderstandings? Would you accept my apology if I took my sweet time calling my mother and just referred to it as a 'misunderstanding'?"

His face reddens even more.

"Surely making everything go away is worth a knee..." I shrug.

He glares at me before quickly dropping his eyes. He knows who's in the driver's seat. "Fine."

But he takes his time, going down as slowly as possible. Probably praying I'll stop him before his knee touches the floor, saying I was only kidding—just testing him.

But I don't have all day. I go around and kick him behind his knee, making him drop to his hands and knees in one undignified flop.

Grace jumps with a gasp. And discretion in the office evaporates as my employees crane their necks to look.

"Ung! What the hell!" Before Nelson can get to his feet, I put a foot on his back and lean my weight into it. He squeals like a pig.

"Finally in the proper position." I sigh with satisfaction. "Now. Apologize."

"I can't do that with you behind me!" he protests.

"More like on top of you, but yes, you can. You owe my wife an apology."

"She's my daughter! I don't owe her shit. You can't make me humble myself to my own child!" His voice rings in the office. He turns to my wife. "What's wrong with you that you're just standing there? I gave you everything, Grace. All I wanted was my dignity!"

Grace shakes her head. "And your money, your reputation and to show favoritism to your other children. I already told you, Nelson. You're dead to me."

"Your mother wouldn't have wanted you hating me. She would've wanted you to rise above that."

"What the hell kind of apology is this?" I don't want to hear these ridiculous arguments. And Grace certainly doesn't need to suffer through this garbage. I put more pressure on his back, but he's undeterred.

He continues, "She would've wanted you to forgive—"

"Don't you *dare* talk about her!" Grace cuts him off. "You aren't worthy. And for the record, I don't hate you. I don't care about you at all. You're about as significant to me as moldy bread. Disappointing that you couldn't be better, but no big loss, either."

"I'm your family! Me, Karie, Mick and Viv—"

"No." She reaches out and takes my hand. "My family is right here."

55

GRACE

EVENTUALLY, security is called and drags Nelson out. "So much for an apology," I say. But his behavior isn't surprising. He's always considered himself better than anybody else. It's a big deal that he dropped to his knees—and hands—even if he was forced to when Huxley kicked him from behind. His pride may never recover.

That alone makes me laugh softly.

"What's funny?" Huxley says.

"Oh... Just thinking about how much his ego must be smarting."

He chuckles. "It makes for a fun way to start lunch."

"You bet." I rest my head on his shoulder. I love how hard and strong his muscles are, how safe and protected he makes me feel. "Ready to go?"

"Not just yet." He tucks a strand behind my ear, then strokes my cheek, brushing his thumb over my lower lip. "There's something I want to tell you."

"You can't tell me over our meal?"

"This isn't something I can share over chocolate cake." The heavy solemnity in his eyes sends jitters through me.

If he were any other man, I might think he was breaking up with me.

But this is Huxley. My husband. The man who tells me he loves me, calls me his and calls himself mine.

So I intentionally keep my voice light. "Ooh, chocolate cake for lunch?"

"It is your favorite. But I think you need this more."

He leads me to his office, then closes the door. The big white urn Claude carried earlier sits on the coffee table. It's plain with a clear glaze. Around it are photos and launch concepts for some products his agency is working on.

"What is it?" I ask. "Don't tell me you bought me more jewelry." Huxley's been buying me too many sets recently. Per Grant, it's Sebastian's doing. Huxley claims it's because every woman needs diamonds. Except he's given me emeralds, rubies, pearls and sapphires as well.

"No. Why don't you sit down?"

What's going on? I take a seat, and he sits next to me. He holds my hand tenderly. "Nelson came to ask me to stop my family from trying to ruin him and his kids."

"Are they really doing that?" I remember hearing about it, but didn't keep up. I want to focus my energy on living my life, not trying to destroy people who've done me wrong. There isn't enough time in the world for me to devote to the new family I've found I belong to. Huxley. Our baby. Emmett and Amy. Grant and Aspen. Griffin and Sierra. Sebastian and Lucie. Nicholas and Molly. Noah and Bobbi. Then there's Jeremiah and Ted. Catalina. Prescott and Akiko. Ares, Josh, and Bryce. And Emma.

Since learning about my mother's death, I've realized that I wasn't letting myself see certain possibilities. I was so focused on my future with her, so convinced that I would have had no one *without* her, that I didn't let the people around me in. And I didn't think that they'd let me in, either.

"Oh yes. You fuck with one of us, and you will pay. That's the family motto."

"I thought it meant loyalty and unity."

"Well, it's in Latin, so it sounds cooler and more noble and all that. But basically, it's 'fuck with us and find out.'"

I laugh.

"Nelson knows that too, so he tried to make a deal with a bargaining chip I couldn't refuse."

"Which was what?"

Huxley squeezes my hand and holds my eyes. "He said that, although your mother was cremated, they never scattered the ashes. They kept them, most likely to use as a leverage for when you found out about her death. Karie and Vivienne might've thought they were smart enough to hide it forever, but Nelson knew you'd eventually discover the truth."

"And..." My eyes flick to the urn.

Huxley nods. "Yeah."

A breath sobs out of me. I cover my face as a cocktail of volatile emotion coalesces around my heart. "Thank you," I croak through the hot lump in my throat.

"You're welcome," he says simply, his comforting hand stroking my back.

I go to the urn and hug it tightly. "Mom..." Tears well. The urn is cold to the touch, but being able to hold something physical that represents her somehow makes the raw pain of loss throb less. "I can't believe I still have tears left."

Huxley puts an arm around me, lending me his warmth and strength. "Don't rush the process. Take all the time you need to grieve and heal."

"Thank you," I choke out. "I married the most wonderful man in the world."

He gives me a grin. "You just figure that out?"

I laugh softly, tears still falling. "I feel like you were right when you told me we were fated to meet and fall in love."

Tender affection replaces the humor on his face.

I take a moment to dry my cheeks. "You remember how you asked me about my vision for the future?"

"Yes. You want to take her to Montana?"

I shake my head. "No. That's too far. I'd like for her to be able to see our children. Watch us be happy. Maybe some place really pretty with lots of flowers, not too far from us."

"I know just the place," Huxley says. "There's a plot next to where Aspen's grandparents are buried. It's absolutely gorgeous out there. We can add more flowers, the ones your mother loved."

I nod. "It sounds perfect. She would love that." I run my hand over the urn, then take his hand and place it against the smooth surface. "Mom, this is my husband Huxley. He's absolutely wonderful, and I love him so much. And he loves me too."

He puts an arm around my shoulders and pulls me close.

"We're expecting a baby now, and I couldn't be happier or more blessed. I have so many new brothers and sisters, too, and they're amazing," I say, starting to cry again. "I love you so much. I miss you even more. I wish we'd had more time to spend together, but Mom. Don't worry about me, okay?" I rest my forehead against the urn. "I met the other half of my soul."

And as I let out the rest of my tears, it seems like Mom's voice whispers, *I'm happy for you, dear.*

56

GRACE

—THREE YEARS later

CHILDREN'S LAUGHTER rings in the cool breeze. Emmett and Amy's daughter Monique is the boss, being the oldest, but Sebastian and Lucie's kid Elise isn't too bad, either. She knows how to bat her pretty eyes and make others agree with her.

Griffin and Sierra's triplets are wrestling on the grass—as usual. "They never seem to get tired," I say, slightly awestruck and stretching my legs on the picnic blanket. Nicholas suggested we have a fall picnic, and everybody agreed. Emmett rented an entire château in Sonoma, and Grant flew everyone up in his private jet.

I close my eyes briefly, letting the sun warm my skin. The weather's just perfect, the sky cloudless. Huxley wraps his arm around me and kisses my temple. "Tired?"

"No. Just enjoying the sun."

Elise says something I can't make out, and Sebastian picks her up and swings her over his head. She lets out a piercing laugh, and Lucie snaps a photo. Aspen just found out she's pregnant, and currently Grant is massaging her nonexistent cankles much to her amusement and embarrassment. He claims it'll prevent her legs from swelling, but we'll see.

Noah and Bobbi's son Steve is only seven months younger than our son Charles. I love it that they're so close in age and get along so well. Not to mention, they always act like they agree with whatever Monique and Elise want, but then do their own thing on the side.

"You really gotta keep an eye on those two," Sierra says.

"No kidding," Huxley agrees, looking at the little boys fondly. They're currently doing somersaults. Their eyebrows pinch together, mouths tight. Then rolling forward they go...although they seem to end up rolling to the side more than forward. Then they stand up, legs together and arms spread, like Olympic gymnasts sticking a landing.

"Perfect!" Noah calls out.

"Flawless," Huxley adds.

"Everyone gets a cupcake!" Bobbi declares, unveiling a big basket of gorgeous cupcakes.

The boys grin. Charlie grabs two and runs up to offer me one. I hug him, feeling his soft weight and smelling the clean sweat of my sweet little boy.

"Where's mine?" Huxley asks.

Charlie gives him a startled look, then dips a finger into the pale blue buttercream frosting and puts it into his father's mouth.

Laughing, Huxley wraps his arms around us. "I have my most precious treasures in my arms," he says, bussing my cheek loudly.

Laughing, I kiss him back, then feel the brush of a rose petal over my forehead. I look up at the clear blue sky to give thanks for all my blessings...and to let Mom know I couldn't be happier, surrounded by my family.

TITLES BY NADIA LEE

Standalone Titles

Beauty and the Assassin

Oops, I Married a Rock Star

The Billionaire and the Runaway Bride

Flirting with the Rock Star Next Door

Mister Fake Fiancé

Marrying My Billionaire Hookup

Faking It with the Frenemy

Marrying My Billionaire Boss

Stealing the Bride

The Lasker Brothers

Baby for the Bosshole

My Grumpy Billionaire

The Ex I'd Love to Hate

Contractually Yours

Finally Forever

Still Mine

The Unwanted Bride

The Sins Trilogy

Sins

Secrets

Mercy

~

The Billionaire's Claim Duet

Obsession

Redemption

~

Sweet Darlings Inc.

That Man Next Door

That Sexy Stranger

That Wild Player

~

Billionaires' Brides of Convenience

A Hollywood Deal

A Hollywood Bride

An Improper Deal

An Improper Bride

An Improper Ever After

An Unlikely Deal

An Unlikely Bride

A Final Deal

~

The Pryce Family

The Billionaire's Counterfeit Girlfriend

The Billionaire's Inconvenient Obsession

The Billionaire's Secret Wife

The Billionaire's Forgotten Fiancée

The Billionaire's Forbidden Desire

The Billionaire's Holiday Bride

~

Seduced by the Billionaire

Taken by Her Unforgiving Billionaire Boss

Pursued by Her Billionaire Hook-Up

Pregnant with Her Billionaire Ex's Baby

Romanced by Her Illicit Millionaire Crush

Wanted by Her Scandalous Billionaire

Loving Her Best Friend's Billionaire Brother

ABOUT NADIA LEE

New York Times and *USA Today* bestselling author Nadia Lee writes sexy contemporary romance. Born with a love for excellent food, travel and adventure, she has lived in four different countries, kissed stingrays, been bitten by a shark, fed an elephant and petted tigers.

Currently, she shares a condo overlooking a small river and sakura trees in Japan with her husband and son. When she's not writing, she can be found reading books by her favorite authors or planning another trip.

To learn more about Nadia and her projects, please visit http://www.nadialee.net. To receive updates about upcoming works, sneak peeks and bonus epilogues featuring some of your favorite couples from Nadia, please visit http://www.nadialee.net/vip to join her VIP List.